DOCTORS, ASSASSINS, AND OTHER TYRANTS

KATHARINE CAMPBELL

To Abby!
Nice to
meet you!

This book is dedicated to St. Augustine, whose awesome name I've stolen on multiple occasions.

PROLOGUE

"Where is it?" Justin hissed.

He grasped Fausta's collar, forcing her up onto her tiptoes. She could feel his fist trembling against her throat as he choked her. His face was scarlet; beads of sweat shimmered on his brow. He was a desperate man and that was exactly what she wanted.

She smiled cooly. "Where is what, brother?"

"The key," he growled, tightening her collar in his fist.

Fausta was standing in front of the door to a storage room. Earlier that day, before Justin returned from his campaign, she had all the liquor in the entire palace locked inside.

"Oh," Fausta continued. "You mean the key to *this* door?" She jabbed her thumb over her shoulder at the locked entrance behind her. Justin swore and forced her up against it. Still, she didn't flinch.

"You wouldn't hurt me, would you?" Fausta asked. "What would Father say?"

Their father almost never lost his temper. He was the type of man who didn't need to raise his voice to be respected. But once, many years ago, Justin had the nerve to strike Fausta, leaving a bruise on her cheek. Their father went into a rage. He threatened to disinherit

Justin, and even had him imprisoned for a short time. Fausta was amazed and delighted. Justin could normally abuse anyone he wanted and the king would look the other way. Apparently, she was the one exception. No one could harm his little princess.

"Damn you," Justin swore. "What do you want?"

Fausta withdrew a roll of parchment from her belt. "Your seal and your signature."

Justin released her and, snatching the parchment, began to skim. Fausta had written the document to be as wordy as possible. There was no way any man desperate for a drink would have the patience to read it in detail. He glanced up at the door.

"There's a pen over there," Fausta stated, pointing to a table a few paces away.

"I could just kill you," Justin threatened.

"Then you'd never find the key," Fausta replied. "And Father would have questions..."

She did not think it possible for a more ravenous hatred to burn in Justin's eyes. He scrawled his signature, then thrust out his hand expectantly.

"Key," he demanded.

"Your seal first," Fausta said.

"What do you need that for?" he snapped.

"Just trying to help," she answered. "I wouldn't want you to die of thirst while waiting for the wax to melt."

Justin plucked his seal off his finger and handed it to her.

Fausta stooped down, pulled a little key out of her shoe, and held it out to him. When he went to snatch it, she caught his wrist and held it fast.

"One more thing," she added. "If I ever even catch you in the same room as Damara or her child, I'll break my own nose and tell Father *you* did it."

Justin knew she would. She had done it before. Fausta took immense pleasure in the terror that flashed in his eyes.

"When I am king, your head will be the first to roll," he hissed.

Her smile broadened. "Justin, you're delightful."

Justin had at least one good quality. He wasn't clever or devious. His desires were simple—animalistic really. It made him prone to violent outbursts, but also easy to manipulate.

He jerked the key away from her and began struggling to insert it into the keyhole. With hands trembling like that, it would be a miracle if he actually succeeded in unlocking the door. He would probably be in the same spot at dawn; either continuing to struggle with the handle or lying face-down across the open portal surrounded by empty bottles.

"By the way," Fausta added. "Damara's son? It's a boy. She named him Augustine."

Justin kept his focus solely on removing the barrier between himself and his only love. If he heard her at all, he made no sign.

"I didn't think you'd care," Fausta grumbled under her breath.

1

THE FIGHT

Augustine's shoulder throbbed. He was clutching it with his opposite hand as his stepfather, King Florian, helped him toward the village doctor's back door. As a young man of seventeen, Augustine never cried. The pain did make his eyes water quite a bit though—enough to cause damp streaks on his cheeks.

Under normal circumstances, Florian would have taken Augustine back to the castle and had the doctor come there. However, the last thing either of them wanted was to be seen by any of the castle residents.

Florian pounded on the door.

"If my mother finds out what happened—" Augustine started. His eyes widened in horror.

Florian looked equally nervous. "You just..." he started thoughtfully. "Fell off your horse."

"She'll never believe that," Augustine continued.

The discomfort in Augustine's shoulder was nothing compared to the embarrassment he felt when Lina answered the door. Lina was the physician's daughter. She was a tiny stick of a young woman with wispy red hair and freckles of various shades on every visible part of her skin.

Augustine adopted her reddish complexion whenever she was around.

She greeted them with a scowl. "Were you jousting again?" she accused.

"No!" Augustine and Florian cried out in unison.

"You see—," Augustine started.

"Augustine rode into a tree branch," Florian finished.

"Do you think I'm stupid?" Lina frowned. She rolled her eyes and beckoned them inside.

"Where is your father?" Florian asked.

"Gone," Lina answered. "In Hersalt, so I'll be taking care of you."

Augustine's cheeks turned even redder. "I would really rather not, I mean... If there's a man who could—"

"Father will be back in three days if you want to wait," Lina informed dryly.

Augustine's face fell.

"It's just your shoulder, right?" Lina asked.

He nodded.

"Can you move your arm?" she pressed.

Augustine swallowed a yelp when he tried. Then shook his head.

"So I'll cut off your sleeve," Lina explained. "Then I'll see only your shoulder."

When she saw his hesitation, she rolled her eyes. "Do you think the sight of your scrawny arm is going to fill me with lustful desires? If anything, it will send me fleeing to the cloister."

Florian laughed. He had a loud booming laugh that Augustine found either endearing or embarrassing depending on the day. In the presence of Lina, it was the latter.

"Do it," Augustine mumbled sheepishly.

She brought him into the surgery and had him sit on the long table in the middle. The room looked like some kind of torture chamber. Knives of various sizes hung on the walls beside other painful-looking instruments.

All the tables, except the one he was sitting on, were littered with vials, ropes, tongs, and an assortment of other horrors. Augustine tried to avoid looking at these instruments because he did not like imagining what they might be for.

Lina cut carefully along the seam that ran from Augustine's shoulder to his neck. The fabric fell down, revealing a motley of black and purple bruising. Augustine's eyes watered a bit more as she felt the area, trying to assess the damage.

Why did it have to be Lina? Augustine wondered if he would ever recover from this humiliation.

"Glad you didn't use actual lances," Lina observed.

"Oh they did," Florian blurted.

Lina shot him an incredulous glare.

"The butts of the lances," Augustine clarified. "I was only trying to teach him a lesson, not impale him!"

"Who?" Lina asked.

"Prince Oswald," Florian hissed. "My idiot brother let his idiot son go gallivanting around on *my* side of the border, where he takes the opportunity to chase after Augustine calling him a slobbering rat-snake among other things."

"That wasn't the worst part!" Augustine snapped. "That swine insulted my mother!"

Florian placed a proud hand on his stepson's good shoulder. "But of course, Augustine wouldn't stand for that so he—"

"Took the bait?" Lina interrupted.

"Taught him a lesson," Florian finished.

"Seems like he taught you a lesson," Lina answered.

Florian and Augustine both laughed.

"You should see Oswald!" Augustine proclaimed.

Lina rolled her eyes and then pointed a commanding finger at the table.

"Lie down!" she ordered.

Augustine's eyes widened. He wasn't afraid or anything, just a little apprehensive.

"Why?" he squeaked.

"Do you want me to fix this or not?" Lina asked.

"Of course he does!" Florian interjected. "Do your worst, he's man enough to take it!"

A subtle smirk touched Lina's lips as she glanced back at Augustine. He was shaking slightly which, he figured, was probably because he hadn't eaten in a while.

He sealed his lips and slowly laid back, the color draining from his face. Maybe if he kept his eyes fixed on the ceiling, he wouldn't have to think about what Lina was going to do.

"Hold him down, will you?" Lina asked Florian.

Florian gripped Augustine's good arm and shoulder, securing him to the table, while Lina took Augustine's hand and started extending his bad arm away from his body. He chomped down on his lower lip as fresh streams of water poured down his cheeks.

Then Lina, still stretching Augustine's hand away from his body, leaned back and gave him a sharp kick in the armpit.

Augustine yelped like a puppy.

"Better?" she asked, releasing his hand.

Actually, it was. Augustine sat up, brushing the water from his cheeks with his wrist.

"Didn't I tell you he could take it?" Florian grinned, giving Augustine a proud swat on the back.

"I hardly felt it," Augustine claimed, swinging his arm back and forth to test the movement.

Lina caught his hand mid-swing. "Are you trying to undo my handiwork?"

"Sorry," Augustine answered.

"Good," she returned. "But I don't trust you. I'm putting you in a sling."

She glanced around the room, looking at the various instruments that lay on tables and hung on walls.

"Wait, just a moment," she ordered before stepping out of the room.

The moment Lina was gone, Florian spoke. "Are you going to ask her?"

"About what?" Augustine shrugged.

"Saint Loudon's day of course!" Florian replied.

Augustine's eyes widened with horror. "It's not the time!"

"Of course it is," Florian insisted. "If not now, when?"

"But—" Augustine started to object. He stopped abruptly when Lina reentered. She had a fabric sling draped over her arm and a needle and thread in her hand.

"What's that for?" Augustine asked, turning pale at the sight of the needle.

"For fixing your tunic," Lina answered dryly. "I'll warn you I'm not much of a seamstress. I'm used to sewing skin."

Florian and Augustine both became slightly green which seemed to amuse her. Lina's smiles were very subtle, but Augustine always noticed them.

"You owe me seven silvers," Lina said as she set to work reattaching Augustine's sleeve.

"Your father only charged us six last time," Florian objected.

"Well seven is my price," Lina stated. "And it will be eight next time, so see that it doesn't happen again."

As she continued sewing, Florian said he had to check on his horse and stepped outside. Lina finished and secured Augustine's arm in the sling. He thanked her and tried to leave, only to find that the back door was stuck fast.

He jerked the handle and it opened only a crack.

"Did you ask her yet?" came Florian's voice in his best attempt at a whisper.

Augustine's face became scarlet. "What? No," he answered.

Florian jerked the door shut and held it closed. Augustine swore under his breath. No effort on his part could budge it.

"Is everything alright?" Lina asked.

Augustine felt a knot in his stomach. *He was going to have to do it.* It wasn't that he didn't want to, it was just that he had a very specific idea of how it should be done. In that picture, his eyes weren't red, his cheeks weren't wet, and she hadn't just seen him shriek like a girl.

He turned around to see Lina staring at him expectantly. Her expression was slightly disinterested, as she polished some claw-like instrument he tried not to think about.

His heart was racing, but he straightened up.

"Lina," he started. He paused briefly, trying to pat down his free-flying curls. "Were you planning on going to the St. Loudon's day festival?"

She shrugged. "Maybe, if there's nothing better to do."

"Are you... going with anyone?"

She shrugged again. Augustine noticed a very subtle smile on her lips. "I might, if someone asked me."

"If I asked you?"

Her smile grew the tiniest bit. "You won't be jousting for me, will you?"

He grinned and shook his head.

"Sparring?"

Again he answered no.

"Brawling?"

He denied it.

"Horse racing?"

"Aren't you going to let me have any fun?" Augustine scoffed.

"You could ask someone else if you think I'm boring," Lina stated.

"I never said you were boring," Augustine answered. "You are sensible, which I admit is similar."

She snorted. "Go home, Augustine."

"Sunday?" he pressed.

She shrugged, but smiled nonetheless. "Alright."

He grinned broadly, then felt stupid for doing so and swung away from her toward the door. It opened easily.

Florian was waiting just outside. Augustine greeted him with a punch in the shoulder. "I'll kill you!"

"Your left punch is pathetic," Florian laughed. "What did she say?"

Augustine answered with a dazed smile. "She said yes."

2

THE SNITCH

A ugustine sat in the armory polishing a helmet. It was surprisingly difficult with one arm. Keeping arms and armor in working order was one of the many duties he had as a squire. With his injury, it was the only one he could perform at the moment.

The work was repetitive and thoughtless but Augustine didn't mind. He liked handling the various implements of knighthood. Though he had never actually seen combat, he liked to think he was formidable with every weapon.

When he was thirteen, he set his heart on knighthood. His stepfather was delighted and his mother was horrified.

As Florian's stepson, Augustine could never be king. Even his status as a prince was somewhat controversial. Of course, Florian had *tried* to make him his successor. Unfortunately, Florian's uncle, the archbishop of Kaltehafen, adamantly opposed him on account of Augustine being a member of the Greek church.

Florian had an argument with his uncle that started out verbal and ended in physical blows and an appeal to the pope. The pope took one look at their case and decided he had neither the time nor the energy to deal with such absurdity. He deferred to the archbishop's judgment and the matter was closed.

Augustine was perfectly happy with the arrangement. Knighthood was much more appealing to him anyway. His blood father, Attikos Hatsi, had been an equestrian in Kalathea who, according to his mother, died defending the crown prince. Augustine imagined his father as some kind of mythological hero who spent his days riding around the Kalathean border saving defenseless villages from raiders. Though he never had the chance to meet his father, he knew he wanted to be just like him—a defender of the innocent.

The sound of tiny feet pattering toward him snapped Augustine from his thoughts. He quickly removed his sling and hid it under the table. He knew the owner of those little footsteps well and she was incapable of keeping secrets.

"'Gustin!" called a little voice. Augustine threw down a mace just as a little girl came barreling into his arms. He yelped as she collided with his bad shoulder, but swallowed his pain. The five-year-old was dressed in a scarlet gown. Her heart-shaped face was framed with bouncy black curls. Augustine smiled into the bright eyes of his younger sister.

"Heidi, you are not allowed in here," he reprimanded. "There are lots of dangerous—"

"'Gustin, are you getting married?" she interjected.

"Who told you that?" he replied, swallowing a second yelp as she slammed her little palm into his shoulder.

"Mama told me," Heidi explained. "Mama said I am not to follow you at the festival because you are taking Lina and need to be alone so you can fall in love."

Augustine snorted a laugh. "Well, I *am* taking Lina."

"Are you going to marry her?" the girl pressed. "I will get the whole wedding ready, I am very good at weddings."

"Not on Sunday," Augustine replied.

"When?"

Augustine shrugged.

"Alright. Well, you tell me when you know," Heidi ordered.

"You'll be the first," Augustine promised. "I mean the second, Lina will have to be the first."

Heidi suddenly grabbed his collar, pulled it down, and gasped.

Augustine jerked away. She must have noticed the bruising that was creeping up his neck.

"'Gustin!" she exclaimed. "You were jousting!"

"No, Heidi," Augustine answered. "I just fell off my horse."

Heidi glared. "Mama says you're a terrible liar."

"Don't tell Mama," Augustine pleaded.

Heidi sprang off his lap with the words, "I'm going to tell Mama!" Then she dashed out of the room before Augustine could stop her.

He sighed deeply as he heard the door slam, wondering if he should warn Florian about the reprimanding that was to come.

3

THE UNICORN

"Promise me you won't do anything dangerous," Queen Damara insisted.

It was the morning of the festival. The queen had made Augustine's appearance her top priority. She wouldn't stop straightening his cloak and fiddling with his hair. He had a groom for that sort of thing, but Damara was never satisfied with his work.

"I've already promised," Augustine sighed.

"What good is a promise coming from a man who lies to his own mother?"

Damara could wield guilt better than Florian could wield a sword. Both Augustine and his stepfather were still sore from the wounds she inflicted after discovering their secret.

"Should I have let Oswald insult you?" Augustine defended.

"You did exactly what Oswald wanted, you know," Damara returned.

"Father was a warrior," Augustine objected. "Why won't you let—"

"Your father died fighting for Kalathea!" Damara snapped. "Defending the prince, no less. You dishonor him by risking yourself over some trivial rivalry."

Augustine looked at his feet. "Yes, Mother."

There was a moment of silence as she unpinned and then repinned his brooch for the fifteenth time.

"Is that really necessary?" Augustine asked.

"Don't you want to make a good impression?" Damara asked. She stepped back, regarding her work, then smiled. "Lina is a wonderful girl, you know."

"I know," he mumbled.

"She's sensible, and that's good for you."

Augustine knew his mother was right but made no response aside from turning a deep shade of red.

Damara scrutinized him again. While he was wondering if and when to attempt an escape, he noticed she was crying.

"What's wrong?" he asked.

She threw her arms around his neck and kissed his cheek. "Nothing's wrong," Damara smiled. "It's just the thought of you getting married..."

"Let's not get ahead of ourselves, Mama," Augustine reminded. "We are only going to the festival."

"I know, I know," Damara replied, wiping her eyes with the base of her palm. "It's just that there were so many times back in Kalathea, when I thought it would never happen..."

Augustine did not like to think about the times she was referring to. It was just the two of them, trying to survive one day to the next under the rule of the ancient gods. Watching their neighbors being taken one after another to be used in the gods' twisted morality experiments. Wondering how long they would last.

Augustine did not let himself fall too deeply into the memories. He squeezed her arm and said, "Here we are."

"Not where you should be," his mother scolded, giving him a gentle swat on the shoulder. "Go on now, don't leave Lina waiting."

"I won't," he grinned. He scurried from the room, hoping that she wouldn't notice she'd wrinkled his cloak.

．　．　．

IT TURNED out there was plenty to do at the festival that did not put Augustine in danger of bodily harm. The town was alive with colors. Banners and flags and tents added to the mosaic. There were acrobats and musicians and entertainers of all kinds.

Augustine wished he could at least watch jousting, but his father had technically banned it. The king still held matches at various remote locations away from the eyes of the queen and her associates.

Florian's knights might have accused the king of fearing his wife except that they all feared her too. Augustine thought this wise, for there was no woman in all the Earth he feared and adored more than his mother.

Archery was one of the few sports the queen tolerated. There was a range set up in a field behind one of the many lines of tents. Augustine stood watching Lina take aim. Her arrow just missed the bullseye. He winced. It wasn't a difficult shot. He could do it easily if both his arms were in working order. She tried again and this time hit her target, just barely. Augustine's fingers itched to take the bow.

"You're good at this," he observed. "But let me show you how it's done properly."

"With one arm?" Lina replied, glancing at his sling. "I'd like to see that."

Augustine jerked his arm free. Lina glared.

She opened her mouth to reprimand him but was cut off by a booming voice.

"Well, if it isn't Alexander the Greek!"

Augustine sighed and spun around to see a pair of monks. One was a bent old man who leaned on a crooked cane. His skin was fair and the little hair he had left was white. The other was about his father's age and had a kindly, weather-worn face, and sandy hair. They were known as Brother Joseph the Elder and Brother Joseph the Younger.

It was the elder who had spoken.

"Brother," The Younger politely corrected. "This is Squire Augustine."

"Augustine who?" The Elder squinted. "No, this is Alexander."

It had become a kind of ritual that occurred every time the Josephs encountered Augustine. The Elder would insist he was Alexander the Greek and The Younger would correct him, growing slightly more embarrassed every second.

Joseph the Elder wasn't the first person to mistake him for the Kalathean king who had lived in Kaltehafen nine years prior.

"Good heaven's boy, you look just like our Alexander," The Elder observed. "Are you related?"

Augustine replied the way he always did. "Only in that we're both Kalathean."

"Are you sure?" The Elder insisted.

"King Alexander is my uncle by marriage," Augustine explained for probably the hundredth time. "He's married to my stepfather's sister. We are not related by blood."

"You look like you could be his twin," The Elder observed. "Or his son."

"Alright," The Younger answered, patiently patting the old man on the arm. "Let's get you back for your nap."

"Alexander the Greek! There's a good man!" The Elder reminisced.

Augustine somehow managed not to roll his eyes. Unless The Younger was willing to forcibly drag The Elder home, Augustine was going to have to listen to him pontificate about how wonderful Alexander was. To Augustine, his uncle was more than just a good man. He was a hero. Still, hearing about it constantly was tedious.

Lina shot Augustine a sympathetic glance as he patiently listened to the old monk praise the only other Kalathean he knew. The Younger finally convinced The Elder to go. As they were walking away, The Elder looked over his shoulder and said, "You just have to be related! You look exactly like him!"

"If I was Kalathean royalty, I think I would know," Augustine answered dryly.

"You're not even Kaltic royalty," a voice called from over Augustine's shoulder. Instantly, Augustine felt anger bubbling up in his chest. He spun around to face his nemesis. Oswald was perched on his horse. He was a sturdy young man who was trying and failing to grow a beard. The result was a patchy unkempt disaster that reflected the rest of him quite well.

He had a black eye and his left arm was in a sling. Augustine smirked, feeling a little proud knowing that these were his handiwork. He almost wished he could boast about it to Lina, but she would never approve.

Lina curtsied politely and said: "Prince Oswald."

"I thought I told you to stay on your side of the border," Augustine snapped.

"It will all be my side of the border eventually," Oswald shrugged. "Unless Uncle Florian has a real son."

"It isn't yours now," Augustine answered. "So are you going to leave, or should Father have you thrown out?"

"Awfully bold of you, calling your king 'Father'," Oswald commented.

Augustine was about to spring forward to rip Oswald off his horse, but Lina caught him by the arm.

"I'm not working today," she whispered. "If anyone gets injured, they're on their own."

Augustine breathed deeply, trying to contain his rage.

"Let's go," he whispered to Lina.

She nodded and without another word, they both turned their backs on Oswald and started toward the village square.

"Halt!" Oswald cried.

They ignored him.

Augustine heard a thundering of hoofbeats and suddenly Oswald was blocking their path.

"I told you to halt," Oswald ordered.

"I don't take orders from foreign princes," Augustine replied. "Now stand aside."

"I'm a foreigner?" Oswald laughed. "Have you looked at yourself lately?"

With these words, Oswald ignited a rage. Augustine was about to launch an attack when he heard a tiny voice.

"'Gustin! 'Gustin!" Little Heidi was running toward them. Augustine looked up the road behind her to see if he could spot Heidi's nurse in pursuit. The girl appeared to be alone.

"Where is Evelyn?" Augustine asked.

"I escaped, 'Gustin," Heidi panted.

"Oh Heidi," Augustine returned. "What have I told you about that? You must stay with Evelyn. She's probably looking everywhere for you."

"I know but this is desperate. Primrose is very sick." The girl's eyes reddened and tears overflowed.

"Did you tell Evelyn?" Augustine asked.

"S-she says we can't do anything," Heidi's bottom lip wobbled and fresh tears wet her cheeks. "She says there's nothing wrong."

"Is Primrose a pet?" Lina asked.

"A unicorn," Augustine answered.

"A what?" Lina blurted. "A real one?"

Augustine nodded, then looking to Heidi said: "I'll come and look. That is..." he glared over his shoulder at Oswald. "If Oswald will let me."

"Only for the sake of the princess," Oswald grumbled. "But we are not finished."

Augustine smirked. Anyone who upset the princess would have to face Florian's wrath and even Oswald wasn't bold enough for that.

Augustine took Heidi's hand. "Lina, will you come with us?" he asked. "If Primrose is sick, perhaps you can do something?"

"I will certainly try," Lina answered. "I've never treated a unicorn before, this will prove interesting."

THE UNICORN LAY on a pile of straw in the barn. The animal was about the size of a doe and had the same delicate legs and slender neck. Its hooves were cloven like a goat's and it had a long thin tail with a tuft on the end like a lion. The way it was lying, Augustine would have thought it dead, but he could see its sides gently moving up and down.

Several months ago, Heidi told Florian that she wanted a unicorn for her birthday. Augustine and Damara laughed at this, but Florian swore that he would not rest until he found one for her. Heidi was beside herself with joy when the huntsman returned with the captive beast. It never sat right with Augustine.

Lina looked over Augustine's shoulder into the barn.

"That's a male," she observed.

"Primrose is a girl," Heidi corrected.

"No," Lina started but Augustine gave her a hard look and shook his head.

"Right, a girl..." Lina continued glancing at the animal's latter end. It was making no effort to hide its masculinity. "Let's see what's wrong with you, Primrose."

She knelt down beside the unicorn and stroked its neck. Then she examined it: looking at the teeth, in the ears, and feeling its stomach. She lay her head on its chest and listened to the heart.

"I can't find anything wrong," she said at last. "How long has he-she been this way?"

"All night and all day," Heidi answered.

Lina frowned

"You know, Heidi," Augustine said. "Maybe Primrose is lonely."

"Can Papa get another unicorn?" Heidi asked.

"Well... um..." Augustine started. "Primrose might already have a family in the forest and she probably misses them terribly."

"Oh, Papa can bring all of them here," Heidi suggested.

Augustine rubbed the bridge of his nose between his thumb and forefinger.

"Heidi..." he sighed. "Unicorns are not like dogs or horses. They aren't happy living here at the castle."

Heidi furrowed her brow.

"What your brother means is," Lina helped. "That unicorns need the forest, they can't survive in a barn."

Heidi's eyes widened. "But I love her."

"Then don't you want... her to be happy?" Augustine pressed.

Heidi sobbed but nodded through her tears.

"Why don't we take Primrose into the forest," he suggested. "I bet she'll perk right up."

Heidi glanced at the imprisoned animal. "But I'll miss her."

"I'll take you to see her any time you like," Augustine said.

"Promise?"

"Promise," he swore.

Heidi threw her arms around Primrose's neck and sobbed into his mane.

4

THE KIDNAPPING

Primrose somehow knew he was about to be set free. When Augustine looped a rope around his neck he stood right up and followed without resistance. Heidi walked beside the animal as they led him away from the castle toward the forest, stifling her sobs in a handkerchief.

"You're being very grown-up, you know," Lina commented. Then she whispered to Augustine. "Do you think it would be unethical to remove the horn before we let him go?"

"Yes," Augustine glared. "Why?"

Lina sighed. "It can cure almost anything. If you grind it into powder and mix it with vinegar."

"I am beginning to think you *are* a witch," Augustine smirked.

"I might be," Lina answered.

Augustine could tell Lina was amused by the way her eyes sparkled when she glanced at him. He had known her since he was nine and had become quite good at reading her subtleties.

All those years ago, on his journey from Kalathea, Florian told him there were lots of children in Kaltehafen. He said his brother Filbert had a son exactly Augustine's age.

He remembered being so excited to meet his new cousin. Unfortunately, Oswald did not like him and the feeling was mutual. They hadn't known each other for an hour before Oswald started mocking Augustine's accent. He was still learning Kaltic at the time and every minor mistake became the subject of his cousin's sport.

Things were no better when they made it to Castle Erkscrim. Most of the Kaltic children had only ever seen other Kaltic children and did not know what to make of the olive-skinned, dark-haired, newcomer. Being the king's stepson did nothing to protect him; in fact, it somehow made things worse. Especially when Oswald was visiting. He convinced the other children that Augustine was a spy.

There was only one other person in the entire village who was treated with equal disdain. That, of course, was Lina. She was the only redhead for a hundred miles. Both her parents looked just like the other Kalts, which convinced the village children she was a changeling or a witch or somehow magical. And both being the subjects of suspicion, Augustine and Lina were friends immediately.

"Here we are, Primrose," Augustine said when he felt they'd gone far enough.

Heidi kissed the unicorn's neck, stroked his mane, and told him she would visit soon. Finally, Augustine removed the rope. The animal looked over his shoulder at the three humans with its ears forward and then bounded away into the forest.

"Look at that, Heidi," Lina said. "She's so excited to see her family."

Heidi sniffled and nodded. "'Gustin, carry me," she ordered. "I am weak with grief."

Augustine managed to swallow a laugh and nod sympathetically instead.

"Your shoulder," Lina reminded.

Augustine stooped down and had Heidi put her arms around his neck. Then he stood up, supporting her with his good arm. He shot Lina a defiant smirk.

"You should know by now that sort of thing doesn't impress me," Lina stated.

"Not even a little?" Augustine asked.

Lina pursed her lips disapprovingly but made no other reply.

"She's impressed," Heidi whispered into his ear.

"I know," Augustine whispered back.

Lina glared at him. He responded with a grin, then the three of them turned and started back toward the castle. They had hardly gone a few paces when Augustine heard a snap in the brush behind him. He ignored it but a few steps later, he could have sworn he heard rustling in the underbrush.

"Do you hear that?" Lina asked.

Augustine rolled his eyes and set Heidi down. "Oswald, show yourself!" he demanded.

The wood was silent.

"Lina, why don't you go on ahead with Heidi?" he suggested, setting the girl down.

"Don't do anything stupid," Lina warned.

"I'll be right behind you," he answered.

Lina took Heidi's hand and continued forward while Augustine scanned the surrounding trees.

Seeing nothing, he followed at a distance. He was sure Oswald would come bounding out at him any minute and was fully prepared for a counterattack.

"Excuse me," came a voice.

Augustine spun around. Behind him stood three friars. The first was like a giant—tall and solid. He was bald but made up for it with a massive black beard. The second, though shorter and slimmer, was no less fierce. He had a keen sparkle in the green eyes that peered at Augustine from below a veil of dark curls. His bearing radiated confidence. Augustine could tell he was the leader of the group, just by looking at him. That and because he was the one holding the map. The last looked like your average Kaltic villager—gangly, sandy-haired, and unsure of himself. He stood with his shoulders slouched while his blue eyes glanced around nervously.

"Do you know how to get to Saint Loudon's monastery?" The green-eyed monk asked.

"Certainly," Augustine replied. "Just continue north—"

"See I told you it was north!" The green-eyed man grinned, jabbing his sandy-haired companion in the ribs.

"You said *west*," the sandy monk grumbled. Then looking toward Augustine he added, "We've been wandering in circles all morning."

"You misunderstood me—" Green-eyes interrupted. Then they both started bickering in low voices and pointing at different places on the map.

Augustine approached. "Please, Brothers. Let me see your map, I'll show you where to go."

"I apologize," Green-eyes answered. "But we have come such a long way and are a bit short-tempered."

"All the way from Kalathea," added the sandy monk.

Augustine was now standing among the three looking at the map. His face brightened at the mention of his homeland. He was about to ask how things were there when the first monk interjected. "That reminds me, I have a message for a man named Augustine Hatsi. Do you know him?"

"You're in luck," Augustine answered. "I am Augustine Hatsi."

At once the bearded monk threw a firm arm around his shoulder and Augustine felt the point of a dagger in his ribs. The green-eyed monk suddenly had a bow in hand with an arrow aimed at Augustine's chest. The sandy monk was pulling a rope from his pack.

Augustine's heart pounded as he drank in the situation.

"What do you want with me?" he demanded.

The green-eyed man made no response but continued watching him with a cold smirk. As the sandy monk brought the rope forward, the bearded monk stooped to remove Augustine's sword from his belt.

Augustine took the opportunity to slip his arm from the sling and elbow the bearded man in the jaw. The man jerked backward allowing Augustine to break from his grasp. Augustine wasted no time, he tore away into the woods.

What happened next was something of a blur. Each second was about outpacing his captors. They were right behind him, snatching at him, trying to grab a hold of his cloak or tunic. Once Augustine heard the whizz of an arrow. It flew past his ear and thunked into a tree trunk. He kept running. If they wanted to kill him, they would have done it already.

Suddenly, he heard the galloping of hooves somewhere to his right. He prayed that it was one of his father's knights. Unfortunately, it was Oswald. The prince slowed his horse so it was running parallel to Augustine.

Augustine suddenly wondered if this entire situation was Oswald's idea of a prank. He quickly dispelled this thought when his cousin spoke in a panicked voice.

"What have you done?" he cried. "Who are these men?"

"I have no idea!" Augustine returned.

Oswald held out a hand, slowing his steed enough that he could pull Augustine onto the saddle in front of him.

"What are you doing here?" Augustine asked as they galloped through the trees. He felt a puff of air on his ear as an arrow whizzed by.

"Looking for you," Oswald answered. "You'll recall we have unfinished business."

Oswald's horse let out a deafening scream and collapsed. The next thing Augustine knew, he was lying on his back staring at the canopy. He leapt to his feet and, drawing his sword, stood facing his pursuers as his heart pounded in his chest.

He glanced sideways. Oswald had also managed to stand and draw his blade. Now, the cousins were strong and capable fighters. Though they were outnumbered, they might have been a match for the three monks except that they were each an arm short and quite sore from the beating they had given each other a few days prior.

"Who are they?" his cousin repeated as two of the three monks closed the gap between them. Augustine couldn't see the bearded monk. He glanced around expecting him to leap out from behind some tree.

"I said I don't know!" Augustine snapped.

"Augustine," the green-eyed man began. "Surrender peacefully and I will let this friend of yours live."

"Friend?" Oswald cried indignantly. "Do you have any idea who you're talking to?"

Augustine glared sideways at him. *"Don't, Oswald,"* he hissed.

"I don't really care," the green-eyed man answered with an amused half-smile. "I was hired to retrieve Augustine Hatsi."

"By whom?" Augustine demanded.

"Him? Why?" Oswald asked at the same time. "He's no one."

"Enough!" The green-eyed man said, holding up a hand. "You can't win. Look at you." He motioned to Oswald's sling. "Now I have no interest in killing your friend, but I will if I have to. What will it be, Augustine?"

"Don't," Oswald whispered. "Surrender and I'll die fighting to save you! Think of how guilty you'll feel then."

Augustine sighed. Oswald was perhaps the only person who could make this situation worse. At least, he thought so until the bearded man reappeared holding little Heidi in his arms. Augustine froze in horror as he watched his sister kicking and biting and struggling in vain. He looked around for Lina but saw no sign of her.

At the sight of the little girl, the green-eyed monk smiled. "Who is this?" he asked.

"I don't know," Augustine lied, but his expression betrayed everything. The green-eyed monk knew he'd caught someone important.

"Drop your weapon," he ordered. "And come forward slowly."

Anger boiled in Augustine's chest, but he did what he was told.

Oswald still clung to his sword with his good hand looking between Heidi and Augustine with an expression full of uncertainty.

"Oswald, drop your weapon," Augustine ordered.

"I won't let them take you," Oswald retorted.

"Do it for Heidi," Augustine pleaded.

Oswald reluctantly threw down his blade.

Augustine's shoulder throbbed as the sandy-haired man forced his hands behind his back and bound them.

"What do we do with him?" the sandy monk asked, looking at Oswald.

"Oh tie him to that tree over there," the green-eyed man answered. "When we're finished here, the girl can let him go."

"Release my brother!" Heidi shrieked, beating the bearded monk with her fists. "He isn't worth anything! He's just a commoner. I'm a princess, you'd get a lot of ransom for me."

If it wasn't for the gravity of the situation, Augustine might have laughed at Heidi's remarks. She was such a fierce little thing.

"Heidi, no," he gently reprimanded.

She glared at him. "I won't let them take you!"

Green-eyes took Augustine by the arm once he was adequately bound and Sandy set about tying Oswald to a tree. Augustine continued scanning the woods for Lina. He desperately wanted to ask Heidi what had happened to her, but didn't want to make his captors aware of her existence.

"The girl is right," Oswald argued. "Augustine is no one of consequence. If it's ransom you want, you'll get a lot more for me. I am the crown prince of all Kaltehafen."

"Shut up, Oswald," Augustine snapped. It was sweet coming from Heidi, from Oswald it was insulting.

"I'm trying to save you," Oswald returned. "Show a little gratitude, why don't you!"

With Oswald safely secured, the bearded man put Heidi down and instructed her to free him once they were out of sight.

"Where are you taking him?" Heidi whimpered looking at Augustine.

The green-eyed man stooped down so he was looking her in the eyes. "What does it matter? As you said. He's no one."

"He's my brother," she answered.

"Do as I ask and we'll take good care of him," Green-eyes responded. There was no sarcasm in his voice. He was making a deal with Heidi, a serious promise.

"My father is going to kill you," Heidi threatened.

The green-eyed man grinned. "Only if he can catch me, sweetheart."

5

A RIDICULOUS CLAIM

Augustine walked in silence, occasionally glancing around the forest for signs of Lina. His captors chatted among themselves mostly about when they were going to eat and what rations they had left.

The green-eyed man was clearly the leader. The others called him Wolf or Wolfy interchangeably. He had the lightest heart of the bunch, laughing and smiling as if he was working at an honest trade he enjoyed. The sandy-haired man was called Mill. He seemed to be close friends with Wolf, from the way they bantered back and forth about everything from the weather, to food, to the state of the world. The bearded man was tasked with guarding Augustine. He never spoke and his face was always expressionless. His name was Faruk.

At last they came to a river where Wolf had a little boat hidden in the brush on the bank. When he found it, he switched places with Faruk, taking Augustine's arm so Faruk could drag the vessel into the water.

Augustine wondered if enough time had passed that he could venture an escape without putting Heidi and Oswald at risk. He noticed Wolf looking at him quizzically.

"You can see the resemblance," he said.

Augustine raised an eyebrow. "Resemblance?"

Wolf looked over his shoulder, then Augustine realized he had been talking to his companions. "Maybe it's the nose," he guessed, cocking his head. "They all had it. Must be Prince Justin's."

"You're imagining things," Mill retorted.

Augustine had no idea what they were going on about.

"What do you want with me?" he demanded.

"Money," Wolf shrugged. "What my client wants, I am really not sure. I wouldn't take it personally. I think it has more to do with your father. If the pay is good, I don't ask questions."

My father? Augustine furrowed his brow. He couldn't mean Florian. If he wanted ransom from Florian he'd have captured Heidi.

"My father... Attikos Hatsi?" Augustine questioned.

"Prince Justin of Kalathea," Wolf corrected.

Augustine tried to recall what he knew about Prince Justin of Kalathea. He was the older brother of Princess Fausta. Augustine's mother was a handmaiden to the princess when he was a baby. His mother still wrote to her, though the princess was in prison for treason among other things... Augustine thought maybe murdering Prince Justin was one of those "other things," but couldn't remember.

"I don't know what you're talking about," Augustine answered. "My father's name was Attikos Hatsi. He was an equestrian, he—"

"Died heroically in some battle or other before you were born?" Wolf cut him off.

Augustine responded with a puzzled stare.

"I've heard it before, kid," Wolf continued casually. "From two of your half-brothers. There's no kind way to say this, I'm afraid. You're the illegitimate child of Prince Justin and some ill-bred temptress."

Augustine lunged for Wolf. He was acting completely on instinct. It never occurred to him that his hands were tied. Wolf stumbled backward, releasing Augustine's arm. Faruk rushed to Wolf's aid and took hold of the prisoner. Augustine thrashed in an attempt to escape from his grip but it was like fighting against solid rock.

"You're difficult," Wolf commented, as he recovered himself. "Hold him there, Faruk."

"Swine," Augustine hissed. "My mother is the queen of this land! How dare you speak of her in such vile terms?"

Wolf pulled a tiny bottle of something from his pack and poured a few drops of the content onto the edge of a small knife.

"I speak of her in accurate terms," Wolf defended. Augustine again attempted to lunge at him, but couldn't break from Faruk's grip. Wolf held up his knife for Augustine to see.

"Do you know what this is?" he asked.

Augustine didn't care. He wanted nothing more than to rip Wolf apart.

"This is venom from a Kalathean rock viper."

Augustine suddenly cared. He stopped thrashing at once and locked his gaze on the blade.

"Now I have your attention," Wolf sneered. "You know what this venom does don't you?"

"Seems an inefficient way of killing me," Augustine replied coldly.

"It would be," Wolf laughed. "But I am not going to kill you."

He leapt forward and sliced Augustine's shoulder. Augustine's eyes widened in horror as he looked at the bleeding wound.

"Normally, viper venom kills you, after paralyzing you," Wolf explained. "But I have discovered through trial and error that very small amounts only paralyze. Now, soon you'll start feeling slightly uncomfortable, then you'll lose feeling, then you'll lose consciousness at which point you will be much more agreeable."

Augustine had once witnessed his uncle suffering from a viper bite. "Slightly uncomfortable" is not how he would have described it.

"Couldn't you have just hit me over the head with something?" Augustine asked.

"Um, no," Wolf answered. "Last time we did that, Faruk hit too hard, said prisoner never regained consciousness, and we didn't get paid. This is better, believe me."

As they pulled Augustine toward the boat, the wound in his arm began to burn.

. . .

LINA RACED TOWARD THE CASTLE. She hadn't a moment to lose. Every second, Augustine was being dragged farther from home. She saw the king and a company of knights gathering on the road before the gates.

Oswald was among them pleading: "Uncle Florian, you cannot make me stay! Augustine's my own flesh and blood—well not technically–, but he's family and I won't be left behind."

"I can have you thrown in the dungeon," Florian snapped. Then he called over the hillside: "Filbert, get up here and control your son."

Lina noticed the queen standing in the gateway, holding Heidi in her arms. The little girl had her head buried in her mother's shoulder. Damara's cheeks were streaked with dark eye makeup.

"My king!" Lina cried as she approached. "They've taken him by boat, down the river that runs through your hunting grounds."

"Where have you been?" Oswald demanded.

"Heidi and I got separated," Lina breathed. "So I went back looking for her and saw those men binding up you and Augustine. When I saw that Heidi was safe, I followed Augustine's captors hoping for an opportunity to set him free. I followed them to the river, but I couldn't keep up with the boat."

"Get her a horse," Florian ordered. "Lead us to the place."

"So she can go, but I can't?" Oswald complained.

"I have half a mind to cut your tongue out," Florian threatened.

"Do not speak to my son that way!" Filbert objected. Then looking at his son, he said: "Oswald, get inside before I cut your tongue out!"

Oswald returned through the gate, swearing under his breath.

"My king," Lina interrupted. "The men who took Augustine... one of them said the strangest thing. I-I think they have him confused for someone else."

Damara suddenly looked up at Lina.

"What was it?" Florian insisted.

"I couldn't hear them clearly, but—they think he's the son of some prince—"

Damara looked at Florian. Florian looked at Damara. And

looking at the both of them, Lina realized they understood exactly what Augustine's captors meant.

Then, a servant approached, leading a horse by the reins and offered it to Lina.

"They're madmen," Florian replied. "And whoever they are, they *will* pay for this."

6

AN UNPLEASANT MEMORY

Augustine became aware. Not of anything in particular—he couldn't see or feel anything. He was like a consciousness floating in darkness. He could hear the steady clop of hoof-beats and a rattling and thumping that led him to believe he was in a cart moving along a dirt road.

Last he remembered, he was curled up in the bottom of the boat feeling, as Wolf eloquently put it, "slightly uncomfortable". His whole body was shaking and burning so that it was a relief when he finally started to lose feeling in his limbs.

"I'm still sore," Wolf's voice laughed from somewhere. "That kid's dangerous even with his hands tied."

"Just our luck, the most important one would be the one who knows how to fight," Mill's voice grumbled. "We should charge double, considering all the trouble he's given us."

"I was expecting trouble," Wolf replied. "I never change my price."

Augustine suddenly heard the distant sound of thundering hooves. His heart swelled with hope and anticipation.

"Knight," growled a beastly voice. It must have been Faruk.

Augustine heard some shuffling above him as the hoofbeats approached.

"Halt!" thundered a booming voice.

Augustine knew it. It was the voice of Sir Albert from his father's court. Relief flooded him. Sir Albert had at least fifteen others with him, if the sounds of the horses were anything to go by. His captors didn't stand a chance.

"To what do we owe this honor, my lord?" Wolf replied pleasantly. He sounded so confident. It worried Augustine slightly.

"I just received word that King Florian's son has been kidnapped," Sir Albert explained.

"How awful," Wolf replied.

"You match the description of the three men who took him," Albert accused.

"We are merchants," Wolf defended. "We are returning to Hersalt from the festival but if it would ease your mind, you may search our cart."

"I appreciate your cooperation," Albert answered.

This was it. They were about to find him. He heard the sound of heavy items sliding across wood, shuffling and creaking. Augustine tried again to move, to cry out, to do something to get attention but nothing happened. It didn't matter, there were only so many places they could hide him in a cart. Rescue was imminent.

"Nothing, sir," someone said.

Again, Augustine tried to move but no amount of willpower made the feeling return to his body. He could only listen helplessly as Sir Albert said, "I apologize for troubling you."

He heard the sound of the company retreating and utterly despaired.

"God speed!" Wolf cried.

As the sound of the hoofbeats faded into the distance, Mill snickered and mumbled, "blind idiots."

"Now Mill," came Wolf's grinning voice. "He may be an idiot, but he is a *noble* idiot. Show a little respect."

"I beg your forgiveness," Mill snorted.

Their snickering faded and the cart continued in silence for a long time. Augustine remained wherever he was, stewing in frustration.

"How long until he comes to?" Mill asked at last.

"We've a while yet," Wolf answered. "And even after he wakes, it will be a good hour before the feeling returns to his limbs."

His captors fell silent again, allowing Augustine to drift into a memory. It was one of those memories he hated recalling but his present situation forced it to the forefront of his mind.

He had been hidden away in a cart by a group of smugglers. They were taking him farther and farther from his mother, from home, from Kalathea. His mother had worked and saved everything she could to hire them. It was far too dangerous for him to stay in Kalathea under the rule of the gods. The smugglers got him out but were horrible in the process. The slightest noise from him resulted in punishment.

Augustine jerked himself out of the memory. This was a different situation entirely. Yes, he was being taken away from home, but he was an adult now and a trained fighter.

He tried to breathe deeply. He wasn't sure if he was successful but he was moderately calmer after the attempt.

So what if Sir Albert missed him? Someone else would find him or he would escape. Everything would be alright. He was going to be home soon. He would tell his mother about how his captors insisted he was the son of some long-dead Kalathean prince and they would have a good laugh about it. Everything was going to be alright.

7
THE ESCAPE

Augustine opened his eyes. Not that it made much of a difference. They had him in some sort of dark, wooden box —though here and there, glimmers of daylight slipped in between the planks.

Sensation was slowly starting to return. He was vaguely aware that he was lying sideways with his hands behind his back. A slight tingling irritated his fingers and toes but he still couldn't move.

His captor's footsteps approached from somewhere, then he heard the shuffling of objects directly above him. A hatch creaked open and the compartment was flooded with light. Augustine slammed his eyes shut.

"Kid?" came Mill's voice.

Augustine ignored him. Even if he wanted to speak, he wouldn't have been able.

"He's still out," Mill said, and Augustine was perfectly content to let him believe it.

"Is he now?" Wolf replied, skeptically.

Augustine could feel himself being lifted. One man was carrying his feet and the other was holding him under the arms. He wanted to see where they had been hiding him. He tried to open his eyes just slightly, but he was facing upward and couldn't see the cart.

They set him down in a sitting position with his back to a tree and his legs stretched out on the ground in front of him. He kept his eyes closed.

"You with us?" Wolf asked.

Augustine made no response, so Wolf slapped him across the mouth. His eyes opened in surprise. He could feel the impact of the blow, but couldn't feel any pain. It was the oddest sensation.

"Thought so," Wolf grinned.

Augustine scowled—or tried to. With so little feeling in his face, he wasn't sure what he actually looked like. They tied him to the tree and went about making camp. Augustine drank in their every move. All the while, he was curling and uncurling his fingers, hoping to bring the feeling back faster.

His captors had abandoned their habits, and by that I mean they had swapped their monk disguises for the attire of common folk. (Unfortunately, they were still compulsive evil-doers.)

Wolf was dressed in a worn green tunic that looked like it had been repaired and repaired many times over. The only thing differentiating him from any ordinary villager was the sword on his belt.

They were in the middle of a deep wood. Augustine couldn't see a road anywhere, but the space between the trees was flat and clear which explained how Wolf's company was able to bring the cart in. Mill built a fire which indicated to Augustine that he was either stupid, or so far away from anything he wasn't concerned about drawing attention to the group.

After a short time, Augustine's sensation returned completely and with it, came a headache and nausea. Despite this, he continued looking around, moving his head very slowly to reduce the throbbing.

A few moments later, Faruk rearranged Augustine's bonds so that his hands were free. He stretched his arms out, relishing the fact that he could move them. Then winced at a sudden jolt of pain in his bad shoulder.

"Your client is going to be deeply disappointed when he realizes you've brought him the wrong person," Augustine commented.

"Oh?" Wolf chuckled. "Are there many young Kalatheans named Augustine Hatsi in Kaltehafen?"

"None that are sons of Prince Justin," Augustine scowled.

"The others didn't believe us either," Wolf answered. "It doesn't matter. I get paid whether you believe me or not."

Faruk offered Augustine some bread and cheese which he accepted without complaint. He would need his strength if he was going to escape come nightfall.

"Who are these *others*?" Augustine pressed, as he took the provisions.

Mill rolled his eyes and grumbled, "Every time, it's always the same questions!"

Wolf didn't answer. Instead, he pulled a book out of his satchel, flipped it open, and started reading it.

"Who are the others?" Augustine repeated.

"No one you need to worry about," Wolf replied, without looking up. "Now you can either eat quietly, or I'll have you gagged and let you go hungry for a while."

"Don't interrupt Wolfy while he's reading," Mill cautioned. "It makes him grumpy."

Augustine obeyed. It wasn't because he feared Wolf, but because if he made his escape that night, he might not be able to eat again for some time. He had no idea where the nearest village was.

As a prisoner, Augustine expected to be fed scraps or even starved but Faruk had been quite generous with what he offered. He noticed that he had exactly the same portion as everyone else. His headache and nausea waned as he ate and before long, he felt almost normal. Escaping would be easy now.

Getting home? Well, that would be another matter. He managed to tuck a crust of bread into his sleeve. It would be meager provisions but better than nothing.

After supper, they bound his hands behind his back again and adjusted the ropes that held him to the tree so he could lie down on his side. Augustine offered no resistance and even obediently moved however they asked him. All the while, he was scanning the camp and the surrounding woods.

Faruk finished retying him, threw a blanket over him, and said, "Sleep."

Augustine lay still but did not close his eyes. He watched the three men, carefully looking for any weakness.

Faruk and Mill lay down to sleep immediately. But Wolf sat up, reading his book by the last remnants of daylight. It was a beautiful little book. The leatherwork on the cover was masterful, inlaid with a large cross. It looked like... *a breviary*? Augustine doubted Wolf did much praying, he was probably interested in the artistry or perhaps he was assessing the value.

Either way, he wasn't watching Augustine and so the latter set to work on his bonds. He started pulling the knots on his wrists with his fingers while twisting his hands to loosen the ropes. It was slow and tedious work. There was also a rope looped at one end around his waist and on the other around the tree behind him. Once he freed his hands he would have to undo this, then free his feet which were also tied together. He closed his eyes as he worked, pretending to be peacefully asleep.

After what seemed like an eternity, he pulled his hands free. He moved them carefully under the blanket and made short work on the knot on his waist. All that was left were his ankles. He opened his eyes very slightly to check on his captors. Wolf had put his book away but was awake keeping watch.

Augustine closed his eyes again and curled backward, trying to reach his feet while moving as little as possible. It was a slow and agonizing process. *He was so close to freedom*, but a single misstep could ruin everything. Just as he pulled his feet free, he heard Wolf's voice. "What's your plan exactly?"

Augustine froze. He opened his eyes to see his captor standing over him with one eyebrow raised and an amused half-smile.

Augustine struck like a snake, lunging forward and snatching Wolf's ankles so he fell on his back. Wolf lay for a moment in stunned silence. Augustine had just enough time to snatch the knife from his belt before Wolf lunged upward, snatching Augustine's wrist while crying out to wake his companions. Augustine struck Wolf in the crook of his arm with his free hand and jerked the other from his grasp before tearing away into the blackness of the forest.

"Feeding yourself to the wolves, kid?" came Wolf's voice. He was in close pursuit, Augustine increased his pace, keeping his arms out in front of him so he wouldn't collide with anything.

"You'll soon wish you stayed with us!" Wolf cried.

Augustine ignored him and continued running until the sounds of his captors had long faded. By this time, the wood was brightening in the early morning light. Augustine could see nothing but wilderness in all directions.

When the sun had fully risen, weariness overcame him. He sank down on the forest floor and fell asleep. It was only when he woke, that the gravity of his situation hit him. His bad shoulder throbbed and he had no idea where he was. He climbed a tree and stared out over the canopy, hoping to see a village or road or some sign of civilization, but all he saw was a sea of treetops stretching endlessly in every direction.

8

DAMARA'S SECRET

Doctor Cleitus Bone had seen a great many things in his time. The most notable of which was a fairy who had fallen through the roof of Castle Erkscrim. He pronounced her dead and then she immediately sat up and started talking as if nothing had happened.

The second most notable thing Doctor Cleitus Bone witnessed was his daughter Lina crying. She hadn't cried since she assisted him with surgery for the first time at the age of ten. He had told her back then that good doctors never cry because it makes their patients nervous.

But on the evening of Augustine's capture, she couldn't help it. Florian sent her home after she showed him where she lost sight of the boat. As she rode back, she kept wondering what she could do to help. The idea of doing nothing was unbearable. She told herself over and over that Florian's company would find Augustine quickly. After all, they were expert huntsmen. He would be home safe by midnight.

Then something occurred to her, Augustine was probably still feeling the effects of the viper venom. He would be weak and nauseous when he returned and she could only imagine what else his captors had done to him since they left. He would need a doctor.

Lina found her father in the surgery, writing in an open book.

"Father," she asked. "Will you come with me to the castle?"

"Of course," Doctor Cleitus mumbled without looking up from his work. She waited a moment but he continued writing as if he hadn't heard her.

"*Father*," she insisted.

He jerked upright and swung around.

"Oh, Lina!" he started. "You're back. Did you have a good day?"

That's when the tears started flowing. Doctor Cleitus raised his eyebrows in alarm. He hadn't displayed that kind of emotion in twenty years.

"Is this Augustine's doing?" he demanded.

"Father, please come with me," Lina insisted. "Augustine's been kidnapped. The king's gone after him and should retrieve him promptly, but when he does, he might be wounded so I thought we could go to the castle and await their return."

"Of course, darling, of course," her father nodded but it was clear from his furrowed brow that he hadn't fully absorbed her words. Lina didn't wait for him to understand. She took a sack and ran around the room collecting medicines and bandages.

She told him the entire story as they traveled. It was dark now. The black hillsides and the silhouette of the forest was illuminated by moonlight. Lina could see the looming black towers of Castle Erkscrim against the starlit sky.

The servant who greeted them at the gate brought them to the great hall where he instructed them to wait. The hall was populated by a small herd of scribes, busily copying notices that described Augustine and the three men who took him.

The only other soul in the room was, to Lina's chagrin, Oswald. He was pacing back and forth swinging his sword in the air in a frustrated rage. The motions were awkward since his right arm was still in a sling and he had to settle for his left.

"So he sent you back," Oswald observed.

"I could offer him no further information, my prince," Lina replied.

Oswald looked at Lina's father.

"You're a doctor?" he questioned.

"Yes, Your Highness," the doctor replied.

Oswald withdrew his right arm from the sling.

"Then tell my mother and Aunt Damara that my arm is perfectly fine," Oswald ordered. "And that I should be with Uncle Florian's company searching for those scoundrels who stole my cousin."

"I will if it's true," the doctor answered, stepping forward to examine Oswald's arm.

"I am the crown prince of all Kaltehafen," Oswald replied. "I'll make it worth your while to say so regardless."

"I am a man of principle," the doctor responded dryly. "And I will do no such thing."

Oswald's face went scarlet, he opened his mouth to reprimand the doctor but stopped short when Queen Damara entered. She was carrying Heidi in her arms. The little girl was sound asleep with her head resting on her mother's shoulder.

The doctor bowed respectfully and Lina curtsied.

"My queen," Lina said. "With your permission, we wish to pass the night here. In case Augustine needs my father's help when he returns."

"Thank you," she answered. The tiny smile she forced onto her lips did nothing to conceal her grief.

"Aunt Damara," Oswald interjected. "Tell my mother I'm alright, I should be with Father looking—"

"Silence, Oswald," Damara hissed.

Oswald fell silent instantly.

"Do you think this waiting isn't torture for me?" the queen continued. "If I didn't have Heidi to care for, don't you think I'd be by Florian's side? I'd tear the very earth apart to find Augustine."

"But—" Oswald started.

"Speak another word and I'll have you thrown in the dungeon," Damara retorted.

Oswald sealed his lips and marched from the room indignantly.

Under different circumstances, Lina would have taken immense delight in seeing Oswald humbled, but as it was she couldn't take much delight in anything. She told herself that Augustine would be back by dawn.

BUT DAWN CAME without any news of him. After what seemed like an endless night, Lina ventured from her room to the great hall. She was hoping to see Florian's company gathered there, all merrily celebrating Augustine's rescue. The morning dragged on. Lina paced across the castle grounds, jumping every time she heard the whinny of a horse, or someone approaching.

"Miss Lina!" A servant called jogging toward her across the grass.

Her heart leapt.

"Miss Lina," the servant said. "The queen wishes to speak to you."

With a quick "thank you" Lina raced toward the castle, her heart pounding with anticipation.

The queen was sitting at a little table in the library with a map spread out before her.

"Is there any news?" Lina asked her as she flew through the door.

Damara shook her head and Lina was hit with a wave of disappointment.

"Will you do something for me?" the queen asked.

"Of course," Lina replied, welcoming any opportunity to help.

"I have people spreading word of Augustine's capture in every village in Kaltehafen. I need someone to take notices to these three villages." She ran her finger down a line on the map that indicated a southern road.

"I can do that," Lina answered.

"There is one other thing I need your assistance with," Damara pressed. "Which may be more of a burden to you."

"Nothing that brings Augustine home is a burden to me," Lina replied.

"I need you to get rid of Oswald."

Lina went silent for a moment, as she tried to comprehend Damara's meaning. She made it sound like the type of task that would require violating the Hippocratic oath. (And since Hippocrates was practically a saint in her mind, she loathed the thought.)

"Get rid of...?" Lina questioned.

"Yes, I am sorry to ask you," Damara sighed. "But I think you are the only person with the patience to do this, and he's been nothing but a nuisance since Augustine's disappearance."

Damara rubbed her forehead between her thumb and forefinger leaving Lina with another awkward moment to ponder what Damara meant by "get rid of Oswald".

"I told Oswald," Damara continued. "That I need him to accompany you on your journey to protect you. I know he isn't much use as protection but I just need him to feel like he's doing something so he'll stop getting in the way of things here."

"Oh," Lina replied, feeling slightly relieved. "Yes, I can manage that."

"I am in your debt," Damara said with a weary smile. She then handed Lina a letter.

"If you encounter the king or any of his knights, please instruct them to send this to Princess Fausta of Kalathea by way of their fastest rider."

"Did you say Kalathea?" Lina asked, furrowing her brow. She must have misheard Damara. Even Florian's fastest rider would take weeks to get to Kalathea.

"Yes," Damara pressed. "No one knew Prince Justin better than the princess. If these men are claiming he's Augustine's father—"

"You found out what prince they were speaking about?" Lina asked eagerly.

"You said the men who took him claimed he was the son of Prince Justin," Damara insisted.

"Oh, I never heard a name," Lina corrected. "Only something about a prince."

Damara's eyes widened in horror, her cheeks flushed red. The strange combination of terror and shame made Lina realize that

Damara knew exactly what prince Augustine's captors were referencing.

Lina had stumbled upon a scandal.

It was probably a fascinating story, but she doubted knowing all the intriguing details would be helpful in bringing Augustine home. She pretended to miss the slip.

"It was probably someone else who suggested Prince Justin," Lina shrugged. "I'd better go. No sense wasting time."

Damara was silent for a long moment. Her head was bent so that she was staring vacantly at the library table.

Lina picked up her satchel and started for the door.

"It wasn't," Damara choked.

"My queen?" Lina asked, turning back to face her.

"No one else suggested it," Damara explained. "I knew they were speaking about Prince Justin because... what they said was true."

Tears escaped the queen's eyes, soaking her cheeks and splashing down onto the table.

Lina kept her face expressionless. Why was Damara telling her this?

"When I was about your age," Damara started. "I was a handmaiden to Princess Fausta of Kalathea. I was always taught that invisibility was the mark of a good handmaiden. My job was to draw attention to the princess; to shower her in compliments, to listen silently as others spoke of her beauty. In all my time at the palace, there was only one person who ever noticed *me*. Only one person ever told *me* I was beautiful."

Damara's hands began to shake. He cheeks reddened with fury.

"Damn it, I was so *stupid!* If the devil himself called me beautiful, I'd have happily mothered his child. I came to learn that Justin was about as close to the devil as a man can be."

Lina allowed herself a moment to absorb the information. "So you know why Augustine was taken?"

"If it's to settle some grievances with his father, it could be..." Damara shrugged. "...Anyone. That's why I must get this letter to Princess Fausta."

Lina nodded thoughtfully. "Does Augustine know about this?" She suspected she already knew the answer and dreaded what the truth would do to him.

A second wave of tears flooded Damara's cheeks as she shook her head and confirmed Lina's suspicions.

"Lina, swear to me that if you see him before I do you won't... you'll let him hear it from me. He deserves to hear it from me."

Lina was feeling strangely numb. It was like a thousand emotions were trying to seize her at once and all blocking each other so that she couldn't feel anything at all. In the near future, when she'd had a little more time to contemplate Damara's revelation, something would break through. The only thing she knew for sure, was that Augustine did indeed need to hear this from his mother. It killed her that she knew and he didn't. She wondered if Damara only told her because she was feeling guilty about not telling him, and needed to tell someone.

"I won't speak a word of it," Lina promised. "Unless circumstances leave me with no other choice."

Damara managed to mouth a thank you.

9

THE MAIDEN

Augustine jerked at the touch of a velvety muzzle. He had been wandering north all morning hoping he would find a road or a village or some sign of civilization. Around noon, he sat down to rest at the base of a tree and that's when he felt the silent animal touch his elbow.

He leapt backward drawing his knife only to see that the creature who touched him was a unicorn. It continued nosing his arm, as Augustine watched in disbelief.

Normally seeing a unicorn was a once-in-a-lifetime experience. What were the chances he'd see another one so soon after releasing Primrose?

It occurred to him that they were almost nonexistent.

Augustine leaned forward to get a better look. It certainly looked like Primrose. Its shaggy, overgrown mane tumbled down its forehead concealing its eyes. One of its ears had a small nick in the side and a quick glance at the underside confirmed this was, indeed, a male.

"Primrose?" Augustine asked.

The creature's ears went forward. It looked up at him for a minute and then started nibbling his sleeve.

"You followed me all this way?" he questioned. Unicorns were sacred animals, deeply intelligent, and magical. Perhaps Primrose had come to repay Augustine for letting him go.

"Primrose," Augustine started. "Will you show me the way home?"

He waited for some sign that the wise creature understood his request, but the animal only stretched its neck out and continued chewing on his sleeve. It was his right sleeve...perhaps Primrose was telling him to go right?

"Sacred creature," Augustine started. "Does home lie that way?" He pointed with his right hand. The unicorn's eyes followed his arm and it snapped at his sleeve with its flat teeth.

"What are you trying to tell me?" Augustine pleaded.

At that moment, the bread crust he had been hiding tumbled onto the ground. Primrose devoured it in two bites.

Augustine leaned his head back against a tree and closed his eyes.

"I'm an idiot," he sighed.

After swallowing the bread, the unicorn curled up on the grass beside him and placed its head in his lap.

Augustine stroked its mane. "They say unicorns are supernatural creatures," he grumbled. "But you, Primrose, are nothing more than an odd-looking goat."

The animal closed its eyes and a moment later, Augustine heard it snoring.

"First, Primrose," Augustine started. "We must do something about your name."

It was early afternoon, and Augustine was continuing his journey north. Primrose followed, perhaps hoping for more bread. Though still bitter about the theft, Augustine was grateful for the company.

"I think it should be a good, strong, masculine name," he continued. He thought for a moment, reviewing the names of mythological figures, heroes, and the like. Finally, he settled on the name of an early Christian martyr who was, in his opinion, one of the manliest people in history.

"St. Polycarp," Augustine declared. "Your name will be Polycarp. But we'll call you Poly for short."

The unicorn made no objections, and so Poly became his name.

Augustine's stomach burned with hunger and the berries he picked as he walked did nothing to relieve him. After a time, he found a brook and followed it upstream. Perhaps, it would take him to a pool where he could fish.

The creek became narrower the farther he went until he could step across it. The terrain was fairly flat, making Augustine wonder where the origin of the little brook was. His curiosity was rewarded. Presently, he came across a crumbling fountain. The water seemed to be flowing from the base.

It had once been a stunning sculpture, with pools at three different levels. It was covered in carvings of animals, trees, and other greenery. When he approached it, the birds in the canopy stopped singing, enveloping him in a suffocating silence.

The fountain stood completely alone among the trees. Augustine couldn't see any other ruins anywhere. Why would someone build a fountain in the middle of nowhere? There had to be something else nearby.

He looked over his shoulder and saw that Poly was waiting for him a few paces away.

"Are you coming?" Augustine whispered. He had no idea why he was whispering. But in this place, it seemed wrong to shout. Poly just paced back and forth bobbing his head up and down.

Augustine circled the fountain. The upper pools were dry, the water was flowing from somewhere on the lower level. He scanned the base for the source.

That's when he spotted another peculiarity. On the ground behind the fountain rested a little silver cage containing a single white dove.

The creature was cooing and bobbing its little round head. Augustine felt sorry for the bird. He glanced around for some sign of the owner but saw nothing. The poor little animal was abandoned. Probably starving... like him.

It occurred to him that he could put an end to the dove's suffering and his own hunger at the same time.

The cage wasn't locked, and the bird did not resist when he reached in and took it. Augustine adjusted his grip on the dove, so he could hold it still with one hand while wringing its neck with the other. As he did so, it turned its head sideways and looked at him with one, beady eye.

Augustine tried not to look into the helpless creature's little face. He wasn't normally the squeamish type, but for some reason, he was getting a strong feeling that he shouldn't harm the stupid and potentially delicious game bird.

He signed deeply and opened his hands.

"You're free," he grumbled, giving the bird a little toss into the air.

A cloud of smoke burst forth from the dove. Augustine stumbled backward coughing and fanning the air with his hand.

The smoke cleared revealing a maiden. She was breathtaking—tall, slender, and fair. Her long hair was such a light gold it was almost white. It spilled down her shoulders and over her spotless gown. She cocked her head and looked at him with a broad grin. There was something familiar about her eyes. They were black, somewhat beady, and lacked intelligence of any kind.

"Is it really you?" she breathed.

It occurred to Augustine that he was looking into the face of the little dove. She had somehow transformed into the goddess that stood before him. The color drained from his cheeks as he realized how close he'd come to wringing her neck and eating her.

"I've been waiting three years for you to save me," she smiled.

While Augustine was still horror-struck by what he had almost done, she wrapped her arms around his neck and pulled him into a kiss. This did nothing to alleviate his anxiety.

He stumbled backward, shoving her away.

"What are you doing?" he exclaimed.

"You are my true love," she giggled trying to pull him back into her arms.

"I don't know what you're talking about," he replied. He scanned the woods over her shoulder looking for Poly. Unfortunately, Poly had abandoned him in his moment of need.

The lady looked puzzled. "You broke my curse and restored me to my human form. You *must* be my true love."

"Well, there are, um, lots of different kinds of love," Augustine stuttered. "Maybe the curse required neighborly love or something?"

"Don't be silly," she giggled, again trying to pull him into her arms. He gave her a firm shove, immediately feeling guilty as she stumbled backward onto the ground.

"I'm so sorry," he said, offering her a hand. "I didn't mean to knock you down."

She accepted his hand with an eagerness that twisted his stomach, and giggled. "That's alright."

"Um, listen," he started, his cheeks flushing scarlet. "Do you have a home somewhere?"

Her face brightened. "Yes! I am Princess Leonore. My father is King Henry of Zoroske."

"Do you know how to get to Zoroske?" Augustine asked.

She glanced around the woods. "It's been such a long time, but... well, I don't think it's far at all."

Augustine felt hope welling up inside him. If he could make it to a village, he could get something to eat and directions back to Kaltehafen.

"Wonderful," he replied. "Let's get you home."

10

AUGUSTINE IS KIDNAPPED BY A PRINCESS

Extracting Leonore's story was a frustrating process. She told it to him in bits and pieces as they walked but always ended up going on tangents about how hopelessly in love she was, and how they would have a magnificent wedding.

"Do you think we can have the wedding tonight?" she asked, in that delicate airy voice of hers.

"Leonore, I cannot marry you," Augustine replied.

"Oh, you're just nervous," she objected. "Wedding jitters."

He was wondering if the curse had affected her sanity. "You were telling me about a witch," Augustine stated, trying to return her to the topic at hand.

"Yes, you see Father threw a feast for my fourteenth birthday," Leonore explained. "And he forgot to invite Lady Mirella—" She trailed off. "Maybe we should wait a day or two," she continued. "I want everyone to come to our wedding. We'll need time to send invitations..."

"Excellent point," Augustine pounced on the chance for delay. "It's really best not to rush these things. Now, you were saying something about Lady Mirella."

"Yes, we'll need to invite her," Leonore stated. "I don't want to get cursed again."

"So Lady Mirella turned you into a dove because she wasn't invited to your birthday party?"

"I've got it!" Leonore exclaimed. "We won't have invitations at all! The wedding will be open to everyone. No one can claim they weren't invited if everyone is invited."

Augustine closed his eyes and rubbed his forehead. His ravenous hunger was giving him a headache and Leonore's relentless love wasn't helping the matter. All he wanted was to get something to eat and then send a letter to his father.

"Listen, princess," he sighed. "I can't marry you."

"Of course, you can," Leonore smiled.

"I am a commoner," Augustine pointed out.

"A common man couldn't break my curse," Leonore giggled. She pulled him closer. He could feel her gazing up at him as she clung to his arm. He kept his eyes fixed on the road ahead.

"You are a lovely person, really," Augustine continued. "But...well, I am already promised to someone."

It wasn't technically true but after everything that had happened, he really wished it was. In fact, he made a decision right then and there that he was going to make it true the next time he saw Lina.

"You forget that my father is a king," Leonore giggled. "That won't be a problem."

Clearly, Leonore was not going to take no for an answer. If he could just get her back home, he could speak to her parents who would surely be more reasonable.

From that point on, he simply ignored her or changed the subject whenever she spoke of her love for him. He thought their journey would never end, but in time, they emerged through the tree line onto a wide grassy pasture. He saw cattle and sheep grazing, and their keepers milling among the herds.

In the distance, the turrets of a great, white castle rose up over the hills. When they entered the village, a crowd of excited residents swarmed around them and news of the princess's return reached the castle long before she did.

The king and the queen met them along the road. Seeing them embrace their long-lost daughter made Augustine think of his parents. He hoped he would have a happy reunion of his own soon.

"Father, this is Augustine," Princess Leonore introduced. "It was he that broke the curse and brought me home."

Augustine bowed politely when he was introduced.

The king placed a grateful hand on his shoulder. "I owe you a great debt," he smiled. "You will be handsomely rewarded for saving my daughter."

"It was nothing, my king," Augustine replied. He noticed Leonore grinning at him and looked away. "I ask only that you help me find my family. I was taken from them by highwaymen several days ago and do not know how to get back."

"Gladly, son! Gladly!" the king replied, smacking him on the back. "But first..."

He clapped his hands and three servants rushed to his side. "Take him inside and get him cleaned up. He must be presentable for the feast tonight."

Augustine allowed himself to be herded away.

SHORTLY THEREAFTER, Augustine was full and sitting comfortably at a table in the room the servants had provided for him. He wrote a letter to Florian, giving him his location and telling him that he was safe. Still, he didn't feel *completely* safe. After everything he had been through, he wouldn't feel safe until he was home.

He was just sealing the letter, when someone knocked on the door. It was Bence, the castle steward. He was a stick-thin and highly excitable man with large eyes that sometimes darted around as if he was being hunted by something.

"It's time!" Bence exclaimed.

"Time?" Augustine asked. It was still a bit early for dinner.

The servant laughed. "For the wedding of course!"

Augustine suddenly had an awful feeling in the pit of his stomach.

"Whose wedding?" he asked.

Bence just laughed.

"Really, whose wedding?" Augustine pressed.

The servant's smile faded. "Yours, my prince."

"Listen, there's been a misunderstanding," Augustine stated. "May I speak to the king?"

"There isn't time, sire," Bence insisted.

"I really must speak to the king," Augustine repeated.

"He'll be at the wedding," the servant answered.

"I cannot marry the princess," Augustine explained. "And I will not come with you until I am allowed to speak to the king."

The servant's face paled, a dread entered his eyes. Augustine noticed his hands trembling.

"Please, sire," Bence begged. "I cannot return to the king without you."

Bence's demeanor fed the fear that was stewing inside Augustine. "I'll come with you on one condition," he bargained.

"Anything!" the servant pleaded.

Augustine handed him the letter. "You promised to have this delivered to my stepfather King Florian of Kaltehafen. Do so at once."

Bence took it. "Of course, sire." As Augustine closed the door behind him, the servant added: "Do be careful, sire. The royals here are a bit..." he glanced around and then lowered his voice. "Sensitive."

"Sensitive?" Augustine whispered back.

Bence nodded. "It would be in your best interest not to offend them."

THERE WAS A TOWERING cathedral in the center of the village with an open square before it. The king, the queen, and Princess Leonore stood on the steps. The square was packed with excited villagers who all cheered at the sight of Augustine.

Bence whispered. "I will do what you've asked. Good luck, sire." He disappeared into the crowd. The king held his hands up to silence the rabble and then beckoned Augustine forward.

When he started up the cathedral steps he noticed the queen staring at him with one eyebrow raised, studying his face carefully. He returned her gaze and when he reached the top of the stairs, she said: "Sorry I didn't mean to stare, but you look exactly like someone I knew a long time ago."

"Your Highness," Augustine said, keeping his voice low. "I was wondering if I could speak with you and the king—"

But the king grabbed his forearm and spun him around to face the crowd.

"This young man has broken my daughter's curse!" the king exclaimed. The crowd cheered once again. "And I can think of no better reward than the hand of my daughter in marriage."

The crowd cheered even louder. Leonore was beaming and bouncing up and down with excitement.

"Your Highness," Augustine whispered. "I really must speak to you."

"Of course, son," The king replied. "After the wedding, we will have plenty of time to speak."

"I must speak to you *now*," Augustine insisted.

But the king ignored him and proclaimed: "Let the wedding begin!"

As the crowd cheered yet again, Augustine jerked away from the king and ran down the cathedral steps.

"No!" he cried.

The people went absolutely silent. Augustine could see dread entering their expressions. It was the same dread he saw in Bence's eyes after he demanded to speak with the king.

The king's face was hard as stone, his cold gray eyes bored into Augustine.

The latter knelt and bent his face to the ground. "I cannot express my gratitude for your kindness, Your Majesty," he said. "It delights me to see your daughter reunited with you. But I cannot accept, I—"

"Is there something wrong with my daughter?" the king growled.

"No!" Augustine replied. "She is beautiful and kind and, and... deserves someone who will love her in a way I can not."

"Why can't you?" the king demanded.

"Because I am already engaged," Augustine answered.

The king threw back his head and laughed. All the people in the square suddenly started laughing also—it was a forced and awkward sound.

"Am I not a king?" he proclaimed. "Consider your previous engagement dissolved."

"I told you," Leonore grinned.

Augustine suddenly felt his fear subside, replaced by a flicker of anger. He stood and, looking the king directly in the eyes, said: "I do not want my engagement dissolved."

"I beg your pardon?" the king answered. He rested his hand on his sword hilt and started down the stairs.

"I love my fiancée," Augustine replied. "And I will not call off my engagement."

The king continued toward Augustine, gripping the hilt of his sword. Augustine instinctively felt for his own weapon, but of course, his previous captors had removed it.

A few of the villagers turned their faces away.

"What woman," the king growled. "Could you possibly love more than my daughter?"

"Are you going to strike me down in cold blood?" Augustine demanded. "Or will you give me a sword and let us settle this fairly."

A few of the spectators gasped. The queen raised her eyebrows in surprise. The princess made a little squeak and covered her gaping mouth with her delicate palm.

"How dare you!" the king exclaimed. "You ungrateful little rat." He kicked Augustine in the chest, sending him backward onto the ground. He drew his weapon and might have sliced Augustine clean in half had not Leonore rushed forward and grabbed his arm.

"Papa, no!" she pleaded. "Can't you see how noble he's being?"

"Noble?" the king questioned.

"Yes!" Leonore insisted. "Dear Augustine is making excuses because he thinks he is unworthy of me."

The anger left the king's expression as quickly as it had entered. He smiled at his daughter. "You are right, precious," he answered. "To think he considers himself so unworthy, he would die rather than be your husband!"

The king offered Augustine a hand. "No man is worthy of my daughter, but you are perhaps the closest we'll ever come."

Augustine was utterly speechless. The king was clearly a madman, and would not see reason. He wondered how long it would take for his letter to reach Florian. If Florian had been tracking his captors accurately, he couldn't be far behind.

Augustine knelt before the king once again and said: "Your daughter has the beauty of a goddess, hair like spun gold, a face as fair as ivory, eyes like... like a dove."

He swore that Leonore was about to swoon.

"Truly, I could never be worthy of one so fair," he continued. "But please, allow me fourteen days of prayer and fasting to purify myself, so that I might at least be less unworthy of her."

The king smiled broadly, snatched Augustine's hand and jerked him to his feet. "Truly, you are the noblest of mortal men. I will grant your request."

The people cheered (albeit nervously).

The king clapped his hands. "Guards! Lock our new prince in the cathedral! Watch the doors to make sure he remains undisturbed in his quest for virtue!"

Augustine walked obediently through the ornate doors and did not look back when they were closed behind him. He marched down the silent aisle of the empty church, his heart pounding in his chest.

When he knelt at the altar rail, the first prayer he uttered in his mind was:

Dear Lord, why me?

11

HANDMAIDENS MAKE THE WORST QUEENS

L ina and Oswald started their journey at a gallop. Lina kept her eyes on the road before her, mulling over Damara's confession. She wished she didn't have such a long ride ahead. There was so much to process, and she had the strangest mix of emotions.

For a little while, her thoughts swept her into a memory. She was a little girl. Her father had sent her out to collect mushrooms that he used in various medicines. She knew these yellow and red mushrooms grew in abundance on the hillside in front of Castle Erkscrim. While she was working, a group of children surrounded her and started teasing her.

"Are those for your witches brew?" one of the boys exclaimed.

She knew from past experience that she could not reason with these children. She tried to ignore them but they kept following her, accusing her of trying to curse them among other things. Then one of the little boys suggested that her magic was in her hair, and that if they cut it off, they could steal her power. The children swarmed her at once, grabbing her hair in fistfuls, pulling it, and cutting it. She fell face forward onto the grass and clasped her hands over the back of her head, trying to shield herself.

Then, a new voice shouted from somewhere outside the swarm. It was the voice of a young boy. He had a very thick accent, she could hardly understand him at all.

The other children laughed and shouted as he jumped into their midst and tried to push her attackers off. He caused enough of a distraction that she was able to slip out from under the swarm pinning her down, and when she had righted herself she got a good look at the newcomer.

He was tiny and dark and utterly ferocious. Lina had never seen anyone like him before. Though completely surrounded, he stood tall and proud holding a stick like a sword. He pointed to each of the boys in turn, telling them that they were honorless cowards for attacking a girl.

Of course, none of them were intimidated. As they prepared to turn their aggression on him, the voice of a grown woman called, "Augustine!"

All the children looked to see the queen approaching at a distance trailed by three handmaidens. Then they fled back toward the village leaving Lina alone with her defender.

She felt her hair, trying to assess the damage. Several large patches were missing and aside from that she was a bruised and muddy disaster. When she saw the queen looking down at her, she turned an even deeper shade of red and wished that the earth would swallow her up.

Augustine started speaking to the queen in a language Lina couldn't understand. To her horror, the queen stooped down and took a strand of Lina's hair in her hand. A wave of embarrassment threatened to swallow her up.

"It's red," the queen said.

The statement made Lina burn with anger. Yes, of course, it was red. She already knew she was a freak of nature without the queen having to point it out to her.

"It's like..." She started snapping her fingers as she tried to think of the correct Kaltic word. She looked at Augustine, and pointing to a red jewel on her neck asked him something in their native tongue.

"Ruby," he replied.

"Like a ruby," the queen finished.

Lina had never really thought about it like that. The queen looked back at Lina, scrutinizing the damage. "I fix."

"Don't trouble yourself, my queen," one of the handmaidens objected. "I am sure I can do something for her."

"Don't touch!" the queen ordered. "She's mine."

The queen beckoned for Lina to follow her back to the castle. Once there, Damara had her sit while she attempted to rescue what was left of her hair. All the while, Augustine paced the room in front of her talking endlessly about Kalathean heroes.

Lina guessed that they were very exciting stories from his enthusiasm, but could only understand about half of what he said because his accent was so thick and he was speaking so quickly. He paused only when his mother needed him to translate something for her.

Lina knew that King Florian had found a wife during his expedition to Kalathea. The whole village was talking about it. No one had said anything about the new queen having a son. She liked him immediately. He seemed so excited about being in this strange new country and his energy was contagious.

The queen trimmed and combed and twisted and braided Lina's hair, shooing her handmaidens away anytime they dared offer assistance.

When she had finished she offered Lina a mirror. Lina's jaw dropped when she saw her own reflection. Her hair was done up, the patches carefully hidden by longer locks that had been combed over or braided up. It was the first time in Lina's nine years that she ever felt pretty.

"You come tomorrow. I do again," Damara explained. "Augustine, take ruby girl home."

"My name is Lina Bone," she corrected curtsying.

Despite this correction, the queen referred to Lina as "ruby girl" for the next three years. Lina didn't mind since Damara meant it as a compliment.

She would go to the castle regularly after that to play with Augustine. He always wanted to be the hero. He rescued Lina from dragons, and ogres, and barbarian hordes until she got sick of playing the victim and insisted on being the enemy general of whatever army he wanted to fight.

When they weren't playing, he would proudly boast about his father Attikos Hatsi. Attikos Hatsi, defender of Lysandria—to Augustine he was Hercules or Perseus. He hoped he would grow up to be just like Attikos.

Lina, now knowing the truth, dreaded what it would do to him.

"We should slow down for a while," she called to Oswald. "So we don't exhaust the horses."

They slowed to a walk. Without the thundering of hooves, the countryside seemed almost silent.

"So..." Oswald began. "You and Augustine."

Lina didn't like wherever this was going.

"Aunt Damara says you're engaged."

Lina wasn't surprised. Damara had been talking like they were engaged for as long as Lina could remember. In response to Oswald, she shrugged and continued staring down the road ahead, hoping he would take the hint.

"Are you?" Oswald pressed.

"My parents haven't said anything to me about it," Lina answered.

"Well it is a good match," Oswald observed.

Lina glanced sideways at him. *Was Oswald complimenting them?*

"A doctor's daughter...An equestrian's son," he continued. "Yes, I'd say you're equals, assuming your father is university trained and not just the village healer."

Those words brought a slight frown to Lina's lips. Augustine would have wisely seen this as a warning. But Oswald, being unfamiliar with her subtleties, didn't notice at all.

"Normally, being the king's stepson might put him out of your reach. But given he's a foreigner and all—"

"Have you ever considered *not* saying everything that pops into your head?" Lina interrupted.

Augustine would have noticed the fury burning in her eyes. In fact, he probably would have fled long before she reached this point.

"I am the crown prince of all Kaltehafen," Oswald replied indignantly. "Who are you to tell me what I should or shouldn't say?"

"I should probably tell King Filbert someone's abducted his son," Lina mentioned.

"What are you talking about? I haven't been abducted."

Lina regarded him quizzically. "Are you sure? Because if someone swapped you with a jackass I wouldn't know."

Oswald's mouth fell open. She kicked her horse and it returned to a gallop. Oswald pursued.

"You do realize that one day I'll have the power of life and death over you and every soul in Kaltehafen! Then I will remember who it was that treated me with respect!"

Lina jerked her horse to a stop and spun around to face him. Oswald's horse reared to avoid a collision, almost throwing him off.

"Do you realize that no one respects you?" Lina hissed. "Certainly, they pretend to appease you, but... let me think... Maybe a week after your coronation, you'll be assassinated or overthrown and not one of your subjects will grieve you. In fact, we'll hail our conquerors as liberators."

"Are you threatening me?" Oswald accused.

Lina smiled. "No, I am simply speaking the truth. Honestly, I don't care enough about you to expend the effort it would take to assassinate you. But don't let that hurt you, my prince." She reached over and gave his shoulder a squeeze. "Someone cares."

Oswald was left dumbstruck. Lina turned her horse and continued forward at a walk.

A moment later, she heard his horse approaching from behind. He rode silently the rest of the way, staring at the ground, his face frozen in a scowl.

12

MAD HENRY

A ugustine spent an uncomfortable night curled up on the floor of the vestibule. He jerked awake to the gonging of the bells somewhere above him. The front doors opened, and villagers started trickling in.

He wasn't sure what day it was but decided it wasn't a Sunday when he noticed the few attendees were all cheery old women. They smiled at him, whispering and blushing as they shuffled in. He heard one say to her companion: "Oh, he's gorgeous! If I was forty years younger..." she giggled.

He stood in the very back corner of the church as he waited for Mass to begin, wondering if the guards were still posted outside and how he could make his escape.

Suddenly he heard a great commotion and the royal family entered. Behind them came first an entourage of servants and guards, then a crowd of villagers who had suddenly regained the piety required for daily Mass attendance.

Augustine prayed Leonore wouldn't notice him, but of course, she did. She spent the entire service watching him over her shoulder, with a smile so radiant it put the stained glass windows to shame. Augustine tried desperately to avoid eye contact.

The priest had hardly finished the dismissal when the royal family and their entire entourage poured down the aisle and out onto the steps. Augustine looked through the open doors, wondering if he could disappear into the crowd. If he could only get past the guards, he could make for the forest and wait for Florian there.

As he was formulating the plan in his mind, he noticed three friars approaching the church on horseback. Though they wore their hoods low over their faces, Augustine recognized them by their stature immediately.

He ducked away from the door, his mind racing. He needed to stay close to the village, so he could meet his stepfather. But supposing Florian didn't get his message? Then in fourteen days, he would be forced to marry Leonore or die. Of course, King Henry was not exactly sane and predictable. He could easily go into a rage and kill him before then or perhaps, Leonore would lose patience and demand he marry her sooner.

Would he be safer in the hands of his former kidnappers? Whoever hired Wolf might also want to kill him. He spent a few moments trying to decide if he would rather die by King Henry's hand or Wolf's. Finally, he decided he didn't want to die at all and settled on a third option.

He would attempt to slip out a side door and flee back into the forest. As he made his way up the left-hand aisle, he noticed the three monks entering. He quickened his pace, swearing in his mind. The three were coming up behind him with their hooded heads bent and their hands folded reverently.

Augustine had no idea how they managed to walk so quickly while still maintaining an air of piety, but somehow they came right up behind him.

"You're in quite the predicament aren't you?" Wolf whispered.

Augustine paused and spun around to face him. "If you do not leave me," he returned. "I will cry out and every warrior in this village will come rushing to my aid."

Wolf grinned. "You really want to become Mad Henry's son-in-law?"

Augustine took a step backward. "Why shouldn't I?" Augustine replied. "Leonore is beautiful."

"True," Wolf agreed. "And as mad as her father, who has a reputation of decapitating people without warning."

Augustine took another step backward toward the side door.

"You must think I am blind," Wolf smirked. "I am not going to let you leave through that door, unless you are in my custody."

Augustine closed his eyes and prayed.

Lord help me, I am about to do something stupid.

Then he bolted, flying through the door with Wolf and company on his tail. Augustine sprang past the guards posted outside, then darted sideways to avoid colliding with a flock of old women.

Wolf was able to dodge the group without slowing down, giving him enough time to draw his dagger and snatch Augustine's wrist.

Augustine struggled to free himself, but Wolf was too quick. He pulled Augustine into a choke hold and pressed the tip of his dagger to his throat. By that time, the guards were almost upon them. Wolf swung his hostage around to face them.

"Another step and I kill him," he threatened.

News of the chase must have reached the front of the church because the king and his entourage were rushing to the scene.

"King Henry!" Wolf exclaimed. "What an honor!"

"Release the prince!" Henry demanded, his cheeks scarlet with rage.

"Oh no, sire!" Wolf objected. "I am doing you a great service."

"I will not listen to this!" Henry cried, but under the circumstances, he didn't have much choice.

"Would you really have your daughter marry Prince Justin's son?" Wolf responded.

Augustine did not think it possible for the king's face to become any redder. He was wrong. At the mention of Justin's name, King Henry's face contorted into an awful shape and became almost purple. He shook with rage.

"Prince Justin of Kalathea?" he snapped.

"The very same," Wolf replied.

"Lies!" Henry shrieked.

"I can prove it to you," Wolf remarked.

"There's no need," came a voice from behind the king. The queen stepped forward.

"It's undeniable," she stated. "He is Prince Justin's perfect image." She looked fondly at Augustine.

"Are you certain, darling?" the king asked.

"Without a doubt," the queen answered. "Why, when I first saw him, I thought he was Prince Justin for a brief moment. That he was returning for me." She smiled dreamily, then added. "I was terrified of course."

The king pointed his blade at Augustine's heart.

"After what Justin did... I have often wished he was still alive," the king fumed. "So that I could rip him apart myself. In his stead, you will suffer tortures neither God nor man can fathom!"

"I'll go with you," Augustine whispered to Wolf.

"I thought you'd see reason," Wolf replied. "On three, we run for the horses."

"Oh, Papa no!" Leonore squeaked from beside her mother.

"One," Wolf whispered.

"No daughter of mine shall ever marry that swine's son!" the king answered.

"Two."

"But Papa! I love him."

"Only because you do not know what his father did to our family!" the king retorted.

"Three."

Wolf released Augustine and they started tearing away through the village. Mill, who was running with Faruk just behind them, whistled. A moment later, Augustine heard horses galloping adjacent to them. Wolf swung into his saddle without breaking his stride.

He held out his hand for Augustine who, taking it, stumbled up the side of the animal and landed awkwardly on his stomach across its upper back. He quickly corrected his position.

The king's men pursued, shouting and firing crossbows. Wolf and his company dodged in and out among the houses as bolts sliced the air around them. Augustine jumped each time he felt a puff of air from a close shot.

Later, when he had time to think, he would be amazed by Wolf's evasion skills. In the moment, he couldn't do much besides hang on tight and pray for deliverance.

They were well into the woods before Wolf determined it was safe enough to slow his horse. He breathed deeply, releasing a victorious chuckle, then said, "That was exhausting, Augustine. Please do not run off again."

13

LINA MEETS LEONORE

Lina and Oswald posted notices in two of the three towns Damara had indicated. They described Augustine and his captors to everyone and anyone they encountered. As they made their way to the final village, Lina noticed the daylight dwindling.

"We'll pass the night in the next town," she stated. It was the first thing she said to Oswald since their squabble.

"Are you giving the orders now?" Oswald grumbled.

"If you have another idea, speak it," Lina remarked.

"Continue," Oswald scowled.

"Then tomorrow we'll go home," Lina answered. "They've probably found him by now."

Lina had an awful feeling there was no news of Augustine. She would go home and just be forced back into the torture of waiting.

When they made it to the inn, Lina spent a sleepless night staring at the wall, hoping and praying that Augustine was alright. Long before the sun rose, she ventured into the village street and walked around a bit hoping that the brisk morning air would clear her head.

Just after sunrise, she met Oswald in front of the inn. They readied their horses and prepared to leave. As Lina was settling into the saddle, she heard the thundering of hoofbeats and saw a company of soldiers approaching.

"That's Sir Albert," Oswald observed. He urged his horse forward. Lina followed close behind.

"Is there any news?" Oswald called.

Sir Albert's company halted.

"I am afraid not, Your Highness," Sir Albert replied. "Your father and uncle were following the captor's trail south last I heard. We've been patrolling the villages, trying to find out if anyone knows the men who took him."

As Albert spoke, Lina remembered Damara's letter. She was reaching into her satchel for it when she heard the thundering of hooves from a single horse along with a frantic, "Sire! Sire!"

She looked up to see a wide-eyed, excitable looking fellow charging toward Albert's company. He was holding a letter of his own, waving it around wildly as he approached.

He halted before Sir Albert.

"Are you—," he paused to inhale deeply. "Are you King Florian of Kaltehafen?"

"No," Sir Albert replied. "But I serve in his court."

The little man coughed a few times as he tried to catch his breath. "I have a message for the king, from his stepson."

Lina felt a prick of anticipation.

"Do you know where he is?" Sir Albert demanded, taking the letter.

"He is at the castle of King Henry of Zoroske," the man replied.

Relief flooded Lina. Augustine had been rescued by a neighboring king. He was safe.

"God help us!" Sir Albert exclaimed, his eyes widening in horror. "Mad Henry's got him!"

Sir Albert charged back down the road and his entourage followed suit.

Lina's relief dissipated instantly. She looked at Oswald. He looked at her. Then they both sent their horses charging after the party.

.   .   .

SIR ALBERT SENT his fastest riders to find the kings while he continued toward Zoroske. Lina and Oswald followed the group, each hoping no one would notice and send them home. No one did. When the company reached the border, the kings and several other knights were already waiting for them.

"Father!" Oswald greeted, as he rode toward the nearest king.

"God help you if you ever call me "Father" again," Florian retorted. "What are you doing here?"

Before Oswald could answer, Florian continued. "Never mind, we'll deal with you later."

Filbert appeared in the crowd behind his brother and motioned to Oswald. He left Lina and moved to his father's side, while Florian addressed the company.

"Gentlemen," Florian began. "We are about to meet with King Henry of Zoroske. As most of you are aware, King Henry is a madman. Unfortunately, he is a madman that is currently sheltering my son. This situation requires diplomatic savvy."

"So let us do the talking," Filbert explained.

"Precisely," Florian agreed. "And until the prince is returned safely to us, you must act as if you agree with everything the king says."

"Do nothing to anger him," Filbert added.

"Right," Florian continued. "If he says fish roam the land, they do. If he says the sky is green, it is. Understood?"

Everyone did and so they fell in line behind Filbert and Florian and proceeded toward the village. No one seemed to notice Lina in the crowd. She was grateful for this. She pulled her hood up over her red hair, hoping the kings would continue to be too distracted to see her following.

When they approached the castle, the company dismounted. The kings picked a few of their knights to accompany them into the hall, while the others waited outside the gates.

Lina tried to follow, but one of the castle guards caught her arm.

"Where are you going?" he demanded.

"I am with King Florian's company," she replied.

"And I'm the pope's aunt," the guard answered. Oswald emerged from the gate behind the guard. "She's with me," he insisted.

The guard looked between Oswald and Lina, slightly alarmed.

"Of course, Your Highness," he said. "I apologize."

Oswald offered Lina his arm and they proceeded inside. Lina said something she never thought she'd say. "Thank you, Oswald."

King Henry was sitting on his throne, with his wife and daughter seated on either side of him.

Lina kept looking around the room, hoping she would spot Augustine somewhere among the nobles and attendants who occupied the hall.

King Henry stood up as Filbert and Florian approached.

"It's good to see you old friends!" he smiled. "I don't think we've spoken since the last invasion! What was it, ten years ago?"

"I remember that!" Filbert smiled. "You laid waste to our southern frontier!"

"Yes, I almost had you didn't I?" Henry laughed.

Filbert and Florian laughed with him as enthusiastically as they could manage.

Henry's face fell. "It's an awful shame we aren't meeting under happier circumstances."

Lina saw the panic in Florian's eyes, but he managed to keep his composure.

"Happier circumstances?" he questioned.

"Old friend, I am afraid I have horrible news," Henry sighed.

Lina felt her heart in her throat.

"Florian, Florian, old friend, I simply don't know how to tell you this..." Henry continued.

"Say it plainly," Florian replied. "There's no sense hiding it."

"It will devastate you," Henry remarked.

"Damn it, Henry!" Florian snapped, losing his composure. "Out with it."

"I am afraid that your son Augustine is..." Henry sighed. "...not really your son."

Lina furrowed her brow. Did Henry not know that Augustine was

Florian's *stepson*? She looked at Florian. She could see relief wash over him before he adopted an expression of absolute shock.

"No!" Florian gasped. "It isn't so!"

"I'm afraid it is," Henry explained.

"How is this possible!" Florian exclaimed.

"Your wife had an affair with none other than Prince Justin of Kalathea," Henry stated.

"It cannot be!" Florian exclaimed.

"But don't worry, Florian," Henry continued. "We will not allow your humiliation to continue. I have men hunting for the boy now, who intend to put an end to him."

"He's not here?" Florian asked.

"The cunning devil slipped through my fingers this very morning," Henry replied. "But fear not, Florian! He cannot be far."

"Oh Henry," Florian continued. "I couldn't ask for a truer friend! But it was I whom Justin duped. If your men capture the boy, let me be the one to end him."

Henry's face reddened. "You are not the only one who has a grievance with that Kalathean rat snake! He almost killed my wife!"

"Did he?" Florian exclaimed, taking a step backward toward the door.

"Seventeen or... maybe eighteen years ago, I caught my wife passionately kissing that devil. I was going to kill her for that, until she explained about the love potion."

The queen blushed.

"Wait, you almost killed your wife, or Justin almost killed your wife?" Filbert asked.

"Justin almost made me kill my wife," Henry explained. "And if I ever catch that child of his, I'll water the earth with his blood!"

"How about we capture the boy alive, and then have a duel to decide who gets to kill him?" Florian suggested. "Or better yet, we can both kill him at the same time."

"Florian, I like the way you think!" Henry praised.

Florian asked Henry in which direction Augustine had gone and where his men were searching. As he spoke, Lina noticed the princess staring at her. She pretended not to notice and continued listening to Henry as he provided the details of Augustine's escape.

Filbert and Florian left the moment they had all the information they could get. Lina and Oswald tailed their party to the door. Just as Lina was about to leave, someone behind her spoke.

"Who are you?"

Lina turned to see the princess. She was a stunning young woman, the model of a perfect princess.

"I am Lina of Kaltehafen," Lina answered with a respectful curtsy.

"Why are you traveling with King Florian's company?" the girl pressed.

"It's a long story," Lina replied.

"Tell it," the princess ordered.

Lina did not want to be delayed. "I am a healer," she replied. "The king was worried his son might be wounded."

"Is that all?"

Lina was frustrated. Now was not the time for such an interrogation. Why did the princess care anyway?

Oswald noticed Lina lingering behind and decided to be helpful. "She's his fiancée."

The princess narrowed her eyes. "I see."

She scrutinized Lina, looking her up and down.

"I mean no disrespect," Lina continued. "But I must leave, we're falling behind."

Without a word, the princess turned and swept back across the hall toward her father.

Lina didn't take the time to think about how strange the exchange was. Augustine was probably nearby and she wanted to do everything she could to find him before Mad Henry's men did. She did not notice the princess whispering something into her father's ear and pointing at her. Nor did she see Henry reply by smiling and nodding and saying, "Of course, darling!"

14

POLY RETURNS

It was late afternoon before Wolf allowed his party to stop and catch their breath. The moment Augustine dismounted, his knees gave way beneath him and he sank to the ground trembling from head to foot.

Wolf offered him a water skin which he gratefully accepted. His captors seemed unfazed by their close escape. As Augustine struggled to keep his hands steady so he could drink, Wolf stood over him looking slightly annoyed.

"We've lost two days, Augustine," he stated.

"How unfortunate," Augustine scowled. "I wouldn't want to be late for whatever horrors this client of yours has planned for me."

"Don't be so dramatic," Wolf replied. "You do not know anything about what my client has planned for you."

"Well, if he was inviting me to dinner, he would have sent an invitation," Augustine shot back.

Wolf was regarding Augustine, thoughtfully stroking his chin.

"Tell me, Augustine," he said. "How should we punish you for the inconvenience you've caused?"

"Having to look at you is worse than any torture you could inflict," Augustine replied.

This comment clearly impressed Wolf, who smiled and raised his eyebrows slightly.

"You should remove that quick tongue of his," Mill laughed. "Before you get hurt."

Wolf regarded Augustine thoughtfully, pretending to consider Mill's suggestion. At least... Augustine hoped he was pretending.

Any second, Wolf was going to say something to indicate he wasn't seriously considering cutting his tongue out... Wolf rubbed his chin thoughtfully and then to Augustine's immense relief, he shook his head.

"No, no, best we keep you in one piece," he grinned. "I have another idea."

He snatched a rope from his saddle.

Augustine, unwilling to show fear, decided to change the subject.

"Wolf," he began.

"Yes?" Wolf responded pleasantly, unwinding a portion of the rope.

"Back at the church, you said that you had proof of my parentage."

"I do indeed."

"Show it to me," Augustine demanded.

"No," Wolf replied. "Now come over here so I can tie you up."

Augustine scowled.

"Now is really not the time to be difficult," Wolf reasoned. "If you delay us, Mad Henry will find you."

"Or maybe my father will," Augustine answered.

Wolf rolled his eyes and motioned to Faruk. Augustine didn't struggle as Faruk pushed him forward but he offered no assistance either. He was too exhausted for a fight, particularly when he knew it wouldn't end in his favor.

Wolf bound Augustine's hands in front of him and left a long lead on the rope. He handed the end to Faruk, who held it as he mounted his horse. Before Wolf returned to his own steed, he gave Augustine a little pat on the shoulder and said, "since you like running so much."

.   .   .

A FEW MOMENTS LATER, Augustine found himself running along behind Faruk's horse as it trotted through the forest. He was somewhat relieved that this was his punishment. The alternatives he'd imagined were much worse.

They were on some sort of a hidden road. He could see faded lines on the ground below him, where carts had passed. A wall of trees loomed on either side and other than the road itself, there was no sign of humanity anywhere.

Mill rode along beside Wolf, chatting pleasantly. Faruk was like a statue, still and silent. Augustine wondered what a man like Faruk thought about. He was probably relishing some sweet memory of pounding helpless serfs into the mud.

Augustine drifted into his own thoughts, trying to process the events of the previous days. What did Wolf possess that made him so absolutely certain of Augustine's parentage?

He thought about Mad Henry's wife, the way she was convinced just by looking at him that he was Prince Justin's child. He suddenly understood. By some unfortunate coincidence, he happened to resemble the prince. So when Wolf was sent to capture the son of Prince Justin, he just assumed it was him.

At midday, they found Wolf's cart just off the path where he had apparently hidden it before setting out to rescue Augustine. (Or kidnap him again, depending on how you looked at it.)

They let him rest while they hitched up their horses. Flopping down on the grass came as a great relief after his long run, but it was short-lived. In a few moments, they set off again with Wolf driving the cart, Mill riding along beside, and Faruk sitting in the back holding one end of the rope that bound Augustine while he jogged along behind.

He didn't think about much of anything during the second half of the day. He focused on keeping his stride, so he wouldn't end up being dragged along the ground.

When evening came, Augustine's lungs were tight and his legs were aching. He wanted nothing more than to collapse onto the forest floor and sleep. But Wolf bound him to a tree in a standing position and left him there all night. Even so, he eventually fell into a shallow and fitful sleep. When they untied him the next morning, he was stiff and sore. They continued the next day and night, as they had the first, with Augustine running along behind the cart and then tied upright all night long.

Several hours into the third day of running, exhaustion completely overcame Augustine and he collapsed into the road behind them. Faruk released the rope so that the horses wouldn't drag him, and Wolf halted the cart and dismounted.

Augustine lifted himself up into a kneeling position, and struggled to keep his head up and his eyes open. Wolf cut his bonds and stood over him with a triumphant smile.

"You're free," he said. "Go ahead, run away!"

Augustine was trembling with anger. He glared up at his captor but said nothing.

"I am not usually so generous," Wolf continued. "If you don't leave now, I won't offer again."

Augustine knew it was impossible. Every muscle in his body ached, even holding himself in a slumped kneeling position was taking the last of his strength. It was clear that Wolf knew it also. Part of Augustine wanted to try running, just to spite him.

"Of course," Wolf continued. "If you don't mind being our prisoner a while longer, we might let you sleep in the back of the cart."

Augustine started falling forward and put his hand out to catch himself before he hit the ground. Wolf took his arm and pulled him to his feet, then helped him up into the cart.

Augustine didn't remember lying down, he didn't remember the cart lurching forward. When he woke, he was in the same place where he had fallen asleep, but it was dark out, and they weren't moving. One of his captors had bound his hands and feet and then kindly covered him in a blanket.

He lifted up his head, just enough to see over the side. Wolf and Faruk were sleeping by a little campfire. Mill was up, keeping watch.

Then, over his shoulder, an animal sneezed. Augustine jumped and rolled over to see what the thing was. He saw a white muzzle and a pair of velvet lips casually gnawing on the side of the cart. But the feature that gave the animal away was the long spiral horn that poked up well above the side.

"Poly?" Augustine whispered.

He glanced back over toward Mill. Thankfully, he hadn't noticed the unicorn.

"Go away, Poly!" Augustine hissed, leaning up to see if he could see the rest of the creature's face. He couldn't quite boost himself high enough.

"Do you know what kind of men these are?" Augustine scolded. The horn of a unicorn alone could make a man rich. Augustine had no doubt his captors would kill Poly if they got the chance. The stupid animal's teeth scratching against the wood seemed to echo through the entire forest.

"*Poly stop*," Augustine ordered.

The animal suddenly froze and then darted away, disappearing into the darkness. Augustine heard someone approaching. It was Mill.

"You're awake," he observed.

Augustine looked up at him without saying a word.

"Trying to chew your way out?" he asked dryly.

"Doesn't hurt to try," Augustine shrugged.

Mill snorted a laugh, then circled the cart, looking under and over it. Grumbling something about "damn rodents", under his breath.

"Well, I definitely heard something gnawing on something over here," he stated. "You see what it was?"

"I told you, it was me," Augustine insisted.

Mill regarded him skeptically. "Quit toying with me, what was it?"

"You want the full and honest truth?" Augustine answered, staring Mill dead in the eyes.

"Out with it," Mill ordered.

"It was a unicorn," Augustine answered. "Gnawing on the wood, just there." He nodded toward the side of the cart.

Mill responded with a cold scowl.

"Do you know what happened to the last man who mocked me?" he growled.

"Nothing you'd dare do to me," Augustine retorted. "Assuming you want to get paid for delivering me to this client of yours."

Mill rubbed the bridge of his nose between his thumb and forefinger. "I hate noble brats," he sighed. He shoved Augustine back down and said, "sleep. If I hear so much as a shuffle over here, I'll see that you run all the way to Anamia."

Augustine furrowed his brow. *Anamia?* It would take them six months to get there, assuming they didn't get snowed in along the way. Who would send men halfway across the world to find him? What made him so important?

15

OSWALD EXPLAINED

Lina and Oswald followed Florian's company as they swept the woods surrounding Henry's capital. Unfortunately, they lost the trail of Augustine's captors shortly after entering the forest. Filbert and Florian divided their group and sent search parties in all directions.

Oswald chose to stay with his father and Lina chose to stay with Oswald. Keeping him out of the way was the one thing she could do to help in this effort, so she intended to give it her all.

Once or twice, Filbert's party encountered a group of Henry's men. Their interactions were polite but brief. As evening came on, they were no closer to finding the trail. Lina didn't know much about tracking, but listening to Filbert and his men talk, she gathered that Augustine's captors had made an art of covering their tracks.

Somehow, during the course of their escape, while being chased by Henry's men, they had left numerous false trails behind them. Each lead ended abruptly, forcing Filbert's men to double back again and again.

Towards dusk, they ran into Florian who looked absolutely awful. His eyes were underlined with deep shadows and he was riding slouched in the saddle. It was clear from his expression and the tone he used with those around him that he was frustrated and irritable.

"You need to sleep," Filbert stated.

"Not until we've found him," Florian snapped.

"You haven't slept in three days!"

"I swore I would not rest until Augustine was safe." Florian intended to take it literally. Lina approved of his spirit but thought it foolish practically speaking.

"He's never going to be safe if you're not rested enough to find him," Filbert pointed out.

Florian continued objecting and Filbert continued insisting until they were shouting at each other.

Filbert drew his blade and cried, "You sleep or I'll make you sleep!"

Lina realized to her horror, that he was threatening to knock his brother over the head. She went rigid as the image of Filbert bringing the hilt of his weapon down directly on the top of Florian's head flashed across her mind. If he hit the bregma– that is, the intersection between the three largest skull plates—she probably wouldn't be able to save him even with the proper surgical equipment.

"Stop!" she cried, as she galloped toward them.

"Lina!" Florian exclaimed. "How long have you been here?"

"I came with Oswald," she explained. "The queen sent me. I–"

Florian interrupted with an irritated sigh. "This is the last thing I need. Augustine will never forgive me if anything happens to you."

Lina blushed.

"King Filbert," she said. "I humbly request that you refrain from hitting your brother over the head. It might knock him unconscious, but it also might kill him or permanently damage his mind."

She looked at Florian. "And even a little sleep would do you good. What use is finding Augustine, if you haven't the strength to defeat his captors?"

"Our quarrel does not concern you," Florian replied. "You are to make camp with Filbert's company, and Oswald will escort you home in the morning."

The king was insufferable sometimes, but he really loved Augustine. Lina knew he wouldn't listen to reason. She decided it was time for a new approach.

"If you do not rest at least a little while, I will ride off alone into the forest," Lina threatened. "I'll probably get devoured by beasts and then you'll have to explain that to Augustine when you find him."

"I'll help her do it!" Filbert laughed.

Florian swore. "Why did Augustine fall for such a–"

"Sensible woman?" Filbert returned. "Because he needed to learn sense from *someone.*"

Florian grumbled his displeasure but ultimately agreed.

THE COMPANY WAS DEEPLY unhappy about having a woman in their midst because it made them feel the need to act respectable. They put up a little tent for Lina and then Filbert and Florian both threatened to kill anyone who so much as looked at her the wrong way.

Lina went inside and lay down without complaint. Despite her worry, she was exhausted and fell into a fitful sleep. Sometime in the dead of night, she woke to the sound of voices outside. The first belonged to one of the two kings. He was attempting to whisper but unfortunately, she could hear him clearly.

"If that damn son of yours hadn't broken his arm, he might have been able to defend himself," the voice accused.

"Well, if *your* son hadn't broken my son's arm, he might have been able to defend him."

Lina took a moment to absorb their words, then decided the first speaker was Florian talking about Augustine.

"If your son hadn't insulted my wife, my son wouldn't have had to break his arm," Florian retorted. "You raised an awful son, Filbert. He is honorless and vile."

"Me?" Filbert exclaimed. "Why does everyone blame me for Oswald's behavior? I hardly raised him. I was always off fighting someone or other—"

"Me," Florian reminded.

"Yes, you! But I saw to it that he had the best nurses and tutors in the world. They never denied him anything!" Filbert sighed despondently. "I don't know why he turned out the way he did."

"Well, do something about him," Florian ordered. "Or it will be a sad day for Kaltehafen when he's crowned."

"Maybe I'll send him on a crusade..." Filbert thought aloud.

They were both quiet for a long while. Just as Lina was finally falling asleep, the kings started speaking again, jerking her back into consciousness.

"Do you ever think..." Florian started. "That maybe it's our fault?"

"Is what our fault?" Filbert grumbled.

"That they fight."

"How is that our fault?"

"I don't know," Florian sighed. "It was something Damara said to me after our sons maimed each other. She said that if I must fight with you, I should leave Augustine out of it."

"Absurd," Filbert answered, "hysterical female nonsense."

Lina, of course, thought that Damara was absolutely right. Filbert and Florian had been rivals for as long as anyone could remember and now that they were getting older, they were using their sons to continue their unresolved feud. It was perfectly obvious, at least to the mind of a hysterical female. She hoped and prayed that they would learn something from Augustine's preventable capture.

The kings went quiet for a few minutes. Lina felt her eyes starting to close.

"Filbert?" Florian started.

Lina's eyes jerked open. She pulled her blanket over her head. This did nothing to block the sound of the conversation.

"Yes, Florian?"

"*Why* do we fight?"

"...I don't know," Filbert mumbled.

"We've been fighting for as long as I can remember," Florian mentioned. "I have no idea what started it."

"They say that every man is at war with himself," Filbert observed. "What if we are actually one man with his internal war–"

"Externalized?" Florian gasped.

They had hit upon a revelation and began to philosophize with enthusiasm. It took some time, but Lina's attempts to ignore them eventually succeeded and she drifted off to sleep.

FILBERT AND FLORIAN were gone by the time she awoke in the morning, along with most of their company. The few men who remained planned to divide into groups and continue searching the surrounding villages for anyone who might have any information about Augustine's captors.

Lina decided to get out of their way as quickly as possible. She found Oswald who seemed to be in a particularly sour mood that morning. He was snippy and short tempered with the men. He kept his expression frozen in a scowl and took his time getting his things together.

"We shouldn't delay," Lina implored, as he slowly tucked a few items in his saddlebag.

He grumbled something she couldn't hear, but eventually mounted his horse. They were just about to leave, when Lina remembered Damara's letter. In all the chaos that ensued during the search for Augustine, she had forgotten to give it to Florian.

She swore in her mind. She failed to do the one thing she was able to do to help with Augustine's rescue.

"Oswald, do you think we can catch up with the king's company?" she asked.

Oswald raised his eyebrows in surprise, then broke into a smile. "Of course!"

He turned his horse south and started charging forward.

Lina caught up to him. "Don't get any ideas about staying with them," she called. "I only need to give the king this letter. Then we must stay out of their way."

They rode at full speed until their horses grew exhausted, then slowed to a walk.

They were now moving along through the forest that surrounded the capital of Zoroske. Suddenly, they heard the thundering of hoof-beats behind them and turned to see a company of Henry's men approaching.

"Halt!" they called.

Lina and Oswald turned to face them. A knot formed in Lina's stomach.

"Do you have news of the prince?" Oswald asked.

The man at the head of the group was dark and stick thin with an angular face.

"No," he frowned. "I am here because King Henry requests the presence of this woman." He looked at Lina.

Lina felt a prick of indignation at being called "this woman". She opened her mouth to introduce herself properly, but Oswald was faster.

"She has a name," he growled. "It's Lina."

"Lina Bone," Lina added. "What does the king want with me?"

"He didn't say," the thin man replied.

"I must apologize to the King," Lina answered. "But I am on an urgent mission by request of Queen Damara of Kaltehafen. I cannot return with you."

"This is not a request," the thin man said.

"Excuse me," Oswald interrupted. "Lina is *my* subject. She doesn't need to take orders from *your* king."

"She does if she's on his land," the thin man threatened. "Now, are you going to come quietly?"

"This is outrageous!" Oswald exclaimed. "You have no right to hold one of my subjects against her will."

"You'll have to take that up with King Henry," the thin man said.

While they were speaking, the thin man's company encircled them, removing any possibility of flight.

"Oswald," Lina whispered. *"I think we'd better go with them."*

16

AN ENEMY WORTH HAVING

Augustine was allowed to ride in the cart the following day, which came as a great relief to him. The party continued along the thieves' highway, which was hidden deep within the forest.

With nothing better to do, Augustine found himself visually examining the boxes and barrels that surrounded him. He thought at first these were just provisions for the journey, but he managed to peer through a crack in one of the crates and saw that it contained jars and bottles. He could smell spices of some kind; apparently, he wasn't the only thing these men had stolen along their journey.

He wished his hands were untied so he could better examine the boxes. Perhaps they contained something that might aid him in escaping. Also, somewhere among the treasures was whatever Wolf considered proof of his parentage. Augustine was dying to see what it was. Of course, Wolf couldn't possibly prove something that wasn't true. Still, Augustine wanted to see what he *thought* was proof so he could laugh about it later.

It was almost evening, when Augustine heard the sound of hoof-beats heading down the road in their direction. His heart pounded.

Were the new arrivals rescuers? His captors didn't seem anxious about the approaching party.

When they finally came into view, his hope of rescue was dashed. These were ruffians, dressed in tattered clothes and carrying a combination of make-shift and stolen weapons.

At once he thought of the valuables that his captors were carrying. The approaching force consisted of at least fifteen men. Wolf's party didn't stand a chance.

As much as Augustine hated his current captors, they seemed to have some interest in his well-being. These highway men would probably kill him without a second thought.

Not only did Wolf seem completely unconcerned about the approaching horde, he smiled pleasantly as they closed in.

"Hello!" he called, with a friendly wave.

The man at the head of the group waved back.

"Well if it isn't ol' Wolfgang the Holy!" he grinned, bringing his horse to a stop.

Augustine looked at Wolf incredulously. He was chuckling at the newcomer. They were clearly good friends and this title "the Holy" had to be some kind of an in-joke. Aside from the fact that he insisted on reading from a breviary every evening, there was nothing remotely holy about Wolf.

"Well if it isn't Liam the Brute," Wolf smiled. "How are things in the village?"

Augustine thought Liam's title was probably more accurate. In fact, if he had to guess, he would say Liam won his position of authority by being the ugliest of the bunch. His face was scared, his beard was patchy, and he was missing every other tooth.

"Lovely, lovely," Liam answered. "Harvest is almost finished, everyone is healthy, no complaints here. Will you be staying for a while?"

"For a few nights," Wolf answered. "Which reminds me..." He turned to Faruk who was sitting in the back with Augustine. "It's probably about time we blindfolded the kid."

Augustine stiffened at this. "Why?" he demanded.

"We won't hurt you if you cooperate," Wolf assured. "It's only so you don't see where we're going. Now it will be much easier for all of us if you don't throw a fit."

Liam rode around the cart to get a better look at Augustine as Faruk pulled a strip of cloth from one of the boxes. The last thing Augustine saw before it was tied over his eyes was Liam regarding him with a twisted frown and a slightly cocked head.

"What did this poor kid do to warrant your involvement?" he asked.

"I think it's more what his father did?" Wolf probably said this with a slight shrug. Augustine couldn't see him but their many hours together had made him familiar with Wolf's mannerisms.

"Is this another one of Prince Justin's?" Liam exclaimed.

"Hopefully the last one," Wolfy answered. "Though I have some suspicions about the princess of Zoroske..."

Liam snickered. "Well, best of luck to you, Wolfy!"

Augustine felt the cart lurch forward and heard the sound of Liam's company riding off into the distance.

"Your friends seem wonderful," Augustine stated.

"Indeed!" Wolfy answered. Augustine could tell he was grinning. "And they tend to be heavily armed, unscrupulous, and hate noble brats so I'd watch your tongue if I were you."

Augustine felt his anger flare up.

"Why don't you come back here and make me?" he shot back. "Before I call you a loathsome base-born worm?"

The moment the words slipped from his mouth, Augustine braced himself for a blow to the face. He received no such punishment.

Instead, he heard a very slight chuckle from Wolf.

"I'm only trying to protect you, kid," he answered. "Not myself. What kind of a coward would I be if I felt the need to shield myself from the insults of a demon-sired swamp rat?"

Mill whistled. "Watch it, kid. You cannot out insult Wolfy. He's spent decades mastering the art."

"Why?" Augustine snapped. "So he could be as vile on the ears as he is on the eyes?"

"No, so I could shatter the egos of chatty little tyrant-spawn," Wolf's tone was brimming with glee. "Though even I may not have blows sufficient to topple your ego."

What Augustine said next, he had learned from his stepfather, and is far too inappropriate to be put in writing. It was the kind of insult he'd been saving for a real emergency. It was so awful, he didn't even think Oswald deserved it.

Wolf received it with effortless class and calmly responded with something equally vile.

And it was at that very moment that Augustine gained a new respect for Wolf. He was the kind of enemy worth having; the cunning, calculating, witty kind. The kind Augustine itched to defeat.

17

LINA'S PANIC ATTACK

Henry's men escorted Lina back to the great hall. Though their thin and highly unpleasant leader assured Oswald his presence was not required, he insisted on coming anyway. Lina tried to convince him to go and get help, but he refused to leave her side. She was some combination of outraged and grateful. As she entered Henry's court with Oswald trailing after her, she was keenly aware that he was her only ally and even an obnoxious ally was better than none.

King Henry leapt up as she entered.

"Well done, Sir Hans!" he exclaimed.

The thin man responded with a tiny bow and a pleasant smile before taking his place by the far wall. Lina, standing in the exact center of the room, under the eyes of the king and his courtiers, wished she could vanish into thin air.

"What is the meaning of this!" Oswald exclaimed, stepping in front of her. Nothing irritated Oswald more than someone else being the center of attention. Under normal circumstances, it was an insufferable trait but in that particular moment, Lina was grateful for it.

"Who are you?" Henry demanded, squinting at Oswald.

"I am Prince Oswald of Kaltehafen, I–"

"Oh, you're Florian's son, aren't you?"

"*Filbert's!*" Oswald corrected.

"Whatever, I can't tell the difference," Henry dismissed.

"How dare you insult–"

"Silence!" Henry bellowed. "I have no interest in you, boy. Hold your tongue or I'll have Sir Hans drag you to the border and toss you back onto your father's side."

"*Oswald, please,*" Lina whispered. "*Listen to him. I don't want to do this alone.*"

Oswald looked over his shoulder at her. His eyebrows were raised slightly in surprise. It was like Lina was the first person to ever sincerely request his company.

"*Hold your tongue just until we figure out what he wants,*" Lina insisted.

To Lina's relief, Oswald replied with a little nod and stepped aside. He stood next to her watching her with an expression of uncharacteristic empathy.

The sound of hurried footsteps echoed from somewhere, and then Henry's daughter burst through a little door adjacent to the thrones.

"Do they have her, Papa? Did they really bring her?"

Before Henry could answer, the princess noticed Lina and squealed with delight.

"Are you sure this girl is his fiancée?" Henry asked his daughter.

"That's what the prince said," she answered, looking at Oswald.

"She can't be," Henry replied, motioning toward Lina. "She's so ugly."

Lina winced. Given the circumstances, this kind of insult should have been the least of her concerns, but for some odd reason, it stung horribly. For a brief moment, that little hurt replaced the fear that preceded it. Lina shook it off. It didn't really matter. Henry was a madman after all.

"I beg your pardon–" Oswald started, but Lina grabbed his arm.

"*Shush!*" she whispered.

"She's all stringy and speckled," Henry grimaced as he continued scrutinizing Lina.

"How could he love her more than me!" his daughter wailed.

"Now, now," the king answered, patting her arm. "It's his breeding, darling. Only the son of that vile Kalathean dog could ever find this ugly wench preferable to you."

"How dare you!" Oswald snapped, jumping back in front of Lina. "You're a repugnant, vulgar, sham of a king!"

While Oswald was still shouting. Henry rolled his eyes, looked at Sir Hans, and snapped his fingers.

"Throw him over the border, will you? I tire of his yammering."

As Oswald was dragged out, screaming insults at the king, Lina's hurt was once again replaced by fear. She was about to be alone in the presence of the king, and she did not expect a good outcome.

"Now what shall we do with her, darling?" Henry asked his daughter.

The princess did not hesitate for a moment.

"I want you to cut her head off."

Lina figured it would be something like that. Still, her expectations did not make the declaration any less unpleasant. Standing there, facing certain death, Lina reacted in her natural way.

There are several natural ways human beings react to traumatic situations. Some people, Augustine for example, react aggressively by either physically or verbally lashing out at whatever is causing the unpleasant emotion.

Lina, on the other hand, was born with the tendency to freeze in the face of a threat. Though her own life had never been in imminent danger before, her work required her to face all kinds of horrors regularly.

She had, therefore, taught herself a little trick for dealing with intense emotions like terror. Whenever faced with some unpleasant situation, she would become completely focused on the technicalities of the medical situation at hand and block out everything else.

After years of training herself to do this, she now did it completely unconsciously. So when Henry responded to his daughter with a warm smile and the words, "Of course, darling! We'll do so at once," Lina became utterly still. Her face lost all expression and she put her full focus on Henry.

She was suddenly intensely preoccupied with the medical mystery he presented. According to Hippocrates, madness occurred when the brain was flooded by bile or phlegm. Violent outbursts (randomly ordering a decapitation, for example) were usually the result of bilious humidity around the brain whereas phlegmatic insanity usually resulted in the patient becoming quiet and withdrawn.

As she mulled over this, she was vaguely aware of a guard taking her arm. Her whole body was sort of limp and she moved as he directed without noticing. The guard was probably about to lead her outside to carry out Henry's order, but she didn't want to think about that.

Besides, she was already busy thinking about how very red and sweaty Henry's face was, further indications of excessive bile around the brain.

They were leaving the castle grounds now and moving into the village. The king and his daughter were following, probably somewhere near the back of the party but that wasn't relevant in Lina's mind. No, she was still focused on determining the cause of Henry's madness.

While excessive bile was the most likely cause, the redness in Henry's face might also be a symptom of stagnant blood.

Patients, particularly male patients, were very good at avoiding their regular bleedings which Lina figured was the reason men as a whole were prone to starting wars, engaging in pointless rivalries, and making all sorts of other unwise decisions.

Lina was now in the middle of a square kneeling before a chopping block surrounded by a crowd of onlookers but that wasn't troubling her at the moment. She was too busy thinking about the fact that even the removal of the stagnant blood might not cure Henry's madness.

Someone was now forcing her down so her neck was stretched

across the chopping block, but that wasn't relevant to the issue at hand. The issue at hand was–

A loud bang and a burst of smoke broke Lina from her musings. She jerked upward. No one stopped her because her executioners were just as alarmed by the spectacle as she was.

The smoke cleared to reveal a goddess of a woman—unnaturally beautiful, her very being radiating power. But the feature Lina found most astonishing was her flowing scarlet hair.

"Mirella!" Henry gasped.

Lina looked toward the voice and noticed Henry standing across the square separated from the villagers by a semi-circle of guards.

"Tell me, Henry," the woman grinned. "What's this poor girl done to warrant such a punishment?"

"Guards!" Henry exclaimed, somehow turning redder. "Arrest this woman!" Then looking at the intruder, he added. "You'll be next, Mirella!"

Mirella rolled her eyes. "Remember what happened last time you threatened me, Henry?" she smirked. "Don't make me enchant your daughter again."

She strolled over and took Lina's arm. Lina hardly felt her touch, she was too astonished to think, or feel, or do much of anything.

The guards surrounding Lina seemed to be frozen in place, unable to carry out their king's order to arrest the enchantress.

A second bang shook the square and Lina was engulfed in smoke. When it cleared, she found herself someplace entirely different. She was in a cozy little cottage. A warm fire burned in the hearth and Mirella was standing beside her.

Lina, who was still on her knees, stood up and drank in her new surroundings.

"You're safe," Mirella smiled. "Sit down for a bit. Let's talk."

Lina blinked. She slowly brought her hand to her neck and felt it carefully. In her professional opinion, she had not been decapitated.

She was not only still intact but out of immediate danger. With this realization, she let out a horrified shriek and crumbled onto the floor in a trembling ball of nerves.

18

THE ESCAPE PLAN

Augustine was in a deeply uncomfortable position. He was lying on his back in the secret compartment on the underside of the cart. It was the same secret compartment where they had hidden him from Sir Albert what seemed like forever ago. Then, of course, he'd been only partially conscious thanks to Wolf's viper venom and didn't realize how painfully small the compartment was. It was just barely deep enough for him to lie in. He was actually grateful for the blindfold over his eyes since it allowed him to imagine a larger space (so long as he didn't move any part of his body at all).

Faruk forced him into the compartment as they approached the place Wolf and Liam referred to as "the village". Augustine couldn't see it, but he heard something that sounded very much like an actual village in the distance—voices, the laughter of children, the bleating of sheep, and the occasional bell.

"Believe me, this is for your own good," Wolf had said as they closed Augustine in.

"I say we let him stay up top," Mill's voice objected. "So what if the people make sport of him? They're not going to kill him."

"Not on purpose," Wolf replied. "No, it's not worth the risk. I want to get paid, don't you?"

Augustine felt the cart lurch forward. As they moved closer and closer, the sounds of the lively place grew louder. Soon Augustine could hear hoofbeats and the creaking of other carts. He tried to distract himself from the unpleasantness of his confinement by painting a picture of their surroundings in his mind.

The roads were dirt, not stone, and from the way the cart jolted in and out of dips and bumps, it seemed like they weren't well maintained.

There was a reasonable population though, he heard a lot of talking and a lot of footsteps.

"Look! It's Wolfy! Wolfy has returned!" someone cried out. Then at once, the cart was surrounded by the sound of happy chatting voices all asking Wolf where he'd been, and what he'd been doing, and how long he was planning to stay.

Augustine marveled. *What sort of village was this?* Why was his ruffian captor so popular here? He would have thought it was some kind of den of thieves but there were just so many people... and women and children too. Was Wolf actually a lord of some sort? Then why wasn't anyone using honorifics with him? Everyone just called him Wolfy.

It took them a long time to move through the happy crowd, slowly the sounds of the busy place faded away. Augustine could still hear voices but they were fewer and far between.

At last, the cart came to a stop. The boards were removed from above him. He breathed deeply, savoring the blast of fresh air as it hit his face.

They led him into a building of some sort. Augustine decided it was made of stone based on the feeling of the floor beneath his feet and the slightly cooler air that enveloped him when he entered. Their footsteps echoed as they walked, it must have been a fairly large empty space, perhaps a long hallway?

He heard the creak of iron hinges and the groan of a heavy wooden door swinging open. They led him forward and then removed his blindfold. He was in what looked like a monk's cell in a monastery.

It was a tiny room. All the furniture had long been removed except for a straw-stuffed mat.

Wolf started undoing the bonds on Augustine's wrists.

"Don't try anything," he said, as he worked. "The people here are *my* allies, not yours, understand?"

Augustine responded with a cold glare.

"What is this place?"

"It was a monastery, a long, long time ago," Wolf answered, confirming Augustine's suspicions. "But now it's... well it's a refuge of sorts..."

"For who? Highwaymen?"

Wolf grinned. "Among others."

The rope on Augustine's wrists went slack. Wolf pulled it off and neatly coiled it while Augustine rubbed the chafing on his wrists.

"Wolfy is technically an assassin," Mill offered from over his leader's shoulder.

Augustine stiffened at this revelation, though he didn't know why it surprised him.

Wolf shot Mill an irritated glance. "I do anything that pays well," he corrected. "And surprisingly, dragging you halfway across the world pays very well." He shrugged. "I'd take it as a compliment, kid."

Somehow, Wolf's comment did not convince Augustine that this entire affair wasn't going to end with his assassination.

Wolf turned to leave but then paused.

"Oh, just a moment." He pulled the pack off of his back and stooped down to rummage through it. Augustine would have taken the opportunity to kick him in the nose and make a run for it, except that Faruk was standing just behind Wolf like a solid wall. He was watching Augustine with those tiny, expressionless eyes of his. What went on in the mind of that brute anyway? Probably not much. If Wolf was doing this for the money, Faruk was probably doing it because he liked kicking people around.

Wolf stood and handed Augustine a tiny jar.

"This will help with..." he pointed to his own wrists and nodded toward the chafing on Augustine's.

"What is it?" Augustine asked skeptically.

"Bee's wax," Wolf shrugged.

"Wow," Augustine answered dryly. "That's so kind. Almost as kind as not kidnapping me in the first place."

"Make yourself comfortable," Wolf said, completely ignoring Augustine's remark. "We'll be here a couple of days."

With that, he pulled the door shut. Augustine listened to the hopeless sound of the key turning in the lock. He heard the footsteps of his captors moving away down the hall. He was alone.

He turned around, drinking in the little room. Opposite the door was a slit-like window. Augustine peered through it observing the silent wood beyond. It was just barely wide enough for him to slip his arm through. He did so and felt the cool evening air against his skin.

Then, he jerked his arm back in and punched the wall in frustration. In hindsight, it wasn't the smartest idea, it left his hand a bloody, throbbing mess. He sank down so that he was sitting cross-legged with his back to the wall, rubbing the injury and swearing to himself.

He could almost see Lina standing before him, looking at him like he was an idiot.

"You punched a rock," he imagined her saying. "What did you think would happen?"

Even though she wasn't really there, he felt embarrassed.

He missed her terribly. He hoped wherever she was, she was safe and not too worried. Soon, very soon, he would find a way back.

He thought of the day he'd asked her to the festival and blushed as he recalled how awkward he'd been. Things weren't always so awkward between them. He used to be more comfortable with her than anyone. They were always together playing games, exploring, telling each other stories... he probably drove her insane with all his stories from Kalathea.

The awkwardness didn't start until about a year ago when one day he looked at her and was hit with a horrifying realization—she was a girl.

It was a silly observation, she had always been a girl. But... had she always been so beautiful or was that new?

And why couldn't he look at her without his stomach flopping and his legs becoming unsteady? Why couldn't he brush against her without his skin tingling where they touched? He suddenly couldn't be around her without feeling a whole wave of awkward emotions.

And the thing that scared him more than anything was that, if he told her how he felt and she didn't feel the same, he would not only be losing the affection of a lovely woman but of his closest friend.

He was still holding the jar Wolf had given him in his good hand. As he glanced around his little prison, he rubbed some of the bee's wax on his wrists.

His current situation made him realize that all of the fear and awkwardness he had felt regarding Lina was a complete waste of time. Life was short, and you never knew when you were going to get carried away by a band of ruffians.

He was going to escape and when he saw Lina again, he wasn't going to waste any time. He would march right up to her and boldly propose marriage. (He smiled as he thought of how excited Heidi would be.)

He set the little jar down and glanced around the room. The big question was, *how* was he going to escape?

His last attempt resulted in him wandering aimlessly through the wilderness, starving, and almost getting murdered. Even if he could get away from his captors, how could he find his way home? Perhaps if he waited until they passed through a real village he could ask someone for help.

Would Wolf be foolish enough to bring him through a village that wasn't entirely overrun by outlaws?

There had to be a way. He had no intention of going to this client of theirs without a fight. Then something occurred to him. If they were going to Anamia, as Mill said, then they would have to cross the Great Sea to get there.

If he could escape on the coast, he could sneak aboard a ship bound for Kalathea. He leapt up and started pacing.

That was it! Once he arrived on Kalathean soil, his aunt and uncle would see that he was safely returned to his parents.

Augustine knew exactly what he needed to do. He was going to be a perfect prisoner, making no attempt to escape until they reached the coast. He would offer his hands when they wanted to bind them. He would speak only when spoken to. He would do anything and everything they asked of him no matter how humiliating. If he gained their trust, they would eventually let their guard down.

It was late summer and would probably be midwinter by the time they reached Greece or wherever they were planning on catching their ship. Assuming that they didn't get snowed in along the way.

Augustine loathed the idea of being in the company of these men for so long. But what choice did he have? And of course, there was always the chance that his father would find him long before then. Perhaps, while being the model prisoner, he would find opportunities to leave clues for his father to follow.

The sound of the key turning in the lock jerked him from his thoughts. Faruk lumbered in. He was holding a crate in his arms with a wooden cup carefully balanced on the corner. Two of his fingers were wrapped around the handle of a bucket, which dangled down below the crate in his arms. One wrong move and everything would come crashing down around him.

The idea of causing an upset flashed across Augustine's mind but he quickly pushed it aside. Certainly, he might be able to brush by Faruk and escape the room but he wouldn't escape Wolf's mob of admirers.

Model prisoner, model prisoner, he repeated to himself.

"Let me," Augustine said, carefully taking the cup and the pail.

Faruk grumbled something that sounded like "thank you", then nodded toward the bucket.

"Eat," he ordered.

Augustine looked inside. It contained a small bowl of stew. About half the contents had sloshed out onto the bottom during transport. It smelled wonderful, though, and Augustine was too hungry to complain.

The cup contained milk. He hadn't tasted fresh milk since his kidnapping, and he had to resist the urge to gulp the whole thing down at once.

"What's that?" Augustine asked, looking at the crate as Faruk placed it on the floor.

"Wolf wants you to put these on," Faruk stated, pointing to the contents.

"You can tell Wolf that—" Augustine stopped himself. "That I will do so promptly."

Emotionless Faruk regarded Augustine for a long moment and then raised one eyebrow slightly. He must have noticed Augustine's suspiciously agreeable change in attitude.

After a brief moment of contemplation, Faruk left without making further comment. Augustine breathed a sigh of relief as the door shut behind him. That tiny little exchange had taken heroic effort on his part. Being a model prisoner was going to be harder than he thought.

19

MIRELLA THE ENCHANTRESS

"I'm sorry, I'm so sorry," Lina mumbled.

She was sitting in a chair by the hearth, trying to hold a cup steady in her trembling hands. Her rescuer was sitting opposite her, casually sipping from a cup of her own.

"I don't know what came over me," Lina continued.

"Probably the sudden realization that you almost had your head chopped off," Mirella suggested.

A little wine sloshed over Lina's fingers. "Oh heavens," she breathed. "That *did* almost happen, didn't it? And you, you... saved me?"

Mirella nodded.

Lina brought the cup to her lips and managed to take a sip. "Wait a moment...how did you save me? There was smoke and...you just appeared and..." Lina regarded her—the magic, the red hair..."*Are you a witch?*"

Mirella laughed. "No. A witch is someone who tries to access power through supernatural means. My powers are a natural gift from a fairy ancestor."

"Oh..." Lina blinked.

All she knew about fairies was what Augustine told her. First, they were not to be trusted, and second, if you ever ran into one you should completely ignore it no matter what it did to get your attention.

Mirella, however, had just saved Lina's life. It didn't mean she was completely trustworthy, but it must have been worth something. And besides, she was only *part fairy*. If Lina had been feeling more herself, she would have taken some scientific interest in this. She had no idea fairies and humans could have children.

"If King Henry had only listened to me when I *tried* to explain this to him," Mirella continued. "We would be on much better terms." She snickered and shrugged. "Or maybe he'd have tried to kill me anyway. I think he enjoys killing people." She took a sip from her cup. "It makes him feel big."

The wine was starting to work its magic and Lina was feeling calmer. With her calmness, came a renewed focus on the problems at hand. She had lost Oswald, didn't even know where she was, and the Princess of Zoroske wanted to kill her for some reason.

"Listen, Mirella–" Lina started.

Mirella leapt up from her chair, dashed across the room, and threw open a little chest.

"Keep talking, I'm listening," she said as she rummaged around inside it.

"You've done so much for me already, and I hate to trouble you, but if you could assist me a little more I am sure I could find some way to repay you."

"Speak," Mirella ordered. She was holding the lid of the chest open with one hand and stroking her chin with the other. "I thought I had cheese in here..." she mumbled to herself. "I hope I didn't eat it. That would be a damn shame."

"I've lost a friend," Lina explained. "He–"

Mirella looked sideways at her. "Was he that entitled, bratty, little tyrant I saw Henry's men dragging through the woods?"

"That sounds like him," Lina answered. "He has fair hair, a roundish face, and he was wearing a blue cape."

"Oh yes, that was definitely him," Mirella answered. "You have an odd taste in friends."

Lina felt a slight smile escape her. "He's not really a friend. He's... well, I'm supposed to be keeping him out of trouble."

"Is that so?" Mirella grinned and raised an eyebrow. "How are you supposed to do that when you can't even keep yourself out of trouble?" The enchantress laughed and shook her head, before adding, "I'll go get him for you."

"Oh, just tell me where–" Lina started.

"The cheese!" Mirella exclaimed, holding up a yellow block. She popped the whole thing into her mouth then vanished.

This time there wasn't a bang or a puff of smoke. She simply disappeared. Lina was beginning to wonder if *she* was going mad or if maybe Henry actually *had* murdered her and this was some sort of strange purgatory where nothing made sense.

Mirella reappeared a few moments later holding a very confused looking Oswald by the wrist. She released him and he stumbled backward onto the floor looking wildly around the room.

While he was orienting himself, Mirella flew back toward the chest, withdrew a biscuit and gobbled it down. "I apologize!" she said between bites. "Magic makes me so hungry!"

Lina rushed over to Oswald.

"Lina!" he exclaimed. "Did this enchantress kidnap you too?"

Lina helped Oswald to his feet. "No, she saved my life," she explained, before snapping her attention back to Mirella. "How did you do that?"

"Do what?" Mirella asked.

"Find the prince... and bring him here so quickly," Lina clarified.

Mirella shrugged and stuffed the last of the bread in her mouth. "I don't know, how do you move your arms?"

Lina was forming an idea.

"You can just move people? Without even thinking about it?" she questioned.

"Well, sort of," Mirella continued. "I have to know exactly where the person is and I can't move people farther than they could travel in a few weeks on foot. *And* it takes a lot out of me." She glanced around the cabin. "Are you hungry?" she added. "Because I think I might go outside and kill a couple of chickens."

Before Lina could answer, Mirella swept out the door.

"What's going on?" Oswald demanded. He was still in a sort of daze, struggling to orient himself.

"I'll explain in a moment," Lina replied before rushing after Mirella. She was not about to let this idea escape her. She needed more information.

"Mirella?" Lina called.

Mirella's house was in a clearing amidst a forest of towering evergreens. A dappled gray mare grazed a short distance away while a couple of tiny white goats followed along in its shadow. Lina envied the tranquil little homestead.

She heard a frantic clucking and flapping coming from around the side of the house which was quickly followed by a deafening silence.

Lina hurried in the direction of the sound and saw Mirella standing among a flock of chickens holding one of their recently deceased brethren by the ankles.

She thrust the bird into Lina's arms. "Pluck that, will you?" she ordered, cheerily.

"Oh, of course," Lina breathed. "But, um Mirella..."

Mirella was watching the other birds, trying to select her next victim.

"If you can move people so easily... well..." Lina started. "There's someone else I've lost."

Mirella raised a quizzical eyebrow. "You really need to do a better job keeping track of your friends."

"He's also a prince," Lina continued. "And I am sure his father will handsomely reward you for recovering him. He was kidnapped from Kaltehafen four days ago."

Mirella suddenly lost interest in the chickens and gave Lina her full attention.

"His name is Augustine," Lina continued. "He's–"

"Augustine Hatsi?" Mirella finished. "Seventeen, stringy, olive skin, dark features?"

"*Yes!*" Lina exclaimed, feeling a surge of hope.

"Ah..." Mirella answered thoughtfully. She bit her lip, gaze dropping to the ground as she mulled something over in her mind. "Tell me..." she said at last. "Who is Augustine Hatsi to you?"

Lina had no idea what to make of this reaction.

"He's my closest friend," she answered.

"Is that how you ended up in Zoroske? Were you looking for him?"

Lina nodded skeptically. Why was Mirella asking these questions? Finding Oswald was such a simple matter for her, why couldn't she do the same for Augustine?

"Tell me about him," Mirella ordered. "Is he a good man?"

"Of course!" Lina was frustrated. Mirella hadn't asked if *Oswald* was a good man. "He's kind, and brave, and he would die to protect the people he loves."

"How do you know?" Mirella continued, the intensity of her gaze somehow increased.

"Because he's always protected me," Lina answered. "When I was a child, the other children in the village tormented me horribly. Augustine took more than one beating trying to defend me."

Mirella was still regarding her skeptically, so Lina decided to continue with another story.

"He was twelve when his little sister was born," she remembered. "The first time he met her, he told me he wanted to be a knight so she'd never have to be afraid."

Just the retelling brought a slight smile to Lina's lips. Augustine, though a bit reckless, had a hero's heart. Lina couldn't help but admire that.

Mirella's gaze dropped. "I see."

She was frowning now and biting her lip slightly.

"The trouble is...I've already helped someone find Augustine Hatsi. And if I were to bring him back to you, it would be a disservice to a very dear friend of mine."

"I don't understand," Lina replied. A knot was forming in her stomach.

"Your Augustine may be a good man, but my Wolfy is a *great* one," Mirella explained, a fond smile spreading on her lips.

Lina stiffened, remembering the last time she had heard the name "Wolfy" was when she was trailing Augustine's captors.

"If Wolfy took Augustine, it's because he had a serious reason. I'm sorry, but I won't stand in his way."

Mirella turned her attention back to the chickens scratching around in the dust at her feet.

Lina was feeling slightly nauseous. Augustine was right. Fairies, even partial ones, were not to be trusted. Her mind raced and she tried to figure out what to do next. Part of her wanted to leave as quickly as possible before Mirella turned on her. But then, Mirella knew Augustine's captors and maybe how to find them. Even if she was unwilling to get Augustine herself, perhaps she would provide some useful information.

Lina looked down at the chicken she was holding. She decided she was going to stay for dinner.

20

POLY'S MIRACLE HEALING SPIT

Augustine looked at the clothing in the crate Faruk provided. They were peasant's clothes, used but not worn out. This came as no surprise to Augustine; they wanted him to blend in. He begrudgingly swapped garments, keeping only his brooch.

It was a small golden, sun-shaped ornament his mother had gotten for him right before they left for Kaltehafen. "To remind you of the Kalathean sun," she had said.

Augustine tried pinning it on the inside of his new tunic where he hoped his captors wouldn't find it. Unfortunately, with the fingers on his right hand bruised and swollen from his clash with the wall, this proved a difficult task.

A gentle tapping near the window interrupted his efforts. He looked over to see a white snout poking through the narrow opening.

"Poly?" Augustine whispered, jumping up and rushing toward the animal. "I told you to leave. What are you doing here?"

The animal stretched its nose in farther and started making little nibbling motions with its lips.

"Really?" Augustine scowled. He stormed over to the place he'd been sitting, picked up a crust of bread, then stormed back to the window and offered it to the grateful animal. It disappeared into the nibbling lips.

"I don't always have treats for you, you know." He sighed deeply and stroked the velvety muzzle. "Why are you following me, Poly? It isn't safe."

Despite his words, Augustine was happy the animal had reappeared. Poly was neither intelligent, nor much for conversation, but he was a connection to home. Talking to him numbed Augustine's loneliness a little.

"If you like humans so much, go back to Heidi." He held out his good hand letting the unicorn nibble his fingers, enjoying the funny tickling feeling of its velvety lips. "She'll spoil you and someone's got to look after her while I'm gone."

Sending the unicorn back gave Augustine an idea. He found a loose thread on his cloak and pulled it until he had a length of string. Then, he took his brooch and tried to tie it onto Poly's horn. This required both hands and while he was fumbling, Poly decided to lick the injured one.

"Ouch!" he exclaimed as its rough tongue passed over his damaged knuckles. "Poly, you're nothing but trouble, you know!"

The reprimand did not stop Poly from licking him. Somehow, Augustine managed to finish fastening his brooch to the creature's horn and pulled his bad hand to safety.

"Now Poly," Augustine whispered. "Go find my father."

The unicorn didn't move. It kept trying to stick its head through the window, extending its tongue toward Augustine's hands. "Or my mother," he added, thinking the animal might be afraid to approach a huntsman like Florian. Still the unicorn remained. Augustine stepped away from the window. "Or Heidi," he suggested.

The unicorn stayed, forcing its nose through as far as it could while stretching its lips and tongue even farther.

Augustine rolled his eyes. "You're useless, Poly," Augustine complained. He slumped down, polished off the last of his soup, and settled down to sleep. The unicorn would leave eventually and then... hopefully it would carry out his orders.

. . .

HE AWOKE ABRUPTLY when his cell door burst open.

"Up kid, up, up, up!" Mill shouted.

It was still dark. Mill was illuminated only by torch light from the halls. His eyes were red and he swayed slightly in the doorway.

"What's going on?" Augustine asked, as he bolted upright.

Mill broke into a drunken smirk.

"I lost a bet just now," he explained. "I was playing that beastly game with this fellow...Brent, Brenton, Bradley..." his voice trailed off for a moment and he mumbled a few more inaudible words. "Brian!" he exclaimed triumphantly. "The keg man, or whatever you call it."

"Tavern keeper?" Augustine suggested.

"That!" Mill agreed. "Wolf said no money, no goods. So I wagered my services and now I've got to water his animals, and his brother's animals, and..." he threw his arms out. "And ALL the damn animals!"

Mill laughed as if he'd just said something hilarious. Augustine crinkled his nose in disgust. The scent of beer was so strong, he worried inhaling would get him drunk.

Mill apparently didn't notice his revulsion, because he kept talking.

"Then I thought to myself, why should I do that when I've got you?"

A rage sparked inside Augustine. He would not be a slave to his captors. Especially, because Mill got drunk and lost a bet. He took a long, slow breath, trying to calm himself. *Model prisoner, model prisoner,* he repeated. He might be able to make this work out in his favor.

"You want me to come out and do your work for you?" Augustine questioned.

"Are you deaf?" Mill nodded impatiently. "I just said that exactly."

"What makes you think I won't run away?"

"Oh, that's not allowed," Mill scoffed. He swayed slightly and tried to widen his drooping eyes. "Besides, if you did run away, I'd kill you."

Augustine wondered if Wolf knew about this. He somehow

doubted it. He stuck his tongue in his cheek to keep himself from smiling at the idea of Mill getting in trouble.

"Don't the people here hate me or something?" Augustine asked. "Isn't that why you hid me in the bottom of the cart?"

"Well, yeah, but you're common now," Mill mentioned, making an unsteady motion toward Augustine's new clothes.

Augustine regarded the drunk man thoughtfully.

"Alright, why not?" he shrugged, stepping out into the corridor. He wasn't going to make a run for it unless he was absolutely sure he could escape. He was sure, however, that this excursion was an excellent opportunity to get more information about his captors and what they intended to do with him.

He hoped his bad hand wouldn't be too much of a hindrance... it wasn't hurting too badly at the moment. Actually, it hadn't been hurting at all since he woke up. Augustine suddenly held up the hand in question, opening and closing his fingers curiously. It was absolutely fine. The torn skin on his knuckles had mostly healed, leaving only a few red scratches. Maybe he hadn't hurt himself as badly as he thought? Or maybe...

He remembered something Lina had said, about how the horn of a unicorn could heal anything if you ground it to powder and mixed it with vinegar. Had Poly healed him somehow?

"Why you looking at your hand like that, let's go!" Mill ordered.

The building was quiet and their footsteps echoed. Augustine drank in his surroundings, hoping to retain as much information about the place as possible.

"If anyone asks, you're my cousin Leo," Mill explained.

"Ah, a fake name," Augustine humored. "Brilliant idea. That way the people here won't know I'm... what exactly is it that they hate about me?"

"The same thing I hate about you. You're a spoiled little lordling." Mill broke into a cruel grin and a burning hatred entered his eyes. "I hope you do run. I'd *like* to kill you."

Augustine eyed him curiously. Why did he get the impression that Mill loathed him on a deeply personal level? When Wolf claimed the kidnapping wasn't personal, Augustine believed him. He was professional in his own way.

Mill was a different matter. Of his three kidnappers, Augustine had interacted with Mill the least. Faruk was usually the one who handled him and Wolfy gave Faruk his orders.

Mill was just sort of in the background chatting with Wolf and doing whatever else needed to be done. But when he did interact with Augustine, his eyes and his tone were full of disgust. Augustine dreaded to think about how Mill would treat him if he was the leader instead of Wolf.

Fortunately, Mill didn't have the makings of a leader. He was weak and weaselly. Drink was the only thing that had given him the confidence he needed to go against Wolf's orders.

Augustine regarded him. If drunkenness made Mill bolder, he might as well take advantage of it. He asked the obvious question.

"Why do you want to kill me so badly? Did I do something to you?"

"It's not what you did, it's what you are," Mill answered.

"Which is?" Augustine pressed.

"A liar."

This did not clarify anything for Augustine.

"I lied to you?"

They were coming up toward the monastery courtyard now.

Mill swayed around and looked at Augustine with ravenous eyes. "My whole life I've been told that people fall into one of three categories." He held up four fingers, stared at them for a long moment, then realizing his mistake, lowered one. "Those who work, those who pray, and those who fight."

Yes, that was the general structure of society. The peasants worked, the clergy prayed, and the nobility fought to defend them. Augustine wasn't sure what this had to do with anything but it probably made perfect sense in Mill's head.

"But I've come to know there are only really two kinds of people," Mill went on. "Those who work and those who lie to them." His smile broadened triumphantly. He was obviously extremely proud of himself.

"Riiiiight," was Augustine's only reply.

"Today, you're going to be one of those who work," Mill grinned. "One of those meager, humble little vermin your kind likes to lie to."

Augustine was suppressing a volcano of rage. Did Mill really think he had never worked a day in his life? That he would swoon if he had to muck out a stall? Was that what he was trying to imply with his drunken ramblings?

Mill's assertion brought Augustine back to some deeply unpleasant memories. Memories where he, at the age of eight, was spending every waking moment doing whatever little task he could to earn a few coins for his mother. For most of his young life, his mother had been handmaiden to a governor's wife. She made a wonderful living that way, until the governor's family was taken by the gods for use in their morality experiments.

Then, all the servants found themselves destitute. Each wondering when they would be taken for use in the god's awful games. Augustine spent all his time wandering around the village doing whatever he could for a few coins or a little food. He carried boxes, cleaned, mended, tended animals; all in the hope that eventually he would have enough to get himself and his mother smuggled to safety. He was always exhausted and always hungry.

As angry as he was at Mill, he didn't want to dignify him by snapping. Instead, he was going to *prove* him wrong. Whatever task Mill gave him he was going to do it better than that ungrateful scoundrel ever could.

They left the monastery and started down the main road toward the town. Augustine drank in the scene, relishing being outside without his hands bound. He looked to his left: *woods*. To his right, he saw an open pasture, some sheep, and more woods. Behind him was the monastery and before him was a village of sorts. Most of the homes were makeshift huts or tents. There were a few buildings and more under construction. These included a windmill and a church.

The sun was almost up and the people in the village were starting to emerge from their dwellings. Augustine could feel them staring at him. He kneaded his hands in and out of fists.

Wolfy could change his clothes but not his dark features. The looks the people gave him reminded him that he was a foreigner and highly suspect. He pulled his hood up to hide his face.

"Here we are," Mill declared suddenly. They had come to a stable on the outskirts of the village. Augustine was glad to go inside out of sight of the suspicious villagers. Although... inside, the building was a mess. A horse stood in the cramped space. Its back was covered in saddle sores and its legs were caked in mud and waste.

Augustine wondered what kind of wretch this Brian was to let his poor horse fall into such a condition.

Mill handed him a bucket and pointed out the door to a nearby creek.

"You sure you want me to go that far?" Augustine asked.

"Stop talking and do it," Mill replied.

"I may not come back," Augustine warned.

"You'll be back," Mill yawned. "Either of your own accord or dragged by the people."

"If you say so," Augustine shrugged and slipped out the door. He actually had no intention of going anywhere, not until he had done something to help that poor horse at least.

21

A CLOSE CALL

When Augustine returned from the creek a few moments later, Mill had fallen into a deep sleep. He didn't stir, even when Augustine emptied his bucket into the horse's drinking trough with a massive echoing splash.

Augustine set the depleted bucket down and walked over to him. "Mill?" he said.

No movement.

"Mill!" he called.

Still nothing.

"Mill, you weasel-faced coward!" Augustine yelled.

The drink had apparently done wonders.

Augustine shrugged and turned back to the horse. He approached the animal slowly, holding out his hand to let it sniff him. The horse nuzzled him half-heartedly which Augustine took as permission to gently stroke its nose. Poor thing didn't have the spirit left for fear or aggression, it had accepted its lot in life. Augustine took it by the bridle and led it outside onto the grass.

He refilled the bucket with water. The only brush he could find was caked in dirt so he had to wash it before he could use it to clean the horse. When he finally started brushing the sorry creature, it leaned into his strokes.

"You like that?" Augustine smiled. "Well, you deserve to feel good for once."

The horse seemed to agree. It closed its eyes and in a few moments, Augustine heard it snoring. He smiled, remembering how his own horseback in Kaltehafen would also fall asleep during groomings.

He worked on the filthy creature for what seemed like forever, removing the dirt and cleaning the saddle sores. When he finally finished, it was a lovely shining copper color with a black mane and tail.

"Aren't you a beautiful girl," Augustine declared. The horse bobbed her head in response—she already seemed a bit more alive. "Now let me see if I can make the barn a little more comfortable for you."

He removed the horse's bridle and left her outside on the grass. If she decided to run off he would fully support that decision.

He mucked out the stall, swept the floor, and organized the tools. The entire time, he was undisturbed. No one came near the little barn and the only indication he got that Mill was alive was the occasional snore.

As he worked, he kept peering outside to look across the field toward the woods. He was using every ounce of his strength not to run—*not yet*. Nothing lay in those woods except death by exposure, starvation, or crazy head-chopping kings. Kalathea was his best chance.

Sometime in the late afternoon, Augustine heard the sound of galloping hooves and a familiar voice crying out, "*Millard!*"

Augustine adopted a smug smile and strolled out of the barn toward the voice.

Wolf sat high on his own horse, eyes burning with fury as he looked around. "*Millard!*" he cried.

"He's asleep in the barn over there," Augustine stated, thrusting a thumb over his shoulder.

Wolf's jaw dropped when he saw Augustine.

"You're still here," he observed.

Augustine shrugged. "I suppose I am. Unless you're as drunk as Mill was when he let me out last night. If that's the case, I might be a hallucination."

Wolf regarded Augustine curiously, raising an eyebrow. He bit his lip in an obvious attempt to conceal a smile.

"Let's go," he ordered. "I'll deal with Mill later."

"Alright," Augustine agreed, approaching Wolf. His obedience only added to the confusion in Wolf's expression.

"What are you up to?" he asked suspiciously.

"Up to?" Augustine returned innocently. "Not much. I spent most of the morning cleaning a horse."

Wolf narrowed his eyes.

"If I walk into that barn, am I going to find Mill murdered or something?"

"If I'd murdered Mill, do you think I would be stupid enough to stand around waiting for you to find out?"

Wolf laughed. "No, I don't think you would. But just in case..." He dismounted. "Why don't you show me where he is?"

Wolf was careful to stay behind Augustine as they walked to the barn. The copper-colored horse was still standing outside the door. Apparently, it had decided against running away.

"Is that Brian's horse?" Wolf asked.

"I think so," Augustine shrugged. "It is whatever horse lives here."

"I didn't know it was that color," Wolf remarked. "Poor thing. She deserves a kinder master."

When they entered the barn, Wolf looked around in astonishment.

"Is this Brian's barn?" he marveled.

"It is whatever barn was standing here when I arrived," Augustine shrugged.

"Nice work, kid," Wolf remarked with an approving nod.

Augustine did his utmost to hide his pride. He kept his expression disinterested, and responded only with a slight shrug.

"Although," Wolf continued, looking at the sleeping Mill. "You still haven't convinced me Mill is alive."

"If he is dead, it was the drink that killed him, not me."

"You know something?" Wolf smirked. "I think I believe you."

He took Augustine by the arm. "Enough of this, let's get you back before you cause any more trouble."

"Cleaning is trouble?"

"I admit," Wolf chuckled. "It's preferable to attacking Mill and making a run for it. Still, I'd like to keep you under lock and key."

They made their way back along the road. Wolf walked beside Augustine, leading his horse by the reins. Augustine could feel the man watching him, waiting for him to make another escape attempt. He found Wolf's caution amusing, it was sort of delightful to know his captor found him threatening.

The sound of chatting voices drew his attention to the road ahead. A small group of men were returning from the fields in the opposite direction, carrying scythes and pitchforks. In the center of the cluster was a donkey pulling a cart full of wheat.

Wolf released a frustrated sigh as they approached and said, "Unless you want to get a nasty beating, stay quiet and let me do the talking."

"Wolfy!" A man at the front called. He was a tall, thin man who looked almost like a living scarecrow.

"Hello, Felix!" Wolfy returned. "How's the harvest?"

"Good, good," Felix answered, but he clearly wasn't interested in talking about the harvest. He was looking at Augustine.

"Who is this, Wolfy?" he inquired.

"This is Augustine," Wolf answered. "He came to us last night seeking asylum."

Felix scrutinized Augustine.

"Where are you from?" he demanded.

Now Augustine knew what he meant, but in response, he smirked and said, "Kaltehafen."

"You're not a Kalt," Felix snapped.

"You didn't ask if I was a Kalt," Augustine retorted, dryly. "You asked wher–"

"Augustine has my complete trust," Wolf interrupted. He put a firm hand on his shoulder and applied a warning squeeze. "It doesn't matter where he's from, he's one of us now."

Wolf's words made Felix back down immediately. He cast his gaze to the ground and said, "Yes, Wolfy."

Having put the farmer firmly in his place, Wolf adopted a more casual tone and changed the subject. He spent a few moments asking each of the men how they were and what had happened since his last visit. He not only knew each of them by name, but also the names and interests of each of their family members.

If Augustine didn't know Wolf was a kidnapper, he would have thought him a very caring and selfless man. After a few moments of friendly conversation, the farmers had almost forgotten Augustine was there. *Almost.* Once in a while, one or the other of them would shoot him a suspicious glance.

Wolf breathed a sigh of relief when the men finally said goodbye and continued on their way. "That was a close call wasn't it?" Wolf whispered.

"Was it?" Augustine asked, hoping he was about to learn something more about Wolf's make-shift feud. "I wouldn't know. You don't tell me anything."

"All you need to know," Wolf continued. "Is that your father is the reason some of our refugees are... well... refugees. You won't find much friendliness toward Kalatheans here and if they knew you were Prince Justin's son..." He threw his arms up. "I don't think even I could stop them from stringing you up."

"So why'd you bring me here?" Augustine asked.

"Because not everything I do is about you," Wolf replied.

"Let me guess," Augustine stated. "It has more to do with my father than with me."

"Wrong," Wolf snapped, turning on Augustine. "It has everything to do with the innocent people who find themselves caught in the middle of the nobility's pointless wars."

They were coming up to the monastery now. Augustine could see two highwaymen acting as sentries by the main gate.

"When I met Mill," Wolf continued. "He was about to be hanged for attempting to assassinate his lord."

For some reason, this did not surprise Augustine in the slightest.

"And do you know why he was attempting to assassinate his lord?" Wolf asked.

Augustine shrugged. Did a man like Mill really need a reason?

"Because his lord failed to do the one thing lords are supposed to do—*protect their people*. When Mill's village was invaded, his lord barricaded himself inside his castle and left his serfs to the enemy's mercy. By some miracle, Mill survived. His wife wasn't so lucky."

Augustine's eyes widened in horror. The idea of a lord neglecting his duty like that disgusted him. No wonder Mill was bitter.

"Mill's lord is an honorless coward," he growled.

"*Was*," Wolfy corrected. "Let's just say I'm a bit better with a bow than Mill." His eyes were sparkling with pride. He pulled back the string on an imaginary bow, miming the shots as he spoke. "First I got Lord Bertok right between the eyes, then I shot Mill down."

"You shot Mill?" Augustine puzzled.

Wolf stopped miming and waved at the guards as they passed through the gate into the monastery.

"No, no, he was about to get hanged, remember? I shot the rope."

"No one can actually split a rope with an arrow like that," Augustine objected.

(He had tried many times, though in his case there was a bag of sand on the end, not a person.)

"I can," Wolf grinned.

"You can not," Augustine insisted.

Wolf paused. They had just crossed the courtyard and were about to enter the corridor that would take them back to Augustine's cell.

"You know what?" Wolf decided. "I'll show you."

"Really?" Augustine dropped his disinterested facade completely.

A child-like excitement entered Wolf's expression, "I'll do it on the first try!"

He turned back toward the courtyard motioning for Augustine to follow.

22

ST. WOLFY THE JUST

The fire crackled beneath the slowly rotating chicken carcass. Mirella had gone outside to tend to her animals, leaving Lina to tend the bird. Oswald had just impaled a second chicken, and was preparing to roast it beside its former associate.

While they worked, Lina told Oswald everything that happened after they were separated in Henry's court. She expected him to be absolutely outraged and declare his intention to take some stupid retaliatory action.

But Oswald did no such thing. As he listened to Lina tell him how close she'd come to losing her head, he became quiet, thoughtful, and almost shaken.

"I shouldn't have left you," he mumbled after a long moment of silence.

"You were dragged off," Lina reminded.

"That's not what I mean," Oswald snapped. "I mean... I should have held my tongue."

Lina raised her eyebrows. Those were words she never thought she would ever hear from Oswald.

"If I hadn't... If I *had* kept quiet they wouldn't have separated us. I could have protected you."

"Unlikely," Lina replied, slightly amused by Oswald's assertion. "But thank you."

"The audacity of that man!" Oswald fumed. "Trying to take the life of an innocent Kalt without so much as consulting her king! Honorless wretch!"

That was more of the reaction Lina expected. She turned the chicken over and let Oswald continue ranting. She only half-listened as he went on and on. Mostly, she was thinking about how she could get some kind of help from Mirella.

Finally, Oswald exclaimed something so indignantly that it snapped her from her thoughts.

"...AND THAT IS JUST NOT TRUE!" he was saying.

"Sorry, what's not true?"

"What Henry said about you being ugly!" Oswald explained.

Lina winced slightly as she remembered what the king and his daughter had said about her. They had called her "stringy" and "speckled" among other things. With Augustine missing, and her own life threatened, a few mean comments from a madman shouldn't have wounded her the way they did.

"You're much lovelier than his awful daughter," Oswald ranted.

Lina glanced sideways at Oswald, "Really?"

"Easily!" he replied. "Why if I had to choose between you and the princess and didn't have wealth or social status to consider, I'd pick you in a second!"

Lina stared at Oswald for a long moment.

"Oswald," she said finally. "I believe that is the nicest thing you've ever said."

It wasn't a compliment, but Oswald seemed to take it as such. He responded to Lina with a warm smile. In a strange way, his words *did* actually help. After all, Oswald wasn't one to conceal his opinions about anything. If *he* said she was pretty, he really believed it.

"Oswald," Lina said. "Will you promise me something?"

Oswald's face brightened. He seemed to like being needed. It was a shame he had no idea how to be useful.

"Name it!" he stated.

"When Mirella comes back, will you let me do the talking?"

Oswald's face fell.

"Please, Oswald?" Lina begged. "She's our best chance at finding Augustine, I have a plan (sort of) but...well, I need to go about it carefully."

"You want me to stay out of the way," Oswald growled.

Lina glared at him. "Remember what happened in Henry's court?"

A hint of guilt touched Oswald's expression. He looked at the floor and grumbled, "*Fine.*"

A SHORT WHILE LATER, they were all sitting together at supper. Lina had been trying to lower Mirella's defenses with some friendly conversation. At the moment, the enchantress was telling them all about her own magic which she clearly took great pride in.

"I have no idea why," Mirella was saying between bites. "People always assume 'true love' is romantic. As if that's the only kind of love!" she rolled her eyes. "When I cursed Princess Leonore, I did it with the idea that her mad parents would have to learn true love in order to break it... Yet here it is broken, and they still seem just as pompous and impulsive as ever." Her brow creased deeply. "And what I can't figure out is... if Leonore's parent's didn't break the curse, who did? It would have to have been a blood relative... I made sure of that." She nibbled on a chicken wing thoughtfully. "And Leonore's only blood relatives are her parents. Henry killed the rest of them years ago."

"Maybe he missed someone," Lina shrugged. While she found the topic fascinating, she wanted to move the conversation to a more pressing matter.

Oswald, through heroic effort, had somehow managed to stay

silent thus far and Lina knew he could only contain himself for so long. She had to act quickly.

"Mirella, you've been very kind to me," Lina began. "I appreciate it."

The enchantress managed to say, "not a problem" between bites. When she swallowed, she added, "I'll take you back to Kaltehafen after this. Don't want you trying to wander back through Henry's territory."

"Thank you, but I won't be going back that way," Lina explained.

"You're not thinking of going after Augustine, are you?" Mirella queried. "That's a hopeless errand; Wolfy's too smart for you."

Oswald turned a deeper shade of red, he was chomping down on his lower lip, and jittering slightly.

"I won't abandon him, Mirella," Lina insisted. "You must understand that."

Mirella responded with an irritated sigh. "You seem like a good person, Lina. Don't waste your life on a hopeless quest."

"Then help me," Lina begged. "What's the harm in bringing Augustine back? I won't ask you to turn Wolf over to King Florian. I'll even speak to the king on Wolf's behalf. I'll convince him to give up the chase."

Oswald's eyes widened at this merciful suggestion. He bit his lip harder and his jittering increased. He was going to blow.

"The best thing I can do to help is take you home," Mirella answered, as she licked the last of the bones clean. (The enchantress had just devoured an entire chicken by herself and was somehow still more of a lady than any woman Lina had ever known.)

She was such a puzzle. One moment she was rescuing Lina from Henry's clutches, the next she was explaining that she couldn't rescue Augustine because of some strange loyalty to a violent criminal. *Why?*

"What makes Wolf such a great man?" Lina demanded indignantly.

Mirella smiled fondly. "He's clever enough to get anything he wants in life. He's accumulated enough wealth to live like a king, but he *doesn't*. Everything he earns goes to the poor. He's a saint, that Wolfy."

That's when Oswald finally lost it. He leapt up from his seat, exclaiming, "He threatened the life of my cousin! She's five!"

Mirella laughed. "Did he? It was a completely empty threat, I promise you. He'd never harm a child."

Lina felt a flicker of frustration. Why did Oswald have to snap right when Mirella was giving them information? She pointed a commanding finger at Oswald's chair and mouthed, *quiet!* He scowled, but took his seat obediently.

Her mind was racing as she looked back at Mirella. The Wolfy Mirella described so fondly, sounded nothing like the man who bound up Augustine and slashed him with a venom-tainted blade. *What was she missing?*

Was Wolfy trying to punish Augustine for his father's crimes? Was he afraid that Augustine would end up just like the infamous Prince Justin? Was everything Mirella said a lie? Why would she fabricate a story like that?

Lina was suddenly struck with an idea.

"Mirella, if you won't bring Augustine to me, will you send me to Wolfy?"

Oswald's eyes widened in horror. His face turned scarlet. He bit his lip so hard it started to bleed.

"Going to fight Wolfy yourself?" Mirella chuckled.

"I'm going to talk to him," Lina answered. "If he's the saint you claim he is, perhaps he'll hear my case."

"How interesting..." Mirella mumbled, drumming her fingers on the table. Lina's heart quickened. The enchantress was actually considering her request.

"Alright," Mirella declared after a moment.

"*No!*" Oswald exclaimed. "I won't allow this! You will not go into the presence of that scoundrel! Do you have any idea what he'll do to you?"

"He'll listen politely and send her home," Mirella shrugged. "But if you're so terrified, I'll send you along to protect her."

"Good," Oswald declared. "Send me to that villain and I'll cut his head off."

Lina silenced Oswald with a single glare. She had never come so close to breaking the Hippocratic oath.

Luckily, Oswald's threat only amused Mirella.

"You're no threat to Wolfy, believe me," she snorted.

"You'll really do it?" Lina pleaded, forgetting her anger.

"Yes, but there will be some conditions," Mirella answered. "And it may not work. Since I don't know where Wolfy is, I can only send you to one of the places I *think* he will go."

"That's alright," Lina breathed. "If there's even a chance, I'll take it."

"There is a village several weeks from here, the lord there is a dear friend of Wolfy's and all the people adore him. Don't think for a moment that you'll be able to harm him there."

Oswald and Lina exchanged a look, both wondering what sort of man Wolfy was that he had earned the loyalty of so many people.

"And you'll have to find your own way back when you're finished."

Lina nodded. Her heart swelled in her chest. It was silly to be so excited. She doubted any amount of talking would convince Wolf to give up his prize, but she would find *some* way to help Augustine escape. And even if she couldn't, at least she'd get to see him again. That alone was worth it.

23

FICTITIOUS FLORIAN

Augustine watched Wolfy as he aimed from the top of the monastery wall. They had stretched a rope vertically from the overhang opposite Wolfy's position to a crate on the walkway.

He fired his bow with a *twang*. A *whoosh* split the air and was almost immediately succeeded by a *thunk*. Though the arrow met its target, it was hardly a victory for Wolf.

"I think Mill is dead," Augustine smirked triumphantly, as he strolled over to retrieve the arrow. It was stuck in the exact middle of the rope, gently swaying back and forth from the motion of the impact.

As Augustine reached for it, a second *twang* sounded from the wall and he felt a puff of air on his hand as a second dart passed over it. The rope snapped, whipping him on the cheek. Augustine leapt backward, unleashing a string of fowl exclamations as laughter rang out from the wall.

"You could have warned me!" Augustine exclaimed.

"No time for that!" Wolf shouted. "Not with Mill's life in the balance!"

Augustine rolled his eyes and rubbed his stinging face. The rope had left him a nasty red blemish.

"That was *two* shots," he grumbled.

"Well this rope is a bit thicker than the one around Mill's neck," Wolf shrugged.

"Excuses, excuses," Augustine mumbled. "How about you let me try? I'll do it in one!"

(This was a completely baseless claim on Augustine's part.)

"Do you really think I'm going to hand you a weapon?" Wolf chuckled.

"What? Are you afraid I'll do it?"

"No, I'm just not an idiot," Wolf replied. "Now, let's get you back to your room before you talk me into wasting more time."

Augustine frowned, remembering that he was a captive. The demonstration had been a wonderful distraction from this fact, and it came to an end too soon for Augustine's liking.

He wondered if Florian could break a rope with an arrow like that. He made up his mind to find out the next time he saw his stepfather.

Wolf came down from his perch on the wall and walked Augustine back to his tiny prison.

Augustine spent the next day pacing back and forth across the room, occasionally going to the window to look for Poly. He should have been relieved when the glorified goat didn't make an appearance. After all, the farther Poly was from Wolf's men the better. Still, Augustine craved the company of some non-hostile presence. His confinement offered no distraction from his loneliness. It nibbled away at his mind, as the day dragged endlessly on.

"Where are you, Father?" he sighed to himself. He wasn't sure if he should be disappointed in Florian for not finding him, or impressed with Wolf for outsmarting Florian. Augustine imagined his stepfather glaring at him in disbelief.

"Do you doubt my abilities, son?" Fictitious Florian gasped.

"Of course not," Augustine answered. "But Wolfy he's–"

"I could take Wolfy in a second if I wanted," Imaginary Florian continued airily. "I'm just waiting to see if you're man enough to escape yourself!"

"I'm working on it," Augustine grumbled.

It was at that point, he realized he was talking to himself. *Lord help me, I'm losing my mind,* he prayed as he flopped backward onto his mat. How was he going to endure months of confinement without completely losing himself?

"You won't have to," Imaginary Florian reminded him. "I'll have you back by dawn."

Augustine pulled his blanket over his head, to block out the mental fabrication that was his stepfather. Maybe he just needed some sleep.

THE DOOR OPENING woke Augustine the following day. Wolfy and Faruk greeted him as he stretched and sat up.

"Good morning, Augustine!" Wolf greeted. "Ready to go?"

"Does my readiness really matter to you?" Augustine yawned.

"Take a moment if you need it," Wolf shrugged.

Augustine rolled his eyes. He slipped on his outer tunic and his cloak then approached Faruk and offered him his hands.

Faruk and Wolf exchanged a glance.

"He's been suspiciously agreeable lately," Wolf explained. "Don't trust him for a second."

Faruk bound his hands in the front. Augustine was grateful for this since it meant he would still have some use of them. (Not that he planned on doing anything.)

Mill was waiting for them at the monastery gate atop his smokey-gray mare. Two other horses were saddled and waiting for their masters.

"We aren't taking the cart?" Augustine asked, glancing around.

"The next part of our journey necessitates lighter travel," Wolf explained.

Augustine felt sorry for whichever horse was going to have to carry two riders. His sympathy was put to rest when Wolf looked at Mill and asked, "Where is our other horse?"

Mill shot Wolf a sour glance. "Brian is bringing it. Should be here any moment."

A thick tension seemed to hover around Mill. Augustine couldn't help but wonder how Wolf had punished him for yesterday's transgression.

"Good, good," Wolf answered cheerily, ignoring the ice in Mill's tone.

By now, they had almost reached the three animals. Wolf's handsome chestnut stallion plodded forward to greet his master who smiled fondly and patted its nose.

"You're going to look after Augustine today, Symeon," he said. The horse nuzzled the side of Wolf's face, nibbling at his ear with its velvety lips.

Wolf motioned for Augustine to come forward.

"Wait a moment," Augustine paused, looking between Wolf and his horse. "You want me to ride Symeon?"

"I wouldn't trust any other horse with you," Wolf answered. "Symeon is completely devoted to me." He stroked the white blaze that ran down the animal's face. "Aren't you, Symeon?"

The horse bobbed its head happily, drinking in his master's love.

"That's right," Wolf cooed. "You'd never dream of running off, would you? No matter what Augustine tried?"

The horse swore his allegiance through more affectionate nibbling.

"Climb up," Wolf ordered Augustine. "If you so much as scratch Symeon, pay or no pay, I'll kill you."

The threat made Augustine gain a new respect for Wolf. He would have said the same if someone borrowed his own horse, Lysander. He smiled fondly as he thought of the coal black stallion he'd left in Kaltehafen. In speed and beauty, Symeon couldn't compare.

Augustine somehow managed to climb into the saddle with his

hands bound. It was an awkward process, and he was actually proud of himself for achieving it as easily as he did.

Just as he had settled himself, he saw a man approaching. Presumably this was Brian; and Augustine recognized the animal he was leading immediately as the copper bay he had cleaned up two days prior.

Wolf paid Brian, and after a brief conversation climbed atop his new mount. Augustine watched him with slight jealousy, he'd grown to like the copper bay during their brief time together.

He wasn't the only one who was jealous apparently. Symeon, feeling utterly betrayed, greeted the copper with a nip on the hindquarters.

"Hey, be nice!" Wolf rebuked, turning to swat Symeon's nose.

Augustine leaned forward and whispered, "If it's any consolation, Symeon, I don't like this arrangement any more than you."

At last, Faruk mounted his horse, a small, shy creature, and an odd contrast to her owner. Augustine had once heard Faruk call her "Buttercup," an unusual name for a mountain of a warrior like Faruk to pick. Perhaps she was already named before he got her. Augustine imagined Faruk stealing the innocent horse from some little peasant girl.

The moment Faruk was seated, he rode up beside Augustine and popped a blindfold around his head.

"How am I supposed to ride like this?" Augustine asked.

"Symeon will do all the work," Wolfy explained. "Just make sure you don't fall off."

"Of course," Augustine grumbled.

He felt Symeon move forward and guessed their journey had begun.

"Don't worry," Wolf continued. "This is only until we've put a little distance between ourselves and the village."

"And if your good friend Felix sees me tied up like this?" Augustine pried. "Won't he have questions?"

Augustine heard a slight chuckle from a short distance ahead.

Symeon must have been following his master very close, it sounded like Wolfy was within arms reach.

"I'll say, Felix, you were absolutely right! I never should have trusted this dirty Kalathean rat! I caught him robbing me last night."

Augustine waited for Mill to laugh at Wolf's comment but he never did. Wolf's genius seemed to go unappreciated.

"I took a liking to this lovely girl after you cleaned her up," Wolf mused.

Augustine hoped that Wolf was talking to him about the copper bay mare.

"I thought she deserved a kinder master than Brian," he continued. "I haven't settled on a name yet... any ideas?"

"Gertrude," Mill suggested. The ice had left his tone, maybe he was starting to forgive Wolf for whatever had transpired between them.

"Rosey," Faruk offered.

Augustine jumped slightly when Faruk made this suggestion, not only because the silent giant spoke, but because of the name he suggested. *Rosey? Really?*

All of the name suggestions thus far were terrible. That copper bay was a beautiful animal and deserved a beautiful name.

"Fotia," Augustine stated. "It means–"

"Fire," Wolf finished. (Of course, he knew some Greek, he seemed to know everything.) "I like that."

With their new addition named, the party continued in silence. Augustine listened keenly to the surrounding landscape. He heard the plodding of the horse hooves, along with their contented snorts. He heard the wind rustling through the canopy, bird song, and the bubbling of an occasional brook. The medley of sounds was beautiful and relaxing even to a blindfolded prisoner getting dragged off to certain doom.

24

LINA THE PATIENT

Doctor Clietus Bone was not a sentimental man. Still, he felt a slight flutter of anticipation in his chest when he received a letter from Lina. She was two days late in returning from her errand. Doctor Bone wasn't worried of course, but he couldn't help but think about all the potential health risks a young lady like her might face while traveling. Being a doctor, he had an extensive mental list of things that could potentially harm her and had been reviewing it almost non-stop since the day she left.

He took a quick breath to quench his sudden surge of emotion then opened the letter with surgical precision.

My Dear Father,

I will be away a bit longer than expected. Please don't worry if you don't hear from me for a while. I received some information about Augustine's whereabouts but I am not at liberty to say more or it could put my entire mission in jeopardy. I promise you, I am perfectly safe, Prince Oswald is here protecting me.

I will be back in the spring. Please remember to check on the miller's youngest daughter to make sure she changes her dressing. Also, I've left

*some ginger root in the surgery, please remember to grind it while it's
still fresh.*
I will write again as soon as I am able.
Your daughter,
Lina

Doctor Bone became utterly still. His face lost all expression and
he became intently focused on the medical mystery at hand, namely,
what would make a sensible girl like Lina put herself in mortal peril?
He began running over a list of ailments in his head, but none of
them proved to be the actual cause.

The real reason for Lina's flight was partially because she, like
most teenagers, was only vaguely aware of the anxiety her actions
would induce in her poor father. The other reason was actually based
on solid logic. Lina's interactions with Mirella gave her exclusive
information regarding Augustine, making her the only person with a
chance of helping him.

She wrote the letter the very evening she convinced Mirella to
deliver her to Wolf. Mirella agreed to send it, on condition that Lina
did not include any information that could be helpful in finding her
beloved Wolfy. Lina wasn't even allowed to use Mirella's name, lest
Florian send a militia to interrogate her. (Florian's men didn't pose a
threat, Mirella just didn't want the hassle of dealing with them.)

Upon completing the letter, Lina gave it to Mirella with the words,
"Thank you so much, I just don't want my father to worry."

Mirella reviewed the letter, presumably to ensure it didn't contain
too much information.

"I'm sure it will put your father's mind at ease," Mirella nodded
approvingly. She folded the letter and placed it on the table.

"In return for delivering this, I am going to ask you to do something for me," Mirella continued.

"What is it?" Lina asked, feeling a twinge of anxiety. Mirella's fairy
blood made Lina a little worried she was about to become involved in
some sort of curse, but what Mirella ended up asking seemed
completely unthreatening.

"When you see, Wolfy, will you give him this?" she asked, taking a little box from a shelf and handing it to Lina. "And tell him Lady Mirella sends her love."

Lina opened the box. The only thing it contained was a red powder that smelled like some sort of exotic spice. It seemed harmless enough.

"I will," Lina agreed.

"Unfortunately, I will only be able to take you partway to the village of Dobze tomorrow," Mirella explained. "It will take another fortnight to reach the place after that and you'll have to wait... probably until winter before Wolfy arrives. Are you certain you want to do this?"

"Absolutely certain," Lina answered.

THE NEXT MORNING, immediately after breakfast, Mirella said goodbye to her guests. Lina hardly had time to respond before the little cabin vanished and they found themselves someplace entirely different.

They were on a dirt road, running through a beautiful valley. Evergreens covered the mountains on either side and bird-song rang out all around them.

"Mirella?" Lina called as she tried to orient herself. But the enchantress was nowhere to be seen. She was probably at home, killing chickens or something.

"Well," Lina stated. "I suppose we'd better be off."

Per Mirella's instructions, they started following the road south. Unfortunately, they had left their horses in King Henry's courtyard and had to proceed on foot.

"What a strange person," Oswald commented as they walked.

Lina hoped she wasn't about to hear a long rant about the woman who had saved her life. Her feelings toward Mirella were complicated. She was frustrated with the enchantress for not bringing Augustine back, but grateful for the rest of the help she provided.

"What do you think she's getting out of this?" Oswald wondered aloud.

Lina shrugged. She would have loved to believe that Mirella wasn't getting anything out of it. That she had helped them as best she could without risking Wolf's life because she was a kind person, still... Lina couldn't help but feel anxious, especially when she thought of the little box she was now carrying in her pack.

Why did Mirella want Wolf to have it? *Was it just a spice?*

Lina decided to change the subject.

"I'm sure my father will tell your mother where you are when he gets my letter."

"My parents probably haven't even noticed I'm missing," Oswald grumbled.

Lina shot him a glare. He was clearly fishing for pity and she wasn't going to bite. She chose to ignore the comment and drink in her beautiful surroundings.

"Do you think if I got kidnapped my father would expend so much effort on me?" Oswald continued.

Lina rolled her eyes. Apparently, she was going to hear a rant whether she liked it or not.

"Uncle Florian cares more about his fake son, than my father cares about his own flesh and blood."

Oswald was clearly suffering from a disease called narcissism. Lina glanced over at his sulky face and frowned. He probably wanted her to say something like, "That's not true, your father adores you!" or "Don't say that, my prince. If you got kidnapped your father would tear the world apart to find you."

After overhearing Filbert and Florian's conversation, she did sort of feel sorry for Oswald but making him aware of that would only make his condition worse.

"Maybe the reason King Florian loves Augustine so much is because Augustine actually cares about people other than himself," she answered dryly.

"I care about other people!" Oswald exclaimed.

"Really? Who?" Lina asked.

"Augustine," Oswald continued. "Why do you think I'm on this godforsaken journey?"

"You're only on this 'godforsaken journey' because you hate the idea of someone who isn't you tormenting him."

Oswald considered this for a moment. "Well..." he started. "I care about *you*. It's why I let you get away with being so disrespectful."

Lina laughed, surprising both herself and Oswald. In the world Oswald had created for himself, where everything revolved around him, this comment made perfect sense. Lina couldn't argue with it. Instead, she shrugged and said, "If you say so, Your Highness."

Oswald stared at her. She could almost see the wheels spinning in his mind. The next couple of hours passed in beautiful silence.

25

CRIPPLE'S RANSOM

Wolf's party spent the next fortnight traveling through the wilderness. They weren't following any kind of road as far as Augustine could see. And they encountered no other travelers. They ate bread and cheese and any small game they were lucky enough to catch.

During this time, Augustine found himself suffering from an unexpected ailment—boredom. The moment they stopped anywhere, his captors would fasten him to a tree where presumably he couldn't cause any trouble.

He had nothing better to do than intently watch the three men as they tended their horses, built a fire, and prepared their evening meal.

If there was any light left after they made camp, Mill would either play cards with Faruk or practice throwing the knife he wore on his belt. If Mill was bad with a bow, he made up for it with his knife throwing. Augustine spent many an evening watching him impale tree trunks with his little blade. He threw with such ferocity, it was like he was channeling all his hatred for his former lord into the weapon.

Wolf never failed to read from his breviary. Even if it was already dark, he'd read it by the light of the fire or of the stars.

One evening, while there was yet a little daylight, Wolf withdrew the precious book and sat with his back to one of the trees. Augustine was tied up nearby. He looked at the beautiful little breviary, then at Wolf.

"Why do you read that?" he asked.

"Doesn't everyone pray the Office?" Wolf replied.

"I didn't think you were the praying type," Augustine observed.

"You have to be in my profession," Wolf replied. "Do you have any idea how hard it is to shoot a man in full armor from the top of a tree two furlongs away?"

Augustine stared at him blankly.

"You don't think our Lord would bless someone in my profession, do you?"

"Um, no." Augustine answered.

"He did say, 'Blessed are the peacemakers'," Wolf continued. "Which is what I am."

"You?" Augustine answered in disbelief.

"Certainly! Nobles start wars, I kill nobles ergo..." He twirled his hand in the air allowing Augustine to fill in the blank.

He chuckled at the confusion in his captive's face.

"Are you..." Augustine started. He wasn't expecting to get an answer to his next question, but he continued anyway. "Are you going to kill *me*?"

Wolf closed his book and gave Augustine his full attention, the air of amusement that always hung around him vanished.

"It depends what the client wants," he answered.

"But if he asks you to, you will?" Augustine pressed.

"Yes."

Augustine felt his anger flare up.

"And God will bless you for it?" Augustine hissed.

"What I do is hardly glorious," Wolf replied calmly. "But it gives the nobles a way to settle their petty disagreements without leaving fields of peasant corpses in their wake. That must count for something in God's eyes."

"We aren't allowed to touch peasants," Augustine corrected. "Our code of honor forbids it."

Mill was standing a few paces away, engaged in his daily knife throwing exercise. At Augustine's declaration, he turned and shot him a glare full of loathing.

Wolf, on the other hand, burst out laughing. "Oh, you're right!" he exclaimed. "If someone had only told your father!"

"Prince Justin is not my father!" Augustine exclaimed. "And I'd never harm an innocent! Why, the very reason I became a squire was so I could protect the innocent from scoundrels like Prince Justin or... evil gods or... anyone else who tries to oppress them."

"And who is going to protect them from your petty rivalries?" Wolf pressed.

Augustine rolled his eyes.

"Don't act so righteous," Wolf accused. "You don't strike me as the kind of man who can walk away from a fight. Someday, some rival of yours will challenge you and you'll charge into battle without once considering the cost."

Wolf opened his book forcefully and turned back to it, leaving Augustine alone with his thoughts.

AUGUSTINE WASN'T WORRIED. If anything was going to kill him on this journey it would be the insanity that came with being a model prisoner. As for Wolfy's client, well, Augustine had no plans of ever meeting him.

The party continued on for another two days, during which time Augustine somehow managed to behave himself.

Then, one morning, he woke to the sensation of someone nudging his ribs.

"Good morning, Augustine," Wolf greeted. It turned out, Wolf was gently kicking him awake.

"Are we getting an early start?" Augustine asked. The sun had only barely started to rise. "Mill and I are," Wolf explained. "Now get up and stand with your back to this tree."

"Why?" Augustine asked, tensing.

"So we can tie you up," Wolf answered. "I don't want you causing Faruk any trouble while we are away."

"Where are you going?" Augustine asked.

"In to town to get supplies," Wolf replied.

"Ah," Augustine answered, standing up obediently. "And I am guessing you can't bring me because this particular town isn't completely overrun by your admirers?"

Wolf didn't answer. Instead, he left Faruk to finish securing Augustine and started readying Symeon. The horse seemed immensely grateful to have his master back—he bobbed his head enthusiastically as Wolf brushed him and fastened on his saddle.

After Augustine was safely immobilized against the tree, Mill and Wolf departed. The sun was fully up by this point giving Augustine a clear view of the campsite. There wasn't much to do, except watch Faruk mill around.

The giant of a man brushed the two remaining horses, giving each one firm but affectionate pats as he worked.

He took a little oil and rubbed it on Fotia's saddle sores. Then brought both horses some branches and flowers to nibble. All the while, he mumbled incoherently to them.

Augustine might have thought Faruk had great affection for the animals if he believed such a man could have affection for anyone. After he had tended to the horses, he rebuilt the fire that had burned down during the night.

The sun had fully risen by the time he finished. The giant squatted by the fire warming his hands for what seemed like an eternity.

Augustine stared at him.

Faruk stared at the fire.

During this unending moment, the sun hardly moved. Augustine closed his eyes and gently knocked the back of his head against the tree where he was bound. *This was going to be a long day.* He almost wanted to attempt an escape just so he would have something to do. Would it really put his whole plan in jeopardy?

"You play?" came Faruk's booming voice.

Augustine opened his eyes and looked at him.

"Play what?" Augustine asked.

"Cripple's Ransom," Faruk said, withdrawing a deck of playing cards from the pouch at his waist.

Cripple's Ransom? Cripple's Ransom was arguably the most complex card game in existence. Few people actually liked it. It was one of those games people only played when they wanted to look smart. Augustine couldn't picture a man like Faruk having any interest in such a pastime.

"Not with my hands tied," Augustine replied.

Faruk untied him. "Tell Wolf, I kill you. Run, I kill you."

"Understood," Augustine answered.

Faruk dealt the cards. "You read?" he asked.

"Yes?" Augustine replied, wondering what that had to do with anything.

"If I win, you'll read to me," Faruk answered.

"Read what?" Augustine pressed.

"Wolfy's book," Faruk answered.

"Would he approve of that?" Augustine asked. The breviary seemed to be Wolf's most prized possession.

"Tell him. I kill you," Faruk answered.

"*Right,*" Augustine mumbled.

"If you win?" Faruk pressed.

"Well, since my freedom isn't an option, let me think..."

"Your freedom," Faruk repeated. "Fine."

Augustine blinked. "Really?"

Faruk responded with a single nod.

Not only had Faruk suggested they play the most complicated card game in existence, he was so confident in his skill that he was willing to let Augustine go if he lost. Now, Augustine was no expert, but he had a reasonable amount of practice. Surely, he could beat someone who couldn't even read.

"So we're clear," Augustine stated. "If I win, I can leave?"

Faruk grunted his affirmation.

"I can take Fotia and some supplies and go home? And you won't do anything to stop me?"

Faruk gave a second affirmative grunt, then added, "Your move."

In Cripple's Ransom, three was the highest card unless you drew a nine of the opposing suit which canceled it out.

"Do you play with rabbits?" Augustine asked. He thought he should check since rabbits was technically a house rule. A rabbit was a four, a six, and queen together which could restore your three if it had been terminated by a nine.

Faruk responded with a scowl Augustine took to mean "no." So the solemn giant was a purist, eh? He was like Florian. Florian insisted house rules were cheating.

Thus the game began with Augustine calculating probability, laying down pairs, and trying to read Faruk's face. The trouble was, Faruk's face was impossible to read even when he wasn't playing cards. He was intently focused the entire time—looking at his hand, looking at the cards on the stump they were using as a table, and occasionally glancing at Augustine. Five rounds in, Faruk laid all four threes on the table thus ending the game in his favor.

While Augustine was still marveling at the man's skill, Faruk marched over to Fotia's saddlebag and removed Wolf's breviary.

Augustine took the beautiful book in his hands, admiring the leatherwork on the cover. He carefully opened it, observing the stunning illuminated script. It really was a work of art. No wonder Wolf valued it so much.

He spent the rest of the afternoon reading aloud from it, while Faruk sat like a statue staring vacantly into the air. Augustine could hardly tell he was even alive. At last, when the shadows grew long, Faruk stood silently.

"Give me the book," he ordered. "Before Wolf comes back."

Augustine nodded. They had read almost the entire thing. Augustine flipped through the last couple of pages drinking in the script and illustrations. Then on the inside of the back cover he noticed something. It was a name written in the same beautiful script that covered each of the interior pages: *Brother Wolfgang the Meek.*

Augustine stared at the name for a long moment, before Faruk's voice boomed, "Give it, now. Wolf's coming."

Augustine did as he was told and when Mill and Wolf returned that evening, they found the camp exactly as they had left it.

26

OSWALD THE KIND

T he first thing Lina noticed about the village of Dobze was how sickly the residents looked. Those she encountered in the streets were pale, thin, and bloated in the middle.

Lina purchased a loaf of bread from an elderly baker and while they were making conversation, the gray-haired woman confirmed Lina's suspicions.

"Yes, it seems like everyone is getting sick these days," she sighed.

"What kind of sick?" Lina pressed. "Fever? Stomach pain?"

As the old woman began to describe cramps, nausea, and vomiting (among other things) in great detail, Oswald suddenly became intensely interested in something farther down the road and wandered away. Lina made no objection; she would find him right after she finished drinking in the detailed descriptions of the symptoms with scientific enthusiasm.

"When did this start?" she asked.

"Oh it's been this way for years," the woman commented. "It's this place, I think. It wasn't this way back in the old village."

"Old village?" Lina pressed, though she thought perhaps, she knew what the old woman was talking about. The road which brought them to Dobze passed directly through a ruin. Most of the buildings had been burned away, leaving only charred stone foundations. The fields all around were barren, save the occasional weed poking up through the sterile ground.

"Yes," the woman nodded. "We used to live down in the valley until the Kalathean invasion about fifteen or twenty years ago. What was the name of that prince of theirs... Jason, I think?"

"Justin?" Lina suggested.

"Was it Justin?" the woman thought. "No, I swear it was Jason."

Lina knew for a fact it was Justin, but she didn't see any point in pressing the matter.

"So this Prince Jason," the woman continued, "came by to settle a grievance with our lord at the time." She scowled. "I remember *that* villain's name. Couldn't forget it if I tried—Bertok, it was.

"When Prince Jason comes, Bertok locks himself up in the castle there." The woman motioned toward a castle, visible on a distant hillside. "And he leaves us to Jason's mercy."

Lina felt a flicker of anger at this, though she wasn't particularly surprised. She imagined Augustine being beside himself with indignation at the idea that a lord would neglect his one duty in life. Poor Augustine had always been a bit of an idealist.

"And since murdering people and burning our homes wasn't good enough for that Kalathean devil," the old woman growled, "he decides to salt our fields. Nothing will grow there now. So we moved here to the eastern end of the valley." She sighed. "But it isn't the same. I swear this place is cursed."

Lina listened politely for a few more moments, while the elderly woman bemoaned the loss of the old village. She described it as a kind of paradise where the harvest was always abundant, the people were in perfect health, and they didn't have a problem in the world.

Finally, Lina realized she'd lost sight of Oswald completely, so she thanked the old woman and excused herself.

She looked for him as she sloshed her way down the muddy street. It was no wonder the people were sickly, it looked like they built their new village on top of a bog.

That's when the obvious cause of their mysterious ailment jumped to Lina's mind—at least, it was obvious to *her*. If the old woman was typical of the people of Dobze, they weren't a well educated bunch. She quickened her pace, eager to confirm her theory.

She almost crashed headlong into Oswald, who was standing in the exact center of the square, being careful to keep a safe distance between himself and the few passing villagers.

"Lina," he said, as she approached. "What did that woman say? Is there a plague? Should we leave?"

"We aren't leaving, Oswald," Lina replied. "If we are going to find Augustine, we need to wait here for Wolf."

"But is there a plague?" he pressed.

"Yes, sort of," Lina answered.

"What do you mean 'sort of'?" Oswald demanded.

"I mean," Lina scowled. "That I don't think it's contagious *and* I think I know how to get rid of it."

"You just used 'think', twice in that sentence which is two times too many as far as I'm concerned," Oswald hissed. "We didn't come here to play doctor."

"I'm not playing doctor," Lina frowned. "I *am* a doctor."

"Women are not doctors," Oswald pointed out.

Lina rolled her eyes. It was technically true because women couldn't go to university, but Lina had been training under her father for as long as she could remember and for all practical purposes was as good as anyone with a degree.

"Fine, I'm a healer," she hissed. "But I'm a damn good one and if I am going to be waiting around here for weeks, I might as well help these people. If you're too afraid to help me, you can leave any time you like."

Oswald stiffened. "I'm not afraid! I just think we should focus on our mission."

While he was still speaking, Lina noticed a woman emerging from one of the nearby homes with a water bucket. She realized a word with this woman might confirm her theory. Lina brushed past

Oswald, intent on speaking with the stranger.

"You *are* afraid," she said as she passed. "I know because you're exactly like Augustine."

"What?" Oswald exclaimed, trailing after her.

"Why is it that the idea of cutting people into pieces on the battlefield doesn't phase either of you in the slightest, but the idea of fixing people...Talk of surgery, and medicine, and stitches, and bile, and pus." Her smile increased along with the discomfort in Oswald's expression. "*That* neither of you are man enough to handle."

Lina increased her speed. The woman with the bucket was a good distance ahead of Lina, and the latter did not want to lose sight of her.

"Now," Lina continued, glancing over her shoulder at Oswald. "I'm going to go and make an inquiry. If you are uncomfortable with that, run off and find someplace to swoon."

In response to this, Oswald grumbled under his breath, but continued to follow her until the woman with the bucket led them to the cause of the mysterious plague.

Just as Lina suspected–it was a pond. A pond with still, boggy-smelling water that was definitely contaminated with toxic vapors. The woman Lina was chasing stooped beside it to fill her bucket.

And Lina took the opportunity to ask her if everyone in the village got their water in the same place. The woman's affirmative answer did not surprise Lina in the slightest.

Convincing the villagers not to drink bog water was a lot easier than Lina suspected. It was just a matter of educating them one friendly conversation at a time. There were other water sources available in the surrounding valley, they were just a bit farther away.

In addition to suggesting alternative water sources, Lina taught the people how to purify water by exposing it to wind, sunlight, or a few drops of any strong drink. As time went on, those who took Lina's advice began to get better, and those who didn't at first, noticed and followed suit.

Lina also offered her services to anyone who needed a healer. It didn't take long for her reputation to flourish, and before she knew it she was spending every waking moment running back and forth across Dobze, bandaging wounds and giving out medicines.

Since, according to Mirella, the local lord was a good friend of Wolf's, Lina thought it best to stay away from the castle and keep a low profile. Oswald reluctantly agreed, and they took up residence with a village family.

The prince was not at all happy about sharing a one room house with four other people and a cow, but it really couldn't be helped. Besides, Lina thought peasant life would offer the future king of Kaltehafen some much needed perspective.

Every morning, Lina would leave before the sun rose to go visit her patients, and every night she would come home exhausted. Oswald followed her on her rounds. Usually, he would stand at a distance while she worked, looking a little queasy. But whenever he found some way to help that did not involve directly interacting with gore or body fluids, he would jump on the opportunity. He would fetch water and medicines, or hand Lina tools while keeping as far away from the patient as possible.

One day, someone called for Lina early in the morning. She left without waking Oswald and didn't see him all day. She remained with the patient late into the night and returned home starving, cold, and exhausted.

To her surprise, she found Oswald waiting up for her with a bowl of hot soup. He gave it to her, had her sit down by the fire and then, fetching a blanket, draped it around her shoulders. She was too tired to question this unusual act of kindness.

During the weeks that followed, Oswald's uncharacteristic thoughtfulness increased. He forgot his position as crown prince and took on the role of Lina's loyal servant. The second Lina began to feel thirsty, he would materialize holding out a cup of water. Anytime, a cool breeze touched her, he would throw his own cloak over her shoulders defensively.

Lina took this as a good sign. Maybe living among the common folk had awakened his sense of compassion? She hoped so, although she noticed his acts of kindness were reserved almost exclusively for her. Still, his being thoughtful to anyone was a step in the right direction. Maybe somewhere, inside that spoiled little noble was the makings of a great king.

27

THE BLIZZARD

The weeks dragged by, the air grew cool, and Augustine became more miserable. His frustration increased with the cold. He was angry at Wolf for kidnapping him, and somehow angrier with his stepfather who hadn't managed to rescue him yet. He would have thought Florian had given up, except that he knew his stepfather was too stubborn to give up on anything.

His loneliness nipped away at him and he frequently found himself thinking of his family. If he continued with his plan, he wouldn't see his sister again for over a year. He hoped she wouldn't change too much—a year was a long time for a little girl.

Mostly though, he thought of Lina. Every time he was overcome with anger, and tempted to lash out at his captors he would picture her glaring at him.

"Be patient, Augustine," she would say. "It's not worth it."

He ate everything he was given because he knew Lina would want him to keep up his strength. He wrapped up warm against the cold because he knew she wouldn't want him getting sick. He took care of himself for her sake. Eventually, he would see her again and when the time came he was going to be the picture of health.

There was one thing Augustine enjoyed, even within his captivity

—playing cards with Faruk. It only happened on the few occasions the party came near a village. Mill and Wolf would tie him to a tree and leave him for Faruk to look after. The moment they were out of sight, Faruk would untie him and let him play Cripple's Ransom for his freedom. On the third such occasion, Augustine had finished reading Faruk Wolf's breviary and they didn't have any other books in their possession.

As he was sitting by the tree stump, waiting for Faruk to deal, the giant looked at him with his great dark eyes and said, "You've read Rouvin?"

"Rouvin...the Philosopher?" Augustine puzzled.

"Yes," Faruk confirmed.

"Um... yes I have," Augustine replied. He had studied the works of Rouvin extensively.

"If I win, you will tell me everything you've learned," Faruk growled.

"That might take a while," Augustine answered.

"Then tell me what he says about the nature of the universe," Faruk continued.

"Can you be more specific?"

Faruk glared at him. "Is the universe made up of triangles or nautilus spirals? Because that Kalathean fellow, Severinus or whatever his name is, says it is made up of triangles but that other Anamian philosopher says it's made up of nautilus spirals and," (Faruk's eyes burned with frustration.) "They can't both be right."

"You've..." Augustine looked up at the quiet terror of a man. "You've read Severinus?"

"Can't read," Faruk answered. "Caught an intellectual and made him do it."

Augustine pictured Faruk threatening to rip the arms off of some prince if he didn't immediately read him the contents of his philosophical library. It... was a strange image.

"What if instead of me telling you what I know..." Augustine started. Faruk loomed tall over him and Augustine hoped his next words would be taken well. "—I teach you to read? Then you can read whatever philosophers you like for yourself."

"Smart people read," Faruk answered. "I'm not smart."

"Well, you must be the way you play Cripple's Ransom," Augustine objected. "Why don't we just try one lesson? If you don't like it, I'll tell you everything I know about Rouvin and the nature of the universe."

Faruk stared at him for a long time. Augustine could see him thinking. He was probably trying to decide whether to accept the offer or beat Augustine to a pulp for daring to make an alternative suggestion.

"We'll try," Faruk said at last.

The game that followed ended pretty quickly. Augustine didn't even try to win. Partly because he knew he couldn't and partly because he *wanted* to teach Faruk to read. Reading would open up a whole new world of hobbies that didn't involve kidnapping noblemen and Augustine thought that would be good for him.

He gave Faruk his first lesson using a flat rock and a piece of charcoal for writing. The giant was a very quick study, he asked intelligent questions, and by the time the day ended, Augustine realized that not only was Faruk intelligent, he was a genius. He had the makings of a great philosopher, the only thing he lacked was education.

The next day, as they continued their journey, Augustine found himself watching Faruk. It occurred to him that the reason the giant was always so quiet was because he was reflecting on the great mysteries of the universe as best he could with the little information he possessed.

Augustine hoped their party would pass another village soon.

WOLF PROVIDED Augustine with warmer clothes, but they were hardly sufficient against the frigid air. He hoped his captors didn't have any crazy ideas about pressing on all winter.

One afternoon, as they pushed forward into the bitter wind, Augustine caught Wolf eyeing the gray clouds that loomed overhead.

"It's going to be close," Mill mumbled.

"We'll make it," Wolf assured.

Augustine wondered where exactly their destination was. The following morning, the first snowflakes began to fall and by the afternoon great flurries danced down from the clouds.

Their poor horses struggled through ever-deepening snow drifts. Wolf repeatedly reassured Mill that they were going to make it somewhere before they got stranded, but of course, he failed to specify where.

Up ahead, Augustine saw something coming into view through the white wall of swirling snow. It was some kind of a building, with the roofs of houses round about it. Perhaps this was the place Wolf was looking for?

As they approached it, Augustine could see that it was a ruin. It had once been a windmill, but the top was mostly burned away leaving only the stone foundation. It was surrounded by the skeletons of other structures—homes and barns and workshops.

The land around it seemed utterly barren. Not that it was easy to tell with the snow flurries clouding his view. Only the charred skeletons of trees remained, and there was no sign of new growth anywhere. Wolf continued through the ruins unfazed; apparently, this former village was not their destination.

"You see this?" Wolf said as they passed the charred structures. "This is your father's handiwork."

Augustine realized that Wolf was addressing him. He took another look around at the place. Even the church in the village center hadn't been spared. Every time he learned anything new about Prince Justin, he was further convinced that there had never been a more evil man. Thank God they weren't actually related.

As the snow fell harder, Augustine kept his head bent down to keep the wind out of his face. Symeon, likely eager for a little warmth, decided he wanted to press up against the side of the horse in front which happened to be Mill's.

Augustine didn't become aware of the animal's intentions until the two horses were almost touching. Then he jerked back on the reins to stop the impending crash and looked up hoping Mill hadn't noticed. The last thing he wanted was to give Mill more reason to hate him.

Thankfully, Mill was oblivious to the near collision. In fact, he seemed oblivious to everything at the moment except a single ruined home a short distance from the road. Though his lips were blue and his cheeks scarlet, he kept his head up so he could continue staring at the sorry remains of the former house. Before they passed by, Mill brought his horse to a stop so he could look at it a moment longer.

Augustine decided not to question Mill's fascination with this particular ruin, and instead quietly directed Symeon around him without drawing attention to himself. After a short time, Augustine glanced back over his shoulder and saw that Mill was following again with his head bent against the wind.

It was almost dark when Wolf pointed out their actual destination. It was another village lying among the trees directly ahead. They fought their way toward it through the ever-increasing volleys of snow.

The night had fallen completely when the four of them stumbled into the inn all soaked through and half frozen. A kindly older woman showed them to their room.

"If you'd like to escape tonight, you are more than welcome," Wolf grumbled to Augustine as he undid the bonds on his wrists. "Tomorrow we'll continue to the house of Lord Ervin."

Augustine had no idea who Lord Ervin was. He didn't even know what kingdom they were in. He doubted anyone in the village could help him or Wolf would not have brought him here. Still, they'd probably be stuck in Lord Ervin's village for some time, perhaps an opportunity for escape would present itself.

28

THE REUNION

Augustine woke the next morning under a roof, completely untied, and somewhat warm. It was the most wonderful feeling in the world. As he sat up and stretched, he looked at his captors who were still sound asleep next to the hearth.

The group was so cold and tired when they arrived, they had just curled up on the floor by the fire and fallen asleep. No one was on watch.

Augustine opened and closed his free hands. Mill was closest to him, and probably still had his knife on his belt. The idea of snatching the weapon and cutting their throats passed through Augustine's mind. He almost immediately dismissed the thought.

Even if he successfully killed them, he had nowhere to go except a village where no one knew him and the lord was a friend of Wolf's. He'd end up getting hanged for murder. Further, he couldn't live with himself if he killed them in their sleep like a coward. If he was going to take someone's life, it would have to be a fair fight.

Augustine tried the door. He wasn't making an escape, he just wanted to have a look around the inn.

There was a tavern on the lower floor. It was unoccupied except for the old woman who had shown them to their room the night before. She was carrying a large wooden bucket toward the entrance.

"Let me help you," Augustine offered.

"Bless you," the old woman smiled. She held the door for him.

"You'll have to go down to the river yonder," she said motioning down the road straight ahead. "The pond is contaminated."

"Alright," Augustine shrugged.

HE DIDN'T MIND the walk. The snow had ceased falling and the sun was starting to rise. He looked around to get the lay of the land. The road into the village was buried in snow and not a soul could be seen anywhere. Even the roosters were sleeping in, all fluffed into balls on the eves.

He filled the bucket in the partially frozen stream and started back. As he approached the main door, he noticed the hooded figure of a young woman entering. He moved slowly as he lugged the full bucket of water and by the time he had entered the tavern, the girl was nowhere to be seen.

He figured she had disappeared into one of the rooms. The old woman was also gone, so Augustine dumped the bucket into the cauldron by the fire and then crouched down by the flames to warm himself.

"Just keep her warm," a voice said. Augustine furrowed his brow. He was definitely losing his mind, he could have sworn the speaker was Lina.

"I've done everything I can for her, I'm afraid," the voice continued. "But if you just let her rest, she'll be back to herself in a couple of days."

Augustine stood up and looked around. The speaker was still in the hallway and he couldn't see her.

"Bless you," a second voice (definitely the old woman), replied.

A moment later, the innkeeper shuffled around the corner, followed by a girl who looked exactly like Lina.

Augustine stared for a long time trying to make sense of this. It couldn't actually *be* Lina, that would be impossible. Either it was a perfect duplicate, or else Augustine had gone insane.

The girl didn't notice him at first. She went to a peg on the far wall to retrieve her cloak.

Meanwhile, the old woman noticed that Augustine had completed his task.

"Oh thank you, son!" she beamed.

At the sound of her voice, the girl turned around and froze. The old woman shuffled away to do some other task leaving Augustine alone with Lina's look-alike.

Neither of them said or did anything for a long moment. Augustine couldn't move. He wasn't seeing a Lina look-alike. Her expression, her features, even the pattern of her freckles was too perfect. He was seeing *Lina*. This was clearly a torturous hallucination.

The girl approached him slowly.

"Augustine?" she whispered.

He opened his mouth but couldn't bring himself to say anything, so he closed it again and continued staring at her in disbelief. Lina extended a hand and gently touched his cheek. Augustine brought his hand up and covered hers, pressing it closer to his face.

He drank in the wonderful feeling of her warm hand. *She was real.* She had to be...but how?

A thousand questions flooded Augustine's mind as he looked into her smiling face. What was she doing here? How had she gotten here? Was anyone else with her? Was he about to be set free?

The questions piled up and swirled around in his head. He was too overwhelmed to ask any of them. Instead, he found himself pulling her close and wrapping her in his arms. She welcomed the embrace by leaning in to him and holding him tight. They stood there in silent joy for a long moment, then Augustine kissed the top of her head.

She pulled away just enough to smile up at him and he took the opportunity to move in for a proper kiss.

Had they been thinking clearly, they might have been more careful about expressing their affections. But Augustine was so overwhelmed with joy he never considered the risks. Lina began to consider them as Augustine was holding her. But when he kissed her, it temporarily subdued her sensible nature and she welcomed the kiss without a second thought.

As they stood there, wrapped in each other's arms, with their lips pressed together, Wolf's irritated voice sounded from the hall.

"Wow, you really are your father's son, aren't you?"

Augustine and Lina jerked apart and swung toward him in alarm.

"We haven't even been here a day and you're already chasing girls," Wolf rolled his eyes. "Just promise me you won't make babies. Because I swear if I have to hunt down any more of Justin's descendants I'm going to throw myself off a cliff."

Augustine's heart raced. *Wolf couldn't ever know who Lina was.* If Lina was here with his stepfather, and Wolf found out, it could spoil their rescue plan.

Augustine took Lina by the arm, spun her toward the door, and blurted, "It was wonderful to meet you, um, what was your name again?"

Lina broke away from him and to his alarm charged toward his captor.

"Are you Wolf?" she demanded.

Augustine froze. *What was Lina doing?* Nothing about this made sense.

Curiosity sparkled in Wolf's eyes. "I am," he confirmed.

"Lady Mirella sends her regards and asks that you would hear my case."

Wolf raised his eyebrows in genuine surprise. "Mirella sent you?" he mumbled.

"And she gave me a gift for you," Lina continued. "Once you've heard me, I will fetch it."

"Then I will hear you at once," he answered.

Augustine had never felt so confused.

29

LINA NEGOTIATES WITH A CRIMINAL

"Augustine, will you give us a moment?" Lina asked.

Augustine reacted exactly as Lina suspected.

"What?" he exclaimed. "I'm not leaving you with him!"

Lina returned the objection with a fiery glare. "Augustine," she stated firmly. "*I need you to trust me.*"

Wolf looked back and forth between the two of them with a slight smile and a furrowed brow. He was clearly just as confused as his prisoner.

The latter didn't move. He seemed to be thinking, trying to figure out what her plan was exactly.

"*Trust me,*" Lina repeated.

Augustine balled his hands into fists.

"We'll be sitting right over there," she said, motioning to a table in the corner of the room. "I'll be alright."

Augustine looked at Wolf. "If you harm her, I'll kill you. I don't care what this 'Lord Ervin' does to me."

"I'd expect nothing less," Wolf replied. "I swear to you, I will not touch her."

Lina breathed a sigh of relief as Augustine moved away down the hall.

"After you, my lady," Wolf said, motioning toward the table in the corner with a sweep of his arm.

She took her seat, regarding Wolf closely as he sat down opposite her.

The first time she saw him, it was from a distance, and her view was partially obstructed by branches and brambles. She thought then, that he had a cruel and arrogant air.

Seeing him clearly, up close, gave her a slightly different impression. He was certainly confident and very handsome. His green eyes sparkled with curiosity and intelligence. But he also had a slight weariness about him. His skin was weatherworn. The lines on his face and the gray streaks in his hair appeared to be the first signs of age; dark circles shaded his eyes.

He had a few minor scars, not the types of things most people would notice. One was across his eyebrow, and one on his cheek. Lina could tell that his nose had been broken at some point and healed improperly. It was slightly crooked.

This man was a fighter, a highwayman, a criminal, a kidnapper, and she was about to appeal to his good nature. Had she completely lost her mind?

God help me, Lina thought. *I can't believe I'm doing this.*

"We'd best keep our voices down," Lina said aloud. "I think..."

"That Augustine is still watching us from the hallway?" Wolf finished. Lina noticed that he was looking over her shoulder. She glanced backward just in time to see Augustine duck out of sight. She smiled. Maybe she should have been annoyed, but his desire to protect her showed that he was still very much himself.

"He's a bit of a pain sometimes," Wolf said with a very slight smile. "But he's hard to dislike."

A moment passed, with Wolf waiting expectantly for Lina to begin. She had been rehearsing this moment for months, it was critical to get it right.

"Lady Mirella told me that you were an honorable man," Lina started. "...and that you would help me if you could."

"And I will," Wolf confirmed. "*If I can.*"

"Can you help me save my closest friend?" Lina asked.

Wolf smiled slightly, and stuck his tongue in his cheek. "As long as his name isn't Augustine Hatsi and it's not myself he needs saving from."

His bluntness caught Lina off-guard. Her mind raced to change tactics. She had rehearsed every possible scenario in her mind but somehow, in the reality of the moment, she was struggling to remember all the perfect arguments she'd spent months constructing.

"You must be very close friends," Wolf commented. "I don't kiss my friends that way."

"Not even Lady Mirella?" Lina accused. It was the type of nosey question she would loathe in normal conversation, but she had a feeling the enchantress was one of Wolf's weaknesses and wanted to test that theory.

Wolf laughed. "That's none of your business."

"She adores you," Lina pressed. "It's why she wouldn't rescue Augustine when I asked her. She said you must have had a good reason for taking him."

Some of the amusement faded from Wolf's expression. He drummed his fingers on the table thoughtfully.

"Mirella seems like a good person," Lina continued. "And she insists you are too. Which is why I think you made a mistake when you took Augustine."

Wolf suddenly scowled over her shoulder and pointed a commanding finger toward the hall. Lina looked backward in time to see Augustine's shape scurrying away.

"Sorry," Lina smiled sheepishly. "He's a bit–"

"Stubborn? Headstrong? Incapable of following directions?" Wolf suggested.

"All of them," Lina admitted.

Wolf laughed. "At least we agree on that point! Now, you were saying?"

"That perhaps there's been some mistake," Lina repeated. "Maybe you took the wrong person."

"No mistake," Wolf insisted.

"But Augustine is an innocent man," Lina explained. "He's done nothing to deserve this. Does it have something to do with..." Lina glanced over her shoulder and lowered her voice. "Prince Justin?"

Wolf furrowed his brow. "How is it that you know and he doesn't?"

"It doesn't matter," Lina stated. "What does matter is that he shouldn't be punished for his father's crimes."

"I don't think punishment has anything to do with this," Wolf shrugged. "All I know is my client is offering a handsome sum for his delivery. What happens to him after that is none of my business."

"Augustine's stepfather is a king," Lina said. "If it's money you want–"

Wolf held up a hand to stop her.

"First, reputation is everything in my business, I never break a contract," he interrupted. "Second, King Florian couldn't pay me half of what my client offered."

Lina's heart was starting to race. Wolf didn't look like the kind of man who valued money as an end. His clothing was simple, worn, and had been patched and repatched many times over.

"Mirella called you a saint," Lina asserted.

At this, a genuine despondency entered Wolf's expression. His gaze dropped to the tabletop.

"Are you doing this to help people?" Lina continued. "Is that why you need the money?"

"I'm hardly a saint," Wolf mumbled. "I've done some very unholy things in my time." He looked back up at Lina. "But when I see the people I've helped, rebuilding their lives... I don't regret any of it."

Lina studied him. His expression was full of sincerity.

"You have no idea what your friend is worth to my client," Wolf continued. "When I finish this job, I'll be able to start another refuge. In exchange for one life, I'll save hundreds."

Lina studied him, thoughtfully.

"Who are you helping, Wolf?" she pried.

"The people whose lives are worthless to the very lords who swore to protect them," he answered. "Serfs, villagers, anyone who has ever found himself homeless or destitute at the hands of the nobility's trivial rivalries."

"That's wonderful," Lina said, and she truly meant it. In a strange way, she sort of liked Wolf. He really believed in what he was doing and his cause was a noble one. What she couldn't figure out, was how a man who cared so much about people, could justify violence against an innocent man like Augustine.

"Let Augustine go," Lina pleaded. "And my king will help you start another refuge. I'll even help you myself."

"I wouldn't need to do this work if it wasn't for men like your king," Wolf answered. His gaze burned into her. "I'm sorry, but I cannot let Augustine go."

Lina felt her fondness for Wolf starting to wane.

"Who is helping *your* victims?" she hissed.

"Every one of my victims, Augustine included, is one less noble for the common folk to fear."

"Augustine isn't like that," Lina started.

"He is a fighter to his very core," Wolf retorted. "I admire his spirit but I dread the damage he'll do when he comes of age." He pushed his chair away from the table. Lina opened her mouth to speak again but Wolf interrupted.

"We're finished," he declared. "I'm so sorry, you seem like a wonderful young lady, but what I am doing is bigger than any one person's happiness. I'll be here for a few more hours and then at the house of Lord Ervin. Don't forget to bring me Mirella's gift."

Lina burned with frustration. It was clear she couldn't reason with Wolf but Augustine was here now and with the snow falling the way it was, he wouldn't be going anywhere for a while. She would find some way to save him.

"Let me talk to him," Lina pleaded.

"Be my guest," Wolf shrugged. "Don't waste too much energy on your escape plan though. It's not going to work."

He got up from the table with a yawn and meandered back to his room.

30

ANOTHER INTERRUPTION

Lina and Augustine left the inn and walked out onto the snow-covered road. It was freezing cold and the snow continued spiraling down all around them. Still, they continued walking, wanting to put some distance between themselves and Wolf.

They found a little storage shack behind the inn. It was locked, but they sat with their backs to the door sheltered by the slight overhang of the eves.

Augustine put his arm around Lina's shoulder and she snuggled into him. He glanced around. He doubted he had anyone to worry about, but still wanted to make sure they would not be overheard.

"Is my father's company near?" he whispered.

Lina's gaze fell, she shook her head. "I'm alone," she answered. "Well...not *exactly*... completely alone..."

"What do you mean?" Augustine questioned.

Lina closed her eyes and released an irritated sigh.

"Oswald is with me."

"*What?*" Augustine exclaimed.

That's when Lina told him her story, how his mother asked her to keep Oswald out of the way, how she was arrested by Henry, how

Mirella saved her, and how she'd convinced the enchantress to send her to Wolf so she could plead her case.

Augustine's heart swelled with admiration for her as she recalled the tale. He knew that Lina was brave, clever, and patient, but now the story made him realize how deeply these virtues were embedded in her nature. The very fact that she had traveled with Oswald so long and not murdered him was an act of heroic endurance.

"Oswald and I arrived a few weeks ago," Lina continued. "We've been working in the village (they don't have a proper doctor here, you know) while we waited for you to arrive."

She lowered her voice. "I knew Wolf might not hear reason so I made another plan." She glanced around. "But I don't want to discuss it here."

They were still close to the inn, and surrounded by trees and boulders where a listener could easily hide.

"I'll need you to trust me, alright?" she finished.

"I do," Augustine whispered. "But, listen, I don't want us to sneak away during this storm. I can't risk your life like that, Lina. Especially, since I've also got a plan."

"You do?" Lina pressed.

"Yes, I dare not talk about it here, but it doesn't involve you and may be safer for both of us."

Lina nodded. He could see her thinking.

"I've got it," she finally whispered. "A way for us to talk safely." A hint of a smile touched her lips. "I can't tell you now, but... soon. Alright?"

Augustine felt himself smiling back. "Alright," he agreed.

"In the meantime, how are you? Have they hurt you?" Her voice was still quiet, but she wasn't whispering.

He shook his head. "I promise, I'm alright."

She grabbed his hand and pushed his sleeve up, frowning when she saw the chaffing on his wrists.

"I was worried about that," she said. "I'll get you something for it."

"Wolf already gave me some beeswax," Augustine answered.

"He did?"

Augustine nodded. "Helps a bit."

"He's..." Lina started. "Such a *strange* man."

"He truly is," Augustine agreed.

Lina was studying his face carefully, wearing the expression she reserved for patients. She was clearly not convinced he wasn't sick or injured. The last thing Augustine wanted was her fretting over him.

"They've been very good to me," Augustine explained. "I mean, as far as captors are concerned. Certainly, kinder than the smugglers who got me out of Kalathea."

"What smugglers?" Lina asked.

Augustine suddenly realized he'd never shared that particular memory. He felt his whole body tense—he hadn't shared it because he hated thinking about it.

It occurred to him that most of what he shared with Lina about Kalathea had to do with the culture, or mythology, or artwork. He told her about how his uncle defeated the gods and how his mother met Florian, but he didn't like talking about his life before all that under the reign of Jace and Acacia.

"Oh...um..." Augustine began. "Back in Kalathea... you know, before King Alexander returned... the gods would take people at random and subject them to all kinds of torture. My mother was afraid I would be taken, so she had me smuggled out of the kingdom."

He hoped she wasn't going to ask for more details. Even with everything that had happened recently it was his worst memory and he had no desire to relive it.

His early life, as far as he could remember, was a daily game of survival. It was a life of hunger, exhaustion, and fear. The only memories from that time he ever chose to revisit were the ones where he was playing with his mother. Where he was squealing as she pinned him down and tickled him, or she was singing him to sleep.

Thankfully, Lina wasn't nosey. In response, she only said, "I see."

They sat there for a while in silence, snuggled into each other. Augustine was bracing himself for the moment one of his captors would show up and drag him away. He had no idea how much time he had left with her and so he made a decision.

"Lina?" he said.

She was resting her head on his shoulder, but she looked up when he spoke. He took both of her hands. Given everything he'd been through lately it seemed ridiculous that this should make him nervous, still he felt his stomach flop as he gazed into her eyes.

"Will you marry me, Lina?" He was actually proud of the delivery, especially since he felt slightly faint. "When we get back to Kalte-hafen, of course," he added.

Lina's jaw dropped and to Augustine's utter alarm tears started rolling down her cheeks. Was this a good sign or a bad one?

"I thought that was a given," she sniffed.

Augustine smiled. "Well, I know what our parents want but..." he blushed. "I realized I never asked if it's what *you* want."

"Augustine," Lina grinned through her tears. "I've wanted to marry you since I was nine years old."

She threw her arms around his neck and kissed him. For a few seconds, Augustine lost himself in that kiss. Time itself stood still.

Then, while he was still holding her, a voice spoke that was colder than the winter air itself.

"I see *he's* arrived."

Augustine and Lina jerked apart and looked at the speaker. It was his cousin Oswald, who was somehow looking more sour than usual.

31

OSWALD MAKES A MESS OF THINGS

"So... does this mean we can go home?" Oswald asked.

His cold eyes were almost cutting into Augustine. Lina spent the last couple of weeks wondering (dreading really) what was going to happen when the cousins were finally reunited. She was hoping Oswald's newfound kindness would extend to Augustine. Unfortunately, his present expression said the contrary.

"Not exactly," Lina answered. "Wolf wasn't in a listening mood."

"So why isn't he locked up?" Oswald asked, gaze still fixed on his cousin.

"Do you want me locked up?" Augustine growled.

Lina jammed her pointy elbow into his ribs. *Why did he always take the bait?*

"Be civil," she hissed.

"I'm rescuing you," Oswald pointed out. "You don't seem very grateful."

"Well you don't seem happy to see me," Augustine returned.

"Augustine," Lina warned. *"Drop it."*

Augustine clenched his jaw and breathed deeply. He laced his fingers with Lina's and squeezed her hand. She winced. He must not have realized how hard he was squeezing.

"I guess this means we need to execute our *other* plan," Oswald stated.

Lina glared at him. Did he have any common sense at all? Did it occur to him for a second that it wasn't the kind of thing they should just talk about openly? Lina locked eyes with him and mouthed, *shut up.*

"Why?" Oswald asked. "It's not like anyone can stop us."

Lina was not convinced that was true. Caution was critical.

"*Timing,*" Lina explained.

"Timing?" Oswald exclaimed. "How about now? Let's go and talk to Lord Ervin."

"What a coincidence," came a voice from up to Lina's right.

She winced. Wolf was strolling down the hill toward them.

"I was just coming to get Augustine," he continued cheerfully. "Because we are also about to go and see Lord Ervin. What do you think? Should we all walk together?"

"This is your last chance, Wolf!" Oswald cried. "Peacefully surrender my cousin or die!"

Wolf bit his lip in a failed attempt to hide a smile.

"You going to kill me?"

The look Lina shot Oswald was burning with contempt, but he was looking at Wolf and didn't see her.

"Lord Ervin will!" Oswald exclaimed triumphantly.

Lina could feel Augustine trembling. He didn't know what their plan was but he understood that Oswald was putting it in jeopardy. Rage burned in his eyes as he watched his cousin. Lina squeezed his hand as tightly as she could.

"*Don't make it worse,*" she whispered.

In response to Oswald, Wolf said, "Really? Well, there's no point in cowering here, I might as well surrender myself. Augustine, let's go!"

"Don't come with us," Augustine whispered. "He won't hurt me, he needs me. He doesn't need you."

Lina nodded. "We'll come after you," she sighed. "I was hoping to do this... more *carefully*... but, well it looks like it's now or never."

Augustine shot Oswald a scowl and said, *"I'll kill him."*

"Oswald is a fool but," Lina glared over his shoulder at Wolf. "He isn't your enemy. *Remember that.*"

"Do I need to get Faruk?" Wolf threatened.

"No," Augustine called back.

He kissed Lina and hurried up to meet his captor.

FARUK AND MILL were waiting in front of the inn with the horses. Augustine was pleasantly surprised when Wolf handed him Fotia's reins.

"Need to remind Symeon he's still the favorite," Wolf explained. "Besides, we aren't going to ride them. It will be hard enough for them to get through these snow drifts without carrying us."

They started off, leading the animals down the buried road. A few curious villagers peered at them from the windows, some smiled and waved at Wolf, but most remained hidden within the warmth of their homes.

After a few moments of walking, Wolf said something that made Augustine tense to his very core, "so you were a refugee..."

"Were you listening?" Augustine exclaimed. He honestly wasn't surprised Wolf heard them, it was his casual admission that caught him off-guard.

"I stepped out for a walk," Wolf shrugged. "I promise you, I didn't catch a word of your escape plan," he grinned. "You did a good job whispering that part."

Augustine had the feeling that he was going to lose control and punch someone before the day was done. He had thought it was going to be Oswald but now he was sure it would be Wolf.

"Tell me something," Wolf continued, the amusement leaving his expression. "When you escaped Kalathea... why didn't your mother go with you?"

Augustine started kneading his hands in and out of fists.

"I thought you already knew everything about me," Augustine grumbled.

"I actually know very little about you," Wolf shrugged. "Your name, the names of your parents, where you were living and so forth... I didn't know anything about you being a refugee." Wolf sent him a sideways glance full of genuine curiosity. "Why did she make you go alone?"

Augustine started trembling, but not from anger. Wolf's words awakened a long buried pain. He tried slamming his eyes shut in a futile attempt to block the memories that came flooding into his mind.

The voice that answered Wolf was that of a frightened child, "she couldn't pay for two." Augustine bit his lip, and glared at the ground. *She lied to him.* He understood completely why she did it. He probably would have done the same in her situation, but his understanding didn't ease the dreadful burning of her betrayal. She promised they would go *together*.

They worked and saved for over a year planning their escape. It wasn't until Damara handed him over to the smugglers that she admitted the truth. The greedy scoundrels wouldn't take them both. He had fought so hard to get back to her, ignoring the threats and blows of those vile men.

And she just stood there watching them drag him away, her face soaked in tears, calling after him with the promise that she would come to him soon. He knew that was also a lie. She could never save enough, not before the gods took her.

"Kid..." Wolf nudged him, jerking him back to the present. Augustine stiffened in horror when he realized Wolf was offering him a handkerchief. *Oh, no, no, no...*he brought his hand up to his cheek and turned scarlet with embarrassment. It was wet. He was sobbing like an idiot. He snatched the cloth from Wolf's hand and turned his face away.

They walked in silence for a while, which allowed Augustine's anger time to simmer. One minute, he was loathing himself for his weakness and the next loathing Wolf for stirring it up. Soon, very soon, he would show Wolf who he really was—not some frightened little child he could bind up and drag across the world for profit.

He was a warrior of noble birth—the son of Attikos—and he would make that villain regret ever setting eyes on him.

His gaze drifted sideways to his captor who seemed to be lost in thought. He was staring vacantly over the road ahead with a furrowed brow. Perhaps the mighty Wolf could sense Augustine's wrath. If that was the case, it was no wonder he looked so troubled.

32

AUGUSTINE PUNCHES OSWALD

By late morning, the combined forces of Wolf and Oswald had drained the last of Augustine's patience. He knew it was only a matter of time before he lost control and punched one of them in the face. As it turned out, while still on the road to Lord Ervin's castle, he exceeded his own expectations and punched them both.

When he left with Wolf that morning, he didn't expect to see Lina or his cousin for several hours at least. However, shortly after Wolf forced him to revisit his most traumatic childhood memory, he heard Oswald coming up the road behind him. To Augustine's dismay, Lina was trailing after him.

Wolf waved and welcomed them with the words, "Decided to come along after all, eh?"

Then he politely insisted they walk in the center of the group where he could keep an eye on them.

Lina took her place by Augustine's side and grumbled into his ear, "I tried to get him to wait."

It was all the explanation he needed. Because of Oswald's impatience, his fiancée was now surrounded by highwaymen. His fragile temper started to crack.

"Don't worry, Augustine!" Oswald started enthusiastically. "She's perfectly safe. I've defended her every moment you've been gone! You wouldn't believe the dangers we faced on our journey."

He went on for another minute listing things like wolves and ogres. The expression on Lina's face told Augustine these stories were highly exaggerated.

"...it was so cold those last few nights," Oswald continued. "But even then I kept her safe by sleeping with my arms wrapped tightly around her. I sav—"

He was interrupted by Augustine's fist slamming into his nose. The blow took Oswald completely by surprise. He stumbled backward into a snow drift where he lay stunned just long enough for Augustine to launch a full-on assault. Then the cousins found themselves rolling around in a nonsensical ball of fists and screaming.

Lina released an irritated sigh and rubbed the bridge of her nose between her thumb and forefinger.

Wolf watched the fight for a few seconds with an expression surprisingly similar to Lina's. Then, glancing at her he said, "Now you see this is exactly the sort of thing I was talking about."

"Blondie deserved it," Faruk growled.

Wolf raised his eyebrows and looked over his shoulder at Faruk. "Well, yes...but...I don't know, let's just break them up. He's no good to us dead."

Wolf was trying to pull Augustine off his cousin when the latter spun around and dealt him a blow to the face. Wolf took it in stride. As Lina correctly guessed, he had been punched in the nose many times.

It only took a few moments for Wolf and Faruk to pull the two apart. Then Wolf tied up Augustine and Faruk tied up Oswald while Lina watched with a reproving scowl.

"No, I'm not helping," she said in response to Oswald's pleading eyes. "You deserve it. You both do."

As far as Augustine was concerned the best thing that came from the incident was that Oswald ended up gagged for the rest of the trip.

When they arrived at Lord Ervin's gate, three of their party were bruised and bleeding. A watchman must have seen them approaching from a distance because the gate started opening as they approached and one of the guards ran out to greet them.

"Wolfy!" The guard exclaimed cheerily. Then, seeing the state of the group, he froze. "Good heavens! What happened to you?"

Wolf wiped the blood from his nose with his shirt sleeve. "Just a minor disagreement," he laughed.

"You want me to lock those two up?" the guard asked, looking at the cousins.

Wolf shook his head. "I think they're ready to behave themselves."

"I think they are," Lina agreed, shooting the pair a warning scowl.

"Miss Lina!" The sentry smiled. "It's so good to see you!"

Wolf glanced over his shoulder at Lina who was greeting the guard with a little bow.

"You know her?" Wolf questioned.

"Of course I do," the guard smiled. "Everyone knows Miss Lina. I swear she was sent by God, Himself."

Augustine looked at his fiancée who was quietly smiling at the ground, then he looked at Wolf's slightly puzzled expression. He felt himself grinning. What had Lina done to warrant such an introduction? And had she become Wolf's rival for village saint? The idea filled him with glee.

The group waited in the courtyard while a servant ran ahead to inform Lord Ervin of their arrival.

Wolf nudged Augustine with his elbow and pointed across the courtyard. There an empty noose hung ominously above a raised wooden platform.

"That's where I met Mill!" he explained cheerily.

Augustine scanned the walls surrounding the gallows and raised an eyebrow.

"Where did you shoot from?"

Wolf pointed to a window in the corner tower.

"I don't believe you," Augustine replied. That was an impossible shot, even for Wolf.

"Ask Mill, he'll vouch for me," Wolf grinned.

"I would if I could," Mill shrugged. "But I didn't see where you were shooting from because I was too distracted by the arrow in my lord's forehead." He smiled fondly and turned his cold blue eyes on Augustine. "May all his ilk meet a similar end!"

Before Augustine had time to process the contempt in those words, Wolf decided to change the subject.

Looking back and forth between Oswald and Augustine he said, "This will be a lot less awkward if you two can walk into the court untied. Do you promise to behave?"

Augustine glared at Oswald. He knew his cousin's comment about sleeping with his arms around Lina probably wasn't true. Even if it was, he didn't think for a second Lina's attempts to survive in the freezing cold were romantic.

He also knew that the only reason Oswald mentioned it was to irritate him. The comment was, what both his mother and Lina would have called *bait*. Bait which he took without a second thought and while so much was at stake. He glanced at Lina and felt he fully deserved her infuriated scowl.

"I promise," Augustine grumbled.

Oswald was still gagged, so he just nodded.

"Can't we just kill him?" Mill asked, pointing his dagger at Oswald's throat.

"We're in enough trouble with Kaltehafen already," Wolf explained.

"Exactly!" Mill begged. "Killing him can't make things–"

"No," Wolf commanded. "You can't just kill everyone you don't like, Mill. Now, Augustine..." Wolf turned his attention to his captive. "You should probably know that Lord Ervin doesn't like Kalatheans and he utterly loathes your father."

Augustine wasn't surprised. It seemed that Prince Justin deserved his reputation.

Unfortunately, by that time Faruk had removed Oswald's gag allowing him to yell,

"What's Augustine's father got to do with anything?"

Wolf ignored him. "I was hoping we could do this without

drawing too much attention to you, but I think your friends are going to make that difficult." Wolf glanced at Lina. "You know, I think it would be much safer for Augustine if you left your prince out here."

"I think you're right," Lina agreed.

"What?" Oswald exclaimed.

"Oswald," Lina snapped. *"Remember Henry's court?"*

To Augustine's surprise, Oswald's entire countenance fell. He nodded submissively, then mumbled, "Lina, may I come if I swear to keep silent?"

"Swear it on your honor as a Kalt," Lina ordered.

"I swear!" Oswald answered.

Augustine was utterly amazed. He didn't think his cousin was capable of willingly submitting to anyone, especially not a commoner like Lina. *What had she done to him?*

"That's an empty promise," Augustine scoffed.

"No it isn't," Lina countered. "And I'll make you swear too if you don't control your tongue."

Wolf was looking at Lina with an expression of genuine admiration. He put a firm hand on Augustine's shoulder and said, "You don't deserve her."

Augustine had to admit, he agreed with Wolf on that point.

33

FAUSTA'S HEIR

"WOLFY!" Lord Ervin's voice boomed as they entered the hall. The lord in question charged forward to greet his friend. He looked more like a farmer than a lord. His skin was rough and sun blemished. The great hands that clasped Wolf's in welcome were well callused.

"Wolfy, you didn't tell me you were coming," Ervin continued.

"Well–" Wolf started but Ervin, noticing Lina, cut him off.

"I see you've met Miss Lina!" he exclaimed, rushing over and kissing her hand. "Miss Lina is an absolute miracle, Wolf! I must tell you!"

"Really?" Wolf said, raising an eyebrow.

"My little son was so sick... I don't know what it was. He was absolutely burning with fever!"

Lord Ervin spoke so quickly, Augustine wondered how he was able to breathe.

"I thought for sure he was going to die! I prayed and I prayed and I *implored* all the saints in Heaven for a miracle!" He threw his arms up toward Heaven to illustrate. "Well, right as I was losing hope, my cook tells me that the baker's sister told him about this little red-headed miracle worker who's been healing people down in the village. So I sent my guards to collect her and she spends three days and nights by my son's bedside working tirelessly until he is cured, *cured!* She's a miracle worker I tell you!"

Augustine looked over at Lina, whose cheeks were currently the color of her hair. "I am not a miracle worker, my lord," Lina corrected. "My father taught me how–"

"Oh she's so humble," Lord Ervin interrupted. "She's a saint, I tell you! Truly a saint!"

"I see," Wolf answered.

Augustine smirked, relishing the envy in Saint Wolfy's eyes.

"My lord," Lina interjected. "I truly apologize for the intrusion but I must speak with you urgently."

Lord Ervin suddenly noticed Augustine and gasped. "Is that... no, it can't be."

"It isn't," Wolf helped, stepping in front of his prisoner. "He is a servant I hired when I was in Kalathea."

"He's lying!" Lina exclaimed.

At her cry, the hall went completely silent. No one, not even Augustine, had ever heard her raise her voice.

"My lord, please hear me," Lina begged. "This man," (she motioned toward Augustine) "is my fiancé."

"A nice girl like you is engaged to a Kala–" Lord Ervin started, but Lina cut him off.

"Wolf took him from our home in Kaltehafen and is holding him against his will."

Lord Ervin didn't seem to know how to take the accusation. He looked back and forth between Wolf and Lina as he tried to process the information.

"My lord, when your son recovered," Lina continued, "you swore to me that you would grant anything I asked. Now, I have no interest in punishing your friend. I only ask that you order him to release my fiancé immediately."

Again the room went utterly silent. Oswald was chomping down on his lip and rocking back and forth on his heels. Augustine was drinking in the picture of Lina, standing bravely before Lord Ervin, pleading for his freedom. She saved his son. How could he possibly say no? Augustine was utterly smitten.

It was Wolf who broke the silence.

"My lord," Wolf started. The hint of amusement in his voice sobered Augustine slightly. "You will recall that, when I helped you rebuild after the Kalathean invasion, shot the lord who left you to Justin's mercy, and established you as his successor, you promised me exactly the same thing."

Wolf glanced sideways at Lina, who stood unintimidated by his assertion. "I bear no ill-will toward this young lady, but she can't possibly understand the reasons behind my actions. I ask that you allow me to keep Augustine in my custody and to continue my journey with him when the storm has passed."

Lord Ervin was now tapping his fingers together as he looked back and forth between his two debtors. "Oh dear..." he mumbled. "...I really need to stop making that promise..."

Finally, he straightened up and said, "Wolfy, can you please explain why you took this young man? Perhaps that would help me, you know..." he twirled his hand in the air as he searched for the right words. "...Make sense of things."

"Of course, my lord," Wolf answered. "And I must apologize for lying to you about him being my servant. As a lord you are so burdened already, I was trying to spare you more worry."

Ervin held up his hand. "I trust you, Wolf. If it wasn't for my debt to Miss Lina, I would let you pass unquestioned."

"You are an honorable man, Ervin," Wolf noted. "For keeping your word to her."

Augustine couldn't help but roll his eyes at this. Wolf was, perhaps, the best politician he had ever seen. He was a self-righteous, cold-blooded murderer whom everyone adored.

"I was hired to collect the sons of Prince Justin of Kalathea," Wolf explained. "Augustine is the last."

"He is the son of that devil?" Ervin's face went scarlet with rage. "I knew it. He looks exactly like him! He deserves whatever you have in store."

That's when Oswald finally exploded. "What are you talking about?" he exclaimed. "Augustine's father is some equestrian fellow!"

Before anyone could reprimand Oswald, Lina swung toward Wolf and cried, "How do you know he's Prince Justin's son? Because your client tells you?"

Wolf opened his mouth to answer, but Lina had turned back to Ervin.

"My lord, whatever Prince Justin has done, it has nothing to do with Augustine. Wolf can't even prove his parentage. He has only the word of some nameless client."

"Actually," Wolf corrected. "I *can* prove it."

"Ah! That settles it!" Ervin interjected, relief washing over him. "Wolf, show me this proof. If I am satisfied, you can do whatever you like with the boy. Feed him to the dogs, for all I care. If I am not satisfied, I will give him back to Miss Lina. Is that agreeable to everyone?"

"A very wise decision, my lord," Wolf nodded.

Augustine looked at Lina. She appeared to be lost in thought. Why was she taking so long to answer? How could Wolf possibly prove such a ridiculous claim? Then again, Lord Ervin clearly adored Wolf, he was probably inclined to believe any nonsense Wolf presented. That must have been what Lina was considering.

"I don't see how it's relevant," Lina said at last.

Augustine raised an eyebrow. Yes, she was definitely trying to counter the lord's bias.

"Even if, somehow, this Prince Justin was Augustine's father..." she continued. "Well that would make Augustine illegitimate. He wouldn't inherit anything from his father. If he can't inherit the prince's wealth or title, I don't see why he should inherit his punishments."

"Because the same violent, greedy, loathsome blood would flow through his veins," Ervin answered. "Oh Miss Lina, you are a beautiful, innocent soul. I could never let you leave here with such a scoundrel."

Lina opened her mouth to object, but Ervin said, "We are getting ahead of ourselves, let's have this evidence."

"Mill, get my box, will you?" Wolf ordered.

Mill slipped out of the hall.

Wolf asked Ervin about his son and then they both fell into casual conversation. Augustine stepped over to Lina and took her hand. "You're wonderful," he whispered. She nodded, but he could tell she was worried.

Augustine took her other hand and gazed into her eyes. "Lina, it's going to be alright," he promised. "Wolf can't possibly prove something that isn't true."

This did not seem to make Lina feel any better. On the contrary, she looked slightly nauseous. It was very unlike her.

"Are you feeling alright, Lina?" Augustine asked.

She squeezed his hands, forced a smile, and nodded.

"Lina, I've been quiet this whole time!" Oswald butted in. "I mean, I said one thing, but that hardly counts! I am the picture of restraint!"

Augustine chomped down on his lip.

"You're doing wonderfully, my prince," Lina answered.

Just then, Mill returned with a little wooden box. It was long and almost flat. From a distance, it looked more like a book than a box. He handed the item to Wolf who produced a tiny key. He had been wearing it on a string around his neck.

He unlocked the box, withdrew two documents, and gave them to Lord Ervin.

Lord Ervin skimmed the first. "Heavens, this is wordy..." he mumbled. He glanced at the second paper, then back at the first.

He pointed to Augustine and then motioned for him to come. Augustine felt his heart pounding as he walked forward. The expression on Ervin's face told him that he was seriously considering Wolf's forgeries.

"What's your full name?" Ervin asked.

"Augustine Hatsi," he answered.

"And your mother's name?"

"Damara Hatsi."

Ervin shot him a cold glance over the top of the papers in his hand.

"What was your mother's occupation when you were born?"

"When I was born?" Augustine questioned.

"You heard me," Ervin pressed.

Augustine glanced over at Lina. Her shoulders were slouched. She was staring vacantly at the floor looking completely and utterly defeated.

"She..." Augustine started. (He was still looking at Lina.) "She worked in the palace, she was a handmaiden to the princess...what does—"

"Which princess?" Ervin pressed.

"Fausta," Augustine answered.

"Well then," Ervin continued, nodding solemnly. "You really are Prince Justin's son."

He handed Augustine the first document.

"Legally anyway," Ervin added. "And looking at you... well, you're either his blood child or much younger twin and one of those is impossible."

Augustine scanned the paper in his hands. It *was* painfully wordy, he skimmed some bits and reread others several times over. In short, it was a letter from Prince Justin acknowledging Augustine Hatsi as his son and bestowing on him all the legal benefits of an heir. It even concluded with the prince's signature and seal. Though how anyone could tell it was Justin's signature was beyond him. He must have scrawled it in a hurry.

While Augustine was still trying to figure out how Wolf got possession of such a perfect forgery, Ervin took the document and handed him another.

It was a letter that read:

> *Senator Clement,*
>
> *Since I am the last of my father's heirs and have no children of my own, I feel it is of the utmost importance to make my legal heirs known so that, in the event of my death, our kingdom isn't left without a*

leader. It is a well-known secret that my brother Justin has children—
a lot of children. Of these children, only two are his legal heirs.

The first is Prince Tarik, son of Princess Amira of Anamia, whom
my idiot brother married on one of his campaigns. My father was
unaware of this marriage and I learned of it only through the letters I
acquired after my brother's death.

I am sure it's perfectly obvious to you that putting an Anamian
prince on the throne of Kalathea would be a disaster. Though this child
belongs to Justin's legal wife, he must never be considered. The law
gives me the right to choose anyone I wish as my successor and so it
follows that I may also exclude anyone I perceive as a threat to the
good of our nation.

Therefore my first choice of heir is Justin's second-born legal son,
Augustine Hatsi, the child of my handmaiden, whom my brother has
claimed as his own in writing. You'll find the acknowledgment
enclosed.

The letter continued on, listing the names of Prince Justin's other
children, the ones he hadn't legally acknowledged but the writer
insisted she could pick anyway.

It was signed at the bottom by Queen Fausta of Kalathea.

Augustine studied the signature. The odd thing was, the handwriting did indeed look like Fausta's. Augustine had seen it many
times on the letters the princess had written to his mother. The only
difference between this signature and the one on those letters was
that Fausta had used the title *Queen* instead of *Princess*. So if the letter
was real (which of course it wasn't) it would have been written during
Fausta's brief reign.

Augustine's head began to pound as he drank in the writing. Why
would Wolf, or Wolf's client, go to the trouble of making up such an
incredible story and then forging such perfect legal documents?

There had to be a reason, none of this could be *true*. That would
mean that Attikos Hatsi, the man Augustine spent his life admiring,
trying to imitate, and even praying to wasn't real. It would mean that

he was the illegitimate child of a monster. That couldn't be true, his father was a hero, not a monster...

It would mean his mother conceived him out of wedlock and it was ridiculous to think that such a God-fearing woman was capable of such debauchery. He was the noble product of a holy union, not some scandalous accident.

His hands began to tremble. If these documents were real it meant that everything he knew about everything was a lie. Therefore, they couldn't possibly be real.

34

THE TRUTH

L ina watched Augustine closely as he reviewed the letter in his hands. His brow was knit, his lips slightly scrunched, and the way his gaze kept moving back up the page led her to believe he was rereading parts over and over again. Whatever the document contained utterly perplexed him.

When Lord Ervin took the letter back, Augustine maintained his expression and the vacancy in his eyes told Lina that he was still reviewing it in his mind. He hardly seemed to notice when the lord gave his ruling.

"The boy is yours, Wolf," Ervin declared, folding the papers neatly and returning them. "I'll put him in the tower until you're ready to depart."

"You can't do that!" Oswald exclaimed. "Imprison him and you make yourself an enemy of Kaltehafen!"

Ervin snapped his fingers and pointed at Oswald. "Guards, remove him, please."

No one made any objection to this.

"I'll find you later," Lina called after him as he was dragged out.

Once Oswald was gone and silence returned to the hall, Wolf spoke up.

"My lord," he said, "I thank you for your ruling, but I don't see any reason to lock Augustine up. He can't go anywhere in this storm."

"I won't have the son of that monster running loose on my land," Ervin replied.

"I understand," Wolf shrugged. "I suppose there's no harm in keeping him here."

While they were still speaking, Lina quietly approached Augustine and took his hand. He still seemed completely lost in his thoughts.

"I don't understand," he mumbled. "Those letters... They were so perfect. Who would go to all this trouble?"

His words crushed her. *He didn't believe it.* He refused to believe it.

She should have known he'd react this way. If Attikos Hatsi wasn't his father, then his entire universe was completely undone. He was ready to cling to Damara's lie to the bitter end.

One of Lord Ervin' guards took Augustine's arm.

"We'll find another way," Lina whispered.

She expected him to put up some sort of a fight while being led away, but he didn't. He followed almost unconsciously, his mind lingering on Wolf's documents.

Lina stood where she was, watching him until he disappeared through a door at the end of the hall. Then she turned her wrathful gaze on Ervin.

"Let me go to him," she demanded.

"My dear Lina," Ervin started. "He's a very dangerous–"

"You made a promise to me," Lina insisted. "Which you just broke in *his* favor." She scowled at Wolf. "So if you do not grant me this, I will return to the village and tell all your people that their lord is an honorless liar whose word means nothing."

"Now, Lina dear," Lord Ervin continued. "You—"

"I've heard all about what happened to their last lord," Lina interrupted. "He was a liar too. Wasn't he?"

Lord Ervin went silent and his gaze dropped to the floor.

Wolf, meanwhile, burst out laughing.

"She makes a good point, Ervin!" he exclaimed. "And I don't see any harm in her request. Let her see him!"

WOLF DID HAVE ONE CONDITION. He insisted that one of his men go to the tower with Lina to "ensure no more heirs were produced." Lina rolled her eyes at this. Wolf had a vile mind.

So it was that as she made her way up the winding tower stairway, a mountainous man named Faruk followed along.

When the guard opened the door, they found Augustine pacing around with his perplexed expression unchanged. He broke into a warm smile at the sight of Lina and ran forward to take her hands.

"Wolf let you come?" he asked.

"Only if I brought him," Lina answered, looking over her shoulder. She noticed that Faruk had stepped into the hall and was pulling the door shut behind him. "Wait a moment, are you leaving?" she called.

Faruk locked eyes with Augustine. "You tell Wolf, I kill you."

"Understood," Augustine replied.

The door clanged shut. Lina and Augustine were alone.

"Why would he do that?" Lina wondered.

Augustine shrugged. "I don't know. We've become friends, sort of...I think." He looked back at Lina, and closing his eyes, touched his forehead to hers. "In any case, now that you're here, we can make a plan. I've been wondering why anyone would go to so much trouble to paint me as the child of this Prince Justin."

Lina's stomach flopped.

"If we can figure that out, maybe we can figure out why Wolf took me and get ourselves out of this mess."

"Augustine," Lina started. She was thinking of her promise to Damara, how she would only tell him the truth if circumstances left her no alternative. "Augustine, have you considered the possibility that...well, that Wolf's evidence is real?"

An awkward half-smile flickered across his face, like he was trying to figure out if he was supposed to laugh.

"What?" he finally managed. "Lina, that's ridiculous."

That's when Lina decided the time had come. Augustine's life was in danger because of his father and he wasn't going to believe any evidence no matter how convincing. She had no choice.

Oh God help me, Lina prayed. She squeezed his hands. Then locking her gaze with his she said, "Augustine, it's true."

He responded with a blank stare.

"Your mother told me after you were taken," Lina continued.

Augustine released her hands and took a step backward.

"She wouldn't tell you and not me," he objected.

So Lina related the entire conversation she had with Damara before setting out on her journey.

"She didn't mean to tell me," Lina finished. "It was only because I caught her slipping up. She made me promise not to tell you because she really wanted you to hear it from her." Lina's gaze dropped to the floor. "I hate that I learned before you."

"You are asking me to believe that my own mother conceived me in some promiscuous scandal and then lied to me about it for years," Augustine seethed.

"She lied to protect you," Lina continued. "All I know is Prince Justin charmed your mother, made her feel beautiful, she fell in love and things got out of hand."

Augustine's gaze burned with anger. "She wouldn't do that," he hissed.

Lina was surprised to feel a spark of indignation.

"Wouldn't what? Make a bad decision? Have you never made a bad decision, Augustine?"

Lina loved Damara and nothing about her confession changed that. Why was it so hard for Augustine to believe that his mother was human and that she made a mistake?

"Did the thought ever occur to you," Lina continued. "That maybe it wasn't her fault at all? Justin was the crown prince, she was his servant! What would he have done if she refused him?"

"My mother is a hero," Augustine stated. "She exchanged her life for a chance, *a chance,* that mine would be spared. And here you are slandering her good name. Lina, why? Has Wolf threatened you?"

She stared at him in disbelief—furious with him and aching for him all at once. His entire vision of reality was crumbling and he was lashing out, just trying to survive.

That's when she remembered Damara's letter, the one she failed to deliver to Florian what seemed like forever ago. She withdrew it from her bag.

"Your mother wanted me to send this to Princess Fausta," she explained. "I don't know what it says but... maybe it will explain things for you."

She held it out to him. Instead of taking it, he stumbled away from her.

"I want you to leave," he ordered.

Those words impaled her heart like a knife. She responded with a silent nod, then looked around for a place to leave the letter. The room was unfurnished except for a straw-stuffed mat, a rickety wooden chair, and a few empty crates.

She put the letter on the chair, then knocked on the door. When Faruk opened it, she took one last look at Augustine. He was standing where she left him, scowling at the floor, kneading his hands in and out of fists.

35

LINA'S DANGEROUS IDEA

Augustine shook with rage as he watched Lina disappear through the door. What had gotten into her? Wolf had to have something to do with it. What Augustine couldn't figure out was *why*. What would Wolf have to gain by forcing Lina to tell such a story?

Maybe she wasn't forced...but then, why would she lie? In all their years together, she'd never once lied about anything. Yet, if Lina was telling the truth, it meant that his own mother had been lying to him his entire life. And his mother never lied to him, except when he was little and... *She was trying to protect him.*

"I'm not hungry," she once said, as she offered him the last of their rations. What parent wouldn't do the same?

"There's nothing to be afraid of," she said one evening, as she held him tightly in her arms. His head was pressed against her chest and he could hear her heart racing and feel the tension in her body. Her gentle smile didn't fool him. She was terrified.

She was only trying to comfort him, what parent wouldn't do the same? It wasn't like she lied about anything important.

He remembered that jar his mother used to keep hidden under her bed. Every evening, they would add to it from the coins they earned that day. And every evening, she would say something like, "We're almost there, Augustine. When this jar is full we can go."

He felt a sting of pain as he remembered *that* lie. The lie she had used to get him to safety.

He looked at the letter Lina left sitting on the chair. His mother wouldn't lie about anything this big, would she?

Augustine's heart pounded. His palms were sweating.

It was definitely his mother's seal on the envelope. He reached out toward it, and stopped himself. *Ridiculous.* She wouldn't lie about his father, not even to protect him.

He walked across the room, turned and paced back toward the chair only to see that stupid letter again.

Why not just open it? Again he reached forward and again he stopped. His heart was somehow racing faster. Why couldn't he open it? Why was he so afraid to look?

He snatched it, tore it open, and began to read.

Princess Fausta,

(It was definitely his mother's handwriting.)

Please excuse my brevity, I am writing to you on an urgent matter. On the feast of Saint Loudon, Augustine was captured and taken away by three highwaymen. One witness to the kidnapping claimed she heard the men say something about Augustine's father, but couldn't hear the details.

Because no one has approached my husband with a ransom demand, I can only assume they meant Prince Justin. Your brother made so many enemies, any one of them could have taken my son.

Please, my princess, think. You knew the prince better than anyone. If you can't figure out who did this, no one can.

The letter went on to describe Augustine's captors and explain Florian's search efforts. Augustine skimmed the rest, then he read the first few paragraphs again, and again, and again. With each pass his heart beat faster and his hands trembled more.

Finally, he tore the letter and thrust the pieces on the floor.

Augustine couldn't think, he could only feel; and what he felt was a fury that burned through every part of his body. He seized the little chair and threw it against the wall with all his might.

LINA WRAPPED her cloak tightly around her as she prepared to walk back toward the village. Faruk silently escorted her to the castle gate. Perhaps she should have been nervous about this. Faruk was, after all, large enough to snap her between his thumb and forefinger.

But, Lina was too preoccupied with Augustine to be afraid of the giant. She also had a feeling that Faruk was not nearly as threatening as he looked.

She would wager that he was the kindest of the three highwaymen. He had gentle, thoughtful eyes. Oddly enough, the one she felt most uncomfortable around was the thin, weasely one. *Mill*, she remembered. *Wolf called him Mill.* They hadn't said a word to each other, but there was something about those cold blue eyes of his she found deeply unsettling.

They had almost reached the gate, when a voice cried, "Miss Lina!"

She turned to see Wolf running toward her across the courtyard.

"I need you to come with me," he finished as he approached.

"Why?" Lina demanded.

"Because Augustine's gone and bloodied himself up somehow and since you're such a miracle worker, I was hoping you could do something about it."

Lina did not hesitate, she followed Wolf back to winding stairs that led up to Augustine's room.

"What happened?" she asked, as the guard unlocked the door.

"I'm not sure, he won't say a word to me," Wolf shrugged. "All I know is that he smashed a chair and got blood all over everything."

It wasn't only the chair Augustine smashed. Everything the room contained that could be smashed or torn had been reduced to debris. The splintered remains of the chair and the crates were speckled with blood.

Augustine was sitting slumped on the opposite side of the room, cradling one lacerated hand in the other. His arms were also covered in scrapes, splinters, and bruises.

Lina turned to Wolf. "Make yourself useful. Get me water and bandages."

Wolf went without a word. He left the door open, and the guard came in and stood watch as Lina cautiously approached her patient. She noticed one half of Damara's letter sticking out from beneath the remains of the chair.

Augustine did not look up as she approached. He was lost in a world of his own.

"Augustine," Lina said. "Let me see your hands."

He didn't respond.

She squatted down in front of him so she was at eye level. He met her gaze but didn't say anything.

"Give me your hands," Lina ordered.

He was holding both hands close to his chest defensively, but he did not offer any resistance when she took one of his wrists and drew it toward her. He gave a little gasp of pain as she tried to uncurl his fingers from the bloody ball that had once been his fist.

"That hurts," he complained.

Relieve washed over her at the sound of his voice.

"Of course it does," she reprimanded. "What did you do? Smash everything and then punch the wall, *repeatedly*? What did you think would happen?"

Much to her surprise and delight, he broke into a warm smile.

"Something like that," he admitted. "I suppose it was a little stupid."

"A little?" she scowled.

She removed a few splinters from his palms and tried to assess the damage.

Augustine kept flinching and trying to pull his hand back, but

Lina held fast and was always able to get him back under control with a quick glare.

Presently, Wolf returned with a basin of water and the bandages Lina asked for.

"Thank you," Lina said. "Set that down and go clean up that debris."

"As you wish, Miss Miracle," Wolf quipped before scurrying away to follow orders.

Lina set to work. For a few minutes, neither said anything. Removing wooden fragments from Augustine's hand gave Lina a welcome distraction from worrying about his internal state.

"Lina," he finally whispered. "I'm so sorry. I was awful to you."

She looked up from his hands to his face. His cheeks were streaked with tears.

"My mother... she only lied to protect me..."

"She adores you, Augustine," Lina reminded. "You know that, don't you?"

His gaze dropped to the floor. "Her life would have been much easier without me," he mumbled.

"Easier isn't always better," Lina commented. She finished wrapping his left hand and moved on to his right. "The way she boasts about you, I'd say she thinks you were worth it."

Augustine yelped, as she pulled another shard from his right palm.

"And..." Lina glanced up into his eyes. "She's not the only person who loves you."

"You knew when I proposed," Augustine mumbled. "And you still agreed to marry me."

"Why wouldn't I?" Lina asked.

"Because I'm the illegitimate child of a tyrannical madman!" Augustine explained. "My very existence is a scandal and everyone wants to kill me. You should want nothing to do with me."

"Augustine, look at me," Lina ordered. He locked eyes with her. "*I don't care.*"

"I do," Augustine insisted. "I won't have you bring shame on yourself because of me."

Lina knew she couldn't reason with him in his current state. He was confused, panicked, and angry.

"How about we focus on rescuing you," Lina whispered. "And discuss our engagement later?"

He nodded.

"No matter what happens, I love you." She needed him to know that. He'd spent months feeling loathed by everyone on account of his father. She didn't want him to forget how much he was loved.

"Augustine, I know you're angry," Lina continued. "But please promise me you'll be more careful."

He looked away from her.

"*Augustine*," Lina pressed. "Should I bring you something else to destroy? Something a little less...splintery?"

"I wish you could bring me my—Prince Justin," Augustine growled.

"You and everyone else," Lina observed.

The corner of his mouth turned upward. "How about Oswald?"

"No," she kissed his cheek. "How about something that isn't alive? Like a pillow or a grain sack?"

"I suppose," he sighed.

She finished wrapping his hands and stepped away to talk to Wolf.

"Do you have any medicines or herbs with you?"

"A little," Wolf answered. "If you come down with me, I'll show you what I have."

"Good," Lina nodded. "I want to give him something to calm him. In the meantime, he shouldn't be left alone."

"I'll send Faruk up to sit with him," Wolf agreed.

They sent the guard into the room and began their descent from the tower. Lina glanced sideways at Wolf. Augustine's well-being seemed to be of the utmost importance to him. He needed to keep him *alive*... at least for now.

A dark thought fluttered into her mind. What would Wolf do if Augustine died now? She remembered what he said to Faruk right before they separated Augustine and Oswald. "He's useless to us dead."

Lina's mind suddenly began to race. She wondered if, among whatever medicines Wolf was about to show her, lay that viper venom he'd used when he captured Augustine.

She was struck with an idea and then quickly dismissed it. Certainly the right dose could make Augustine *look* dead, but the wrong dose would actually kill him.

The idea kept nipping at her as she walked along beside her enemy. Try as she might, she couldn't get it out of her mind.

36

FROM THE ASHES OF HEARTBREAK

A ugustine lay in the corner facing the wall, trapped in a state of numb oblivion. Someone, probably Faruk, must have draped a blanket over him at some point because he was gripping the corners of one. He couldn't eat, couldn't sleep, and couldn't even pray. For all he knew, God was just another one of those people his mother made up to make him feel good about himself. He'd spent years praying to the soul of Attikos Hatsi—where had all those prayers gone? He would have felt sick if he could feel anything at all.

As the endless hours dragged by, he slipped away into a memory. His eight-year-old self had found a wonderful hiding spot. It was a little cave in the rocks below the Lysandrian palace.

His mother had gone to live there when Queen Ilona moved in four months prior. It was then, Augustine made it his personal mission to explore every inch of the colossal structure.

During his exploration, he discovered a secret stairwell which brought him to a cave underneath the palace. There was a rock plateau at the bottom of the stairs, and if you sat on the end of it, you could dangle your feet in the water and stare out the cave mouth that opened onto the sea.

The mysterious cavern had likely been used as a boat launch in ages past, now it seemed completely forgotten. Little Augustine spent many long hours sitting in that spot, splashing his feet in the water. At some point during each visit, he'd usually jump off the plateau and swim around in the surf.

This was his special secret place. He was convinced he was the only person who knew about it. That is until one day, as he was sitting on the edge of the little plateau, he heard the sound of footsteps patting down the stone stairway.

Alarmed, he lowered himself into the water and swam around behind a rock so whoever the newcomer was wouldn't see him. A young man came into view carrying a small wooden panel under his arm. It took Augustine a second to recognize him partly because the light was dim and his view was obstructed, but also because the man was wearing a simple knee-length tunic covered in ink stains.

Augustine was used to seeing him in the longer, gold and purple garments of a king. For the man was King Alexander, recently rescued from captivity. He set the panel down on a rock, undid his sandals and sat down at the end of the plateau dangling his feet in the water.

Augustine was overcome with curiosity. Only a few days ago, the boy had witnessed the king's death and now here he was in perfect health. Augustine couldn't help but wonder if he was a ghost.

There was only one thing to do. It was disrespectful and his mother would certainly kill him if she found out, but he needed to do it for his own peace of mind. He grabbed a pebble and threw it at the back of Alexander's head.

"Ouch! What?" Alexander blurted. He looked over his shoulder rubbing his hair where the pebble hit.

Augustine was so pleased with his aim, that he forgot to duck out of sight before the king spotted him.

"Oh, hello Augustine," the king smiled. "Did you just…"

Augustine leapt out of the water like he was some sort of frog and landed in a kneeling position. "I'm sorry! I just needed to see if–" Augustine stopped himself. He felt silly.

"If...?" Alexander pressed.

"If you were a ghost," Augustine mumbled.

"I am not," the king promised.

When Augustine continued regarding him suspiciously, he held out his hand.

"You can pinch me if you like, I promise I'm alive."

The boy took his hand and squeezed it until the king winced. He definitely felt real.

"Did you really die?" Augustine asked, then remembering his manners added, "Your Majesty?"

"You don't need to call me that, you know," Alexander replied. "We're practically related thanks to your mother's engagement. Call me 'uncle'."

"Yes, Your Majesty," Augustine blurted.

The king swallowed a laugh but didn't correct him.

"But um," Augustine continued. "But you weren't really dead, were you? How could you be?"

"I really was," the king responded.

The boy's jaw dropped in wonder. "Did you see God?"

Alexander smiled. "If I had, nothing in the world would have brought me back."

"Then what *did* you see?" Augustine pressed.

"That's private."

When Augustine recalled this memory in later years, he always felt so embarrassed. It never occurred to the eight-year-old version of himself that it wasn't polite to interrogate people about their experience being brutally murdered and brought back to life.

Still, his uncle never seemed annoyed with him. During the entire conversation, his tone alternated between matter-of-fact and slightly amused.

Alexander began sketching on his wooden panel with a scrap of charcoal.

"It's my turn to ask a question," he smiled. "What brings you down to my favorite hiding spot?"

"This is your hiding spot?" Augustine gasped.

"You even answer questions with questions!" the king chuckled. "You'd make an excellent philosopher!"

"Really?" Augustine exclaimed. "I never thought of that."

"Yes, this is *my* hiding spot," Alexander asserted. "I was younger than you when I found it."

"Are you hiding from someone now?" the boy interrogated.

Alexander shook his head. "No, I'm just thinking. You see ever since... Well, for the past few days, I've been trying to draw my mother but I just don't think..." He made a few aggressive strokes with the charcoal. "...I can ever do her justice."

The boy looked over the king's shoulder. He had no idea why Alexander wasn't satisfied, even the rough sketch of the beautiful queen seemed perfect. Alexander threw down the charcoal with a sigh, rested his cheek in this hand, and scrunched his lips as he regarded the image.

Augustine giggled because when the king's fingers touched his face, he got charcoal dust all over himself and he didn't seem to notice at all. After a minute of scrutinizing his work, he looked back at Augustine.

"Are *you* hiding from someone?" he asked.

Augustine's gaze dropped to his feet. He didn't want to say, but he also didn't want to lie to the king.

"My mother," he admitted. "She's all frantic with packing."

"Well, she probably needs your help," Alexander commented. "The two of you have a long journey ahead of you."

Augustine had heard from his neighbors that Kaltehafen was a wild, mannerless country overrun with filthy uneducated ruffians. Leaving civilization to live in such a place was the most wonderful and exciting thing the boy could imagine.

"Do you think I'll like Kaltehafen?" he asked, his whole face brightening.

Alexander thought for a moment. "Do you like camping?" he asked.

"Yes!" Augustine exclaimed.

"Then you'll love it," Alexander answered. "It's like camping all the time."

"My mother's going to marry the king of Kaltehafen!" Augustine announced proudly. "Because when the gods threw her in a pit, he climbed in and rescued her."

"Did he?" Alexander stated flatly.

Augustine nodded before continuing his litany of admiration. "And then he hid us, and took care of us, and protected us with his very life! He's a real hero."

Alexander was drinking in the boy's ramblings with his tongue in his cheek.

"King Florian certainly is a hero," Alexander agreed. "But so is your mother."

Augustine considered this. His mother was plenty brave, but when he thought of a hero, he usually pictured a demigod in glistening armor locked in combat with some kind of beast. King Florian matched that description a bit more than the frazzled handmaiden that raised him.

"Your mother is every bit as strong and as brave as King Florian," Alexander continued. "Maybe more so, because she stood up to the twins without a weapon. Don't ever forget that."

Those words didn't make much of an impression on Augustine at the moment, but the older he grew the more he understood them.

As he sat in his tower prison, now knowing the truth about his father, he found himself reflecting on his uncle's words all the more. His mother wasn't perfect, the wounds her lies left were still open and bleeding. He was so deeply angry with her and yet... he couldn't say he wouldn't have done the same in her position.

Used and abandoned, she welcomed him into the world. Her love for him was born from the ashes of heartbreak. She was willing to sacrifice everything for the sake of that love. The lies she told were the fruit of desperation.

Only with the truth revealed did Augustine realize the depth of her heroism. And yet, even the strongest of heroes were capable of making grave mistakes.

37

AUGUSTINE'S QUESTIONABLE RECOVERY

The day after Lina patched up Augustine's hands, she returned to check on his progress. The air was bitter cold when she left the house, which brought her some comfort because it meant conditions wouldn't be suitable for travel for a while yet.

She found Augustine lying on his mat, buried under a pile of blankets, staring vacantly. She was glad Wolf had the decency to bring him some extra covers. The tower was freezing.

Faruk was sitting against the far wall like a statue, his dark eyes staring into space. Lina couldn't help but wonder if the giant had been sitting like that all night. Didn't he ever get bored? He got up and left the moment she arrived. Probably so he would have something to do.

Augustine hardly moved the entire day. He didn't speak and refused to eat. So Lina just sat there next to him, wrapped up in her cloak, praying he wouldn't get sick. The only good thing about this situation was that it probably wouldn't be difficult to convince Wolf that Augustine was ill and then, once she'd administered the venom, that he was dead.

The next day passed very much like the first, with Lina sitting quietly in that little tower room, trying and failing to get Augustine to eat.

On the morning of the third day, the sun came out. She hoped and prayed this wasn't the beginning of a thaw. She realized she was going to have to at least mention her plan to Augustine and hope he acknowledged her. She couldn't do this to him without his consent. The thought of using the venom at all made her sick.

Augustine was in his usual place with a cold bowl of stew next to his mat.

She knelt down beside him and waited for Faruk to leave.

"Augustine," Lina whispered. She didn't know why she was whispering. Faruk was gone, and no one could hear them. "I have an idea for getting you out of here."

Augustine did not respond, he continued staring vacantly at the gray stone.

"It's dangerous though..." Lina continued. "I don't want to do it unless... we can't think of anything else."

Augustine didn't answer.

"I stole Wolf's little vial of snake venom. The right dose will paralyze you, it will slow your heart and your breathing enough that you might appear dead and then, Wolf wouldn't have any use for you. He might–"

Augustine's eyes widened slightly.

"I've just realized something..." he mumbled. "Uncle Alex is my actual uncle."

Lina was delighted just to hear his voice.

"Um, yes, I suppose he is," she commented, hoping this realization would be helpful to him. After all, his uncle was one of his greatest heroes. Still, she didn't understand what, if anything, it had to do with her plan. Had he been paying attention at all?

"My uncle died from a viper bite, did I ever tell you that?" Augustine continued.

So... he had *sort of* been paying attention. He heard the part about venom anyway.

"Many times," Lina answered. Then, hoping to bring the topic back around to her idiotic rescue plan, she added, "He may not have been dead, maybe he was just paralyzed."

Augustine rolled away from the wall onto his back and looked up at her. "Oh no, he was definitely dead. I asked him." He smiled slightly and stared off into the memory. "I was a horribly nosey kid. My uncle has the patience of a saint."

Lina decided this sudden tangent was a good thing. Maybe knowing his father's side wasn't completely evil would help him come to terms with it. She glanced toward the window wondering how much time they actually had to make a decision about her escape plan.

Augustine suddenly sat up and stretched and picked up the cold bowl of stew.

"We are not faking my death," he declared.

Lina wasn't sure what to make of this new development. He not only had been paying attention, but he was up, talking, and about to eat, that was good. Still, she wished he would say something to convince her his mind was alright. He'd been through enough to make anyone insane.

He winced when he tried to pick up his spoon in his swollen hand.

"Damn it," he swore. "I need that stupid unicorn to lick me."

This comment did nothing to put Lina's mind at ease.

"Augustine... are you feeling alright?" she asked.

"Perfect," he answered cheerily, managing to take a few bites of his soup. "But I'm not escaping... not yet."

"Augustine—"

"You are going to go back to Kaltehafen and tell my mother to meet me in Lysandria."

"Lysandria?" Lina marveled.

"Yes," Augustine confirmed. "I have a plan for getting there, but I'll have to let Wolf take me a little farther."

"I don't think you should go anywhere with that man," Lina objected.

"I need you to trust me, Lina," Augustine insisted.

Lina needed to see evidence that his mind was sound before she could trust him with anything.

She sighed. "Well, we have a few days to decide anyway. Maybe longer."

"I already have," he declared. "I need some answers and Lysandria is where I am going to get them."

"Answers?" Lina questioned.

"About Prince Justin and my mother, about whoever this client is, and all these half-siblings I supposedly have, and... well... who I am." Augustine finished eating and set the empty bowl down. "My mother said in her letter, no one knew Prince Justin better than his sister, so that's who I am going to talk to."

"Isn't she the one who–" Lina started.

"Killed him?" Augustine finished. "Yes, I'll be sure to thank her for that while I'm there."

"I think it might be wiser," Lina began slowly. "To go back to Kaltehafen first and start with your mother."

"I'm halfway to Lysandria already," Augustine objected. "I'm not going back without answers. Besides, my mother's been talking about going back forever. Now she has a reason."

Lina opened her mouth to say something else, but Augustine suddenly stood and walked over to the place where Faruk had been sitting.

"Ah good, he's been practicing his alphabet," Augustine smiled looking at the floor.

Lina approached him and noticed some letters drawn in charcoal on the stone.

"Lina, he's brilliant!" Augustine whispered. "He can't even read yet he understands more about the philosophers than I ever will."

Lina was beginning to wonder if she was the one losing her mind.

"The whole time he's been here looking after me, he's been practicing," Augustine continued. "Whenever he hears the door opening, he hides the charcoal. I don't think he wants anyone to know how intelligent he is."

At this point, Lina was utterly lost. "That's...um... what an interesting person," she mumbled.

"Isn't he?" Augustine smiled. "And I think he's my key to freedom."

He suddenly took Lina's hands. "I need you to promise me that you'll go home after the thaw and tell my mother what I asked."

"No," Lina answered. "I'll send a message to your mother but if you're going to Lysandria, then I am going with you."

38

A TREATY BETWEEN COUSINS

Back in Kaltehafen what seemed like an eternity ago, Augustine had a very clear idea of how the world worked. Nobles protected their people. The clergy didn't need to become assassins to serve the poor. Knights rescued ladies (never the other way around) and his father, Attikos Hatsi, was a good man.

As it turned out, Attikos Hatsi was a fantasy. His real father was a horrible person, and the rest of the universe was upside down and backward.

The only thing in his life that seemed unchanged was Lina. She was, as she had always been, his closest friend and his greatest ally.

Lina knew she wouldn't be able to follow Wolf. He was cunning and if Florian couldn't find him with a lifetime of tracking experience, there was no way she could. She explained to Augustine that when she inevitably lost his trail, she would go directly to Lysandria and meet him there. Augustine tried again and again to dissuade her but he couldn't convince her to give up and go home.

It wasn't only that he was worried about her making the long journey, it was that he didn't want her giving so much of herself to him. Only a short time ago, he longed to make her his wife. Now, though he loved her to the very depths of his soul, he no longer knew who he was. Did he have anything to offer Lina as a husband aside from the loathing of his father's enemies?

He couldn't marry her or even move his life forward until he got a clearer picture of who his father really was. When Prince Justin died, Augustine was three years old and living in the palace with his mother. His father must have known him or at least, he must have seen him around the palace. Did the prince ever acknowledge his existence? Did he even care that he had a son living under the same roof?

Clearly Fausta knew he was Justin's child. He wondered about his grandfather King Basil. Did he know or suspect? Did he just look the other way?

Half of Augustine's family story was just missing. What burdens or benefits would his father's lineage add to his life? He couldn't marry anyone until he had some idea.

He didn't want Lina going on a long and dangerous journey and then waiting around for years while he tried to put together the missing pieces. He wanted her to do what he couldn't—disassociate herself from Prince Justin and move on with her life.

So, when he noticed water dripping from the eves outside his tower window, and the air growing warmer, he made a torturous decision. He sent for the only person he could count on to get rid of Lina —*Oswald*.

Since both Wolf and Lina were doing their utmost to keep the cousins apart, Augustine had to bribe Faruk to set up the meeting.

"I've memorized the entire Epic of Eyad," Augustine told him, as they sat in the tower playing cards.

"The world's oldest poem?" Faruk marveled.

"The oldest *known* poem in history," Augustine corrected. "If you find some way of sneaking Oswald up to see me, I'll recite it for you."

The bribe worked.

· · ·

THAT VERY NIGHT, the door to Augustine's tower opened and there stood his cousin.

"Oswald," Augustine greeted, with a curt nod. He then waited for his cousin to start hurling insults at him.

But Oswald did no such thing, he just stood awkwardly for a moment before saying, "How are you?"

Augustine blinked. He had never heard Oswald use those three words that way. And his cousin's expression, it was filled with... *genuine concern*. It almost seemed like Oswald was actually interested in his well being.

Reality as Augustine knew it was truly folding in on itself.

"I um..." Augustine started. "I'm fine."

He braced himself for Oswald to spring some kind of a trap.

"Good," Oswald continued. "Lina said you were sick because of your... because of Prince... she said you were melancholic."

Augustine did not want to dwell on this topic. Oswald possessed an exhaustive mental list of derogatory terms for people with unmarried parents which he had used to insult Augustine even before he knew the truth. The latter had no interest in learning how his cousin would use these insults now.

"I've moved on," Augustine lied then, before Oswald could say anything else, he got right to business. "I know you and I haven't always gotten along but... well... I need you to do something for me."

"Anything," Oswald answered, further confusing Augustine. "After we've rescued you."

"You're not rescuing me, Oswald," Augustine corrected.

"Of course we are!" Oswald insisted. "Lina had a plan about faking your death!"

Augustine sighed. This was exactly why he couldn't tell his cousin his personal escape plan: Oswald had an annoying habit of blurting things.

"*Oswald*," Augustine growled. "Even after I escape Wolf, I am not returning to Kaltehafen. Not for a long time. And... I am not going to marry Lina."

"What?" Oswald gasped. "Why not?"

"Because–" Augustine started.

"Is it because you think you're too good for a doctor's daughter now that you're Kalathean royalty? Is that it?"

Augustine was utterly taken aback. *Kalathean royalty*? Is that how Oswald had interpreted the revelation about his father? If he was Kalathean royalty, he was the kind the rest preferred not to talk about.

"After everything she did for you, she deserves to be a queen!" Oswald exclaimed angrily. "I'm the crown prince of Kaltehafen and I would marry her!"

"You... what?" Augustine started in disbelief. "You called her an ugly witch!"

"I was ten," Oswald rolled his eyes.

"What about when you were fifteen? And you said she looked like a spotted red devil!"

"I didn't mean it, I say that sort of thing to everyone," Oswald shrugged.

"Which is why no one likes you, Oswald!" Augustine snapped, his patience expended.

Oswald's jaw dropped.

"One moment you're spouting cruel nonsense, the next minute you're wondering why no one wants you around!"

Oswald opened his mouth to object, but stopped and closed it again.

Augustine could see his mind racing. *Had he actually gotten through to his cousin?*

Augustine kneaded his hands in and out of fists, wincing slightly. (His hands were still badly swollen from his confrontation with the furniture.)

"Do you know what I think?" Augustine growled. He was about to say something he'd suspected ever since he met Oswald behind the inn. At the time, he didn't want to say it, or even think it because of how it angered him but well... everything was different now.

"I think you've grown to love her."

Oswald crossed his arms. "What if I have?"

Augustine was shaking slightly. He was using every ounce of his will to avoid lashing out.

"If you had," Augustine started slowly. "You would see to it that she is safely returned to Kaltehafen that she doesn't try to follow me."

The moment he closed his mouth, he turned away from Oswald. He didn't want to see the mockery that would enter his cousin's eyes when he said the next part. "I've asked her not to wait for me. I don't know if I'm ever coming back."

Oswald was strangely silent. Augustine turned back toward him and for a brief moment saw it again—that expression of genuine concern. But Oswald wiped it away the second he realized Augustine was looking at him.

"You know something," Oswald smirked. "As the crown prince of Kaltehafen, I can marry anyone I want."

Augustine went rigid then winced as his fists closed tightly. He remembered how Lina looked at him after he damaged his hands. He also knew that Oswald's comment was nothing more than bait. He couldn't force Lina to marry him. Florian would protect her and he hadn't the nerve to stand up to Florian.

Augustine breathed deeply, diluting his anger, letting it dissipate. Then he said something that caught Oswald completely off guard.

"So be it. She deserves to be a queen."

Oswald stood in stunned silence.

"Keep her safe, Oswald," Augustine concluded. "That's all I wanted to ask."

"You're just going to let me marry your fiancée?"

"That's not my decision," Augustine shrugged. "The question you should ask yourself is, will Lina let you marry her?"

"You're not even going to try and stop me?"

Augustine shook his head.

"You really are ill..." he mumbled.

Augustine felt a strange little prick of pleasure at Oswald's bewilderment. He had, with heroic effort, avoided breaking his cousin's face. In the process it seemed he broke his cousin's mind. Somehow it was more satisfying.

He knew that Oswald, though entitled and confrontational, possessed at least enough honor to bring Lina home safely, and that was all Augustine wanted.

39

A TORTUROUS GOODBYE

I t was pitch black and freezing cold, but Lina waited anyway. She was standing outside the castle wall wrapped in her cloak. The sun would rise very soon, and before then Wolf's party was going to try and sneak Augustine away.

Lina healed many of Lord Ervin's people during her time in the village. Among these were some of his own guards. Though none dared help her free Augustine (*typical*), they were willing to tell her exactly when, where, and how Wolf planned on leaving.

So, just before dawn, Lina stood outside the southern gate, waiting. The ground was still covered in snow, but it had been receding each day. Soon, her patience was rewarded, the gate opened and out rode Wolf and his company. In the dim light, she saw Augustine riding adjacent to Wolf.

She waited for them to proceed a little ways from the castle, and then followed at a distance, hoping they wouldn't be able to hear the sound of her boots crunching against the snow. Keeping up with them would be an impossible task. Sooner or later, they would increase their speed, and she would lose them. Still, she hoped she could overhear something useful before then—maybe their actual destination or who their client was.

She moved parallel to the road and within the tree line where possible. They were long out of the village before anyone dared speak.

"I thought we'd never see the last of that place," Wolf quipped. "It's wonderful to be moving again!"

"I can't wait to get away from this damned snow," Mill grumbled in reply.

Wolf and Mill went back and forth for a few moments filling the time with idle talk. Lina took the opportunity to sprint closer. But the sound of their voices wasn't enough to mask her hurried footsteps.

Wolf suddenly held up a hand to silence his companions. Lina froze.

"Stay here a moment," Wolf mumbled to the others. He turned his horse around and galloped back up the road a few paces, pausing parallel to Lina's position.

"Miss Miracle, is that you?" he called.

Lina winced. He knew. How did he always know everything?

Slowly, she emerged onto the road, greeting Wolf with a scowl. At the sight of her, Augustine turned his horse and brought it up beside Wolf's. Mill and Faruk looked on without following.

"Miss Miracle, you are the bane of my existence," Wolf rebuked.

"Good," Lina replied. "It's time someone was."

She glanced at Augustine, hoping he wouldn't be angry with her for following. If he was, it didn't show. He looked worried more than anything.

"What exactly were you hoping to accomplish by following us all by yourself?" Wolf asked.

"I thought a saint like you would have the decency to let me say goodbye," Lina snapped.

Wolf sighed. "I was trying to save you both the pain."

"Don't act so noble. You wanted to save yourself the trouble of dealing with me. There you failed so you might as well give us a moment."

"Make it quick," Wolf sighed. "And then Faruk will take you back to the village. You shouldn't be out here all alone."

"No," Lina agreed dryly. "I might have a run-in with highwaymen."

She noticed a slight smile flicker across Augustine's face, but she maintained her frown. Every word that came out of Wolf's mouth fueled her anger. He was worried about her being alone on the road, which she wouldn't be if he hadn't heartlessly dragged off her fiancé.

Everything he did was justified because he had a noble cause. Injustice in the name of justice was permissible when the almighty Wolf declared it so. She almost wished he was just a greedy scumbag.

Wolf turned his horse back toward his waiting companions, but before returning to them, leaned over toward her and said, "Don't think you're the only person who has given up love for the sake of my cause. I wouldn't ask anything of you that I hadn't done myself."

"You're a *martyr* now?" Lina marveled. "It is such a privilege to stand here basking in your holiness."

Wolf responded with a scowl and then spurred Fotia forward to give the couple a little space. Augustine, whose expression was now bursting with admiration, dismounted and approached her.

That's when she noticed the shackles on his wrists, presumably a gift to Wolf from Lord Ervin. The chain that connected them gave him some range of motion, though not enough to cause trouble.

He stood close to her, his gaze locked in hers. Neither of them said anything for a long moment. Then, Lina reached out and took his hands. His smile vanished. While he didn't pull away, he didn't close his hands around hers either.

"Um...where is Oswald?" he asked matter-of-factly.

"Probably sleeping," Lina shrugged. "Do you think I would have made it this far if I'd told him where I was going?"

A smile briefly touched Augustine's lips.

"You've been wonderful, Lina," he said. "I swear if Wolf drags me to every corner of the world, I'll never find a woman half so admirable. Thank you."

Lina responded with a warm smile. She tightened her grip on his hands and leaned forward to kiss him. Then Augustine did something that crushed her. He pulled his face away.

In response to her questioning glance, he brought her hand to his lips and kissed it, with the words, "Marry someone who will bring you the honor you deserve."

If Wolf had brought Lina to the breaking point, Augustine pushed her over.

"Honor..." she hissed as fury flared in her eyes. "That word is nothing more than an excuse to protect your delicate ego."

Augustine's gaze dropped.

"In the name of honor you fight with your cousin and injure your-self and make stupid rash decisions...and..." now tears were boiling over. "And now it's me you've hurt."

He didn't say anything but the pain was plainly visible in his eyes. She'd wounded him.

"You *are* worth loving, no matter what your father did," Lina insisted. "Having the humility to admit *that* would be honorable."

Augustine was completely at a loss for words. He stood in silent shame before her wrathful gaze. A tense moment passed.

Then, they heard hoofbeats approaching and looked over to see Faruk making his way toward them.

Augustine snatched her hands.

"I won't marry you, Lina," he said. "But I will never stop loving you. If I searched the whole world over I'd never find a heart as pure, a mind as clever, a spirit as brave, or a face as beautiful."

The litany of complements might have softened Lina except that Augustine concluded by saying, "I am not worthy of you."

Anger radiated from her as she looked up into his sorrowful, brown eyes. He had spent his whole life romanticizing everything—his rivalry with Oswald, his role as a defender of the people, and most of all his imaginary late father, the mythical hero. Now, slapped by reality, she was the last thing he had left to romanticize. Of course he didn't think he was worthy of this perfect goddess of a woman he imagined her to be.

She didn't want to be angry with him. Not now, when they were about to be separated, but she couldn't help it. Still, she didn't resist when he squeezed her hands and kissed her forehead.

"Go home, Lina," he said. "Be safe."

"Be safe, Augustine," she answered, then locking her fiery gaze with his added, "I will see you in Lysandria."

40

AUGUSTINE DOES NOT THINK ABOUT LINA

A ugustine rode with his back straight and his head high. He had a mission now and if he put all his focus on that, he wouldn't think about Lina. Thinking about Lina was like getting stabbed in the heart repeatedly, and like getting stabbed repeatedly, it was something he wanted to avoid.

It was now late morning, the sun was well above the horizon and the air was a bearable temperature. Mill and Wolf were making idle talk as they usually did to fill the time. Faruk hadn't returned from his brief detour back to the village.

Augustine stared off into space observing the blue sky, the open road, the shrinking piles of snow. Carefully observing his surroundings meant he was focused on the mission at hand, and not thinking about Lina.

While he was thus engaged, he heard galloping hooves on the road behind him and turned to see Faruk approaching.

"There you are!" Wolf smiled. "I was worried she'd cut you to pieces with that sharp tongue of hers."

Augustine smiled slightly. He almost made a comment about how it was Wolf who had been torn to pieces by Lina's tongue, but then he realized that talking about Lina was dangerously close to thinking about her so he resisted.

Wolf withdrew a little wooden box from his saddle bag. "Now that you're back, we can use this."

He opened the box, from what Augustine could see it contained only a crimson powder.

"Hmm..." Wolf said, taking a pinch of the powder and tossing it across the road behind him. "You know what's ironic?"

"What's that?" Mill asked.

"Mirella sent Miss Miracle to find us on condition that she deliver this box to me," he explained. "And Miss Miracle only agreed to Mirella's terms because she wanted to find Augustine. Now, the very thing that helped her find him, is going to ensure she can't find him again."

"What are you talking about?" Augustine demanded.

"Mirella made this powder for me. It contains a powerful spell," Wolf grinned. "It's the reason your stepfather hasn't been able to track me. Miss Miracle came at just the right time, I was almost out."

Wolf tossed a little more of the powder over the road behind him. "Our tracks and our scent will vanish in a few moments."

"Until now, I thought it was your wit that helped you evade my father," Augustine stated. "I suppose you aren't as clever as I thought."

"A little wit, a little magic," Wolf shrugged. "I get the results I want. Right now, I want to escape your lady."

Augustine felt a twinge of pain.

"She's not my lady," Augustine corrected and continued down the road with only a slight shrug. He was doing his utmost to appear emotionless, but his best efforts left him with the expression of a man who'd just been punched in the stomach.

"My apologies," Wolf said, urging his horse onward. As he passed Augustine he looked him in the eyes and added with a tone of genuine compassion, "You did the right thing, you know. It was admirable."

Augustine gritted his teeth. He didn't want anyone to praise him for rejecting Lina, especially not Wolf.

Mill caught up to Augustine and fixed a frigid gaze on him. "Just take comfort in knowing she's still alive," he hissed.

He could feel Mill's loathing burning into him. At least now he understood the man's resentment. Augustine was the son of the man who destroyed his village, why shouldn't he be resentful? After a moment, Augustine decided that this fact fell into the Lina category of thoughts to be avoided, so he became intensely interested in the scenery again and didn't think about anything for a while.

Mill and Wolf rode at a slightly faster pace than Augustine and so they ended up a short distance ahead. After a while, boredom compelled them to speak to each other. Faruk took the opportunity to come up just behind Augustine and growl, "I think you're a fool."

Augustine jumped. While he was aware that Faruk was right behind him, he wasn't expecting him to speak. He looked over his shoulder at the man and raised an eyebrow.

"I'd never met a woman before your red girl," Faruk mumbled.

"Wait, what?" Augustine questioned. "How–"

"I believed the words of Rouvin the Philosopher." He was keeping his voice so low, even if Wolf and Mill heard him, they probably could only make out a low grumbling. "I believed women were incapable of reason."

"Never any women?" Augustine persisted. "What about your mother?"

"*Silence,*" Faruk hissed. "I'm talking."

Augustine sealed his lips obediently.

"When she spoke to you about honor, she spoke with more wisdom than any man I've ever known. If Wolf doesn't kill you, you should marry her."

Augustine swallowed hard. Why did the conversation keep coming back to Lina?

"Faruk?" Wolf called over his shoulder. "Is everything alright back there?"

He must have heard a grumbling sound coming from the giant's direction.

"Chain is loose," Faruk called back. "I fixed it."

"This is why we keep you around, Faruk!" Wolf grinned, then he returned to his conversation with Mill.

"Faruk," Augustine whispered, trying to distract himself from the stabbing pain in his heart. "You are very wise. Why do you work so hard to conceal it?"

"No one would hire me if they knew I was intelligent," Faruk explained. "I wouldn't be able to travel the world and catch educated men to read for me."

"You can almost read yourself," Augustine pointed out. "Perhaps you don't need this job anymore."

"Books cost money," Faruk grumbled. "I need this job."

"Or...the friendship of a man with access to the Lysandrian library..." Augustine suggested.

Faruk's eyes widened slightly.

Wolf glanced over his shoulder in their direction. He must have heard them talking. Augustine had an idea.

"How dare you threaten me, you vile oaf!" he exclaimed at Faruk.

Faruk, being a brilliant man, caught on immediately.

"Then stop squirming," he barked.

Wolf slowed his horse, until he was parallel to the pair.

"Now, gentlemen," Wolf said. "What is the subject of your disagreement?"

"Ever since Faruk returned he's been back here whispering threats and insults!"

"Is this true, Faruk?" Wolf asked.

"Yes," Faruk confirmed.

"I'm surprised you aren't man enough to take it, Augustine," Wolf commented.

"It's wearing on me," Augustine answered.

Wolf rolled his eyes. "Faruk, you take the lead. I'll ride back here with Augustine for a bit."

Faruk glanced back at Augustine for a minute as he urged his horse ahead. His mustache twitched in a way that led Augustine to believe he had smiled briefly. Augustine smirked back, then bit his lip when Wolf glanced over at him.

The little exchange filled him with the hope that when he broke from Wolf's party to make for Lysandria, Faruk would be with him.

41

DRUNK DOES NOT GET FAIRIES

The air warmed as Wolf's party continued south. The mountains and the evergreens gave way to lower hills covered in shorter twisted trees. Augustine was hit with a wave of nostalgia. He hadn't been this close to his homeland since he left eight years ago. The sights, the smell, even the taste of the air reminded him of his childhood.

Wolf kept his route a secret, so Augustine didn't know where they actually were at any given time. Once in a while, he felt so close to Kalathea he was tempted to try escaping and making his way there by land. He knew this was folly though. He kept reminding himself to be patient. If he made a move too soon, he would lose his opportunity. It would be easiest to wait until they reached the Great Sea.

He continued playing the model prisoner and it worked. Wolf started giving him jobs to do when they stopped to make camp. Augustine built the fires, cooked, and tended the horses. Eventually, Wolf started removing the shackles during the day to make it easier for him to use his hands. Everything was falling into place.

Augustine took every opportunity to speak to Faruk about the Lysandrian library, tempting him with all the knowledge it contained. Certainly, he could escape on his own but it would be a lot easier with

Faruk's help; and honestly, he had grown fond of the brilliant giant. Perhaps it was only bad luck that forced him into a life of crime.

After several weeks of travel, the company's supplies waned. Wolf started rationing the food and the party grew irritable.

"We should have reached a village by now," Mill complained one afternoon as they were making their way through the woods.

"If we keep going, we'll reach Trapzi by nightfall," Wolf assured him.

As the daylight faded, they saw no sign of the promised village, only trees stretching endlessly in every direction.

"I think we're lost," Mill grumbled.

"We aren't lost," Wolf snapped. "It's here, I swear it. Keep moving."

After a short while, Augustine noticed an orange light glowing up ahead. Wolf kicked Fotia, bringing her to a trot.

"See! I told you!" he called over his shoulder. "It's just ahead."

The rest of the party increased their speed. As they came closer, they heard the sound of music and laughter echoing through the forest. Wolf slowed as he approached the tree line, then stopped. He suddenly went rigid.

Augustine, coming up beside him, saw what alarmed him. The source of the light was not a village but a single bonfire in the middle of a clearing. Around the blaze a group of nymphs and satyrs danced, some playing on flutes and lyres while the rest pranced around drinking deeply from golden goblets.

This was one of those old-style Greek parties Augustine's mother always warned him about. There was loud music, excessive drinking, inappropriate dancing, and unfortunately, almost everyone was naked.

Thankfully, the furry goat legs of the satyrs made them look like they were wearing pants. As for the nymphs, they had very long hair that fell in exactly the right way to provide the necessary coverage. It was like some invisible being was doing her utmost to keep the scene of flagrant debauchery appropriate.

Wolf, no doubt, was alarmed by the satyrs but Augustine's attention was drawn to the most human looking of the party-goers who lounged on the grass before the dancing flames. *Fortunately,* the two of them were wearing clothes (in the style of the ancient Greeks). *Unfortunately,* they were the very gods who had brought so much misery to Augustine's early life—Dythis and Areti.

"We need to go," Augustine breathed, hoping no one would spot them through the tree line. Presently, the false gods were laughing at something, clutching their stomachs and gasping for breath. They hadn't noticed the human intruders at all.

"Agreed," Wolf whispered, his eyes still fixed on the satyrs.

The company started turning their horses. Augustine had only rounded partway when Symeon froze beneath him. He kicked the animal, trying to urge it forward but it wouldn't move. Then the air around him seemed to constrict holding him in place.

Glancing at Wolf, Mill, and Faruk, he realized they were in the same predicament. Unable to do anything else, Augustine tried turning back toward the clearing. The tension gave way immediately and both horse and rider found themselves staring into a pair of gleeful faces.

Augustine's heart raced, his hands trembled. Why was it, that after everything he'd been through, it was these two that scared him senseless?

They're not gods, they're fairies. Augustine reminded himself. *Their real names are Jace and Acacia and they cannot hurt me unless I engage with them.*

The image of his uncle lying on the ground writhing in pain flashed across his mind. He quickly pushed the memory aside. *They can't hurt me, they can't hurt me...* he reminded himself. *...At least, not easily.*

"Where are you four going?" Jace exclaimed, throwing his arms out. The force of his own motion, made him sway slightly. "Come back here and sit down! Have a..." he blinked his eyes a few times like he was trying to clear his head. "...A drink."

"Do as they say," Wolf whispered, urging his horse forward. "We have no idea what these beings are capable of. If we play along they might let us go."

"No!" Augustine cried.

All eyes, including those of the twins, fell on him.

"Ignore them," Augustine exclaimed. "They can't hurt us if we don't engage."

"Is that our good friend Alex?" Acacia questioned, taking a few unsteady steps forward.

Her brother followed, squinting at Augustine. "Oh no, sister, it's that one lady..." He snapped his fingers as he tried to find the memory. "...that pit lady... her kid."

"Pit lady?" Acacia burst out. Then they both doubled over laughing as if it was the funniest joke in the world.

"No, no, no," Jace said, recovering himself. "That one girl who had that thing with Prince Justin no one talked about? Her kid."

"Ooohhh!" Realization dawned in Acacia's eyes. She looked at Augustine. "You're named after that hippo philosopher or something, right?"

Jace burst out laughing all over again which set Acacia off.

"Hippo philosopher..." he breathed. "I can't..."

Augustine looked in disgust at the twins. Were they... they couldn't be... could fairies get *drunk*?

"We are extremely sorry for intruding," Wolf apologized. "We are lost. If you would kindly point us back to—"

Wolf couldn't finish his sentence. He was jerked from his horse by some invisible power and landed face first on the grass before the fire. The fairies busted up laughing again.

Wolf rose to his feet with all the dignity he could muster, wiping blood from his nose with his sleeve.

Augustine glanced at the twins. Jace's nose was bleeding in exactly the same way.

The latter ran his finger over his upper lip and observed the blood.

"Oh, that was stupid," Jace sighed, shaking his head.

"You're drunk," Augustine pointed out. "Let us go, before you accidentally kill one of us and yourselves in the process."

Acacia straightened up and held up her figure authoritatively, then with her eyelids drooping and her body swaying, she proclaimed, "Drunk does not get gods!"

A laugh burst through Jace's closed lips, making a raspberry sound. "Except you, sister!"

"Could a drunk god do this?" she grinned.

A force threw Jace across the clearing and sent him smashing into a tree. At the same moment, Acacia fell over onto the grass in a fit of hysterics. Most of the satyrs and nymphs were too lost in their merry-making to notice the newcomers and those who did see them only looked on gleefully.

Augustine dismounted and ran to Wolf. Mill and Faruk were already beside him, ensuring he was alright and waiting for orders. Wolf was always the one with the plan, but now... well the look on his face indicated that he was far outside his area of expertise.

"You saw that, right?" Augustine whispered. "When he hurt you, he received a matching wound."

Wolf nodded. "You know what they are?" he whispered, motioning toward the twins.

"And how to defeat them," Augustine confirmed. "Well, sort of."

"Speak," Wolf ordered.

"Ignore them," Augustine explained. "No matter what they do, don't react. Eventually they'll lose interest and let us go."

"How long will that take?" Wolf hissed.

Augustine shrugged.

"Don't be absurd," Mill hissed at Wolf. "He's trying to get us killed so he can make his escape. There has to be something we can do–"

"You three are greedy, murderous, demon-sired, villains" Augustine stated. "But I'd be your prisoner forever if it meant escaping those two. You've got to believe me. They tried to murder my mother."

Wolf was regarding him thoughtfully.

"I'll explain everything later," Augustine pleaded. "You've got to trust me."

Wolf thought for a moment, then answered with a silent nod.

"First, do not accept anything they offer," Augustine started. "It's all part—." He was interrupted when he felt himself flying backward. He crashed into Acacia who only stumbled slightly at his impact.

"You've gotten handsome since I last saw you," she grinned, spinning him around to face her. "You look just like your father."

Augustine jerked against her grasp. She released him with a laugh and they both stumbled away from each other.

Jace came up beside his sister and smirked, "You know what would make him look more like his father?"

"What's that?" Acacia asked.

"A knife in his back!"

The two fairies both melted into hysterical, convulsing puddles. As Augustine regarded them, he felt something he wasn't expecting —pity. This is what the 'almighty gods' had come to? This is where they fled? The thought that he'd spent so much of his life living in fear of these two was depressing. Yet another of Augustine's realities had just been turned upside down. He wondered if he should start keeping a list.

"Poor, poor little..." Acacia sat up and pointed a finger at Augustine. "What was your name again?"

"Augustine," Jace reminded. "Like Augustine the Hippo."

Augustine waited patiently as the twins suffered another bout of suffocating hysteria.

"Augustine *the* Hippo," Acacia choked, wiping a tear from her eyes. "I can't..." She inhaled trying to calm herself. "Now, what was I saying?"

"Poor Augustine," Jace helped. "He never knew his father."

"We have Madhuri's hourglass. We could take you back in time," Acacia offered. "You could get to know him."

Augustine made no answer. He had no idea what Madhuri's hourglass was and the fact that they thought he *wanted* to meet his father, led him to believe they were much drunker than originally suspected.

"No, no, no, sister," Jace rebuked, accepting a fresh goblet from a passing satyr. He sipped. "That one!" He thrust a finger at Wolf.

"That's a man with big ideas! A man who could use our powers to do some good in this world."

Jace took another gulp and said. "We can give you anything you like, you know—money, power, anything! Think of all the people you could help with us by your side."

Wolf seemed to think for a moment before replying, "Perhaps we can discuss that in the morning."

"How about over dinner?" Jace suggested. He clapped his hands and at once everything changed. Augustine found himself seated on a cushion beside a low table. It was very long with enough room for everyone including all the nymphs and satyrs.

In the center of the table, surrounded by colorful bowls of fruit, crisp brown bread, and steaming vegetables, was the largest serving platter Augustine had ever seen. Upon this, was a golden-brown, roasted hippopotamus with a watermelon in its mouth.

The four travelers regarded the thing with hanging jaws.

Acacia squinted at the animal. "Wh-why is there a hippo there?"

Jace stared at the thing for a moment then laughed and shrugged. "I wanted to make a pig, peacock, or another... you know bird thing, but you had me thinking about hippos so..." he threw his arms out triumphantly. "Here we are!"

Acacia snorted a laugh. All the satyrs laughed.

Wolf wiped the astonishment off his face, closed his mouth and stared into space.

"Time to eat! Time to eat!" Jace proclaimed cheerfully.

A few of the satyrs leapt forward to carve the hippo. Though Jace urged everyone to eat, *he* only seemed interested in drinking. Augustine wondered how much more he could stomach. Would he lose consciousness soon? One could only hope.

A satyr placed a slice of hippo before Augustine who immediately decided eating fairy food was probably a bad idea. He also wasn't sure he liked hippopotamus.

"Now," Acacia grinned, looking at the travelers. "Delight us with tales of your adventures!"

"There's nothing to tell," Wolf replied. "The weather was fair, the road was smooth, we made good time."

"That's wonderful, just wonderful," Jace interjected. "After all, as we've already mentioned, you've got a mission, don't you? Tell us aaalll about it."

"There isn't much to tell," Wolf shrugged. "I'm a potter."

"You're a liar," Acacia accused.

"You're correct," Augustine interjected. "He's a tax collector."

"Ooooo, I bet no one likes you–" Acacia started.

"Which reminds me, I just read the most fascinating book!" Augustine interrupted. "It's called *The History of Kalathean Tax Law*."

Wolf locked eyes with Augustine. "That does sound interesting. Do tell."

"How about we don't do that," Jace suggested.

But Wolf and Augustine did. They went back and forth for what seemed like forever talking about rates and deductions and how they changed slightly over the centuries until Acacia completely lost interest and aggressively kissed the satyr on her opposite side.

The moment she did so, Jace launched himself over the table with the words, "Unhand my sister you filthy, dirty, vile..." he snapped his fingers as he searched for a really creative insult. Unfortunately, with his mind flooded the best he could come up with was, "shirtless goat-man!"

Augustine and company sat quietly as Jace sent the satyr hurtling through the air.

The satyrs who were still sober enough to use their legs rose to their comrade's defense. A drunken brawl broke out, with Jace throwing the goat people in all directions while Acacia fell backward laughing herself senseless.

Augustine slowly rose. Wolf and company followed suit. Then, they quietly found their horses and started away. When they were out of sight of the firelight, they brought their horses to a gallop.

Once they put some distance between themselves and the merry-makers Wolf began to laugh. "Tax law! Really?"

"It was the most boring thing I could think of," Augustine shrugged.

Then he started laughing and even Faruk smiled. Mill was the only person who didn't seem even slightly pleased by their unlikely escape. He thanked Augustine with a venomous glare.

42

LINA'S BAD DAY

Lina ran to find Oswald the moment Faruk set her on the ground. As she suspected, he was still sleeping. She woke him and had him collect his things, then ran to make her own preparations.

Shortly after Lord Ervin broke his promise to Lina, she requested a horse for both herself and Oswald. Ervin was still feeling guilty about denying her first request and was happy to oblige.

Lina had the two cedar-colored bays ready and waiting when Oswald met her in the village square.

She was about to climb up into the saddle, when Oswald caught her shoulder.

"We are leaving, but we aren't going after Augustine."

"What are you talking about?" Lina scowled.

"I am taking you back home," Oswald asserted.

"You're giving up?" she exclaimed. "That's not like you, Oswald."

"Giving up? Hardly!" he retorted indignantly. "But neither Augustine nor I think this is the type of quest appropriate for a lady."

Lina narrowed her eyes. "Did Augustine put you up to this?"

"No, no!" Oswald insisted. "Augustine and I just happened to agree on this particular matter."

"At least you agree on something," Lina grumbled.

Oswald put his free hand on her opposite shoulder. "Lina, I know he broke off your engagement. I see no reason for you to endanger yourself chasing a man who will give you nothing in return."

Lina thought for a moment. Oswald was certainly strong enough to drag her back to Kaltehafen by force. He would probably try if she refused to go willingly. Unfortunately, the two of them were Augustine's only allies with any clue to his whereabouts. As far as Lina was concerned, she had to follow him as long as she could. She had an idea.

"Of course Augustine told you that," she stated. "He probably doesn't think you're man enough to protect me."

Oswald's eyes widened. Lina could see the wheels turning in his mind.

"You may be right..." Oswald mumbled.

"Prove him wrong, Oswald!" Lina demanded. "When Augustine finds that I've arrived safely in Lysandria, he'll realize he was a fool for not trusting you."

Oswald bit his lip. He was jittering.

"I know what you're doing," he stated.

"Going south?" Lina grinned.

"Curse you," Oswald grumbled. "Fine, I'll protect you but I don't want you to get your hopes up. He's still not going to marry you after all this."

"You sound very sure of that," Lina noticed.

"Well, he sounded sure of it when he spoke to me," Oswald insisted.

Lina glanced sideways at him, wondering when and how the cousins had managed to meet.

"Whether he marries me or not is irrelevant," Lina stated. "He's my closest friend and we are his best chance. I'm going after him."

She climbed up into the saddle and started south.

As they continued their journey, Oswald boasted about his swordsmanship, promising Lina again and again that he could protect her from whatever obstacles they faced along the way.

Lina smiled and nodded, but didn't really hear him. She was too busy looking down at the hoof prints Wolf's company left in the muddy road. It wasn't until they were well out of town that Oswald got Lina's attention.

"Lina?" he said. "*Lina?*"

"Sorry, what?" Lina asked, looking sideways at him.

"You seem distracted," he noticed.

Lina just shrugged. "What was it you wanted, Oswald?"

"I was just saying that... well now that Augustine's broken your engagement..."

Lina furrowed her brow. Oswald's cheeks were slightly pink.

"Well, you're probably worried about how you're going to support yourself..." he continued. "You know... without a husband..."

This was actually the furthest thing from Lina's mind. Healers were always in demand so she was perfectly capable of supporting herself, husband or no. In fact, for the past few weeks, *she* had been supporting Oswald.

"I... um..." Oswald's cheeks reddened.

Was he struggling for words? That was very unlike him. Normally he blurted out the first thing that came to his mind without a second thought.

"I just want you to know that you don't need to worry about that because..." He gripped the reins tightly and straightened up. "I've decided that since my cousin so heartlessly cast you off, it's my duty to marry you."

Lina froze.

"What?" she demanded.

"I'm going to marry you," Oswald continued. "I'm Augustine's only relative who is available and close to your age so... it's my duty."

Now, Lina was in a state of shock. Where was this coming from?

"Oswald..." Lina started. "Do you..." She couldn't believe what she was about to ask. "...have feelings for me?"

Her question filled Oswald with a strange boldness. He pulled back on the reins to stop his horse and waited for her to do the same. She did, giving him her full attention.

"Not just feelings, Lina," he said. "I love you."

When Augustine was dragged away that morning, Lina thought the day couldn't possibly get any worse. Unfortunately, Oswald's declaration of love proved her horribly wrong.

She took a deep breath, and narrowing her eyes, locked her gaze with his.

"Tell me something," she said. "Would you love me if I wasn't Augustine's lady?"

"You aren't Augustine's lady anymore," Oswald pointed out.

"If I *never* was Augustine's lady," Lina clarified. "If he'd never met me, would you still love me?"

"Why does that matter?" Oswald asked.

"Because I don't think you really love me," Lina explained. "I actually think this has very little to do with me. I think it's the next contest in your ongoing rivalry."

Oswald didn't know how to respond to that. For a long moment, he just sort of stared.

"That's not true," he finally managed.

"I think it is," said Lina, spurring her horse forward. "You see an opportunity to take something from Augustine and you're using it."

"Why shouldn't I?" Oswald suddenly exclaimed. "He has everything!"

She looked over her shoulder at him, his eyes were burning with anger and hurt.

"*He* has everything?" Lina remarked dryly. "Aren't you the 'crown prince of Kaltehafen'?"

"Yes, but what does that matter?" Oswald fumed. "You said it yourself, no one respects me, no one likes me. And Augustine, he, he..." his face somehow reddened more. "*Everyone* likes him! Uncle Florian isn't even his real father and he loves him more than my father loves me!"

Lina actually felt sorry for Oswald who was suddenly being forced to face the consequences of his upbringing.

"And he has *your* love," Oswald continued. "The love of a brave and beautiful woman who will stop at nothing to get him back. Can you blame me for being jealous?"

They rode in silence for a moment. Lina occasionally glanced in his direction thoughtfully. There was a good man somewhere inside the haughty prince. Despite their ongoing rivalry, he seemed sincere in wanting to rescue Augustine and he had done his best to take care of Lina on their journey. He wanted to be helpful, he wanted to love and be loved, he just didn't know how and it was clearly frustrating him.

"You can have all of those things, Oswald," Lina reassured. Then, realizing how it might be interpreted, she quickly added. "Not *my* love, I mean. But... the love of another woman. And friendship, respect, all of it."

Oswald looked at her expectantly.

"But you've got to stop behaving like you're the center of the universe."

Oswald's gaze dropped to the ground. "I don't mean to... I just..." he sighed, dropped the reins and threw out his arms. "How? How do I do that?"

"Well, you're listening to me and considering my words," Lina smiled. "I'd say that's a good start."

43

WHAT'S THE MATTER WITH WOLF?

"You knew exactly how to handle those two," Wolf said to Augustine. "How?"

It was the morning after their escape from the twins and they were all sitting around a campfire consuming the last of their rations. Augustine was untied, sitting among the three highwaymen like he was one of their own.

"I lived under the rule of those beings for years," Augustine explained. "They posed as our ancient gods and oppressed us. Didn't you hear about any of this?"

"Certainly," Wolf answered, dipping a stale biscuit into a bowl of water. At this point in their travels, the biscuits were *so* stale, they were inedible unless softened. Even then, they were only edible if you were starving.

"But I heard all sorts of strange rumors in my travels," Wolf shrugged. "I confess I didn't give the one about the evil gods returning much weight."

"Well, it was true," Augustine answered. "Sort of." He proceeded to explain the nature of fairies to Wolf. How a magical law prevents them from directly harming humans and how some of them come up with creative ways to work around that problem.

"Since no one knew they couldn't harm us," Augustine went on. "The army, the guards, everyone followed their orders. My mother's master at the time dared to question them and his entire family was arrested. My mother was left without a home or a job. We moved from place to place, my mother taking whatever work she could."

Wolf set his bowl aside, and continued listening with his fingers laced and his thumbs tapping together thoughtfully.

"While King Alexander was in exile, he learned about Jace and Acacia's true nature and came back to help us. That's how I learned."

Wolf continued prying, asking for the rest of Augustine's story, how his mother met Florian and what exactly happened after Alexander's return.

"And now the twins spend their days drinking in the woods with satyrs?" Wolf questioned. "How the mighty have fallen!"

"From one cheap thrill to the next," Augustine grinned. "In a strange way, I feel sorry for them."

Wolf responded with a brief smirk and then seemed to lose himself in thought.

THANKFULLY, the party made it to a village that very day. Wolf, per his usual custom, left Augustine with Faruk.

The moment Wolf was out of sight, Faruk untied him and reading lessons commenced. Augustine kept bringing up the beautiful city of Lysandria and its extensive library. He couldn't tell if he was making any headway with Faruk, but he didn't worry. The coast was nowhere in sight, he had time.

Another two weeks of travel passed. The farther they went, the more Wolf's usual cheer began to subside. He started being unusually kind to Augustine and short tempered with Faruk and Mill. It was the strangest thing. Augustine had no idea how to make sense of the man. Mill, by contrast, became more cheerful over time. When Wolf snapped at him, he would respond with a laugh or a little quip.

One evening, as they were all settling down to sleep, Faruk approached Augustine with the shackles to secure him for the night.

Augustine was obediently offering his hands, when Wolf looked up from his breviary and said, "That's not necessary. He has nowhere to go."

"Have you lost your mind?" Mill objected. "He'll murder us in our sleep, steal our horses and go wherever he likes."

Wolf shot Mill a look that silenced him immediately. "Augustine is a man of honor," Wolf asserted. "He would never kill a man while he slept." He looked over at Augustine, his solemn eyes asking for affirmation. Augustine nodded. He wouldn't kill anyone, not even in self-defense, unless it was a fair fight.

"Put those things away," Wolf ordered Faruk. The giant stowed the shackles in one of the packs and left Augustine loose.

"Honor," Mill scoffed. "A man of honor, just like his father!"

Wolf snapped his breviary shut. "Not a word from you until morning," he ordered Mill.

That night, Augustine was able to stretch out and sleep in a somewhat normal position. It was such a little thing, but after months in captivity, he relished every little freedom he got.

When he woke the next morning, Wolf greeted him with the somber words, "I see you're still here."

Augustine furrowed his bow. Wolf's downcast expression and tone indicated... disappointment. It was almost like he *wanted* him to escape. He couldn't make any sense of the man's behavior.

Later that morning, he decided to test the boundaries of Wolf's benevolence by speaking to him about something that had been nipping at his curiosity for months. So after helping himself to a refreshingly soft biscuit, he took a seat on a tree stump near Wolf and said, "So you were a monk?"

"Have you been reading my breviary?" Wolf asked. To Augustine's surprise, he didn't seem angry. His tone was matter-of-fact.

Still, Augustine wasn't ready to confess to the crime just yet.

"Um, I hear people talking."

Wolf smirked. "Who? I haven't told anyone. Either you looked at my breviary, or..." He looked over at Mill who was standing at a distance, practicing with his throwing knife, then at Faruk who was brushing the horses. "Or else they did and told you." That's when irritation entered his expression. "If they touched it, I'll kill them."

"I did it," Augustine blurted. The last thing he wanted was Faruk getting in trouble.

"As I thought," Wolf chuckled, his pleasantness restored.

"So... you'll kill them, but not me?" Augustine puzzled.

Wolf's countenance fell, his gaze dropped to the ground and he mumbled, "Well, you're my prisoner, I don't exactly expect you to be on your best behavior."

Then, he seemed to swallow his despondency. He straightened up and said, "Yes, I was a monk a very, very, long time ago."

"Why did you leave?" Augustine pressed.

Wolf's jaw tightened. "Our abbot was less interested in serving the poor and more interested in pleasing the rich. While the common folk worked themselves to death in the fields, we were exchanging prayers for land and gold. In those days I was a lot like you—naïve, idealistic..."

(Augustine felt a twinge of annoyance at this comment, but was too interested in the story to say anything.)

"I thought if I only reminded the abbot about our vows of poverty, it would solve everything." Wolf chuckled bitterly. "But the abbot only seemed interested in one vow, *my* vow of obedience. He rebuked me for my boldness and told me to be silent." Wolf shrugged. "So I left and found my own ways of helping people."

"Your ways seem just as corrupt," Augustine observed.

He was expecting Wolf to snap at him for this comment but he didn't. He looked at Augustine sadly, then at the ground and mumbled, "Maybe... maybe you're right."

Unfortunately for Lina, Oswald was talking again. They had long since lost Wolf's trail and were now traveling directly to the Kalathean capital. If Augustine wasn't there when she arrived, Lina planned on telling King Alexander everything she learned along her journey.

In the meantime, she was stuck in the wilderness with Oswald, whose favorite topic of conversation was himself. He went on and on about the various contests he'd won, his royal lineage, and everything else he could think of boasting about. Finally, she interrupted.

"Prince Oswald, remember what we've been talking about?"

At once, Oswald stopped speaking and gave Lina his full attention. Ever since his declaration of love, Lina had been working with him, trying to help him overcome his upbringing as best she could.

"You've been boasting about yourself all morning," Lina explained. "If you want to be respected, you need to take an interest in other people."

"What do I do?" Oswald asked brightly. He had the look of a little puppy eager to learn a new trick. Lina appreciated his enthusiasm.

"Ask *me* something," Lina suggested. "Maybe something about my family."

"Right," Oswald replied. He thought for a moment, then blurted, "Is your mother dead?"

Lina closed her eyes. "Why would you start with that?" she sighed.

Oswald seemed confused. "I'm trying to show an interest! And... well... you only ever talk about your father, so naturally I wondered if..."

"Try again," Lina ordered. "If you want to win a lady's heart, it's best not to start with a subject that might be painful to her."

"Oh..." Oswald realized. "I didn't think about that."

Of course he didn't. Lina breathed deeply, reminding herself to be patient.

"How about this," Oswald tried. "Do you have any brothers and sisters?"

"That's better," Lina smiled. "Yes, I have two brothers, but they went away to study at university, so it's just me with my parents now."

"Your mother isn't dead?" Oswald exclaimed. "Why don't you ever talk about her?"

Lina bit her lip, hiding a very subtle smile. He was trying so hard, poor prince.

"Now *that's* prying," she explained.

"But you said I should show an interest," Oswald objected.

"Yes, but not *too* much," Lina continued. "You ask for too much information all at once and it frightens people."

Oswald ran his hand through his hair. "This is complicated."

"You'll learn," Lina reassured him. "We've got plenty of time to practice, now try again."

As they rode on and on, Oswald kept practicing and Lina patiently corrected him. As horrified as she was by his declaration of love, she was actually glad it happened. It gave her the opportunity to understand his frustrations a little more and to help him.

She couldn't say for sure whether or not narcissism was a disease, but she decided to treat it like one. Challenging his ego, while providing constructive advice seemed to be an effective treatment. Most importantly, he wanted to be cured and took her words to heart. If he hadn't, she couldn't have done anything to help.

He made a little progress each day and Lina eventually found his presence not only tolerable, but sort of enjoyable sometimes. She supposed his true test of character wouldn't come until he'd been reunited with Augustine. If those two could get along, Lina would consider him cured.

44

THE CLIENT

It was now or never. Faruk was tying Augustine to a tree, meaning Wolf was about to take Mill and go into town.

The evening before, as the company was making camp, Augustine noticed the smell of salt in the air. Climbing a nearby hill, he spotted a glimmer of blue on the horizon. The warm sandy wind blew up from the water, filling the air with the taste of the sea.

Now was as good a chance as any he would get. All he had to do was wait for Wolf and Mill to leave. Then he would suggest to Faruk that they make a run for it. Assuming the giant agreed, they would ride along the coast until they figured out where they were and how to get to Lysandria.

If Faruk refused, Augustine would wait just a little longer until they reached a port. Wolf was being so lenient with him lately, escaping wouldn't be difficult. Then it would just be a matter of finding the right ship.

His heart was racing as he considered everything that could go wrong. One mistake and the trust he'd spent months working to build would be lost along with his opportunity for freedom. *He could do this.* He had escaped before and he could do it again.

"Faruk," Wolf said, as the giant finished securing Augustine. "You're with me today."

Augustine stiffened. Faruk raised a questioning eyebrow.

"Don't worry, Faruk," Wolf explained. "We won't be gone long, and I trust you've bound him tightly. Mill can handle him. I need you."

Faruk just nodded and prepared his horse.

Augustine looked at Mill who was regarding him with a slight smirk.

This is alright, Augustine assured himself. He would find some other opportunity to speak to Faruk. None of the others knew the giant could read, perhaps he could pass him a note.

Before Wolf mounted Symeon he gripped Mill's shoulder and hissed, "Do not touch him. If I find the tiniest scratch on him when I return, I swear I'll kill you."

Mill returned the threat with an eye roll. "I'll treat him like the prince he is!"

That comment was somewhat ominous coming from Mill. Fortunately, not much came of it. The blue-eyed criminal kept himself busy as the first hour slipped by, brushing the two remaining horses and organizing supplies. Once he'd completed these tasks, he practiced with his throwing knife, brutally impaling tree trunks.

Augustine couldn't do much of anything in his position except think and look around. He wiggled a bit, testing the ropes, just wondering if it was possible to escape (not that he was going to try). Faruk, of course, did an excellent job binding him, he could hardly move at all, let alone break free. He was completely at the mercy of the bitter weasel named Mill.

The whole morning Augustine had an odd feeling, a feeling that something was deeply wrong. It wasn't just that Wolf had taken Faruk with him. Something was troubling Wolf. Augustine could see it in his stature—he was anxious and preoccupied like he was trying to work through some complicated problem in his mind.

Nothing seemed to be troubling Mill, he was still whistling away as he practiced with his throwing knife. Augustine couldn't help but admire his skill, he never missed.

"Someone's in a good mood," Augustine said finally. He was expecting Mill to glare and insult him. Instead Mill turned to him, grinned broadly, and went to retrieve his knife for the hundredth time. This did nothing to put Augustine's mind at ease. He decided to avoid conversation, no matter how bored he got.

Only two hours had passed when Augustine spotted Wolf returning around the base of the hill. That was unusual; normally when Wolf went into town he was gone at least half a day. Augustine craned his neck, looking for Faruk but couldn't see him anywhere. When Wolf dismounted he had the expression of a man defeated. He was downcast, his shoulders slouched.

"Where is Faruk?" Augustine asked.

Wolf didn't immediately answer, instead, he approached Mill and said, "Get your things and ride east along the water until you see the Anamian encampment. Tell the princess I will be there soon."

Augustine felt his heart starting to race. *Anamian encampment?* This wasn't right. None of it was. He began to struggle against his bonds.

"Can you handle him on your own?" Mill whispered.

"Would I have ordered you to leave if I couldn't?" Wolf snapped.

Mill threw up his hands defensively. "Alright, I'll see you there!" he laughed. He snatched his pack, plucked his knife from the tree where it was lodged, leapt up on his horse, and galloped away leaving Augustine alone with Wolf.

"*Where is Faruk?*" Augustine demanded.

Wolf slowly approached Augustine until he was standing opposite him.

"I've paid and dismissed him," Wolf answered.

"What? Already?" Augustine questioned. "We still have a long way to go, don't we?"

Wolf shook his head. "No, Augustine. My client is very nearby. I saw no reason to keep Faruk from..." Wolf thought for a moment. "...I doubt he has a family actually..." he shrugged. "Whatever it is Faruk does."

"We aren't going to–"

"Anamia?" Wolf interrupted. "No."

Augustine's eyes widened.

"But you thought that, didn't you?" Wolf continued. "You thought that if you could gain our trust you might escape along the coast and flee to your uncle."

Augustine's heart was hammering in his chest. Rage and frustration boiled inside him. *How did Wolf always know everything?*

As if reading his mind, Wolf mumbled. "It's exactly what I would do in your position."

His gaze fell. Though he had outsmarted Augustine, he lacked his usual smugness. A pain lingered in his eyes and his tone was laced with bitterness.

Augustine clenched his jaw while kneading his hands in and out of fists.

"So you've won," he managed. "What happens now? You're going to drag me to this client all on your own? Try, I dare you!"

Without a word, Wolf unsheathed his dagger. He rolled the hilt in his hand. Augustine found his gaze drawn to the blade. Wolf studied him for a moment almost clinically, looking from his face to his throat, down to his chest, and back up. Then he slammed his eyes shut and began pacing.

"I owe you an explanation," he mumbled. "After everything we've been through... it's the least I can do..."

Augustine fought harder against his bonds. He knew it was useless, but he couldn't stop himself. His every instinct was telling him to fight.

"You'll recall that your father was married to the princess of Anamia," Wolf stated.

Augustine vaguely recalled something about that.

"She is the one who hired me," Wolf explained. "...to kill the sons of Justin." His gaze dropped. "You are the last, Augustine. Once I've brought her your body, she'll pay me and this whole nasty business will be over."

Augustine's anger flared up. "You're going to kill me here?" he cried. "Coward! Cut me loose and then if you want my life, take it in a fair fight!"

"I was going to kill you this morning," Wolf sighed. "I was hoping I could do it quickly, before you woke but, well there were two complications. First, Faruk had grown attached to you and I was worried he might turn on me when the time came. Second..." His shoulders slouched. "*I've* grown attached to you, Augustine. I couldn't live with myself if I didn't at least ask the princess for your life. I offered to sell you as a slave in some distant corner of the world where you'd never trouble her. She refused." His sorrowful green eyes met Augustine's. "So you know what I have to do now."

As Augustine struggled in vain to break free, the tiny voice of reason spoke in the back of his mind. *You can't fight your way out of this, Augustine. He's conflicted. He's stalling. Breathe.*

Augustine did, calming himself just slightly.

"I shouldn't have told you all that," Wolf mumbled. "The longer I talk, the longer you'll have to think of a way out of this mess."

As he said this, his eyes were almost pleading with his captive.

"You don't have to do this," Augustine managed, trying desperately to suppress the tsunami of rage and fear that swelled inside him.

"This is bigger than my own feelings," Wolf explained. "There are people, lots of people who depend on my work, you've seen that." Wolf rubbed the bridge of his nose between his thumb and forefinger. "Princess Amira is a brutal woman, a perfect match for her late husband, I might add. If I do not do as she asks, she will see that as a betrayal. It could be the end of everything I've built."

He's still talking, came the internal voice of reason. *He doesn't want to do this. He feels trapped. Offer a mutually beneficial solution.*

It occurred to Augustine that his internal voice of reason sounded just like Lina and, with the thought of Lina, came a mutually beneficial solution.

"What if you could get paid for killing me *and* get paid ransom for my safe return?" Augustine suggested. "Think of all the good you could do with that money."

Wolf's eyes brightened hopefully. "I'm listening," he replied.

"Do you have any more of that viper venom?"

"It's not like I use it a lot," Wolf nodded.

"Paralyze me with the venom," Augustine suggested. "And then give me a wound that looks lethal. Once you've shown me to Amira and collected your pay, offer to dispose of the body. I'll wake up in a few hours, then you can ransom me back to my uncle. You'll be safely out of Amira's reach by the time she realizes what happened."

Wolf stuck his tongue in his cheek and furrowed his brow.

"You know how risky that is?"

"It's definitely less risky than you murdering me right here and now," Augustine pointed out.

"For *me*, not for *you*," Wolf clarified.

"If I show signs of life too soon..." Augustine started. "Just, um, act alarmed and stab me a couple of times until I'm really dead."

"I can't have a corpse wake up while I'm collecting from a client," Wolf complained. "That will make me look like a terrible assassin!"

"The fact that you haven't killed me yet, already makes you look like a terrible assassin," Augustine pointed out. "So why don't you just accept my offer, or kill me while I'm tied here like the honorless coward you are."

A slight smile touched Wolf's lips. Then he removed his pack and started digging through it.

"Alright, Augustine," he said. "Since you're so insistent we'll try this crazy plan of yours." He found his little box of medicines, then added, "Doubt it's going to work, though, so you'd better take a moment to beg for God's mercy."

Augustine did, praying for the first time since he learned the truth about his father. He was a little ashamed of this fact, but every time he tried to pray, he thought of Attikos Hatsi and fell back into wondering if God was another of his mother's lies. He hoped not. After all, not everything that he knew was wrong—and the things he was wrong about weren't all bad. Wolf, for example, wasn't *as evil* as he originally thought. He was… *complicated*.

Then there was Lina who remained the same loyal, sensible friend she had always been. He hoped God fell into the Lina category of things in life that still made sense.

As he watched Wolf apply a drop of venom to his dagger, Augustine realized he would probably know for sure by the end of the day.

"When you start to wake up," Wolf said. "Continue lying still until I tell you it's safe, understand?"

Augustine nodded apprehensively, his eyes fixed on the blade. He knew that what came next wasn't going to be pleasant.

"Wolf…" Augustine asked. "Why does Amira want to kill Justin's sons?"

"Jealous, perhaps?" Wolf shrugged. "If the pay is good I don't ask questions."

He lunged forward, slicing Augustine on the shoulder.

45

THE LISTENING CORPSE

Augustine became aware. Not of anything in particular—he couldn't see or feel anything. He was like a consciousness floating in darkness. Voices murmured in the air around him, at first they blurred together incoherently, then they became clearer.

"He looks just like Father," came a strong masculine voice.

"Just confirms that Wolfy brought us the right person," a woman replied.

"Of *course* Wolfy brought us the right person," the man said. "He's Wolfy!"

"Will you cover him up?" the woman ordered. "I don't like seeing him."

"Oh, yes, Mother," the man answered.

The voices suddenly became slightly muffled and the air a little stuffy. Augustine searched his mind, trying to make sense of things. Where was he? Who were these two?

He remembered Wolf and something about venom... it all came flooding back to him.

He was paralyzed and probably somewhere in Princess Amira's encampment. He wondered if she was the woman speaking.

"We don't really need him, you know," the man continued. "It's clearly troubling you, Mother. I'll just have Wolfy get rid of him."

"No, we are not changing the plan," the woman objected. "And it only bothers me because he looks so much like your father. It's like seeing *his* corpse." There was a brief pause then she added, "We're saving Fausta for last. She's going to suffer for what she did."

"If you say so, Mother," the man agreed.

Augustine heard someone get up and footsteps crunching over what was probably rocky ground.

"Oh Tarik," the woman called.

The footsteps stopped.

"Will you send Wolfy in here?"

"Of course, Mother," the man answered.

Things were silent for a long time after that. Augustine could hear the woman adjust herself in her chair occasionally. He heard a slight scratching sound, probably a quill moving over parchment.

Tarik, that was one of Justin's sons, wasn't it? Augustine remembered seeing the name on Fausta's letters. Fausta had explicitly excluded him from inheriting the Kalathean throne. Apparently, he'd also been excluded from Amira's kill list. Figures she'd spare her own son.

After a short time, Augustine picked up the sound of footsteps approaching.

"Ah, Wolfy!" the woman greeted.

"Princess," the familiar voice answered respectfully.

"How are you feeling, Wolfy? Rested and refreshed, I hope?"

"You're servants have been wonderful, my lady," he replied.

"Good," the princess continued. "Wolfy, I have another job for you."

"My lady, I couldn't ask for an honor greater than serving you. But now that I've brought you the last of Prince Justin's sons, I wish to retire."

"Don't be silly, Wolfy," Amira laughed. "You wouldn't know what to do with yourself."

"With all due respect, my lady–"

"You wouldn't refuse me, would you, Wolfy?"

There was a short silence.

"Never, my lady."

"I've sent a message to King Alexander," the princess explained. "I told him, I found a body that matches the description of his missing nephew. I expect him to be here by tomorrow morning at the latest."

"You want me to kill him?" Wolf questioned. "I've heard he's hard to kill."

"Why do you think I'm hiring *you*, Wolfy?" Augustine could almost hear her smile.

"You flatter me, princess." Wolf hesitated for a moment, then added. "Forgive my boldness, but I fear for your safety. The king is well loved, and we are far from your own country. Where will you flee once he's dead?"

"I have the matter well in hand," Amira asserted, her tone warning Wolf not to ask further questions.

"As you wish," was his only response.

Augustine heard his footsteps going back the way they came. But when the sound was right beside wherever Augustine was, it paused.

"Lady," came Wolf's voice from somewhere just above him. "Let me get rid of him for you. I swear to you that Alexander will be dead before he gets within a hundred paces of this body, there's no sense keeping it around."

"It stays until the king is dead," Amira stated. "Because if you fail me, I'll tell the king to come in here and identify it and then while he's looking down at it I will *stab him in the back!*"

"Princess," Wolf laughed. "When have I ever failed you?"

"He stays until the king is dead," Amira insisted. "Then you can dump them both wherever you like."

Wolf left without another word.

Augustine did the only thing he could do—lay there in darkness mulling over the complexity of his situation. He wondered if Wolf was going to make any effort to smuggle him out now. Probably not. It would be too risky for him. If anything, he'd deem the plan a failure and sneak back in to finish Augustine off before he could wake up and maim Wolf's reputation.

The minutes dragged by with Augustine lying utterly helpless, praying Wolf would have a major conversion experience in the next hour or two.

Finally, someone else entered the tent. Before the newcomer could say anything, Amira stood (somewhat aggressively from the sound of her chair being thrust backwards).

"Everything's in place," she hissed. "The king will be dead by midmorning and my maidservant is ready to assassinate the rest of his family tomorrow night. You'd better be ready to declare your right to the throne before dawn on the following day. Is that clear?"

"Yes, Mother," came Tarik's voice. "But... won't it be obvious that we orchestrated the whole thing?"

"Of course, it will be obvious," Amira snapped. "But it won't matter, you'll be the only heir left!"

Tarik sighed. "This all seems so underhanded, Mother. I wish we could have just done the honorable thing and invaded."

"You see this is why men can't conquer a kingdom without destroying half of it in the process," Amira scoffed. "We do things my way and the city stays intact. Understand?"

"Yes, Mother," Tarik mumbled.

A moment passed before Amira continued. "This is exactly what your father wanted, you know."

"I know, Mother."

"He was a wonderful man, your father." Amira sighed deeply. "When he rescued me from that harem, he cursed our backward ways and swore to me that I would be his one and only wife."

She pounded her fist on something, alarming Augustine.

"Once all this is over, I might have Wolf hunt down all those vile temptresses who led him astray!"

"Of course, Mother," Tarik agreed. "If that will make you happy."

"We should go eat something," she suggested cheerfully. "It's getting late."

They continued talking as they walked past Augustine leaving him alone. At least, he assumed he was alone, he couldn't hear anyone. He tried moving his hand but still couldn't feel anything. He wondered how much time it would take for the venom to wear off. It would be a few hours before he could even open his eyes. Then longer before he could move normally.

Augustine wasn't even slightly worried about his uncle. Wolf wouldn't be the first person to make an assassination attempt. Alexander would be on his guard. But his family... Queen Ilona and their children...

Amira had a maidservant in the palace. How long had she been stationed there? The princess sounded so confident. Whoever this maidservant was, she must have Queen Ilona's trust. Alexander's children were still small. He had four: the oldest was seven and the youngest wasn't even two. They would be easy prey for a skilled assassin, especially if she was one of the maids who tended them.

Augustine tried again to move. Still no luck. They had to be close to Lysandria. If by some miracle, he could escape Amira *and* Wolf, perhaps he could get to the palace with enough time to warn the queen.

Unfortunately, all he could do in the moment was lie there, a prisoner in his own body, holding on to the knowledge that his uncle's family was in mortal peril.

46

WOLF'S CHOICE

The hours dragged by with Augustine lying in his place, hoping and praying that the feeling would return to his body soon. While he waited, he tried to paint a picture of his surroundings based on the sounds he heard.

Human voices murmured at a distance, both men and women alike. There was music and laughter. This didn't sound much like a military encampment. Surely, Amira had some armed guards with her for protection, but she knew better than to take an army onto Kalathean shores.

Augustine paid special attention whenever he heard the whinny of a horse. He would need to steal one if he was going to make it to Lysandria with time to warn the queen. Amira's conversation with her son led him to believe he was within a day's ride of the city.

After a time, he started feeling a tingling in his fingers that filled him with hope. He tried curling and uncurling his hands to return sensation faster, but he couldn't tell if his attempts were successful. *Why was this taking so long?*

Eventually, the sounds of the camp began to die down, Augustine guessed that evening was approaching. In the morning his uncle would come looking for him... *This was torture.*

He suddenly realized his eyes were opening. He blinked and tried to squint, hoping it would bring something into view. Unfortunately, the only thing he could see was the fabric that was draped over his face. It was probably an off-white color, but it appeared gray in the dying light.

Moving his head proved too ambitious for the moment. At least the tingling sensation was starting to spread to the rest of his body. Maybe he'd be able to move soon? He just had to be patient. *It was killing him.*

The night deepened, the camp was now totally silent save for an orchestra of chirping insects. Augustine became aware of a strange feeling at the base of his neck. It was like a line of stinging and prickling pins running horizontally across his throat. It wasn't painful but it wasn't pleasant either.

Suddenly, he heard two pairs of footsteps approaching.

"He's here," whispered Wolf's familiar voice.

Augustine wasn't sure whether or not he should feel relieved. He closed his eyes and stopped trying to move. Until he knew who was with Wolf, he was going to act as dead as possible.

A quick whoosh and a cool draft told Augustine that the canvas had been lifted away.

"Alive?" Faruk's voice bemoaned. *"You cut his throat!"*

Relief flooded Augustine. If Faruk was here, it meant Wolf was indeed going to rescue him.

Augustine opened his eyes to see the giant standing beside him with his hands around Wolf's neck.

"He is–I–" Wolf gasped. "I swear, Faruk! I-" (He choked.) "I needed to make it look convincing! It's... not as bad as..." (He gasped.) "...it looks!"

Faruk released him and he crumpled to the ground. That's when the giant noticed Augustine looking up at him.

"Kid?" he said, a tear spilling down his cheek.

"You satisfied now?" Wolf grumbled as he picked himself up.

"You alright, kid?" Faruk asked, ignoring Wolf.

"No, he's dead until I say otherwise," Wolf ordered. "Augustine, close your eyes."

Augustine obeyed. He heard the canvas frumpling and then Wolf said, "Come on, Faruk help me roll him up."

A prickling sensation whirled through Augustine's body at even intervals. He assumed it was from Wolf and Faruk rolling him in the canvas but had no way of knowing for sure.

Then Faruk must have lifted him because his head fell backward causing painful little prickles to erupt across the base of his neck. *Did Faruk say something about throat cutting?* Augustine really hoped not. He tried to move his hand up to his neck to check, but the most he could get it to do was flop a little.

He bounced around as Faruk raced across Amira's camp. With every little bump, a wave of pins and needles radiated through him. He was getting nauseous.

"You're safe, kid," Faruk whispered. "You're going back to King Florian."

"*Shush,*" Wolf whispered from somewhere off to the left.

Augustine's stomach flopped as he felt himself being flung down on what he guessed was the back of a horse. He was draped over it, with his head resting next to its side.

As the animal started walking, Augustine decided he was not looking forward to getting feeling back. He couldn't imagine there was a single muscle in his body that wasn't going to hurt after this. Poor Faruk was trying to be gentle but that was like expecting an elephant to be gentle. After a long time on horseback in the most awkward position imaginable, Faruk laid him on the ground and unrolled him.

"Alright, kid," came Wolf's voice. "We've put a little distance between ourselves and Amira. Are you alive?"

Augustine opened his eyes and looked up into the starry night sky. They were hidden in a little brushy valley between some dark hills. The landscape seemed to be turning before his eyes.

Augustine had a little feeling back by this time, enough that he could roll on his side and puke.

"You're looking much better," Wolf stated dryly. "As in, not dead."

Augustine groaned, then realizing he had managed to make a sound, tried to speak.

"Y've" Augustine said. What he was trying to say was, "You've got to let me go so I can warn the queen her life is in imminent danger!" Unfortunately, "Y've" was all he could manage at the moment.

"Don't speak," Faruk ordered. "Rest. I'll carry you."

Then Augustine realized he was being lifted again. Faruk managed to get Augustine up into the saddle on his own horse and climbed up behind him.

Then, they continued riding into the night for a long time. Faruk rode with one arm around Augustine to keep him from falling off.

While it was preferable to being draped over the saddle on his stomach, Augustine was still assaulted by millions of little pins every time the horse took a step.

They continued for several hours through the hill country until they found a little grove of trees. Wolf ordered Faruk to halt.

The giant lay Augustine on the ground and then made a bed for him with a blanket and the canvas he had used to transport him. When Augustine settled comfortably, Wolf stooped down beside him.

"How are you feeling, kid?" he asked.

"I'd-ah-go!" Augustine tried, thrashing a little.

"Stop that," Faruk ordered, pointing a commanding figure at Augustine. "Lie still."

"Faruk's right, Augustine," Wolf nodded. "You look awful. Get some rest."

He stood and, going to Faruk, said, "I can't sleep. I'm going to ride for a while to make sure we are secure. Take care of him. I'll be back by dawn."

Faruk responded with a nod and Wolf was gone.

Augustine lay quiet for a moment, drowning in frustration. Now it was not only Wolf holding him captive but the entire universe. He looked over and saw Fotia standing next to Faruk's horse. The moment he could move, he was going to take her and go.

If Faruk tried to stop him he would fight to the death.

Now the prickling feeling in his neck felt more like a burning. His muscles ached, his head pounded. He had no idea what time it was but the sky was slowly brightening. He probably didn't have more than twelve hours to get to Lysandria before Amira's assassin made her move.

LINA COULDN'T SLEEP. She was camping in the forest a short distance from the road. Supposedly, they were within a day's journey of Lysandria. It was killing her how close they were. She was exhausted, but she just wanted to continue their journey. Oswald was lying a short distance away, sound asleep. At least one of them would be well rested in the morning.

A rustling in the trees snatched her attention. As she turned to look, she could have sworn she saw Wolf out of the corner of her eye. Now she knew she was going crazy because when she looked through the tree line she saw only shrubs, branches, and yawning darkness.

Still... it couldn't hurt to have a look around. She got up and moved a few paces from the camp scanning the woods apprehensively.

"Is someone there?" she asked.

The breeze rustling in the branches was the only answer she received. She must have been more exhausted than she realized. Sighing she returned to her place, lay back down, and drifted into a fretful sleep.

47

EVERYTHING IS AWFUL AND THEN
IT STARTS TO RAIN

A s the rest of the night dragged by, Augustine hoped and
prayed and longed for the feeling to return completely.
When it finally did, he wished it hadn't. The pounding in
his head and the pain in his muscles had increased tenfold. The
wound in his throat was screaming.

Despite his pain and anxiety, he must have drifted off to sleep
because when he woke, the sun was well above the horizon and he
heard Wolf talking to Faruk.

"You'll never believe who I saw camping in the woods last night,"
Wolf was saying.

Augustine didn't wait to hear who it was. He leapt to his feet and
immediately crumpled back down.

"Kid," Faruk growled. "Don't do that. You're hurt."

Augustine sat for a moment with his head in his hands and his
eyes slammed shut, waiting for the scenery to stop spinning.

"I have to go," he said.

"No, you have to sleep," Faruk ordered.

Augustine looked up from his hands to see his two captors sitting
on the hillside, eating a breakfast of biscuits and dried meat.

"Wolf," Augustine pleaded. "You have to let me go."

"Patience," Wolf yawned, he glanced up at the sun and said. "Amira and your uncle are probably meeting as we speak and without my help, I'll wager this will end in the king's favor."

"Amira has an assassin in the palace," Augustine blurted. "She is going to kill the queen and her children tonight unless I can warn them."

"That's just politics, kid," Wolf shrugged.

"*Politics?*" Augustine cried. "Killing children is politics?"

"Who is killing children?" Faruk asked.

"*Amira's assassin,*" was Augustine's exasperated reply. He then told them what he had overheard in her tent.

Wolf became very quiet. Augustine could see him thinking as he stared up at the sky.

"You dreamed it," Faruk offered.

"I did not," Augustine objected. "Why do you think she's had you running across the world murdering Justin's sons? She wants to make sure Prince Tarik is the last person with any claim to the throne."

"How old are Alexander's children?" Wolf asked thoughtfully.

"The oldest is seven, the youngest is only a baby."

"That's unfortunate," Wolf responded thoughtfully. "But even if I was willing to let you go, you're in no position to go to Lysandria. It's more than a half day's journey from here and you can hardly stand."

"Then you go, or Faruk," Augustine pleaded.

"Not a chance," Wolf replied. "Amira has people all over that city, if one of them stops either of us after what we did yesterday, we're finished. Do you have any idea how much I've risked for you?"

"Then I have to try," Augustine insisted, stumbling to his feet. He doubled over clutching his stomach for a moment, waiting for a wave of dizziness to pass. Why was it taking so long for him to recover? It didn't take this long the last time Wolf used the venom. Then again, last time he didn't have a slash across his throat and he hadn't spent the entire night being tossed around by a well-meaning giant.

"You're still my prisoner, you know," Wolf reminded.

"I swear to you," Augustine said, straightening up. "If you let me deliver this warning I will come back. You *will* get your ransom."

Wolf furrowed his brow, then said, "Faruk, I'll be back in a few moments. Tie him up if you have to but make sure he doesn't leave."

The moment he was gone, Augustine used every measure at his disposal to attempt escape. First, he tried to fight, which was ridiculous in his condition. Faruk had pinned him down immediately and then tied him hand and foot.

Then, Augustine tried reasoning with Faruk and even bribing him, in response to everything, Faruk just said, "You can't go. You're hurt. You'll kill yourself."

Augustine kept trying. He was going to fight with all his strength until he ran out of time. King Alexander had given everything to rescue his people and Augustine wasn't going to lie idly and let Kalathea fall into the hands of another tyrant. And fight he did, much to Faruk's annoyance.

The giant kept trying to cover him with a blanket and then force-feed him, but Augustine kept thrashing and rolling in a vain attempt to escape.

Then something happened that was simultaneously hopeful and horrible. Wolf returned holding Lina at knife-point. He had her sitting on Symeon in front of him, while he held his dagger in one hand and the reins in the other.

Her jaw dropped when she saw Augustine. "What did you do to him?" she cried.

"I kept him alive," Wolf answered.

"By cutting his throat?" Lina exclaimed.

"Yes, actually. It's a long story." He looked at Augustine and added, "Now that I know you'll return, you may go and rescue those little cousins of yours."

"He can't go," Faruk objected. "He'll kill himself."

Wolf looked back over his shoulder, rolled his eyes, and called out, "That's too close, Blondie! Do you want me to cut her head off?"

"Is Oswald with you?" Augustine cried.

"Unfortunately," Wolf sighed. "I can't get him to stop following me."

"He won't hurt you, Lina," Augustine assured her.

"I know," Lina answered, then she looked back and shouted, "He's all talk, Oswald! Saint Wolfy doesn't kill women."

"Where'd you hear that one?" Wolf asked.

"From your lady friend," Lina hissed.

"Slight correction," Wolf continued. "I don't kill children, women... eh, maybe I'll make an exception for you Miss Miracle." Wolf looked at Faruk. "Set Augustine free, he's got a long ride ahead of him."

"*No!*" Faruk growled. "He'll kill himself!"

"He's right," Lina agreed, fixing her eyes on Augustine. "He can't go anywhere after what you've done to him. Whatever this is, Oswald can do it. Send him!"

By now, Augustine could see Oswald at the top of the hill a fair distance behind Wolf.

"Oswald doesn't speak the language," Augustine asserted. "But he can help me."

He looked at Faruk. "Oswald will keep me safe. He'll help me reach Lysandria safely."

Faruk glared at him. "If he doesn't, I'll kill him."

He cut Augustine's bonds.

Augustine looked up into the giant's brown eyes. "Look after Lina," he ordered.

Faruk nodded.

As Augustine staggered to his feet, he noticed Lina studying him, looking from his face to the wound on his neck and back up again, trying to assess his situation as best she could from where she was.

"Augustine, whatever this is, it can wait," she said.

"There's a plot to kill Queen Ilona and her children," Augustine said. "I'll explain ever–"

"Then go," Lina interrupted.

Augustine smiled and left her without a word. He had to keep himself from running to Fotia. His legs were very unsteady, if he ran he might fall over and Faruk would probably change his mind and hold him hostage. Then Oswald would have to deliver the message in Kaltic or his terrible, terrible Latin and hope someone understood.

He struggled onto Fotia's back. Once seated, he slammed his eyes shut allowing the dizziness to pass. When Augustine felt his head clear he turned his horse toward Oswald and trotted forward.

"Good heavens, what happened to you!" Oswald cried, as he approached.

"Long story," Augustine said, halting briefly. "I need you to come with me to Lysandria, before the Anamians assassinate our uncle's family, understand?"

"What?" Oswald exclaimed. "You're just going to leave Lina with–"

"Faruk will take care of her," Augustine remarked. "Just follow me and make sure I get to the city."

"But–" Oswald started, with a look of complete bewilderment.

Augustine urged Fotia forward. He didn't have time to argue with Oswald; it was already past noon and he had to keep moving. Lina would send Oswald along soon.

It was strange, there was a time it would have been torture to leave Lina with Wolf. Now, knowing Wolf a little better, he didn't expect him to lay a hand on her. The assassin considered himself a moral man. All he wanted was money to fund his work, and to him, Lina was just a guarantee that he would get it. He wouldn't harm her, especially since Augustine planned to make good on his word. He was going to deliver his warning and come right back.

As Augustine rode, he slumped forward over Fotia's neck, holding on with his knees and his hands, tangling his fingers in the poor animal's mane. It wasn't something he would normally do, but her every movement sent jolts of pain through his body.

As he continued, desperately clinging onto the animal, he noticed dark clouds gathering above him. His homeland was in danger, he felt like he was barely alive, and now it was going to rain.

When the droplets finally started to fall, he sighed. How could things possibly get any worse? He probably shouldn't have asked the question, because he got an answer in short order.

As Fotia was galloping through the downpour, already cold and on edge, a thunderclap startled her. She reared sending her rider flying through the air. He crashed down hard on the muddy road.

Augustine struggled to his feet, wincing as he felt a sharp pain in his side. Fotia was galloping back the way they came in a panic, ignoring his calls. He could only look helplessly after her, as she disappeared into the downpour.

He was wounded, trembling, and dizzy. How could he possibly reach the city in time on foot? If he didn't, not only would his uncle's family die but, there was a real possibility his homeland would fall into the hands of another tyrant. The memories of the fear and hunger that plagued his early life flashed in his mind. It wouldn't happen again—not when he could stop it. He breathed deeply, swallowing his pain, and started running down the road in the direction of the city.

As he ran, he kept looking over his shoulder, hoping to see Oswald catching up to him. After several long minutes, he noticed a hooded figure coming up the road toward him. It couldn't have been Oswald though, because the stranger was coming from the wrong direction.

Still, hope swelled in his chest. Whoever it was would probably help him. As Augustine stopped to call to the man, a wave of pain and dizziness hit him. He stumbled down into the mud, catching himself on his hands and knees.

Augustine heard the stranger's boots splash down as he dismounted, then, a hurried sloshing as he made his way toward him through the muck. The stranger took his arm and helped him to his feet.

Augustine, still dizzy and slightly nauseous, kept his head bent toward the road and his eyes slammed shut as stood.

"Thank you," he finally managed.

At the sound of his voice, the stranger stiffened and jerked backward.

"*You,*" the man breathed.

Augustine's gaze snapped to the man's face—it was Mill.

"No," Mill mumbled. "No, you can't be here. You're dead. Wolf killed you. He..."

The terror in his expression contorted into rage. His hand flashed down to the knife on his belt. Augustine flew forward, catching his wrist before he had a chance to throw it.

"You're dead!" Mill cried as he struggled to free his hand from Augustine's grip. "Dead!"

Augustine swore in his mind as he tried to twist the blade out of his enemy's hand. He didn't have time for this, but he couldn't run away or he'd end up with the knife in his back.

If he was going to stop Amira, he had to either disarm Mill or incapacitate him. Augustine jerked his arm, pulling his enemy forward, and struck him hard on the side of the head with his free hand.

Mill fell but continued gripping the blade. Not daring to give him a chance to throw it, Augustine fell upon him again, pinning him down with his body weight while he tried to pry the knife free.

Augustine's hands trembled violently as he fought his enemy's grip. Mill's cold blue eyes bore into him as they struggled, burning with a loathing only blood could satisfy.

"You don't get to live," he hissed. (His wrist was trembling now, any minute he would drop his weapon.) "You don't get to live when she didn't."

Though pain radiated through his entire body, Augustine fought with all remaining strength. *Why wouldn't he drop it? How was he so strong?*

In truth, it wasn't Mill's strength that made the task difficult. It was Augustine's weakness. The viper venom, the wound on his throat, and exhaustion from his sleepless night were taking their toll. Still, he fought. Innocent lives were in danger, *his people were in danger*. He would fight to the death to protect them if he had to.

He tried to deal Mill another blow to the head hoping to knock him out, but as he brought his fist back to strike, his opponent jerked his wrist hard, freeing it from his opposite hand. The sudden movement sent a wave of pain and dizziness through Augustine's body. He fell down sideways, clasping his head.

Mill had just enough time to roll away and stumble to his feet before Augustine was back on his own. They were now standing about three arm's lengths apart. Augustine kept his gaze fixed on the knife his enemy clutched, waiting for him to raise it. If he could make his move right before the throw, he could take Mill down again.

But the moment Augustine was waiting for never came. The sound of thundering hooves and the stern warning of a strong voice stole Mill's attention.

"Back!" Oswald cried, as charged toward them sword in hand, ready to strike. Mill fled to his horse and leapt into the saddle. He hesitated long enough to send Augustine a loathing glance, but seeing Oswald was nearly upon him, he decided to urge his horse forward and make his escape.

"Leave him," Augustine cried, as he saw his cousin looking after Mill. "Nothing matters but Lysandria!"

Oswald obeyed, stopping his horse by his cousin's side.

"Are you hurt?" Oswald asked as Augustine fell forward onto his knees. Under the circumstances, it was a stupid question.

"No," Augustine groaned, which under the circumstances, was a stupid answer.

"Where's your horse?" Oswald pressed.

Augustine had no idea, he looked around but couldn't see her anywhere.

"She's probably wandering back to Wolf," Augustine breathed. "Take me on yours."

Oswald helped Augustine up into the saddle and then climbed up behind him.

"You need a doctor," he said, as they started toward Lysandria.

Augustine shook his head. "I'll deliver this message, then go back and save Lina."

"Are you insane?" Oswald argued. "You'll deliver this message, then *I'll* rescue Lina."

Augustine was too tired to argue. He closed his eyes, clenching his jaw as he was jolted around in the saddle. He couldn't remember much about the hours that followed. He was vaguely aware of seeing the lights of Lysandria from a hilltop somewhere.

Then he remembered Oswald calling out to the watchmen on the wall.

"I am Prince Oswald of Kaltehafen," he cried. "This is Prince Augustine of Kaltehafen, he needs help."

"I don't understand you," one of the watchmen called back. "Do you speak Latin?"

At those words, Augustine snapped awake just enough to call to the watchman in his native tongue.

"I am Augustine Hatsi, stepson of King Florian the Kalt. Queen Ilona's life is in danger!"

He opened his eyes a little, enough that he could see the watchman disappear from his perch atop the gate.

A few moments later, Augustine found himself lying on the floor in the guard house, staring up into the faces of Oswald and two watchmen.

Everything that happened next was a blur. He knew that he delivered his message and that it caused a great deal of excitement, but he couldn't remember the exact words he used. All he knew was that his message had been received. With that knowledge, he slipped out of consciousness.

48

VENGEANCE

When Augustine had left, Oswald didn't immediately follow. First he tried to continue toward Lina. But after much urging on her part, and an explanation from Wolf about the imminent threat to the queen, Oswald reluctantly turned and rode after his cousin.

Once he was safely out of sight, Wolf lowered his blade and had Lina sit down on a large boulder while he cleaned up camp.

"We need to move," Wolf explained. "In case either of those two decide to bring an army back."

"An army to capture two highwaymen?" Lina stated. "Don't flatter yourself."

Wolf only grinned in response.

"Perhaps, Your Holiness," Lina scowled. "You would like to explain to me why the man I love is running around with his throat slashed."

"Because I was careful to avoid cutting anything important," Wolf boasted.

Lina was not amused. "If you do not explain everything immediately," she hissed, "I will become the most difficult hostage you've ever had to deal with."

"Well, we wouldn't want that," Wolf chuckled. "As you wish."

He proceeded to tell Lina everything, about how Amira hired him to kill all of Prince Justin's sons and how he saved Augustine for last since he lived halfway across the world. He told her how Augustine saved his company from Jace and Acacia.

"I thought traveling for months with someone would make me *want* to kill them more," Wolf finished as he lifted Lina into Symeon's saddle. "But... well I know it's unprofessional, but I got attached. And I was in his debt after he saved me, what was I supposed to do?"

The sky was gray by the time they left the campsite and Lina could feel the occasional droplet.

Wolf finished his story as they started riding, telling her how they faked Augustine's death and smuggled him away from Amira's camp. It made Lina wish she had never suggested using the venom on Augustine.

They came to the top of a hill and Lina could see the road to Lysandria in the distance. Beyond it was the forest where she had camped with Oswald the night before. All Lina could think about as they descended the hill toward the road was all the lasting effects the venom might have. Tremors, numbness, a permanent tick... she continued the list in her mind while simultaneously reminding herself that Augustine was young and strong and would probably make a full recovery.

By the time they reached the road the rain was pouring down, drenching the little party through their cloaks and hoods.

"I don't suppose you saw any kind of shelter when you were here last night?" Wolf asked Lina casually.

Before Lina could answer, Faruk said, "look there."

Lina and Wolf both looked down the road and saw at a distance a hooded figure on horseback coming in their direction.

"Come on," Wolf urged, spurring Symeon forward into the trees. "We don't want any trouble."

They left the road and ventured into the woods. The forest canopy provided some relief from the downpour but they were still soaked and freezing. Wolf kept looking for a cave or house or some form of shelter, but in the end, he gave up and had Faruk help him stretch a canvas between a couple of trees to make a tent.

"Do you know how often it rains in Kalathea?" Wolf complained, as he tightened one of the ropes.

"Never," Lina answered dryly, as she took her seat below the makeshift roof. "It's a perfect sunny paradise *all the time.*"

"Sounds like Augustine's been lying to you," Wolf smirked.

"He's prone to exaggeration," Lina commented. She pulled her soaking cloak around her and then questioned why she even bothered.

"I'm sure he also told you that the scorpions are elephant-sized and that every single Kalathean is a philosopher," Wolf quipped.

Lina smiled very slightly. She had to admit, Wolf knew Augustine well.

"Many of the greatest philosophers are Kalatheans," Faruk mumbled.

Wolf shot him a sideways look and raised an eyebrow. "Since when have you–" he stopped abruptly, his attention stolen by the sound of twigs snapping in the direction they had come.

The cloaked rider from the road was approaching. As his horse lumbered forward, Lina noticed a second riderless horse following behind. Her heart started pounding when she realized it was a copper bay, exactly like the horse Augustine took when he left.

"Hello!" Wolf called, stepping forward to face the man. His tone was friendly but his manner was tense. He wanted to get rid of the intruder.

The person removed his hood. Lina immediately recognized Wolf's third companion—Mill.

She glanced at Wolf and then Faruk, and from their expressions immediately determined that Mill had been deliberately excluded from their most recent scheme.

Mill's cold blue eyes were drilling into Wolf, burning with disdain.

"You lost a horse," he stated, holding aloft the reins of the bay.

"I've been looking everywhere for her," Wolf said. "Thank you, Mill."

"I know who took her," Mill offered.

A tense silence passed before Wolf fabricated a laugh and said, "Well, are you going to tell me who or not?"

"I think you already know," Mill seethed. "I've been thinking about it ever since I saw him lying in the road with that ugly wound across his throat."

Lina felt herself stiffen, *lying in the road?* Had he fallen? Was Oswald there with him?

"You're a trained killer, Wolfy." Mill was shaking with fury now. *"You don't make mistakes."*

He looked at Faruk briefly and then rested his gaze on Lina for a moment.

"You let him go," Mill accused.

Wolf, realizing he was caught, dropped the ruse with a sigh. "He saved us, Mill. I was in his debt. You got your pay, let's forget the whole thing and go home."

Mill removed a coin pouch from his belt and flung it at Wolf's feet.

"I don't do this for the money, Wolf!" he cried. "I do this because Prince Justin's horde burned my home and killed my wife while my lord cowered behind his walls!" His cheeks flushed with rage. "I do this to see Justin's blood spilled over and over again as each of his filthy children dies!"

Wolf rested his hand on the hilt of his dagger. "We've avenged her, Mill," he insisted gently. "Many times over. How much blood will it take to satisfy you?"

Lina stood perfectly still as she watched the exchange. Her instincts told her to avoid drawing attention to herself. Though she was frozen in place, she wasn't feeling fear. She was feeling pity. Mill's pain was enough to make anyone lose their sanity. She had seen some of her own patients lose themselves completely over less.

She wished she could do something to help him but unfortunately, grief wasn't something that could be treated easily in the best of circumstances and it couldn't be treated at all when the patient was uncooperative.

Mill didn't answer Wolf's question. Instead he glanced at Lina. The corner of his lip turned upward into a sly smile as the fury melted from his face. An unsettling calm overtook him as his frigid stare bore into her.

Lina noticed Wolf's hand slip down and grip the hilt of his blade.

"This is better actually," Mill realized. "If Augustine is going to live, he can live with my pain."

Then two things happened almost simultaneously. Wolf lunged at Mill as the latter snatched something from his belt and hurled it at Lina.

The item Mill threw slammed into Lina's chest, knocking the wind out of her. She fell to her knees and then doubled over, flinging her arms out to catch herself before she hit the ground. She remained frozen on her hands and knees for a second in shock, trying to make sense of things.

Mill released a horrible cry and a second later, Lina heard him fall into the brush. After that, the wood fell silent save for the pattering of raindrops on the canopy.

Lina felt something slip from her chest and land on the forest floor with a gentle thump. She stared at it for a long moment before she understood. It was a little throwing knife, its blade crimson with blood. Lina inhaled sharply, triggering a deep pain that radiated out across her chest. Then, crumpling onto her side, she lay curled up on the ground with her hands pressed tightly over the wound.

That's when Wolf finally broke the silence. He swore.

49

HIS STEPFATHER'S SON

"L*ina*," was the first word on Augustine's lips as he drifted back into consciousness. Before he knew where he was or what had happened, he got a sense that she was in some kind of trouble. When he finally opened his eyes the memories came flooding back.

He found himself lying in the most comfortable bed in the universe. He wasn't sure if this was an objective fact, or if he would have thought the same of any bed after being dragged around in the wilderness for months. If he hadn't been so eager to rescue Lina, he would have been content to lay there forever.

He was in a room constructed of marble and cedar, portioned off from some larger space with richly embroidered curtains. The surroundings were so strangely familiar... he felt like he had seen the room before but couldn't attach it to any specific memory.

Such a room could only be in the Lysandrian palace. Ilona, at least, must have survived the night. If Amira's people were in power, someone would have killed him by now. The queen was safe, he had accomplished his mission. It was time to go rescue Lina.

He tried to jump out of bed but immediately fell backward with a groan. While very sore, he wasn't as sore as he had been the prior morning. His wounds were washed and bandaged. He was probably fine. Rescuing Lina wouldn't be a problem, he just had to move more slowly.

He coughed. It was one of those horrible rattling coughs that shook his whole body. He must have caught a cold from riding through the downpour, another minor inconvenience.

He sat up ignoring the aches and pains, swung his legs over the side of the bed, and carefully rose to his feet pausing a moment to let his head stop spinning. He put all his focus on Lina hoping the thought of her would give him the strength he needed to attempt a rescue.

As he took a step forward, a thin man in the long blue robe of a Kalathean physician popped through the curtain.

"Lie back down, Your Highness," the doctor ordered. "You've been badly wounded."

"I have to save, Lina," Augustine croaked. He grimaced at the raspy sound of his own voice.

"You're in no condition to rescue anyone," the doctor objected. "You need to rest."

The doctor, commanding him to stay in that little room, ignited a flame of indignation. For months other people had told him where he could and could not go. They'd controlled him, restrained him, treated him like an animal.

He tried to brush past the man but the doctor caught him by the shoulders. He was elderly and very thin. Under normal circumstances, Augustine could have forced past him in a moment, but in his weakened condition, they were evenly matched.

"I have to save, Lina! Wolf has Lina!" Augustine insisted.

"We know," the doctor replied, struggling to push Augustine back to his bed. "Prince Oswald explained everything, the queen is sending people for her."

Augustine ignored this assurance. The harder the man tried to restrain him, the more he fought to escape. He didn't want to hurt the old man, but he *needed* to escape him.

Finally, the physician's assistants rushed to his aid and managed to return their rebellious patient to his bed.

He lay there for a moment, under the watchful eyes of his healers, trying to recover from a coughing fit. Then he tried to escape all over again.

The old doctor stepped away through the curtain while his younger assistants struggled to keep Augustine still. A few moments later, the doctor returned with the queen, herself, in tow.

"Lie still!" she ordered, thrusting a commanding finger at Augustine.

He ceased struggling immediately and regarded his aunt. She stood with her head high and her shoulders back and spoke with such authority, Augustine obeyed unconsciously.

"You've got to let me go," he pleaded. "Lina is–"

"I know," Ilona interrupted. "Oswald told me everything."

"Then you know why–"

"If you think a wounded, sickly, squire is more capable of rescuing her than thirty of Kalathea's best, you insult me and your entire homeland." Ilona rubbed her forehead with an exasperated sigh. "You really are your stepfather's son. You think the world can't spin unless you're turning it!"

She had a point but it did not sit well with him. His cheeks reddened and he cried, "I am not your captive and you cannot hold me here!"

The moment those words had left him he went utterly silent, alarmed by his own disrespect.

The irritation melted away from Ilona's expression.

"You're not a prisoner, Augustine," she assured him.

With those words, Augustine understood why he had been so combative. Of course the queen's men were more equipped to rescue Lina, but his struggle to escape wasn't just about her.

"I'm so sorry," Augustine mumbled, going pale with embarrassment. "You're right."

Ilona pulled a chair to the side of his bed, seated herself there and gave Augustine's hand a squeeze.

"You saved my children," she smiled. "I think I can forgive you for being a little irritable."

"Did you catch the assassin?" Augustine asked.

Ilona nodded. "She was a maid of mine, who had been in my service for years. I wouldn't have suspected her for a moment. If you hadn't warned me..." Ilona breathed deeply. "When the watchmen brought me your warning, I took the children from the nursery myself and hid them in another part of the palace. Then the guards concealed themselves in the nursery and waited to see who would come. They caught my maid armed and ready to carry out Amira's orders."

"What about the king?" Augustine pressed.

"He's alright," Ilona answered.

"He's returned then?"

"No, I haven't heard a word from him," Ilona shrugged. "But someone or other is always trying to kill him. He'll be back before dark."

Augustine managed a slight smile, but it quickly faded as the reality of his situation hit him. He was doomed to spend the next few hours lying around while other people rescued the woman he loved. The most evil man in the universe couldn't have invented a more perfect form of torture.

50

FARUK SPEAKS

Lina had a serious problem—she didn't have any vinegar. She also had no idea if her idiot captors had any idea how to treat a stab wound and she couldn't explain it to them because she could hardly breathe, let alone talk.

Even she, an experienced healer, would have struggled to treat a patient under these conditions. Without vinegar or wine or something of that nature, she couldn't clean the wound. They didn't have any proper bandages, and all available fabric was wet and muddy.

Faruk was pressing a wad of cloth over her chest in an attempt to stop the bleeding. Even if he managed to do so, she would probably die of fever in a couple of days.

She hoped she could at least survive long enough to tell Augustine it was Mill that threw the knife and not Wolf. Otherwise, Augustine would take her death personally and waste his life hunting down Wolf on some idiotic quest for vengeance.

She actually felt sorry for Wolf. He was kneeling beside her opposite Faruk assuring her over and over again that she was going to be alright. His expression said quite the contrary. He was forcing a slight smile, but his eyes betrayed the truth. He was seconds from completely falling apart. Calm, cool, sainted Wolf, who was always one step ahead of everyone, was desperately searching his mind for options. The fact that he had just killed a former friend in a vain attempt to defend her, only aggravated his condition.

Faruk had Wolf hold the cloth while he cut the rest of his cloak into long strips. Then, with Wolf's help, he lifted Lina off the ground just enough to wrap the strips around her. The man clearly had no idea how to properly apply bandages, he was tying them much too tight. Whatever blood they contained was going to stagnate.

By the time they laid Lina back down on the ground, she was feeling very lightheaded.

Her eyes began to close but Wolf tapped on her cheek.

"Keep your eyes open, Lina," he ordered. "Look at me."

Lina guessed he was only doing that because he didn't know what else to do. Faruk, on the other hand, must have realized he'd done everything he could. He sat back regarding Lina for a long time through his dark, thoughtful eyes. At last, he turned to Wolf and said, "I'm taking her back."

"Back where?" Wolf snapped.

"To Augustine," Faruk answered.

"He's in Lysandria, Faruk. You'll be arrested."

"*I'm taking her back,*" the giant repeated.

"They'll kill you, Faruk," Wolf hissed.

"So be it," Faruk's voice boomed.

Wolf went utterly silent, he stared at Faruk with eyebrows raised in alarm.

"You told me..." Faruk continued, bringing his voice down so he was barely speaking above a mumble. "You told me you only hurt people who were a danger to others. Warriors and nobles and people who abused the vulnerable... Not only is this girl innocent of such crimes, she lives to heal. She helped all those people back in Dobze and never harmed a soul. If she dies, all the people she could have helped die with her."

"I never would have harmed her, Faruk!" Wolf exclaimed. "You know that!"

"*But we did,*" Faruk retorted. "I'm taking her back. If you're the saint they say you are, you'll come with me. If they kill us, we deserve it."

Wolf's fragile facade was crumbling, he trembled visibly. He looked around as if the trees or the rain would bring some brilliant solution to mind. Then he forced a laugh.

"You've really thought a lot about this... haven't you, Faruk?" he grinned. "If you want to throw your life away, that's your business! But I've got people who need me."

"You're a coward," Faruk accused.

Wolf's gaze dropped to the ground. *"Maybe... maybe..."* he mumbled under his breath.

Lina couldn't be sure if he was speaking to himself or to Faruk. Still trembling, he began to gather up his things.

"If you're going to Lysandria, I see no point in staying here," Wolf answered.

"Where are you going?"

"You think I'd tell you right before you go marching into the arms of our enemies?"

Faruk didn't say anything in response. He just continued watching Wolf as he scurried around the little camp. When he had finished collecting his things, he wrapped up Mill's body in one of the blankets and had Faruk help him lay it over the back of his horse.

"I killed the idiot," Wolf grumbled. "The least I can do is find someplace to bury him properly."

The annoyance he forced into his voice, did nothing to mask his grief and anxiety. Calm, cool, suave, Wolfy the Saint was coming apart at the seams.

He tied Mill's horse into line behind his own. Then, right before climbing onto Symeon's back, he turned to Faruk.

"It occurs to me that young Augustine may be compelled by some strange sense of honor to return to me as promised," he said. "So if you see him, tell him that he'll never find me, even if he searches every corner of the Earth."

With that, he made off.

If Lina had been herself, she would have been disgusted with him. As it was, she wasn't feeling well enough to be disgusted with anyone. She had watched the entire conversation in a slight daze.

Faruk knelt back down beside her and said, "When the rain stops, I'll take you back. I don't want you getting cold."

He knew as well as she did there was no point in rushing her anywhere. There wasn't a village around for miles and carrying her off into the rain would do nothing except make both of them colder and wetter than they already were. She was at the mercy of her own body now. Either it would heal on its own, or she would die.

Faruk touched her cheek with the back of his hand. "You're already cold," he mumbled. Then, he searched among his things and on the backs of the two remaining horses for anything dry enough to use as a blanket.

When he couldn't find anything, he lifted her up into his arms and sat down under their canopy with his back against a tree holding her like she was a baby. She was probably warmer that way, but she couldn't remember.

As the night deepened and the rain pattered on the leaves, she had only fragmented memories that may just as well have been dreams.

She remembered Faruk speaking to her, reassuring her that he would take her back again and again. Then she remembered him mumbling rhythmically, like he was reciting a poem or saying a prayer. She couldn't understand him because he was speaking in a foreign language. She realized it was Arabic when he used the word *Allah*. Then again he was reassuring her, and then singing softly in Arabic.

Then, something happened she did not expect—she woke up the next morning.

THE SUN HAD BEEN UP for several hours when she came to. She was laying under the canopy carefully tucked in under a damp blanket and she felt... *better*. Not completely, her chest was still very sore and her head was still foggy.

She looked around trying to put things together. The rain had long stopped, but drops still fell from the leaves overhead. Faruk was walking around the camp, looking at the ground, and swearing under his breath. Some kind of an animal had gotten into his pack and strewn the contents everywhere.

Lina lifted her blanket and looked down at her chest. The bandages Faruk tightly applied the evening before were gone. She could see one of the strips of cloth through the trees at a distance, as if dragged away by some predatory creature.

What in the world had happened? Was she really awake or was this a fever dream? She didn't feel like she was dreaming. It all seemed so real. She lifted the collar of her dress so she could get a look at the wound itself.

The sight of it left her perplexed. It was mostly closed, dry, and slightly pink around the edges like it had been healing for several days instead of one night.

She pulled her head back above her blanket.

"Faruk?" she called. Speaking still hurt, but it was bearable.

The giant looked up at her in surprise and then ran to her side.

He didn't say anything, just looked at her and put the back of his hand against her cheek like he was trying to check for a fever.

"What happened?" Lina groaned.

"Something got into our camp while I was asleep," Faruk explained. "It..." He knit his brows as if he couldn't believe what he was about to say. "Tore off your bandages, then got into my pack and stole the biscuits."

Lina blinked. "What?"

"Nothing about this makes sense," was Faruk's exasperated response. "I was holding you all night, it didn't wake me. Why didn't it frighten the horses? And now you're alive? How?"

Faruk's logical mind was racing for solutions.

Lina looked around at the various items strewn about. It looked like the work of a bear, but as Faruk said, the animal hadn't frightened the horses.

"Did it leave any prints?" Lina asked.

"Deer prints," Faruk answered. "And look at this." He held up a biscuit with little nibble marks all over it.

"That does look like a deer," Lina shrugged.

"But why would a deer take your bandages off?"

The unanswered questions were breaking poor Faruk's quizzical mind. Lina had no idea. She was less interested in the deer thief and more curious about her miraculous healing. She asked Faruk if he had given her any medicine or done anything else to treat her. He hadn't. The inexplicable incident occupied the two scientific minds for a long time afterward.

51

FLORIAN'S FOOLISH PROMISE

Augustine was trying to behave himself almost as much as he was trying not to worry about Lina. He spent the first part of the day resting quietly. By the afternoon, he was feeling a little better and decided to try walking around.

He wasn't going to do anything stupid, at least, he hoped not. He was bored and wanted to tear his idle mind away from the woman he loved. There was a wide window in the wall next to his bed, he got up and, peering through it, got a sweeping view of the grounds in front of the palace. He looked out over the open space taking in the stone walkways, the statues, the fountains, and the emerald grass that filled the expanse between the palace itself and the outer wall.

Beyond the wall, he could see the city skyline and the top of the obelisk that stood in the center of the Forum of St. Valerian. To his right, he could see the cathedral with the front all covered in scaffolding. To his left, he could see the open sky where the amphitheater used to be.

Suddenly, the golden gate at the front of the grounds opened and a person rushed through it. Augustine knew immediately who it was by the armor he wore and the purple cloak that billowed behind him as he ran. It had to be King Alexander. The fact that he was racing across the grounds toward the palace led Augustine to the conclusion he had not been assassinated.

Servants and guards came pouring toward him from every direction. Augustine could hear the king speaking to them urgently but couldn't make out what he was saying. Then, Augustine saw three children running out from the palace toward the king. At the sight of them, the king forgot everyone else. He pushed through the crowd, and caught them in his arms, embracing them and kissing each one in turn.

While he was still fussing over his children, the queen approached holding a baby in her arms. Noticing the new arrivals, the king flew to them, threw his arms around them both, and after kissing the baby's head, he pressed his lips to the queen's.

Augustine was so busy watching the happy reunion, he didn't notice someone else rush in just behind Alexander. That person got swallowed up in the crowd and Augustine may not have noticed him at all if he hadn't marched up to the happily kissing couple, grabbed Ilona's shoulder, and started interrogating her in an all too familiar voice.

"Where is my son?"

Augustine was alarmed that he could make out the words from such a distance. Then again, even when Florian wasn't excited you could hear his voice from two rooms over. Augustine's mother complained about it regularly.

Ilona had hardly answered him, when Florian tore off into the palace. Augustine broke away from the window. His first instinct was to run down to meet his stepfather but a horrifying realization struck him—what if Florian didn't know?

Had Augustine's mother lied to him also? What would he do when he found out?

He stood frozen in place, imagining the worst possible reactions, his stepfather getting angry, disowning him and his mother. There was a time when he could never imagine Florian doing anything like that, but so much of his life had turned upside down and it seemed like everyone hated him now on account of Prince Justin.

The sound of hurried footsteps echoed from somewhere in the distance. Augustine jumped back into his bed and closed his eyes, pretending to be asleep. It would have been a true miracle for anyone to sleep in the same building with Florian running around in such an exasperated state.

He heard the curtain fly aside, followed by a couple of hurried footsteps.

"Aug–" Florian stopped himself. He must have believed his stepson's act and thought him asleep. Augustine knew it was a stupid deception, but he needed to buy himself enough time to think about how he could broach the horrible truth.

Florian was trying (and failing) to approach quietly. A chair scraped across the marble floor toward Augustine's bedside. After falling into it, Florian actually managed to stay silent for a moment. Then he sniffled and grumbled under his breath, *"they'll pay dearly for this."*

Augustine would have continued pretending to be asleep, but his stepfather reached over and squeezed his hand. It was doubtless meant to be a gentle act of affection, but at Florian's best he was about as gentle as a raging elephant.

"Ouch!" Augustine winced.

"Augustine," Florian blurted. "Did I wake you? I'm sorry!"

Augustine turned his head and looked up at his stepfather. He was very pale, his shoulders were slouched, and he had deep shadows under his eyes. His cheeks were streaked with tears.

"What did they do to you?" Florian demanded. Augustine realized he probably wasn't a pretty sight himself. Before he could answer the question, Florian said, "This is all my fault. I never stopped looking for you, not for a moment."

Looking at his stepfather, Augustine was tempted to take this literally.

Florian's head fell into his hands. "...And I still failed! I'm not worthy to be your father!"

"They–" Augustine started, but Florian was still talking.

"I'm a failure as a huntsman and a king and–"

"They used–" Augustine tried again.

"I should have warned you about Prince Justin's crimes," Florian continued. "Then maybe you would have known to be vigilant but–"

"They used magic, Father!" Augustine interrupted. "It isn't your fault. Wolf knew this enchantress who gave him...wait a moment, *you knew?*"

"About what?" Florian asked.

"About Prince Justin being my father?"

Anger flashed in Florian's eyes. "That animal isn't your father. If he *was* your father, he would have married your mother like he promised and raised you." Florian shook his head. "Throwing away your mother's love was the most foolish thing that scoundrel ever did!"

Augustine thought that the thousands of serfs whose homes Justin leveled would disagree. Still, it was a romantic sentiment on Florian's part and it brought Augustine great relief. Apparently, his stepfather was in the same category as Lina, the category of things in his life that hadn't completely turned upside down. Florian, for better or for worse, was still Florian.

Augustine's relief was suddenly replaced by a tiny prick of resentment.

"How long have you known?" he asked.

Florian went silent. He wasn't good at hiding his emotions and Augustine could see his guilt plainly as he desperately searched for words.

"I've known since I proposed to your mother," Florian admitted.

Augustine glared at the ceiling. "She told you all those years ago," he grumbled. "And she never told me."

"You must not hold that against her," Florian ordered. "She did it to protect you and...well it's my fault really."

Augustine glanced sideways at his stepfather and was surprised when he found himself trying to conceal a smile. Amusement was the last thing he expected to feel but the moment Florian claimed fault for the long buried secret, the words of Augustine's aunt popped into his mind. What was it she said? It was something about Florian thinking the world wouldn't spin unless he was turning it? Of course he thought *he* was somehow responsible.

"How is it your fault?" Augustine asked, biting his lip slightly.

"You see... well... it happened like this," Florian explained. "When I proposed to your mother she burst into tears, not happy tears, no. She was very upset. I thought at first it was because I was about to go away on a mission to find that fairy fellow and save your uncle's life but that wasn't it at all! Before I could ask her what was wrong, she said, 'you don't know what I've done. You would never love me if you knew.'

"Then I took her in my arms and said, 'Damara, you couldn't have done anything so horrible it would shake my love for you!'"

Augustine knew his stepfather well enough to know that this retelling was likely embellished in such a way as to make him seem like some kind of romantic demigod and his mother Aphrodite. Florian was incapable of speaking about his relationship with Damara in any other way.

"When your mother told me about her love affair with Prince Justin, I was furious. I swear if that scoundrel wasn't already dead, I'd have hunted him down and killed him myself."

"You and everyone else," Augustine murmured.

Florian was so angry at the very memory of Justin, he didn't hear Augustine's comment and continued his own story.

"Then I made a very foolish promise," Florian continued. "I kissed your mother and swore to her that she would never have to think about that devil again." The anger melted from his face and was replaced by the guilt of a man who was singularly responsible for all the world's horrors. "There were times when I thought we should tell you but whenever I thought of mentioning it to your mother I remembered her tears and my own foolish promise..."

That was when Augustine realized he couldn't hold a grudge against his stepfather. It was partly because Florian was angry enough at himself for both of them and partly because Augustine was just so happy to be back in his company.

Though so much of what Augustine believed to be true had

changed, water was still wet, the sky was still blue, and Florian still loved him like he was his own son.

"Your mother is on her way here now," Florian said.

"She is?" Augustine asked, suddenly overrun with a whirlwind of emotions.

"She's still a few weeks away," his stepfather explained. "She came to the same conclusion I did, that the best hope of finding you was in Lysandria."

Florian's gaze dropped to the floor and he tapped his thumbs together nervously. "I'm glad she won't be here for a while, I'm not ready to face her after failing you so miserably."

Augustine thought now would be a good time to explain to Florian about Mirella's magic and how Wolf used it to cover his trail. Florian was both horrified and greatly relieved he hadn't completely failed as a huntsman.

"It doesn't matter," Florian asserted. "Even when I failed you, I never lost hope. I knew that you would escape because you are just like your mother—brave, resourceful, and strong." Florian beamed proudly at Augustine. "And I was right!"

52

FARUK SPEAKS AGAIN
(THIS TIME IN PERFECT GREEK)

"How are you?" Oswald asked.

It was the afternoon now, and Augustine had been trying his utmost not to think about Lina. Despite his best efforts, the second Oswald stepped into the room, he blurted out, "Is there any news of her?"

"No, and Aunt Ilona won't let me go after her!" Oswald fumed. "Something about, 'your father's sick with worry,' and 'if you vanish again on my watch, he'll kill me!'" Oswald rolled his eyes.

Augustine glared at the ceiling. "This waiting is torture," he grumbled. "I feel so–"

"Useless!" Oswald finished for him.

"Exactly!" Augustine agreed.

They shared in a moment of silent brooding, before Oswald said something that took Augustine completely by surprise.

"This is my fault," he mumbled.

Did Oswald just admit fault? Augustine still didn't know what his cousin was pleading guilty to, but that didn't matter. Oswald taking responsibility for anything was a miracle.

"I was supposed to protect her, but Wolf came so quietly," Oswald rambled. "I didn't even wake until I heard him dragging her away through the brambles."

Augustine didn't answer. There was a time when he would have eagerly affirmed Oswald's guilt, but after everything he'd been through he didn't think such an action would be productive. He also had failed to outsmart Wolf on numerous occasions, so who was he to judge?

They both fell into another moment of silent brooding and while they were thus engaged, the curtain that separated Augustine's room from the hall flew aside and in marched King Alexander, beaming like it was Christmas morning.

The first thing he did, to both cousins' alarm, was hug Oswald. Then turning toward Augustine, he gripped his hand and greeted him brightly with the words, "Welcome back to civilization!"

The two princes both stared at their uncle in shock.

Looking back and forth between the two of them, the king said, "You two saved my family, I am forever in your debt."

"You owe me nothing," Augustine corrected. "Since you saved mine first."

"So it's only Oswald, I owe?" Alexander grinned. "Now we're deeper in debt to the Kalts. The people will never forgive me!" He shrugged then added, "If either of you need anything at all, name it."

"Is there news–" Augustine started.

"Have you heard–" Oswald said at exactly the same time.

Then they both finished with the words, "about Lina!"

"Nothing more than what the queen's already told you," Alexander continued. "But I have complete confidence in my equestrians. She couldn't be in better hands."

When the king saw the disappointment on their faces, he added, "This waiting must be awful for you."

Their crestfallen expressions confirmed Alexander's suspicion.

"The watchmen at the northern gate will likely be the first to see them returning. Oswald, why don't you go and wait with them? At the first sign of my men, send someone back here to tell Augustine."

Oswald tore from the room.

Augustine knew better than to try to follow. The physician and his assistants were always nearby and seemed to have the power to materialize from thin air. There was something he wanted to ask his uncle about anyway.

"Uncle Alexander," Augustine started. Even though he'd called the king "uncle" for half of his life, the title suddenly brought an uncomfortable reality to the forefront of his mind.

The king smiled expectantly.

"There's something–" Augustine started but before he could proceed, their attention was captured by the sounds of a commotion rising up from the courtyard below the window.

"There they are!" Alexander announced.

Augustine half jumped, half fell out of bed, then sprang off the floor toward the window.

A dozen Kalathean riders were crossing the emerald grounds. In the very center of the group was Faruk. Lina was sitting sideways in the saddle in front of him, with her arms wrapped around his neck.

Augustine blinked wondering if he was delirious. What was Lina doing? Why was she riding with Faruk and why was she clinging to him like that?

At this point, nothing about Faruk surprised Augustine. If, during the one day he was with Lina, he had somehow won her undying love, Augustine wouldn't be able to do anything except shrug and congratulate him.

"Why don't I go see what's going on?" Alexander suggested. "I'll have someone report back, promptly."

Augustine nodded but did not move from the window.

THE SIZE of Lysandria might have completely amazed and overwhelmed Lina, if she had not been so focused on shielding Faruk from her rescuers.

That morning the Kalathean equestrians met them on the road to the capital city. Lina was still too weak to ride on her own, so she was sitting in front of Faruk when they spotted her. She had called out to them, trying to explain that Faruk had betrayed Wolf and saved her. Unfortunately, none of the Kalathean riders spoke Kaltic. They only saw a young woman crying out to them while being carried off somewhere by a giant.

They surrounded Faruk and started shouting at him. Lina, while she could read in Greek thanks to a lifetime of studying Hippocrates, couldn't understand it when it was spoken aloud.

Apparently, Faruk could understand the equestrians because he spoke to them in their own tongue. One of the riders cautiously brought his horse up beside Faruk's and tried to take Lina.

"I've told them you're injured," he explained to her. "This man is going to take you."

"Did you tell them that you saved me?" Lina asked. "And that you're taking me to Lysandria?"

Faruk didn't answer, he just dropped his gaze to the ground.

"I'm not going anywhere until you tell them you're innocent," Lina ordered.

"But I'm not," Faruk mumbled.

The rider beside Faruk said something kindly to Lina and tried to take her again. She gently pushed his hands away and, turning herself sideways in Faruk's saddle, she put her arms around his neck defensively.

She knew that if they took her they would arrest Faruk. He would probably be chained up and beaten and thrown into some awful dungeon to await execution.

"I'm not going to move until someone with authority promises me you won't be harmed," Lina explained.

Try as they might, neither Faruk nor the equestrians could get Lina to move. So the riders allowed her to stay where she was and surrounded Faruk while they all returned to the palace. She was on her guard the entire ride back, terrified to let go for a moment.

Lina looked around at the beautiful stone walkways, the emerald lawns, and the fountains that decorated the palace grounds. Augustine had described the place to her many times, but his descriptions didn't do it justice. (And she had always assumed he was exaggerating.) She had no idea such a colossal place could be built by the hands of men.

A group of guards came out from the palace to greet them and to these men, Lina called, "Does anyone here speak Kaltic?"

"I do," came a voice from somewhere near the back of the group.

The crowd parted respectfully revealing a man who looked exactly like Augustine. He was a little older, had a slimmer build, larger eyes, and a gentler manner. It was obvious by his attire and the way the people around him behaved that this was the king. It was also obvious to anyone with eyes that this man was a blood relative of Augustine's. It was amazing to Lina that Damara even bothered trying to hide the truth.

"Your Majesty," Lina said, still clinging to Faruk. "This man saved my life and I will not release him until you swear to me that no harm will come to him."

Faruk said something to Alexander in Greek, snapping the king's attention to him. His eyes widened in amazement as the giant continued. The king replied to Faruk with what seemed like a question.

They went back and forth a couple of times before the king returned his attention to Lina.

"This man just confessed to some very serious crimes," Alexander explained. "He seems to think he deserves to be punished."

"The man who deserves to be punished is making his escape as we speak," Lina objected.

The king asked Faruk something else and again marveled at the response he received.

"In all my life I have never heard such wisdom," he mumbled. Then, snapping himself from his trance, he looked at Lina and added, "I will thoroughly investigate this matter and until then, Faruk is under my protection. Do you find that agreeable?"

Lina released Faruk. "Thank you, Your Majesty."

53

BATTLE OF THE SAINTS

ugustine watched from the window as one of the palace guards took Lina from Faruk's horse and carried her into the palace. Why were they carrying her? Was she wounded somehow? He ducked through the curtain into the hall and would have run down to her had the doctor not caught him and sternly ordered him to lie down.

He returned to bed and lay staring vacantly at the ceiling as anxiety nibbled away at him. He was boiling hot, slightly dizzy, and still struggling through regular coughing fits. He had escaped Wolf only to have his own body hold him hostage. Did the whole universe hate him or something?

After what seemed like an eternity, but was actually only twenty minutes, news came to him from the mouth of Lina herself.

He heard her approaching from somewhere in the distance along with a small army of maidens who kept saying things like, "You're hurt, miss!" and "Come with us, miss!" and "Please stop running, miss, you've got a knife wound in your chest!"

Augustine sprang out of bed. *Did that maid say "knife wound"?*

He flew through the curtain and saw Lina scurrying away from the women. In response to them, she was saying, "I don't speak Greek! No Greek! I'm fine. *Augustine, Aw-gus-tin!* Where's Au–"

Noticing him, she ceased negotiating with her pursuers and flew into his arms. Augustine was so happy to see her, he forgot that he was trying to distance himself and received her in a tight embrace.

She was freezing cold, her clothing was soaked and she was all muddy. Augustine separated from her just enough to look her up and down. There was a thin tear in the front of her dress surrounded by a dark stain that expanded outward and covered her entire front.

"What happened?" he breathed, looking at the injury in horror.

Lina was regarding him with her brow furrowed, her hand resting on his cheek.

"You're burning up, Augustine," she remarked.

"You've got a knife wound in your chest!" he exclaimed.

"I knew I shouldn't have let you go riding through a downpour in your condition," she grumbled. "Latin or no Latin, Oswald could have handled it."

"But Lina, you–" he motioned to the blood on her dress.

"Back to bed, Augustine!" Lina ordered. "I didn't chase you halfway across the world so you could die of fever!"

"It's a fever, not a knife wound!" Augustine objected.

"Both can kill you, back to bed!" Lina demanded.

By now, the flock of maidens had caught up to Lina and were standing a short distance away, grumbling to each other and shooting the pair frustrated scowls.

"I'm alright, I promise," Augustine coughed. "But you're–"

"No, you're not." Lina scowled. "I swear you think you're immortal but you–"

"Tell me what happened to you and I will do anything you ask," Augustine argued.

"Do you promise?" Lina asked.

"I swear it," he answered.

Through Augustine, Lina told the maids that she would surrender to them peacefully after she had had a moment to speak to him. They reluctantly agreed, seeing that, despite appearances, she wasn't in immediate danger of death.

Augustine obediently tucked himself back in while Lina pulled a chair up beside his bed.

Now he was truly convinced that the universe had it out for him. Here Lina was, running all over the palace grounds with a gaping hole in her chest while he was confined to bed because of a few scrapes and a slight fever.

He should have been happy now that Lina was back safely, but hearing her story made him utterly nauseous. All he could think about, as she concluded her tale, was that if he hadn't let Mill go, she never would have been wounded in the first place.

"I don't know how I survived," Lina concluded. "When I woke, the wound was already healing, and by the time Faruk and I arrived at the palace I felt completely normal. No one believed me when I told them I could walk on my own."

"Did you say something got into the biscuits?" Augustine puzzled.

"Odd, isn't it?" Lina answered. "It removed my bandages without waking Faruk, and then pulled his things apart looking for scraps. It didn't touch the meat though."

Augustine's eyes widened and he broke into a broad grin. "That damn unicorn," he mumbled. Then he sprang out of his bed crying out. "That stupid, damn unicorn!"

Throwing the curtain aside, he called out to one of Lina's waiting maids. "Go at once to the kitchen and gather as many biscuits as you can."

"Your Highness?" the perplexed woman questioned.

"Then take that basket deep into the forest and leave it there," Augustine continued.

Before the confused maid could ask any more questions, he swung back through the curtain with the words, "I love you, Poly! You stupid, ugly goat!"

It was then that Augustine realized something. Unicorns were indeed sacred, magical, and deeply intelligent. There was no reason at all an animal couldn't be all of those things *and* also be a mangy, awkward, nibbling, bread-thief.

Lina was clearly troubled by Augustine's giddy outburst.

"That's delirium," she mumbled. "Augustine, in bed! Now!"

He obeyed without complaint. His excitement was wearing off now, leaving nothing to distract him from his weakness and pain. If only he could find that biscuit-stealing freak of nature, he wouldn't have to deal with such a long and tedious recovery.

"I don't care what Wolf said," Augustine mumbled, as he sank into his pillow. "I will find him one day. I will see that he pays for abandoning you."

Lina rolled her eyes.

"Can you at least wait until you've recovered before running off on your stupid vengeance quest?" she requested.

"It's not vengeance," Augustine grumbled. "I am going to catch him and turn him over to the law."

"So your stepfather?" Lina pressed.

"He is the king," Augustine shrugged.

Lina sighed. "Just take some time to heal first, promise? And talk to your mother?"

"Fine," Augustine croaked, closing his eyes. By now, he had a pounding headache. The room felt like the inside of an oven. Why in the world was it so hot?

AUGUSTINE DIDN'T REMEMBER Lina leaving his side. One moment, he was looking up at her, clinging to her hand, and the next he had fallen into a fitful dream.

He was standing in the very center of a burning village. The homes around him withered and collapsed in the soaring flames. The air was thick with ash that filled his lungs and choked him.

As he struggled to breathe, gasping and coughing, he saw faded figures emerging from the walls of fire that surrounded him— villagers with pale faces and withered skin. Their blackened bones were visible here and there, where fire had eaten away their flesh.

They drew closer, cursing him and reaching out for him with their charred hands. The flames burned hotter, the ash fell thicker, sweat poured from Augustine's brow as he slowly backed away from the mob of undead.

"Death to Justin!" they cried, as they moved in slowly. "And death to all his kin! Our bodies fueled his fires, now his blood will water the earth!"

"Augustine!" called a familiar voice through the blackness. He looked over the crowd and saw Lina charging toward him. He cried out to her desperately, begging her to leave, but she did not heed him.

The horrid beings ignored her, until she broke from their midst, came up beside Augustine, and took his hand. Then the villagers cursed her too, calling for her blood along with his.

"She has nothing to do with me!" Augustine exclaimed, turning to Lina, he ordered her to flee, but in response she tightened her grip on his hand and shot him a gentle smile.

He had to get her to safety. Augustine looked over his shoulder desperately. A slight gap between two walls of flame offered his only opportunity. As he dragged Lina through it, his skin seared and his chest ached with coughing.

At last, they burst from the inferno. Augustine gasped, drinking in the cool night air. His relief was short lived, for as the smoke cleared, he saw an army looming before them. At the head, a Kalathean prince sat proudly on horseback, looking over the burning village.

"You shouldn't be here, Lina," Augustine urged. "This is my burden, not yours."

She looked at him, her expression peaceful and pleasant despite the dangers looming all around her. "I want to help you bear it."

She may as well have ripped his heart out and crushed it in her fist. He looked at her for a long moment feeling love and terror more deeply than he'd ever felt anything. He glanced over his shoulder at the warrior prince on the hill behind him. He had turned his cold expressionless face toward them.

Augustine shuddered. *They had the same face.*

He had to get Lina away. The burning village and Prince Justin's army surrounded them on three sides; there was only one direction they could run. Augustine gripped Lina's hand and turned only to find their final escape route blocked by an all too familiar green-eyed assassin.

"You really think you can escape him?" Wolf laughed. "Your veins run thick with the blood of that monster!"

Wolf glanced toward the village, as the largest of the buildings caved in, releasing a shower of embers. A few stray sparks leapt from the ruins searing Augustine's skin.

The white shapes of the undead emerged from the flames passing through the skeletal buildings unhindered.

"I can save them, you know," Wolf said, pulling his knife from his belt. "With your blood, I can restore them to life."

There was something so deeply twisted about this Wolf. He wore a crooked smile, his confidence radiating from his core. But he was also very pale and had a weary look about him. It was like he was oblivious to some lethal consuming sickness.

"That's not your choice to make," Lina hissed. "You have no right to weigh the value of his life against theirs."

"What life?" Wolf laughed. "He's a mistake, the byproduct of a vile man's lust!"

"Only God can give life," Lina replied, her gaze burning into Wolf. "And He doesn't make mistakes."

Augustine snapped awake. Or at least, he thought he did. He was back in his room sitting up in bed trembling violently. The only hint that he was still caught up in a bizarre fever dream was Faruk. He was standing at the foot of his bed looking like a saintly intellectual dressed in a toga and bathed in a halo of glowing white light.

The giant rested his dark eyes on Augustine and in a warm, rich, booming voice declared, "Your red girl is full of wisdom. Marry her."

Augustine's head fell into his hands. How he wanted that! He wanted it more than anything.

54

DAMARA WRESTLES WITH GOD

T he fever lasted a fortnight, during which time Augustine was plagued by similar dreams. He was surrounded by towering flames and watched again and again as the world around him withered away and collapsed in on itself.

During the final dream, he saw the flames creeping up his arms devouring his flesh. They flared up and surrounded him, consuming his body. Then, everything went black.

A moment later, Augustine found himself lying in the ashes of the fallen village. His mother was looking down at him, her cheeks streaked with tears and her eyes burning with fury. She squeezed his hand so tightly he thought it would break and turning her face toward Heaven, she cried, "Don't You dare take him back!"

His mother had gotten into trouble on more than one occasion for lashing out at authority. Now, undeterred by past punishments, she was screaming at the ultimate Authority with a wrath that made Augustine shrink.

"You gave him to me," she seethed. "Why would You give him to me, only to snatch him away?"

She brought Augustine's hand to her lips and held it there. Her cool tears landed on his fingers and then trickled down his arm.

Then Augustine woke.

He was lying in his room, damp with sweat and utterly exhausted. His mother was kneeling by his bed clutching his hand to her forehead hissing, "Don't You dare take him. Oh God, don't take him," under her breath.

Glancing over he noticed that his hand was covered in black and gold eye makeup.

"Mama?" he mumbled, still not convinced she was really there.

She looked up at him and burst into tears. Then she threw her arms around him and kissed his cheeks and his forehead until he had splotches of gold and black all over his face.

He normally would have put a quick stop to such an expression of affection, but after everything, he thought she'd earned the right to fuss over him.

"I'm so sorry," she wept. "I should have told you... I should have told you..."

He replied by wrapping her up in his arms and pulling her close to his heart. For a long time, he just held her and they both wept. All the while, she kept mumbling, "I'm sorry" over and over again.

He wanted so badly to tell her that it was alright but he couldn't. It wasn't alright; her lie had wounded him so deeply. So instead, when he could finally bring himself to speak, he said, "I understand."

Then, releasing her from his embrace, he squeezed her hand and added. "But I need to know the truth now."

The truth wasn't particularly surprising. After everything Augustine had been through, he could have guessed most of it.

It was the story of a young maiden catching the eye of a handsome prince. The prince showered her in the kind of praise reserved for nobility. He treated her like a princess and promised that one day she would be his queen.

She was completely taken with his charm. Nothing terrified the girl more than losing the affection of her prince, so she gave him everything he asked for. She let him treat her like his wife, though he'd done nothing to earn such a privilege.

"The kind of wife," Damara recalled bitterly. "That you have to sneak into your bedroom to avoid causing a scandal." Shaking with rage, she added. "It's so obvious to me now but... I was so young then. I should have listened to the princess when she ordered me to stay away from him."

"Did he ever try to see me?" Augustine asked.

"No," Damara replied. "When I told him I was pregnant, he acted like he didn't know me." She scowled at the memory as a few fresh tears burned their way down her cheek. "I couldn't get anywhere near him after that."

"But we lived under the same roof for three years," Augustine pressed. "He never acknowledged me at all?"

Damara shook her head. "Princess Fausta was careful to keep you apart. She didn't think it was safe for you to meet, and she was probably right."

Considering the type of man Justin was, this shouldn't have hurt Augustine as much as it did. He just couldn't imagine having a child and then deliberately ignoring its existence.

But then, everything Augustine knew about fatherhood he learned from Florian. A man who had chosen to be his father, when he had no responsibility to him, no blood connection, and came from a completely different corner of the world.

As Augustine healed, his room was crawling with visitors. Apparently, his mother arrived several days before his fever broke and refused to leave his side until she was sure he would make a full recovery.

There was also Florian and Lina and his uncles and aunt. Even Oswald came to see him once in a while. *His* visits were always a little awkward. While he wanted to connect with Augustine, Lina had convinced him to give up the only methods he was familiar with: threats and bullying.

Instead he would come in, ask Augustine how he was, and then ramble on about things he had seen while wandering around Lysandria.

"There are a lot of holy men here," Oswald mentioned one day.

"I suppose," Augustine shrugged. He hadn't really thought about it. It wasn't like Kaltehafen didn't have holy men.

"I saw a holy man on top of a pillar outside the city," Oswald marveled. "Apparently he's been there for ten years, praying and fasting! Can you believe that?"

"I've heard of stranger things," Augustine shrugged. He wondered how long this conversation would continue, and where in the world it was going to end.

"I don't think I could ever be a hermit," Oswald mentioned.

Augustine raised an eyebrow. "Did someone suggest that to you or something?"

"No!" Oswald cried defensively. "Why would anyone suggest that? That's crazy!"

"Sorry," Augustine shrugged, turning his attention back to the open book on his lap.

"Of course..." Oswald continued.

Augustine glanced back up at him, hoping the irritation he felt wasn't bleeding into his expression.

"I could see how someone might choose that life to do penance for..." Oswald shrugged. "I don't know... being awful or something... It would probably be an excellent way to purge out selfishness... if that's something you'd struggled with, you know."

Oswald seemed to be talking to himself more than to Augustine, so the latter returned to his reading, nodding occasionally as Oswald rambled.

"Can you honestly picture me *(me!),* wandering in the desert alone with a robe and a staff!"

"Mmm hmm," Augustine nodded. "That would be... completely ridiculous."

Given Augustine's recent influx of visitors, he was starting to see the appeal of being a hermit. In fact, he made up his mind that the first thing he was going to do when he was allowed to leave his room was return to his favorite hiding spot.

55

THE PHOENIX

T he moment he was allowed to leave his room, Augustine went for a walk alone. His body was fully recovered, but his spirit still needed time.

Now, out of immediate danger, he was becoming ever more aware of the fact that his reality had been completely shattered. Florian had convinced himself that the truth about Prince Justin didn't matter in the slightest. As far as he was concerned, he was the only father Augustine had.

The problem with Florian's assertion was that it wasn't true. Or, wasn't *completely* true. Certainly, Florian was his father in the ways that counted most but Justin, for better or for worse, would always be part of him. He looked exactly like him for one thing. Maybe they had other similarities. Augustine often wondered if the man had any good qualities at all. He had to. Everyone had *something* good about them, even the most evil of men.

He wandered through the palace halls toward the passageway that would lead him down to the secret dock below the palace. As he went, he drank in the carvings, the curtains, the ornaments... Everything seemed so familiar.

He came to a massive tapestry that triggered a long-forgotten memory. It was a stunningly intricate piece depicting a forest filled with animals. A much smaller version of himself had spent many a long moment drinking in the scene. He remembered the stag in the center, that stood across from a rearing unicorn.

The wise-eyed lion in the lower left corner was the most familiar of all the animals. It occurred to Augustine that it was probably exactly at the eye-level of his three-year-old self.

He felt himself smiling as he bent down to look at it more closely. Though the memory was very faint, he knew the lion had been his favorite detail.

After a moment, he straightened up and noticed something in the upper right. Unsurprisingly, he had no memories at all of the upper portion of the tapestry. His gaze ran along this new section taking everything in.

A mountain rose up above the woven trees and at the top was a little hollow containing a phoenix. The scarlet bird stretched its wings as it rose up from a nest of crimson flames. It reminded Augustine of those strange and awful dreams where everything around him was on fire.

This phoenix was at home in the flames; it was, after all, born from them.

Augustine smirked bitterly. In a way, he was like the little woven bird—they were both born from destruction.

He returned to his walk, finding the hidden tunnel where he remembered it, and making his way down to the subterranean dock.

When he stumbled into the open cavern, he found his hiding place was already occupied. His Uncle Alexander sat on a large rock beside the water, sketching away on a wooden panel.

Augustine would have tried to slip back up the passage unnoticed, but he hadn't exactly come quietly. His uncle looked up as he came into view.

"Hello, Augustine," Alexander said pleasantly. "It's good to see you up and about!"

"Um, thank you," Augustine mumbled, taking a few steps backward. "Sorry I didn't mean to intrude."

"It's alright," the king shrugged. "It's not you I'm hiding from."

"You're hiding?" Augustine questioned.

"Well, not hiding so much as thinking, I suppose..." the king answered. He took his stick of charcoal and made a few strokes on the panel on his lap. "Actually, you might be just the person to help me."

"Um... alright?" Augustine shrugged.

"All those people," the king continued. "Wolf's refugees... I know he wouldn't let you see where they were but you still might remember something that can help me find them."

"You want to find them?" Augustine questioned.

"Once you're well, of course!" the king added. "I don't want to force you into anything too soon." He continued sketching on the wooden panel.

"I'll try my best..." Augustine answered. "But finding Wolf's refugees won't help you find Wolf himself. Our best chance of catching him is to speak to the enchantress who keeps him hidden."

"We are doing everything we can to catch Wolf," the king promised. "But that's not why I am interested in his refugees." He set his charcoal down and looked up at Augustine. "I want to help them."

This declaration made Augustine wonder how in the world the man before him was related to Prince Justin. They were practically opposites. Alexander was as kind as Justin was cruel.

While Augustine was ashamed of being Justin's son, he was proud of being Alexander's nephew. How could that be when one was impossible without the other? The universe was full of puzzles like that.

"I'll do everything I can to help," Augustine promised. He truly meant it. The prospect excited him actually. Wasn't that why he wanted to become a knight in the first place? To protect the innocent?

He took a seat on the plateau and dangled his feet in the water. Then he spoke to his uncle for a little while about what he remembered about the refuge from his journey and what he thought could be done. The king didn't push him, he was insistent that Augustine take the time he needed to heal before they made any solid plans.

After a while, they stopped talking and the king became

engrossed in his sketching. Augustine was left to face a thought that had been troubling him for a long time.

"Uncle?" he said. "My stepfather says you are a philosopher."

"Your stepfather thinks that all Kalatheans are Greeks and that all Greeks are philosophers," Alexander pointed out.

Augustine couldn't help but chuckle at this. "You aren't then?"

"I never said that," the king smirked. "What's your question?"

Augustine's smile faded. He bit his lip and thought for a moment.

"If Prince Justin..." he started. He inhaled deeply. "If *my father* had been obedient to God's laws, I would not exist..."

Augustine paused, unsure how to express the awful thoughts that had been gnawing away at his heart.

His uncle must have understood though. He set his panel down and gave his nephew his full attention.

"Augustine," the king replied. "You are not a product of Justin's sin. You are God's victory over it."

The king's gentle brown eyes were full of warm sincerity.

"You were in the mind of God from eternity, you are His beloved child and a gift to our family. Don't ever forget that."

Augustine thought for a long moment trying to process his uncle's words. For some reason, his mind kept returning to the little phoenix on the tapestry rising up from the flames.

After a few moments, Augustine said. "Uncle, will you do something for me?"

"Name it," Alexander shrugged.

"I need to design a coat of arms," he explained. "For when I am knighted, you know. I had always thought I would use a horse to represent Attikos Hatsi but obviously..." Augustine sighed without finishing the thought. "In any case, I think instead I'd like to use a phoenix. I was hoping maybe you could design it for me?"

The king's face brightened. He set his panel down, and kneeling began to sketch directly on the stone floor.

Watching Alexander work was like watching some kind of magic. At first, Augustine saw what seemed to be only a few disconnected dark strokes, then with another stroke or two, the king brought forth the great firebird.

"Sorry, this is a bit rough," Alexander apologized, as he surrounded it in swirling flames.

Augustine had no idea how the masterpiece on the floor was "rough", but he mumbled, "Oh, it's alright."

After a few more strokes his uncle stepped back regarding the image with his head cocked.

"It's perfect," Augustine gasped.

"Excellent," Alexander grinned proudly. "Of course, the final version will need color... I was thinking Tyrian purple."

Augustine looked at his uncle in alarm. In Kalathea, only those with royal blood could wear Tyrian purple. Even visiting kings from foreign nations weren't allowed to wear it while on Kalathean soil.

"Tyrian purple?" Augustine mumbled.

"We could do a different color if you like," Alexander mentioned. "I only suggest it to satisfy my own vanity."

Augustine continued staring at his uncle confused.

"For what it's worth," the king shrugged. "I'm proud that we're related."

A SHORT WHILE LATER, Augustine received a gift from the king. It was a long silk tunic with the Tyrian purple phoenix on the front. He smiled as he drank in the intricate detail. Suddenly his uncle's charcoal sketch did indeed seem "rough". The actual symbol was better than he ever could have imagined.

And the timing of the gift couldn't have been better. He had arranged to speak with Lina and he wanted to show it off. Slipping on the tunic, he ventured down from his room to the emerald grounds.

As he made his way toward the fountain where Lina was waiting, he noticed Heidi zipping after her seven-year-old cousin Thekla. The little girl was like a tiny, female version of Alexander, except that she had Ilona's bright blue eyes. Augustine smiled as he passed the two gleefully squealing girls. They were too caught up in their own game to notice him at all.

He felt a knot in his stomach as he approached Lina. Since their reunion, he had been a little distant. Certainly, she had come to see him while he was sick but with so many relatives and servants about, they hadn't been able to talk alone.

She had also spent a great deal of time with her parents who had come with Damara to Kalathea. They had been so overwhelmed with worry, they never willingly let her out of their sight.

"Hello, Augustine," Lina smiled, when she saw him approaching.

Augustine returned her smile. She looked like a princess in her gown of white and green silk. Her red hair was styled in the local fashion beneath a thin veil.

He sat down beside her on the edge of the fountain and for a few moments they made idle talk. Their cheeks were scarlet as they commented on the weather and shared stories of palace happenings. Lina was clearly waiting for Augustine to move the conversation to a more important topic, but Augustine took his time working up the courage.

"Lina?" he said, finally.

She smiled expectantly.

"Did you mean what you said about..." Augustine dropped his gaze to the ground. "Not caring about my... lineage?"

Lina rolled her eyes. "I think you're the only person who cares about that, Augustine."

"You're right, Lina," he admitted. Not one of his family members treated him with less love or respect because of his father. The people who hated him for it were people who did not know him.

"Why do you ask?" Lina pressed hopefully.

"It's just that..." Augustine started. "Well, our families are here all together, I doubt that's ever going to happen again..." He turned a deeper shade of crimson. "I thought it might be a good time for a wedding."

"Are you sure, Augustine?" Lina asked. Her furrowed brow communicated concern. She was asking if he was ready—ready to accept the truth about himself with a humble heart. Ready to let her love him.

The truth still hurt. Maybe it would always hurt... but Augustine embraced it. It was what made him who he was, and who he was was someone worth loving.

"I am sure if you are," he answered.

Lina broke into a warm smile. "I've always been sure."

Augustine took her hands and sealed their engagement with a gentle kiss.

"I KNEW IT!" came Heidi's voice.

Augustine and Lina jerked apart to see Heidi and Thekla watching them. The two little girls were jumping up and down squealing and clapping their hands.

"'Gustin! 'Gustin!" Heidi cried. "Are you getting married?"

Augustine looped his arm around Lina's shoulder.

"Yes, Heidi," he grinned. "So you'd better start planning!"

EPILOGUE

Amira's attempted assassination resulted in months of investigations, negotiations, and interrogations. Working through the mess left King Alexander wondering why so many people wanted his job.

The Anamian king, who happened to be Amira's brother, was not at all happy with Alexander for arresting her, even though she had tried to stab him in the back. He demanded the immediate release of his sister and her son.

Alexander was hesitant to grant this request, primarily because Amira was responsible for numerous murders among other things. However, he was keenly aware that if he refused, her brother would launch an attack. Since war posed a greater threat to his people than the release of two criminals, Alexander reluctantly chose the latter option.

No sooner had he banished the pair, then another hostile force arrived on his northern border. It was King Henry of Zoroske with one simple demand—the immediate surrender of Prince Justin's son.

Alexander eagerly explained to King Henry that he had just released Prince Justin's son to the Anamian king and that he'd have to take up the matter with him. He then showed King Henry the records of Justin's marriage to Amira, gave him directions, and sent him on his way.

Thus Kalathea was spared from war twice in a single month. Many of the people attributed this miracle to the prayers and fasting of their newest celebrity holy man—Oswald the Hermit.

Crowds of people came from all around the kingdom to watch the prince in sack-cloth live a life of solitude. Considering Oswald had become a hermit to separate himself from the undue praise that had turned him into a narcissist in the first place, he found the presence of these followers deeply frustrating. Eventually, a wise visitor by the name of Faruk suggested to Oswald that maybe the frustration itself could be his penance. It was only then that Oswald found peace.

Augustine also started a new life. Eventually, he planned to capture Wolf and bring an end to his crimes. Then he would find the outlaw's refuges and work with his uncle to help the people Prince Justin hurt. He would protect and serve the innocent just as he always planned. But first, he needed to spend a little time resting, a little time healing, and a little time alone with his wife.

ACKNOWLEDGMENTS

- First, I need to thank Amelia who has been a beta reader on all of my books from the beginning of time. Amelia, you are the best!
- Thank you, Cecilia Lawrence, for once again blowing my mind with your cover art! You'd think I'd be used to getting something ten times better than what I originally asked for by now. How is it that you always surprise me?
- Thank you to everyone in the LegendFiction community who supported me and left me notes, especially Grace and Max who read the early version and kept me motivated with their fan art!
- Miriam, thanks again for being my medical consultant. Since you still have a nursing license, I assume your medical knowledge is more up-to-date than Lina's.
- Helen thank you for taking on the horrifying and near-impossible task of proofreading for me.
- Dominic, thank you for putting up with all my questions about font size and line spacing. You were basically my cover-design tech support. I am forever in your debt!
- Joe, thank you for being there to support me, encourage me, and look after the tiny barbarian horde.
- And finally, I would like to thank Hippocrates for being the father of modern medicine. I think everyone should take a moment to appreciate Hippocrates now and then.

THANK YOU FOR THE FAN ART!

Florian and Family by Max Woods.

Heidi leads Poly to Freedom by Grace Woods

Augustine will return in
The Phoenix and The Wolf

CPSIA information can be obtained
at www.ICGtesting.com
Printed in the USA
JSHW082121200423
40654JS00001B/7